Please turn to the back of this book for a preview of Donald E. Westlake's upcoming novel, *Put a Lid On It.*

more . . .

By Donald E. Westlake

NOVELS

Put a Lid On It ◆ The Hook ◆ The Ax ◆ Humans
Sacred Monster ◆ A Likely Story ◆ Kahawa ◆ Brothers Keepers
I Gave at the Office ◆ Adios, Scheherazade
Up Your Banners

THE DORTMUNDER SERIES

What's the Worst That Could Happen? ◆ Don't Ask
Drowned Hopes ◆ Good Behavior ◆ Why Me
Nobody's Perfect ◆ Jimmy the Kid ◆ Bank Shot
The Hot Rock

COMIC CRIME NOVELS

Smoke ◆ Baby, Would I Lie? ◆ Trust Me on This
High Adventure ◆ Castle in the Air ◆ Enough
Dancing Aztecs ◆ Two Much
Help I Am Being Held Prisoner ◆ Cops and Robbers
Somebody Owes Me Money
Who Stole Sassi Manoon? ◆ God Save the Mark
The Spy in the Ointment ◆ The Busy Body
The Fugitive Pigeon

CRIME NOVELS

Pity Him Afterwards ◆ Killy ◆ 361 ◆ Killing Time
The Mercenaries

JUVENILE
Philip

WESTERN
Gangway (with Brian Garfield)

REPORTAGE
Under an English Heaven

SHORT STORIES

Tomorrow's Crimes ◆ Levine ◆ The Curious Facts Preceding My
Execution and Other Fictions ◆ A Good Story and Other Stories

ANTHOLOGY
Once Against the Law (coedited with William Tenn)

DONALD E. WESTLAKE

BAD NEWS

WARNER BOOKS

An AOL Time Warner Company

WARNER BOOKS EDITION

Cover design and art by Tony Greco

Warner Books, Inc.
1271 Avenue of the Americas
New York, NY 10020

Visit our Web site at www.twbookmark.com.

 An AOL Time Warner Company

Printed in the United States of America

Originally published in hardcover by The Mysterious Press
First Paperback Printing: March 2002

10 9 8 7 6 5 4 3 2 1

I would like to dedicate this novel, with apologies, to all of the translators who've had to deal with my language in their languages over the years. I have not made it easy for them. For instance, they're going to have to deal with the "verisimilitude" remark in the first chapter of this current book. Therefore, one dedication and two aspirin to Laura Grimaldi, Jiro Kimura, Jean Esch, and all my other artful collaborators. Thank you.

1

John Dortmunder was a man on whom the sun shone only when he needed darkness. Now, like an excessively starry sky, a thousand thousand fluorescent lights in great rows under the metal roof of this huge barnlike store building came flickering and buzzing and sqlurping on, throwing a great glare over all the goods below, and over Dortmunder, too, and yet he *knew* this vast Speedshop discount store in this vast blacktop shopping mall in deepest New Jersey, very near Mordor, did not open at ten minutes past two in the morning. That's why he was here.

Speedshop was a great sprawling mass-production retailer stocked mostly with things that weren't worth more than a quarter and didn't cost more than four dollars, but it had a few pricier sections as well. There were a pharmacy and a liquor department and a video shop and an appliance showroom. Most important, from Dortmunder's point of view, there was a camera department, carrying everything from your basic low-price PhD (Push here, Dummy) to advanced computer-driven machines that chose their own angles.

In two Speedshop tote bags, canvas, white, emblazoned in red with the Speedshop slogan:

! SAVE FAST !
at
!! SPEEDSHOP !!

Dortmunder could fit ten thousand dollars' worth of such high-end cameras, for which he would receive, no questions asked (because the answers are already known), from a fellow in New York named Arnie Albright, one thousand dollars in cash. Ten minutes inside the store, no more, after he'd bypassed the loading dock alarm systems, and he'd be back in the Honda Platoon he'd borrowed forty minutes ago from an apartment complex farther up the highway, and well on his way home to the peace and quiet and safety of New York City.

But, no. As tote bags full of cameras dangled from his bony hands and he loped down the silent, semidark aisles—little night-lights here and there guided him along his way—he was suddenly bathed in this ice-water deluge of a harsh white fluorescent glare.

Okay. There must have been something, some motion sensor or extra alarm he hadn't noticed, that had informed on him, and this big store would be filling up right this second with many police officers, plus, probably, private Speedshop security people, all of them armed and all of them looking, though they didn't know it yet, for John Dortmunder. Didn't know it yet, but soon would.

What to do? First, drop these bags of cameras behind a kids' sneaker display rack. Second, panic.

Well, what else? He'd come in from the loading docks

at the back, which they surely knew, so *they* would come in from the back as well, but they would also come in from the front. And they would leave guards at every entrance, while the rest of them fanned out to search inexorably forward like volunteer Boy Scouts in pursuit of a lost hiker. Any second now, groups of them would appear at the ends of aisles, visible far away. And he would be just as visible to them.

Hide? Where? Nowhere. The shelves were packed full and high. If this were a traditional department store, he could at least try to pretend to be a mannequin in the men's clothing section, but these discount places were too cheap to have full entire mannequins. They had mannequins that consisted of just enough body to drape the displayed clothing on. Pretending to be a headless and armless mannequin was just a little too far beyond Dortmunder's histrionic capabilities.

He looked around, hoping at least to see something soft to bang his head against while panicking, and noticed he was just one aisle over from the little line of specialty shops, the pharmacy and the hair salon and the video rental and the optician.

The optician.

Could this possibly be a plan that had suddenly blossomed like a cold sore in Dortmunder's brain? Probably not, but it would have to do.

As the individual all those legislators most specifically had in mind when they enacted their three-strikes-you're-out life-imprisonment laws, Dortmunder felt that any plan, however loosely basted together, had to be better than simple surrender. His wallet tonight contained several dubious IDs, including somebody's credit card, so, for almost the first time in his life, he made use of a credit card in a discount store, swiping it down the line between door and jamb leading to the optician's office, forcing the striker back far enough so he could push open the glass door in the glass wall and enter.

It wasn't until after the door snicked shut again behind him that he realized there were no knobs or latches on its inside. This door could only be opened or closed or locked or unlocked from the outside, because the fire laws required it to be propped open anytime the place was open for business.

Trapped! he thought, but then he thought, wait a second. This just adds whadayacallit. Verisimilitude. Unless that's the color.

The optician's shop was broad and narrow, with the front glass wall facing the rest of Speedshop, plus white walls at sides and back, liberally decorated with mirrors and with color photographs of handsome people with bad eyesight. A glass counter and display case full of spectacle frames faced the door, and little fitting tables with mirrors and chairs stood to both sides.

Against each side wall was a small settee where customers could sit and wait for their prescriptions to be filled, with magazines stacked on a nearby table. The light in here at this time of night was only the long, dim bulbs inside the display racks, mostly showing the frames on the glass shelves.

Dortmunder dashed around the end of the counter and found the cash register, which for once he didn't want. But under it was the credit card swiper, which he did want. He found the blank receipts, swiped one with the credit card he'd used on the door, filled in the receipt with

some stuff—$139.98, that seemed like a good number—
looked at the name on the credit card, and signed it more
or less the way it looked on the back: Austin Humboldt.

Customer copy, customer copy; here it is. Glancing at
the windows across the way—no cops out there yet—he
pocketed the customer copy, found the stack of used receipts under the cash register, and added Austin Humboldt's near to but not at the top of the pile. Out of his
wallet and into his shoes went all the IDs not named
Humboldt. Then he started around the counter again.

Wait a minute. If he was buying glasses, he was somebody who'd *wear* glasses, right? A display on the rear
wall was two-thirds full of glasses; he grabbed a pair at
random, slapped them on, and realized he was looking
through nothing. No glass, just frames.

Try it? No; up close, it would be obvious, and he had
the feeling he'd be inspected up close very soon now.

Time, time, time—there was no *time* for all this. Down
to his left, another display of glasses, and these bounced
dim light at him from a hundred lenses. He lunged down
there, praying they wouldn't be blind-as-a-bat prescription specs, threw on a pair of delicate but manly tortoise-
shell frames, and looked through glass. Clear glass, clear.
Okay!

Now he could run around the counter, collapse onto
the nearest settee—it wasn't very comfortable—grab a
three-month-old *People* from the little table, open it face-
down on his lap, and flop, eyes closed.

It took them three minutes to find him. He slumped
there, unmoving, telling himself to relax, telling himself,
if worse came to worst, he could probably eventually es-

cape from prison, and then he heard the rattling of the metal knob on the glass door.

Don't react, he told himself. Not yet, it's too soon. You need your sleep.

Banging and knocking on the glass door and the plate-glass wall. Indistinct, muffled shouting.

Dortmunder started, like a horse hearing a pistol shot, and stared around at the optician's shop, at the magazine sliding off his lap, and at last at the glass wall, which had become an active mural of cops peering in at him, staring pressing faces to the glass, waving and yelling—a horrible sight.

And now he realized these glasses he'd put on were not *exactly* clear lenses, not *exactly*. They were some kind of magnifiers, reading glasses or whatever, which made everything just a little larger than usual, a little closer than usual. He not only had this horrible mural of Your Police In Action in front of him, he had them in his lap.

Too late to change. Just stagger forward and hope for the best. He jumped to his feet. He ran to the door, reaching for the nonexistent knob, bruising his knuckles against the chrome frame surrounding the glass, because it wasn't exactly where he saw it, then licked his knuckles. Cops crowded close out there, the other side of the glass, calling, intensely staring.

Dortmunder stopped licking his knuckle to show them his most baffled face. He spread his hands, then pointed at the door, then made a knob-turning gesture, then shrugged like Atlas with an itch.

They didn't get it yet. They kept yelling at him to open up. They kept pointing at the door as though he didn't know where it was. He did his little repertoire of gestures some more, and then two of them, one at the door and one at the wall next to the door, pressed their faces to the glass, so that they now looked like fish in police uniforms, and squinted to try to see the inside of the door.

Now they got it. And now Dortmunder, once they understood he was locked in here—it's a locked-room mystery!—began to exhibit signs of panic. He'd been *feeling* panic all along; it was nice to be able to show it, even though under false colors.

He bobbed back and forth along the wall, waving frantically, gesturing with great urgency that they should release him. He pointed at his watch—do you people realize what *time* it is?—he mimed making rapid phone calls—I got responsibilities at *home*!—he tried to tear his hair, but it was too wispy to get a grip on.

Now that *he* was excited, the cops all became calm. They patted the air at him, they nodded, they made walkie-talkie calls, they came close to the glass to mouth, *Take it easy.* Easy for them to say.

It took them fifteen minutes to unlock the door; apparently, none of them was a good credit risk. While more and more of them, cops and rent-a-cops both, came streaming in from all the aisles of Speedshop to stare into this one-man zoo, Dortmunder kept ranting and raving in pantomime, flinging his arms about, stomping back and forth. He even ran around behind the counter and found the phone, intending to call his faithful companion, May, sleeping peacefully at home in their nice little apartment on West Nineteenth Street—would he ever see it again?—just so the cops could see the frantic husband was calling his worried wife, but a recorded announcement told him he could make only local calls from that phone, which was even better. Let May sleep.

At last, another team of cops arrived, with special vinyl jackets in dark blue to show they were supercops and not just trash cops like all these other guys and gals, and they had several strange narrow metal tools with which they had at the door.

God, they were slow. Dortmunder was just looking around for a helpful brick when at last the door did pop open and maybe twenty of them came crowding in.

"I gotta call my wife!" Dortmunder yelled, but everybody else was yelling, too, so nobody could hear anybody. But then it turned out there actually was someone in authority, a gruff, potbellied older guy in a different kind of important uniform, like a blue army captain, who roared over everybody else, "That's enough! Pipe down!"

They piped down, surprisingly enough, all of them except Dortmunder, who, in the sudden silence, once again shouted, "I gotta call my wife!"

The man in charge stood in front of Dortmunder as though he were imitating a slammed door. "Name," he said.

Name. What was that name? "Austin Humboldt," Dortmunder said.

"You got identification?"

"Oh, sure."

Dortmunder pulled out his wallet, nervously dropped it on the floor—he didn't have to pretend nervousness, not at all—picked it up, and handed it to the boss cop, saying, "Here it is, you look at it, I'm too jumpy, my fingers aren't working."

The cop didn't like handling this wallet, but he took it,

opened it up, and then spent a couple minutes looking at several documents the real Austin Humboldt would be reporting stolen six hours from now. Then, handing the wallet back, waiting while Dortmunder dropped it again and picked it up again and returned it to his pocket, he said, "You broke into this building half an hour ago, came in here, got locked in. What were you after?"

Dortmunder gaped at him. "What?"

"What were you after in this shop?" the cop demanded.

Dortmunder stared around at all the displayed eyeglass frames. "My glasses!"

"You break into a store at—"

"I didn't break in!"

The cop gave him a jaundiced look. "The loading dock just happened to be open?"

Dortmunder shook his head, a man besieged by gnats. "What loading dock?"

"You came in through the loading dock—"

"I did not!"

Another look. "Okay," the cop decided, "suppose *you* tell *me* what happened."

Dortmunder rubbed his brow. He scuffed his shoes on the industrial carpet. He stared at his feet. "I don't *know* what happened," he said. "I must of fell asleep."

A different cop said, "Captain, he was asleep when we got here." He pointed at the settee. "Over there."

"That's right," said several other cops. "Right over there." They all pointed at the settee. Outside the plate glass, some of the other cops pointed at the settee, too, without knowing why.

The captain didn't like this at all. "Asleep? You broke in here to *sleep*?"

"Why do you keep saying," Dortmunder answered, drawing himself up with what was supposed to be an honest citizen's dignity, "I *broke* in here?"

"Then what *did* you do?" the captain demanded.

"I came in to get my prescription reading glasses," Dortmunder told him. "I paid for them, with a credit card, two pair, sunglasses and regular, and they told me to sit over there and wait. I must have fell asleep, but how come they didn't tell me when my glasses were ready?" Looking around, as though suddenly realizing the enormity of it all, he cried, "They *left* me here! They walked out and locked me in and left me here! I could of starved!"

The captain, sounding disgusted, said, "No, you couldn't of starved. They're gonna open again in the morning, you can't starve overnight."

"I could get damn hungry," Dortmunder told him. "In fact, I *am* damn hungry, I never had my dinner." Struck by another thought, he cried, "My wife is gonna *kill* me, I'm this late for dinner!"

The captain reared back to study his prisoner. "Let me get this straight," he said. "You came in here earlier today—"

"Around four this afternoon. Yesterday afternoon."

"You bought two pairs of glasses, you fell asleep, and you want me to believe the staff left without seeing you and locked you in. And it was just coincidence that somebody *else* broke into this building tonight."

"Somebody broke in?"

Nobody answered; they all just kept looking at him,

looming outside these glasses, so finally Dortmunder said, "How often does that happen, somebody breaks in here?"

The captain didn't deign to answer. Dortmunder looked around, and another, younger cop said, "Not a lot." But he sounded defensive.

"So it happens," Dortmunder said.

"Sometimes," the younger cop admitted, while the captain glowered at this underling, not pleased.

Dortmunder spread his hands. "So what kind of a co-incidence is that?"

The captain leaned closer; now the glasses made him look like a tank with eyes. "How did you pay for these glasses? Cash?"

"Of course not." Now the damn glasses slipped down his nose, and he finger-pushed them back, a little too hard. Oow. Blinking, eyes watering, which didn't help, "I used my credit card," he said.

"So the receipt should still be here, shouldn't it?"

"I dunno."

"Let's just see," the captain said, and turned to one of his flunky cops to say, "Look for it. The credit card slip."

"Yes, sir."

Which took about a minute and a half. "Here it is!" said the cop, pulling it out of the stack he'd placed on the counter.

In stunned disbelief, the captain said, "There's a credit card slip there?"

"Yes, sir."

Dortmunder, trying to be helpful, said, "I've got my copy in my pocket, if you want to see it."

The captain studied Dortmunder. "You mean, you really did come in here this afternoon and fall asleep?"

"Yes, sir," Dortmunder said.

The captain looked angry and bewildered. "It can't be," he insisted. "In that case, where's the burglar? He has to be in the building."

One of the rent-a-cops, an older guy with his own special uniform with stripes and epaulets and stars and awards and things on it to show he was an important rent-a-cop, a senior rent-a-cop, cleared his throat very loudly and said, "Uh, Captain."

The captain lowered an eyebrow at him. "Yeah?"

"The word went out," the senior rent-a-cop said, "that the burglar was caught."

The captain got that message right away. "You're telling me," he said, "no one's watching the exits."

"Well, the word was," the senior rent-a-cop said, "he was, you know, caught."

Dortmunder, honest but humble, said, "Captain, would you mind? My wife's gonna be really, really, really irritated, I mean, she doesn't like me to be *ten minutes* late for dinner, you know, and—"

The captain, furious at everybody now, snapped, "What? What do *you* want?"

"Sir," Dortmunder said, "could you give me a note for my wife?"

"A *note*!" The captain looked ready to punch a whole lot of people, starting with Dortmunder. "Gedaddahere!"

"Well, okay," Dortmunder said.

2

May didn't like to be critical, but she just had the feeling sometimes that John didn't really want a nest egg, or a financial cushion, or freedom from money worries, or even next month's rent. She felt somehow that John needed that prod of urgency, that sense of desperation, that sick knowledge that he was once again dead flat, stony, beanless broke, to get him out of bed at night, to get him to go out there and bring home the bacon. And the pork chops, and the ham steak, and maybe the butcher's van as well.

Oh, he *made* money sometimes, though not often. But it never got a chance to burn a hole in his pocket, because it burned through his fingers first. He'd go with a couple of his cronies out to the track, where obviously the horses were smarter than he was, because *they* weren't betting on *him,* were they? John could still remember, as he sometimes told her, that one exciting day when he'd almost broke even; just the memory of it, years later, could bring a hint of color to his cheeks.

And then there were the friends he'd loan money to. If he had it, they could have it, and the kind of people they were, they'd take his two hundred dollars and go directly to jail.

So it was no surprise to May, this morning, that John's great triumph last night, over in New Jersey, was that he'd escaped. Not with the loot he'd gone over there for, of course; just with himself.

"Hundreds of them," he told her. "More uniforms than a convention of marching bands, and I walked right outta there. I almost got them to give me a note to tell you how come I missed dinner."

"But you missed the swag," she pointed out.

"Oh, the cameras," he said. They were having break-fast—black coffee and half a grapefruit for her, corn-flakes and milk and sugar in a ratio of 1:1:1 for him—so there were pauses in the conversation while he chewed and she swallowed. After the next pause, he said, "See, the thing is, May, by then I was a guy buying eyeglasses. If I try to walk out with fourteen cameras, it doesn't go with the image."

"Of course not," she said. She didn't say that was the reason she held on to her cashier job at Safeway super-market, a job she was going to have to leave here for in a few minutes, because what was the point? He'd only feel bad, and it was so rare that John felt good, she couldn't bring herself to spoil it. He'd gone out last night to raise some ready and he'd come back empty-handed, but the triumph was, he'd come back. Fine. She said, "Andy called last night."

Andy Kelp was a not unmixed blessing in their lives, reflected in the way John immediately lowered his head closer to his bowl, shoveled in a whole lot of cornflakes and milk and sugar, and only then said, "Nrrr?"

"He said he had a little project," she told him, "simple and easy."

"Ne-er," John said.

"Well, you never know, John, be fair."

"I know."

"He's coming over this morning," she said, "to tell you all about it."

"What time?" he asked, as though considering two escapes in twenty-four hours, and a third voice said, "Morning. Hi, May, is there extra coffee?"

"I made enough, because you were coming over," May said, and Andy Kelp, a sharp-featured, bright-eyed fellow in a black windbreaker—because it was October outside—crossed over to the stove, where the coffeepot simmered. May told his moving form, "I just told John you called."

"Thanks, May."

John said, "Andy, you still don't use the doorbell."

"I've heard your doorbell, John," Andy told him, bringing his coffee over to join them at the kitchen table. "It's an awful sound, it's a nasty buzz. It's like one of those sounds they describe on *Car Talk*, why would you want to start your day listening to a nasty noise like that?"

Complaining to May, John said, "He uses our apartment door to practice his housebreaking on. And the building door."

"You gotta keep those muscles exercised," Andy said.

May said, "I don't know, John, I don't mind it anymore, especially if he calls ahead, like today, so there won't be any, you know, embarrassment. It's almost like having a pet."

John looked Andy over, as though considering him as a pet: Keep him, or have him put to sleep?

After a minute, Andy decided to hide behind his coffee cup awhile, and then to clear his throat a lot, and then to say, "Did May tell you I had us a little job?"

"Breaking and entering?" John asked. "Like you do here?"

"Now, John," May said.

"No, nothing like that," Andy told him. "It's just a little digging. It's hardly even illegal."

"Digging?" John swallowed some of his own coffee, to have his mouth absolutely clear as he said, "You want me to dig ditches, is that what this is?"

"Well, it's kind of a ditch, I guess," Andy said, "but not exactly."

"What is it exactly?"

"A grave," Andy said.

"No," said May.

John said, "Grave robbing? Andy, I'm a robber, I'm not a grave robber."

"It's not grave *robbing*," Andy said, "it's more, you know, *switching*."

"Switching," John said, while May just sat there, saucer-eyed, looking at Andy Kelp, her grapefruit and her job at Safeway both forgotten. She didn't like graves, and she certainly didn't like the thought of people digging in graves.

Meanwhile, Andy explained a little more, saying, "See, what it is, out in that big cemetery out in Queens, one of them out there, there's this grave. Kind of an old grave, guy's been in there quite a while."

"I don't think I wanna hear about this," John said, and May nodded in silent agreement.

"We're not gonna *look* at him, John," Andy said.

"Well, *I'm* not."

"We don't open the box at all," Andy assured him. "We dig down to it, we pull it outta there, we put it in the van."

"We got a van."

"It's the employer's van."

"We got an employer."

"I'll get to that," Andy promised. "What we do, we go out there with this van, and there's already a coffin in it."

"I bet this coffin is full," John said.

"You got it," Andy told him. "Absolutely. This guy was already dug up out west someplace, and whatever they had to do to fix him up for whatever this is—"

"Whatever what is?" John asked.

"The scam, what's going down."

"And?" John asked. "What is this scam? What's going down?"

"Well, I'm not in the loop on that," Andy said. "We're dealing with a real pro here, John, and he does this on a need-to-know basis, and that's something we don't need to know."

"I don't need to know any of it," John told him.

But by now, May had gotten over her first shock and disgust, and she *did* want to know. She said, "Andy, what is this? You dig a coffin out of a grave and put another coffin down in there instead?"

"That's it," Andy agreed.

John said, "So, what is it? These guys look alike?"

"They do now," Andy said.

May decided not to follow that thought. Instead, she said, "Andy, what are you and John supposed to do? Just do the digging and that's it?"

"And the filling in again," Andy told her. "And put the other coffin in the van, and I guess it goes back out west, or wherever."

May said, "And nobody opens any of these coffins."

Andy said, "Not while *I'm* around."

John said, "Why us? Why me? Why you?"

Andy explained, "He needs people in our kinda business, you know, on the bent, that'll keep their mouths shut and not ask any questions or show up to the party wearing a wire, and then maybe he'll have another job somewhere down the line."

May said, "Well, at least it would be healthful."

John looked at her in disbelief. "Healthful? Hanging around a graveyard?"

"Out in the air," she said. "Getting some exercise. You don't get enough exercise."

"I don't want enough exercise," he said.

Andy said, "He'll pay us a gee apiece."

Pleased, May said, "There you are, John! It's your cameras!"

Alert, Andy said, "Cameras?"

"He had to leave them behind," May explained.

"The point is," John said, "I escaped." Then, obviously preferring to change the subject, he said, "Who is this employer guy?"

"I met him on the Internet," Andy said.

"*Oh* boy," John said.

"No, come on, he's okay," Andy insisted. "As soon as

he understood the situation, he stopped scamming me. That second."

"Great."

"And offered me the job."

"And what's this peach's name?" John asked.

Andy said, "Fitzroy Guilderpost."

3

Fitzroy Guilderpost said, "Do we have the shovels?"

"In the van," Irwin said.

"Both shovels?"

"In the van," Irwin said.

"And the Mace? The pistol? The duct tape?"

"In the van. In the van. In the van," Irwin said. "And so's the tarpaulin and the rope and the canvas strap."

"In other words, what you're saying," Guilderpost summed up, "is that everything is in the van."

"Except you," Irwin said.

Little Feather said, "Shouldn't you boys get moving?"

"Just dotting our eyes, Little Feather," Guilderpost assured her. "Crossing our tees."

"Before you start tilding your ens," Little Feather told him, "maybe you oughta get moving."

"I love these little glimpses of your education, Little Feather," Guilderpost told her, and patted her leathery cheek, not too hard.

The three conspirators were gathered here, just before midnight, in a motel room on Long Island, just over the border from New York City, not far from Kennedy Airport. They'd been here two days, in three consecutive but nonconnecting rooms, of which this was Guilderpost's. It was still as neat as when he'd first entered it, or even neater, since he'd more perfectly aligned the phone and its pad on the bedside table. The only evidence of his occupancy, other than himself, was the slightly ajar ThinkPad on the round table beneath the swag lamp; the ThinkPad glowed quietly to itself down in there, thinking its own slow thoughts.

By contrast, Irwin's room next door, within half an hour of their arrival, had begun to look like a men's shop after the explosion, and Little Feather's room, one beyond, while comparatively neat, was, nevertheless, piled high with her possessions, her clothing, her cosmetics, her exercise tapes.

Guilderpost had interposed Irwin between himself and Little Feather deliberately. It was his rule never to mix business with pleasure, and that went double when dealing with as attractive a package of rat poison as Little Feather.

The three were more than an odd couple; they were an odd trio. Little Feather, the former showgirl, Native American Indian, was beautiful in a chiseled-granite sort of way, as though her mother were Pocahontas and her father Mount Rushmore. Irwin Gabel, the disgraced university professor, was tall and bony and mostly shoulder blades and Adam's apple, with an aggrieved and sneering look that used to work wonders in the classroom but was less useful in the world at large.

As for Guilderpost, the mastermind looked mostly like a mastermind: portly, dignified, white hair in waves above a distinguished pale forehead. He went in for three-piece suits, and was often the only person in a given state wearing a vest. He'd given up his mustache some years ago, when it turned gray, because it made him look like a child molester, which he certainly was not; however, he did look like a man who used to have a mustache, with some indefinable nakedness between the bottom of his fleshy nose and the top of his fleshy lip. He brushed this area from time to time with the side of his forefinger, exactly as though the mustache were still there.

Now he said, "No need to be overly hasty, Little Feather. The reason my operations invariably succeed is because I am an absolute stickler for detail."

"Hurray," Little Feather commented.

Irwin said, "What about the bozos? They gonna be as easy as the ones in Elko?"

"Easier," Guilderpost assured him. "I've only met the one, of course, but he's bringing a friend, and it isn't hard to imagine what a friend of Mr. Andy Kelly's will be."

"Another bozo," Irwin said.

"A couple of gonifs," Guilderpost agreed. "Strong backs and weak minds. They do the heavy lifting, and then we're done."

Little Feather cleared her throat and said, *"Tempus fugg-it."*

Guilderpost smiled upon her. "Very well, Little Feather," he said, "you're undoubtedly right. Traffic into Manhattan can be uncertain, even at this hour. If Irwin is ready—"

"Been ready," Irwin said.

"Yes, fine," Guilderpost said. He would have preferred more subservient assistants, but where do you find them? Everybody's got attitude. And in fact, Little Feather's background was absolutely perfect for the part she was to play, and Irwin's scientific knowledge was invaluable. So one took the rough, as it were, with the smooth.

All three left Guilderpost's room, and he tested the knob to be certain the door was locked. The black Econoline van with dubious California plates waited in front of them. Irwin's Plymouth Voyager with the equally dubious South Carolina plates, in which he would follow the van, stood next over, in front of Irwin's room.

Little Feather nodded at them and said, "See you at breakfast."

Irwin said, "You don't want a report tonight?"

Guilderpost believed Irwin actually had designs on Little Feather, which just shows how recklessly advanced degrees are handed out these days.

Little Feather offered Irwin her version of a smile; a faint temporary crackling in the glaze. "There isn't any doubt, is there?"

"None," Guilderpost answered. "We'll place grandpa where he can be of help, use and deal with these final assistants as we have the others, and then we'll be off, at long last, to collect our reward."

"Goody," Little Feather said.

4

For the life of him, Dortmunder couldn't figure out how he'd been bamboozled into this. Standing on the southeast corner of Thirty-seventh and Lex at one in the morning, waiting to be driven out to a cemetery to dig a grave. And then undig it again. It wasn't right. It was menial, it was undignified, and it didn't fit his history, his pattern, his MO. "I'm overqualified for this," he complained.

Kelp, waiting cheerfully beside him as though ditch digging were the height of his ambition, said, "John, it's the easiest grand we'll ever take in."

"It's manual labor," Dortmunder said.

"Yes, I know," Kelp agreed, "that's the downside. But look at it this way. It's also illegal."

"It's more manual than illegal," Dortmunder said, and a black Econoline van came to a stop in front of him. The driver's door was at the curbside, and out of it immediately popped a portly man in a dark gray three-piece suit, white shirt, narrow dark tie. He had completely tamed white wavy hair, like a lawn in Connecticut, and he looked to Dortmunder like an undertaker.

"Andy!" this fellow said, with the kind of rich voice

that goes with that kind of rich hair, and stuck out a portly hand.

"Fitzroy," agreed Kelp, and they shook, and then Kelp said, "Fitzroy, this is John. John, Fitzroy."

"Harya."

"How do you do," said Fitzroy, with a gleaming but brisk smile, and when offered his hand, Dortmunder found it warm and pulpy, like a boneless chicken breast in a sock.

Kelp said, "Right on time."

"Of course," Fitzroy said, and to Dortmunder, he said, "I'm sorry, John, you'll have to ride in back."

"That's okay," Dortmunder said. At this point, what difference did it make?

Fitzroy led the way to the back of the van and opened one of the doors there. "Nothing to sit on but the floor, I'm afraid."

Naturally. "That's okay," Dortmunder said, and bent forward to climb in on all fours, feeling the rough carpeting beneath his palms.

"All set?" Fitzroy asked, but he didn't wait for an answer, instead slamming the door the instant Dortmunder's heels had cleared the area.

Dortmunder propped his left forearm on a wooden box taking up most of the space back here, so he could scrunch around and get into a seated position, legs folded in an extremely loose version of the lotus position. Then he looked around himself in the dimness.

There were no windows back here, only up front, the windshield and the windows in the doors flanking the front seats. In this space back here were two shovels, a coil of thick rope, some other stuff, and this long box he was leaning his forearm on, which was . . .

A coffin. Very dark brown wood, scuffed-looking, with pocked brass handles and a faint redolence about it like basements, like a greenhouse in winter, like freshly turned earth, like, well, like a grave.

Dortmunder took his forearm off the box and put it on his knee. Of course; this was the coffin that would go into the grave once they took the original inhabitant out. And I, Dortmunder thought, get to ride out to the cemetery with him. Great.

The other two got into the front of the van, and Fitzroy made the left onto Lex, then the left onto Thirty-sixth, and headed for the Midtown Tunnel. The darkened city bounced by, beyond those two heads.

It was May's fault, Dortmunder decided. So long as she'd been against him taking this job, it'd been easy to say no. But when she came to the conclusion there was something mystical or something about this being exactly a thousand dollars, the exact same amount as the profit he'd had to leave behind in the Speedshop, there was no hope for him. He wasn't a ditchdigger, he wasn't a grave robber, and he wasn't a guy given to manual labor, but none of that mattered. It was the thousand dollars coming around again, so he was supposed to grab it.

All right, so he'd do it and get it over with, and come back with the thousand, and never touch a shovel again for the rest of his life, so help him. In the meantime, Kelp and Fitzroy sat up front, jabbering about how useful the Internet was—sure, you could meet people like Fitzroy Guilderpost there, with shovels—while Dortmunder and the fellow beside him in the back had nothing to say to each other.

Dortmunder found, if he raised his knees and put his crossed forearms on them, and then rested his chin on his forearms, he could look out the windshield past those two happy heads and watch the city unreel. Also, in this position, he could watch their recent history in the large rearview mirrors beyond both side windows; large because there was no interior mirror, since there were no windows at the back of the van.

They were approaching the tunnel now. Traffic was light, mostly big panel trucks with 800 numbers on the back that you could call to rat on the driver if he wasn't doing a perfect job. Dortmunder wondered if anybody was ever fink enough to call one of those numbers. Then he wondered if anybody ever called one of those numbers to say the driver was doing a great job. Then he wondered at how bored he was already, and they weren't even out of Manhattan yet.

They ran through the tunnel, and Dortmunder noticed there was no one on duty at any of the glassed-in police posts along the way; a hardened criminal could actually change lanes in here. He looked in the rearview mirrors and saw a car appear, way back there. He noticed that the left headlight on that car was a little dimmer than the right. He realized he had to break out of this tedium right now; it wasn't healthy.

So he sat up straighter, ignored the rearview mirrors, and broke into the Internet conversation—they're doing E-mail in person up there—to say, "This box here come a long way?"

Fitzroy automatically looked at where the interior

mirror would be, to see the passenger in back, then looked out at the tunnel again and said, "Out west."

"Oh, yeah? A long way. You don't have to, uh, refrigerate it or anything?"

"No, that's old in there," Fitzroy assured him. "That's almost seventy years old. Nothing more's going to change in there."

"I guess not. And the one we're switching? That's old, too?"

"Two or three years older, in fact," Fitzroy said. "You won't mind, John, if I don't tell you the entire operation."

"Not me," Dortmunder said. "I'm just making conversation."

But Fitzroy was full of his caper, whatever it was, and both wanted to talk about it and didn't want to talk about it. "It's the linchpin, I'll tell you that much," he said. Then they were out of the tunnel and at the tollbooths, and he said, "Excuse me."

"Sure," Dortmunder said. Polite guy, anyway.

It took Fitzroy, being portly, a while to get at his wallet, and then to hand over some bills to the attendant and wait for his change. Dortmunder leaned his chin down to his knees again to look in the outside mirrors, and the car with the one fainter headlight was moving very slowly toward another open booth. Very slowly. That driver must be trying to get to his money before he reached the booth. The car was a gray Plymouth Voyager, a passenger van, the kind of suburban vehicle mostly used for hauling Little League teams around and about, though this one had only the driver, a guy, indistinct inside there.

Fitzroy at last got them moving again, and Dort-munder sat up to say, "So this is the linchpin, huh?"

"We couldn't do the operation without it," Fitzroy assured him. "But with it, we win. We have to be ab-solutely secret about it, though, absolutely. We daren't risk a *word* getting out."

Kelp said, "Well, you know you can count on John and me. We'll never say a thing about this."

"Oh, I haven't the slightest doubt on that score," Fitzroy said, and turned his head to smile at Kelp. Seen in profile like that, from the back of the van, smiling, he looked more like a hungry wolf and less like a portly man.

It was only ten minutes along the Long Island Ex-pressway, and then they were passing among the ceme-teries, a huge necropolis spread across Queens, different cemeteries for different religions and ethnics, clustered together for companionship, like campfires on the Great Plains. For the one they wanted, they had to stay on the highway to the far end, then take the exit there and cir-cle back. Dortmunder, who'd been getting bored again, once Fitzroy wouldn't talk about his scam anymore, had gone back to the chin-on-knee posture, and now he saw that same Plymouth Voyager with the gimpy headlight, well back there, but with his right turn signal on, prepar-ing to take the same exit as them.

Is this guy following us? Dortmunder wondered if he should mention it to Fitzroy, if this was maybe some problem with his secrecy that he should know about, but then he thought, Fitzroy's been looking in the same mir-rors as me. I've seen him check those mirrors a lot, all the way out, so if he's that hipped on secrecy tonight, he's already noticed that car. So if it's somebody that *is* following us, Fitzroy already knows about it.

Dortmunder thought about that.

Taking a side street that cut between two different cemeteries, Fitzroy said, "They lock these places at night for some reason, which could be a problem for us. We don't want anyone ever to know that anything happened here tonight. Fortunately, up ahead here, a portion of the fence is broken. Not done by us. Much earlier. Drug dealers possibly, or lovers."

"Or vampires," Kelp said.

"Yes, very good," Fitzroy told him. "But more likely ghouls, I think. Vampires prey on the living. It's ghouls that eat dead flesh."

"Well, so do we," Kelp said. "You know, beef and like that."

To distract himself from the conversation, Dortmunder leaned down again to look in the mirrors. No lights but the wide-apart streetlights, so the Voyager had voyaged elsewhere. No, here it came, around the corner, well back. Came around the corner, and right away the headlights switched off.

Funny place to park.

Dortmunder looked out front. They were on a bumpy blacktop street flanked by eight-foot-tall wrought-iron fences of two different designs, with tombstones visible beyond them both. The street ran straight up a gradual slope, and it looked to Dortmunder as though the land tipped down again farther ahead.

But they didn't go that far. On the right, a section of fence sagged inward, away from one of the support bars, leaving an opening wide enough for a person to walk through, or maybe even two people abreast, but not wide enough for a car. Nevertheless, Fitzroy angled toward this opening, bumping up over the curb and sidewalk—why had the city bothered to put sidewalks on a street like this?—and stopping just short of the fence.

"Now, Andy," Fitzroy said, "if you and John get out and pull on that fence, you can open it wide enough for me to drive through. Once I'm in there, it would be best to close it up again."

"Sure," Kelp said, and opened his door.

Fitzroy said, "You'll have to open the back door for John, there's no knob on the inside there."

The optician at Speedshop again. Dortmunder wriggled about to face the back, trying not to lean on the coffin more than absolutely necessary, and Kelp came around to open the door. Dortmunder clambered out and the two of them walked over to the fence, which was black wrought iron designed with daisy shapes between the vertical bars at waist level and again at head level. These shapes made good grips. As they grasped handfuls of daisies, Dortmunder said, without moving his lips, "A car followed us."

"I know," Kelp said, without moving his lips.

The fence moved more easily than they'd expected. It was heavy, but once they got the end lifted from the ground, it swung without trouble.

There were a few old graves here, sunken, with tilting tombstones, but they weren't in the way. Fitzroy steered slowly around them and stopped when he reached the gravel roadway.

Dortmunder and Kelp moved the fence back to position number one, and Dortmunder said, without moving his lips, "He likes absolute secrecy."

"Absolutely," Kelp said, without moving his lips.

They walked over to the van, where Fitzroy had opened his window so he could tell them, "It isn't far, it'll be just as easy to follow me."

"Lead away," Kelp said.

Fitzroy drove slowly along the gravel roadway, and Kelp and Dortmunder walked behind, speaking without moving their lips. "They can try whatever they want," Dortmunder said, "just so he's actually got that thou."

"He's got *some* dough," Kelp said. "I took a look at his wallet at the tollbooth."

"They won't make their move until the switch is done," Dortmunder said, "so we still gotta do all this digging."

"Maybe that's good," Kelp said. "Maybe their scam gets to be our scam."

"I dunno about that," Dortmunder said. "I don't like hanging out with dead bodies."

"Well, they're quiet," Kelp said, "and you can trust them. We'll see how it plays."

The brake lights went on in front of them, and Fitzroy angled off onto the grass so that his headlights shone on a small pale stone in front of another slightly sunken grave. Dortmunder and Kelp walked around the van, read the stone, which said:

JOSEPH REDCORN
July 12, 1907–
November 7, 1930

"Died young," Kelp commented.

"There's a lesson in that," Dortmunder said.

Fitzroy had gotten out of the van to go around back and open both its doors. Now he came toward them, carrying a folded canvas tarp, saying, "We want to be very careful we leave no traces of our digging. We'll spread this on the next grave and put all the dirt there. Also, I'll ask you to remove the sod very carefully, so we'll be able to put it back."

Meaning somebody else would be coming along, probably pretty soon, to dig the guy up again. And for Fitzroy's scam, the guy they dug up had to be the ringer from out west, instead of the actual Joseph Redcorn. Almost seventy years he'd been lying down there, old Joseph, minding his own business, and now he was getting evicted so somebody else could pull a fast one. Dortmunder almost felt sorry for the guy.

Kelp said to Fitzroy, "I was saying to John, he died young, this fella."

"Well, he was an American Indian, from upstate," Fitzroy told him. "You know, those are the people that work in construction on the skyscrapers, up on the tall buildings. Mohawks, mostly, some others."

"This one was a Mohawk?"

"No, one of the minor tribes the Iroquois controlled, the Pottaknobbee. But Redcorn was a steelworker alongside them, on what they call 'the high iron.' "

Dortmunder said, "And something went wrong."

"He was working on the Empire State Building, while they were putting it up," Fitzroy explained, "and one day in November, it started to rain. Help me spread this tarpaulin, will you, John?"

"Sure," Dortmunder said.

They spread the tarp while Kelp got the shovels out of the van. Dortmunder looked around, saw nobody, knew there was somebody nearby just the same, and took the shovel Kelp handed him.

5

Irwin sat on a tombstone, but the stone made his butt cold and there was nowhere to lean his back. So he sat on the ground in front of the stone, leaning against it, but the ground made his pants wet and the stone made his back cold. So he stood and leaned against a tree, but the bark was rough and uncomfortable, and his legs got tired. So he tried sitting on the stone again.

Meanwhile, over there, in the glare of the van's headlights, the bozos were working up a pretty good sweat. They were stripped to the waist now, both excessively unlovely, both shovels working, dirt flying up and out of the hole and onto the tarp on the grave next door. These two were better than the bozos in Nevada, harder workers, more willing, and much more trusting.

Irwin walked around in the darkness, trying to dry the seat of his pants, and thinking how the word *trust* and the name Fitzroy Guilderpost just naturally didn't belong together. Well, *he* was no bozo, Irwin Gabel was no bozo, and when *he* outlived his usefulness for Guilderpost, he'd have something to say about it.

His partners had no idea that Irwin had routinely wired himself for every single one of their meetings, including the events in Nevada and including the events yet to come tonight. All those tapes were very safely and securely tucked away, not to be mentioned until that inevitable moment when Fitzroy Guilderpost thought he and Irwin Gabel had come to the parting of the ways.

If only he could team up with Little Feather, but the bitch was so cold and hard, it was like trying to chat up one of these tombstones here. But she was the one he'd need, when the end of the partnership with Guilderpost was reached. It was Little Feather who was going to be the rich one, and if Guilderpost really thought he had her tied up with that contract they'd all signed, he was crazy. Try enforcing *that* in court.

But if Irwin and Little Feather could combine, life would be a lot easier and a lot safer. Guilderpost would be out and gone and forgotten, and Irwin would be in, and life would be easy forever after. Millions, an eventual payout of millions, and coming in steadily, endlessly, over their lifetimes and beyond. It was worth all the effort they were putting into it.

The problem was, Little Feather's relationships with men had been too narrowly focused over the years. She just naturally assumed Irwin's interest in her was sexual, which it emphatically was not. Get into bed with that, you'd probably break something. But until he got her on his side, it was too dangerous to tell her what he really had in mind. She would probably believe she'd be better off siding with Guilderpost, who'd thought up this scheme in the first place, not realizing that Irwin Gabel was the real brains of the operation.

Well, there was still time to sort everything out.

Over there at the grave, Guilderpost was now turning

the van around, so they were ready for the switch. Yes, here came the Redcorn coffin up out of the grave, the two bozos tugging and hauling on the ropes attached to the thick canvas strap they'd lashed around the middle of the box. Out it came, with a certain amount of heavy breathing and muttered curses, and now they removed the strap and headed for the open van.

Irwin dared to move cautiously a little closer to the scene, because this was the part that mattered. How they banged around the Redcorn coffin didn't concern him, but the Elkhorn coffin had to be used gently. It shouldn't go into the grave with any fresh dents or dings on it. Irwin had explained that very carefully to Guilderpost, and he could only hope Guilderpost was explaining it just as carefully to the bozos.

Well, apparently so. Good. The two pulled the box out of the van, laid it carefully on the ground, strapped it, roped it, then lowered it with care into the grave. Excellent.

The rest took no time at all. The dirt went back into the hole a lot more quickly than it had come out. When the bozos went to their knees to start carefully replacing the sod, like assembling a jigsaw puzzle, Irwin turned away. Nothing would go wrong from this point. At the end, they'd put the Redcorn coffin in the van, to be taken to the disposal site, and then they'd leave.

Irwin walked briskly, still hoping the air movement would dry the seat of his pants, and went out through the hole in the fence and down the long block of Sunnyside Street to where he'd left the Voyager. He got into it, U-turned, and then, back at the corner, he went left, away from the highway. A hundred yards from the corner, he

U-turned again, parked, switched the lights off, and waited for the van to come out. Once again, he would stay well back as they headed out the island to the disposal site. It wouldn't be a good idea to let the bozos know Guilderpost wasn't alone out here tonight.

6

This new coffin smelled a little nastier than the first one, a little more dank, probably because the bits of dirt clinging to it had more recently been underground. Otherwise, it was a very similar coffin, a little timeworn in the same way; nevertheless, Dortmunder found it less appetizing to sit beside, and he tried to scrunch over as far to the left as possible, away from the aura of the thing.

Up front, as they drove back onto the Long Island Expressway, eastbound, away from the city, Andy said, "So what are we gonna do with Mr. Redcorn, now that we got him?"

"About half an hour from here," Fitzroy told him, "there's a bridge over to Fire Island, the western end of Fire Island. It's almost never used this time of year, because, mostly, Fire Island is seasonal, summer cottages. There's a pretty quick channel under the bridge, water from the South Bay going out to sea."

"I get it," Kelp said. "We toss it off the bridge, it floats for a while, and it's heading out to sea, and then it sinks."

"Exactly."

And us, Dortmunder thought, we just sink, right there in the channel.

The Voyager's headlights hadn't appeared in the mirrors until they'd gotten back up on the expressway, but they were there now, keeping a certain distance, trying to remain unremarkable in this sparse traffic. After two in the morning, even the Long Island Expressway wasn't getting much action.

And the traffic only got sparser as they headed east, so that the Voyager had to hang farther and farther back. They left Queens and crossed Nassau County, all the little bedroom communities asleep, and by the time they got to Sagtikos Parkway, that distant Voyager was the only light at all in the rearview mirrors.

Fitzroy turned south on Sagtikos Parkway, which was empty in both directions as far as the eye could see. They crossed the Southern State Parkway, and then they came to a very long and elaborate bridge, which couldn't be the one Fitzroy had in mind.

No. This one crossed the Great South Bay, the long strip of seawater between the southern shore of Long Island and its line of sandbar beaches. At the end of this bridge, you could turn right and go eventually to Jones Beach, or you could go straight, over a much smaller and shorter bridge crossing a narrow inlet over to Fire Island, a long strip of sand with seasonal communities, no real roads, and very few vehicles, so that this bridge wasn't used much even in season.

There had been no headlights in the mirror since they'd reached the first bridge, so the follower must be driving with his lights out. A whole lot of effort these people were putting in, and it seemed to Dortmunder the reason had to be something more than just stiffing a couple guys out of a thousand dollars. They wanted *nobody*

to know Joseph Redcorn was AWOL from his grave, replaced by an alternate. Meaning that when that coffin was
dug up again, by somebody else, there would be some
publicity in it, something of value connected to it.

But what? A guy falls off the Empire State Building,
and seventy years later he's important? How can that be?
And how can slipping a proxy in there in his place do
anything for anybody?

Well, we'll find out, Dortmunder thought. Eventually,
we'll find out.

This smaller bridge was steeply arched, and Fitzroy
stopped the van at the top of the hump. "All we have to
do now," he said, "is toss it over. Andy, would you open
the doors back there?"

"Sure," Kelp said, and got out, and Dortmunder
reached forward to give Fitzroy a neck hold in the crook
of his left arm while he reached for Fitzroy's pistol. One
crime a fat guy usually can't commit is carrying a *concealed* weapon, so Dortmunder had known from the beginning that Fitzroy's pistol was in the right-side pocket
of his suit jacket, handy to his right hand. Handy to Dortmunder's right hand, too. He pulled it out, a neat little
Smith & Wesson .32 six-shot revolver with a cover over
the firing pin, so it wouldn't snag in a pocket.

Taking his bent left arm away from Fitzroy's Adam's
apple, so the guy could start to breathe again, substituting
for it the barrel of the pistol, touching Fitzroy's head just
behind his right ear, Dortmunder said, "Put both hands
on the steering wheel, okay? Up high, where I can see
them."

Obeying, Fitzroy said, "What was—" But he had a little trouble with his throat, had to cough and *ahem* before

he could start again. "What was that for, John? What are you— Why are you doing this? What are you doing?"

"At the moment," Dortmunder told him, "I'm waiting for Andy to come back with your pal in the Voyager. Then we'll see what happens next."

Fitzroy kept trying to see Dortmunder in the nonexistent interior mirror. "You— How did you . . ." But then he ran down, had nothing more to say, and merely shook his head.

"Just lucky, I guess," Dortmunder said. "Listen, would you like to tell us the scam now?"

"What? Absolutely not!"

"Well, later then," Dortmunder said, and the door behind him opened and a strange voice, talking very fast, said, "Well, I certainly don't know what this is all about, I mean, a man should be able to park by the side of the road, a little meditation in the, in the darkness, I certainly don't know what you people want from me."

Still watching Fitzroy, Dortmunder said, "Andy, hit him with something."

The voice stopped, and Kelp, behind Dortmunder in the doorway, said, "He was wired."

That galvanized Fitzroy. He spun about, ignoring the pistol held to his head, and yelled at the people behind Dortmunder, *"What?"*

"I have no idea who you are, sir," the new voice said, "and I would prefer to have nothing to do with whatever's going on here tonight."

"Irwin?" screamed Fitzroy. "You've been *tape-recording* us? You miserable sneak!"

There was a little pause. Fitzroy's face was now inches from Dortmunder's, his eyes focused in wrath toward the

people in back. Then the focus shifted, and he and Dortmunder gazed deeply into each other's eyes. Dortmunder
smiled amiably and showed him the pistol. "Just go with
the flow, Fitzroy," he advised.

From behind him, the new voice said, "One has to protect oneself around you, Fitzroy."

"Miserable, miserable sneaking . . ."

Kelp said, "I think this is what they call a falling-out
among thieves."

Dortmunder said, "Bring yours around, Andy," and to
Fitzroy, he said, "When they get here, time for you to step
out."

Fitzroy was doing his best to get his cool back. "My
friend," he said, pretending he'd been calm all along,
"John, I have no way of knowing, of course, what misap-
prehension you have about this evening. Irwin was
merely to observe, to be a backup in case there was trouble."

"There's no trouble," Dortmunder assured him, and
the door beside Fitzroy opened, and Kelp said, "Come on
out, Fitzroy."

Dortmunder clambered past the coffin and stepped out
onto the bridge. He shut the door, and when he came
around to the front, the pistol easy at his side, Kelp had
what must be Irwin's pistol in his right hand and the other
two were standing unhappily together by the rail. Irwin,
the new one, was as scraggly as Fitzroy was plump, and
no more appetizing.

Dortmunder said to Kelp, "Do you have the Voyager
key?"

Kelp held up his left hand, to show a chain with a car

key dangling from it. "Yes . . ." he said, and tossed the key over the rail, ". . . and no."

"No!" cried Irwin.

"Too late," Kelp told him.

Dortmunder said, "Fitzroy, do you by any chance have our two thousand dollars?"

Fitzroy actually looked embarrassed. "Not all of it," he said.

Dortmunder pocketed Fitzroy's pistol and held out his hand. "Wallet, Fitzroy."

"Can't we," Fitzroy said, "can't we discuss this?"

"Sure," Dortmunder said. "What's the scam?"

"No."

"Wallet, Fitzroy, or I'm gonna shoot you in the knee, which you won't like at all."

Fitzroy didn't like turning over his wallet at all, either, but grudgingly he did, and Dortmunder counted the bills in it, then gave Kelp a disgusted look. "Four hundred thirty-seven dollars."

"I apologize, John," Kelp said. "I didn't think he was that much of a jerk."

Dortmunder pocketed the money and gave back the wallet, then turned to Irwin: "Hand it over."

Irwin looked astonished and outraged. "Me? Why me? *I* didn't promise you any money!"

Dortmunder leaned closer to him. "Irwin," he said, "you remember the threat with the knee?"

Irwin, grousing and complaining, throwing Fitzroy angry looks as though it were all *his* fault, pulled out his shabby wallet and handed it over. Dortmunder counted, gave the wallet back, pocketed the cash, and said to Kelp, "Another high roller. Two thirty-eight."

Fitzroy said, "I can get you the rest of the money. Absolutely."

"No, Fitzroy," Dortmunder said. "The way it stands right now, you can't pull your scam without us, because if you try to pull it without us, we'll blow the whistle on you."

"Pull the plug," Kelp said.

"Point the finger," Dortmunder finished. "So what it is, we're your partners now. So all you have to do is tell us the scam."

"Never," Fitzroy said.

"Never's a long time," Dortmunder commented. "Let's go, Andy."

Fitzroy called, "What are you doing?" But since it was obvious what they were doing, they didn't bother to answer him. What they were doing was, they were getting into the van, Dortmunder behind the wheel. Then they were making a K-turn on the bridge, while Fitzroy and Irwin stood staring at them. Then Dortmunder was lowering his window, so he could say, "When you want to talk to us, you know how to get in touch with Andy. On the Internet." He closed the window, then drove back toward Long Island, saying, with deep scorn, "On the Internet."

"There's bad apples everywhere, John," Kelp said.

"*I'm* a bad apple," Dortmunder pointed out, "but you won't find me on the Internet."

"Oh, I know," Kelp agreed. "I can barely get you to use a telephone. What are we gonna do with this vehicle?"

"Long-term parking at La Guardia for tonight. Tomorrow, we'll move it. Or maybe you will, you got us into this."

Kelp sighed. "Okay, John."

Dortmunder shook his head. "I can't wait," he said, "to tell May how the thousand dollars worked out."

7

Guilderpost was too furious to speak. He watched his van drive away, over the bridge toward Long Island, with Joseph Redcorn aboard, and when he could no longer see those departing taillights, he turned to glare at the indefensible Irwin. There were lights on this little bridge, enough for Irwin to feel the full extent of that glare, which he at first ignored and then returned with as much force as a miserable, cowardly little sneak could muster.

It was Irwin who spoke first: "How did you screw up?"

Guilderpost restrained himself from leaping at that bony throat. "*I?* How did *I* screw up?"

"You did something that tipped them off."

"They saw you following! *You!* From the beginning!"

Irwin tried to look scornful: "Those bozos?"

Beginning to calm down—that's the trouble with speech, it drains some of the heat out of rage—Guilderpost looked toward Long Island and the disappeared Andy and John and the gone van. "I don't think, Irwin," he said, "those were quite the bozos we took them for."

"They're digging a grave! They're not rocket scientists!"

"Yes, yes, I know," Guilderpost agreed. "We had every reason to expect brainpower equivalent to our late assistants in Nevada. But somehow we wound up with people who were rather more than that."

"When that son of a bitch came out of the dark," Irwin said through clenched teeth, "to where I was standing beside the car, and stuck his fingers in my nose, I goddamn well couldn't believe it."

Guilderpost frowned. "Stuck his fingers in your nose?"

"It's painful as hell, let me tell you," Irwin said. "All of a sudden, he was there, brought his hand up, you know, palm toward himself, first two fingers right into my nose, and kept lifting."

"Lifting."

"I'm on tiptoe," Irwin said, patting his nose in pained remembrance, "and he's still lifting, and with his other hand, he's frisking me, and found my gun."

"*And,*" Guilderpost added, remembering, getting furious all over again, "your goddamn wire! Irwin, are you taping *this*?"

"He took the tape," Irwin said. "But there's nothing on it, I don't tape myself sitting alone in a car."

"You so mistrust me—"

Irwin looked scornful. "Fitzroy," he said, "everybody on earth mistrusts you, and every one of them is right."

"And you're telling me," Guilderpost said, "if you were to go out and be run over by a city bus, nothing to do with me, those tapes would go to the authorities?"

"If I'm dead," Irwin pointed out, "what do I care?"

"I thought," Guilderpost said, more in sorrow than in anger, "we had attained some level of trust between us."

"You're not that stupid," Irwin said, and looked around. "Do we live here now, or are we gonna get off this bridge?"

"Where's your car?"

"Over there," Irwin said, waving vaguely. "And you know where the key is."

"You don't have a spare key in the car?"

"No."

"But you could start it anyway, Irwin, you're a scientist, you'll know how to jump wires, or whatever that is."

"The doors are locked."

"Well, we'll have to break into the car, then," Guilderpost said, and firmly started to walk off the bridge, saying, "Come along."

Irwin came along. As they walked toward the car, he said, "Can you find that guy Andy again? Not in the computer, I mean, but in the world. Can you find where he lives?"

"I don't know. Possibly."

"And if you can't?"

Guilderpost glowered at the darkness all around them. He still didn't see the Voyager. He said, "Then we'll have to make them partners, won't we?"

"Temporary partners, you mean."

"Naturally." Guilderpost stopped. "But, Irwin," he said, "I must insist you stop taping our activities and destroy all the tapes you've already made."

"Not on your life," Irwin said, and looked back at him. "Now you want to stand *there,* in the middle of the road?"

Grumpy, Guilderpost started walking again. "Where did you leave the car, Irwin?"

"Out of sight."

"Irwin, those tapes are too dangerous."

"You're damn right they are," Irwin agreed.

"You won't destroy them?"

"Not a chance. But I tell you what," Irwin said. "Now that you know they exist, I won't make any more. Nevada and New York are both death-penalty states, there's enough on tape already to have them fighting over you."

"What a nasty piece of work you are, Irwin. And I recall how little you've tended to say, at certain moments. Ah, there's the car, at last."

They had walked some distance down the road toward Jones Beach, and there was the Voyager, dimly gleaming beside the road. Guilderpost began walking around it, looking at the ground, as Irwin said, "What do we tell Little Feather?"

Guilderpost stopped. "I think, for the moment," he said, "Little Feather needn't know about tonight's minor setback. No need to upset the poor girl. After all, the right body *is* in the grave, there's that. And there's still a chance I can lay my hands on Andy." And he started walking and looking at the ground again.

Irwin said, "Do you know his last name?"

"I doubt it," Guilderpost said. "He said it was Kelly. The other one didn't give a last name at all."

Irwin said, "Fitzroy, what are you looking for?"

"A rock," Guilderpost said.

Irwin recoiled. "You wouldn't dare!"

Guilderpost gave him an exasperated look. "To get into the car," he said.

Irwin liked that idea almost as little. "You're going to smash my car window? With a rock?"

"If I don't find one soon, I'll use your head," Guilderpost told him. "Help me look, Irwin."

8

Until Anne Marie Carpinaw, an extremely attractive semidivorcée in her late thirties, became his fairly significant other, Andy Kelp had never had much dealings with holidays. He pretty much did what he felt like each day, regardless. But now, in addition to curtains on the windows and place mats on the tables, there were these dates on the calendar to think about.

The latest one was Thanksgiving, which would be on a Thursday this year, or so Anne Marie said. "We'll have some people in," she said.

Kelp had no idea what that phrase meant. "People in? What, like, to fix something?"

"For dinner, Andy," she said. "You know what Thanksgiving dinner is."

"I know what dinner is," Kelp said.

"Well, I'm going to invite May and John, and J.C. and Tiny."

Kelp said, "Wait a minute. To eat here, you mean. Come eat dinner with us."

"Sure," she said. "I don't know what you used to do for Thanksgiving—"

"Neither do I," Kelp said.

"—but this year we'll have a traditional Thanksgiving dinner."

So apparently, there was even a tradition connected with this. Kelp said, "Okay, I give. What's a traditional Thanksgiving dinner?"

"Turkey, of course," she told him, "and cranberry sauce, and sweet potatoes, stuffing, gravy, brussels sprouts, creamed onions, marshmallow and orange salad, mince pie—"

"Whoa, whoa, whoa," Kelp said. "What was that one?"

"Mince pie."

"No, back up one."

"Marshmallow and orange salad," Anne Marie said, and studied his face, and said, "Not in New York, huh?"

"Not even in New Jersey, Anne Marie."

"I don't know what New Yorkers have against things that taste sweet."

"It confuses them," Kelp suggested.

"Well, it's too bad," Anne Marie said. "Marshmallow and orange salad is a big hit in Lancaster, Kansas"—she being from Lancaster, Kansas—"though, come to think of it," she added, "I don't remember ever seeing that much of it in D.C.," she also being from Washington, D.C., her father having been a congressman until God imposed His own personal term limits.

"So far as I know," Kelp told her, "marshmallows aren't allowed in this neighborhood."

"So you probably don't want them on the sweet potatoes, either."

Kelp said, "Tell me you're joking, Anne Marie."

Anne Marie said, "What about oranges?"

"For breakfast, sometimes," Kelp told her. "If you get

up feeling extra strong and you wanna rassle with something, an orange is good."

"I'm glad I asked you," Anne Marie said. "I don't want to get this wrong."

"You could check with May, maybe," Kelp advised.

"Oh, I'm going to," Anne Marie said, and she went away to make lists, the food list and the seating arrangement list and the beverage list and the phone call list. She also, over the next week and a half, kept reminding Kelp, just about every time she saw him, about Thanksgiving coming up on that Thursday, and about May and John and J.C. and Tiny all being invited to dinner, and the sheer mass of reminders had their effect, because at five minutes past four on that Thursday afternoon, when the apartment doorbell rang, Kelp, in a clean shirt, crossed the living room and pulled open the door.

Tiny and J.C. were the first arrivals. J.C. (for Josephine Carol) Taylor is a pleasure to describe. A statuesque, pale-skinned, dark-eyed brunette, she'd trained herself to look hard and efficient in her dealings with the world of business, where she ran a number of iffy mail-order outfits and had her own country, Maylohda*, somewhere in the Pacific, a place that came in for its share of Third World developmental seed money. Only when around Tiny did the stony surface crumble and another person appear, hardly scary at all.

Tiny Bulcher is another matter. A man mountain, with a body like an oil truck and a head like an unexploded bomb, he mostly looked like a fairy tale character that eats villages. "Hello, there, Kelp," this creature rumbled.

*Don't Ask

"Whadaya say, Tiny?" Kelp greeted him.

"I say," Tiny rumbled, "you got some rude cabdrivers in New York."

Kelp raised an eyebrow at J.C., who grinned and shook her head and said, "He'll be okay. A couple days' bed rest, he'll be right back in the cab."

"Good," Kelp said, and shut the door.

Tiny looked around at the empty living room. "We ain't early, are we?"

"As a matter of fact," Kelp told him, "you're a few minutes late."

Anne Marie, coming in from the kitchen, wearing the apron that Kelp liked when that was all she wore, but also wearing her party slacks and blouse, which was probably just as well, said, "Andy, people are supposed to be a few minutes late, it's polite."

"Oh," Kelp said, and the doorbell rang. "Here comes more politeness," he said, and went over to let in May and Dortmunder, while Anne Marie took Tiny's and J.C.'s coats. "Hey, there," Kelp said.

Dortmunder said, "May wouldn't let me pick the lock."

"Not on Thanksgiving," May said.

"Feel free," Kelp told him.

May went farther into the room to greet the others, while Dortmunder said, "We'd of been here before, but May made me walk around the block."

"For politeness, I know about that," Kelp told him. Then, as Dortmunder would have joined the others, Kelp detained him with a hand on his forearm and leaned close to murmur, "Tell me something. Am I getting civilized?"

Dortmunder looked him up and down, contemplating this idea, then shook his head. "I don't think so," he said.

"Good."

"I don't think you oughta worry about it," Dortmunder told him, and they started toward the others, and a bell rang.

For just a second, Kelp thought this was more politeness at the door, but then he realized it was the phone, and he said, loudly enough for Anne Marie to hear, "I'll get it, I'll take it in the bedroom," and hurried into the bedroom. The phone there was cordless, so he picked it up and walked around with it while saying, "Hello?"

"Andy Kelp?"

The voice was familiar, but Kelp couldn't quite place it. "Yeah?"

"Formerly Andy Kelly?"

Whoop. What blast from the past was this? A number of potentials crossed his mind. He stopped pacing to hunker over the phone and say, "Possibly."

"This is Fitzroy Guilderpost," said the voice, and then Kelp recognized it, and yes, that was the voice of Fitzroy Guilderpost.

It had been five weeks now since the night of the switcheroo in the graveyard. Kelp, being the one who'd gotten them involved in this thing in the first place, had been in charge of the van with the coffin in it, taking a train north once a week to move it from one commuter railroad station to another, where they all had free parking, and a vehicle that didn't stay more than a week would never attract any official body's attention. So far, the van had been in Dover Plains and Croton Harmon and Poughkeepsie and Peekskill and Pawling, and Kelp had begun to wonder just how much longer he was going to be prepared to go on doing this. There would come a time when he and Dortmunder would have to agree that they were unlikely ever to hear from Guilderpost, and decide it was time to park the van in front of a police station somewhere and the hell with it.

But here was Guilderpost now, and the man had apparently been a busy little beaver these past five weeks. He knows Kelp's real name, and he calls him at home. This is not something Kelp found enjoyable; he liked this apartment, especially now that Anne Marie had it all fixed up, and he didn't want to move. And he also didn't want to have to explain to Anne Marie why a move would be a good idea. Therefore, all cheerful amiability, he said, "Well, hello there, Fitzroy, I've been wondering about you."

"I believe we've been wondering about each other."

"And here it is Thanksgiving," Kelp said.

"I wanted to be sure to catch you at home," Guilderpost told him. "And it was just two days ago I learned how to reach you."

"Yeah, I'd love to know how you did that."

"The Internet," Guilderpost explained. "We all leave trails, Andy. I admit yours was fainter than most, but still. It's no longer really possible to hide, you know."

"Yeah, I guess you're right."

"Which means, more than ever," Guilderpost said, "we should all strive to compromise, to come to agreements, not to let hostility and bad feelings fester and grow. Not now, when anybody can find anybody."

"So I could find you, too," Kelp pointed out.

"Of course you could! I'm not exempt, I know that. But Andy, would you have any reason to pursue me?"

"Not that I can think of."

"No. So I'm comfortable, here in my little home. And how about you, Andy? Can you think of any reason I might have to pursue you?"

"Not if we come to an agreement," Kelp said. "By the way, did you find John, too?"

"Not yet. Of course, I know less about him. Does John have an E-mail address?"

Kelp laughed. "John barely has a snail mail address."

"Not an enthusiast of the new technologies, I take it."

"John's still dubious about the internal combustion engine."

"That's here to stay," Guilderpost assured him.

"That's why he's dubious. You want to include him in the conversation now? He's here."

"Oh, really?"

Kelp said, "Well, it's Thanksgiving. We thought we'd get together, cut up old jackpots, count our blessings. We were wondering if— Hold on."

Kelp walked back into the living room, where Dortmunder and May and J.C. and Tiny were now seated on most of the chairs, with Tiny on most of the sofa, talking away about something or other. Anne Marie must be in the kitchen with the turkey and all that. To Dortmunder, very up and cheerful, Kelp said, "Guess what, John? It's Fitzroy Guilderpost!"

"No kidding," Dortmunder said. "Tell him I said hello."

"John says hello," Kelp told the phone, "and about these blessings we were counting, you know, as a matter of fact, we were just wondering if *you* were one of those blessings, or if you were the other thing."

"I'm prepared to pay—"

"No, Fitzroy, wait." To Dortmunder, Kelp said, "I think he wants to talk money, like a payoff."

Dortmunder shook his head. "We want in."

"I heard that," Guilderpost said, "and Andy, I'm sorry, but it isn't possible. There are already people involved—"

"Well, there's gonna be more, Fitzroy," Kelp interrupted. "I know John, when he sets his mind to something. What we're gonna need from you right now is a rundown on the scam, and then—"

"I'm not going to do that!"

"Listen, Fitzroy," Kelp said. "It's pretty clear, what you're doing is gonna go public, you're expecting some kinda splash, so we'll know the score then, anyway, so we might as well know it now, see what we think of it, do we wanna help out some way or just take a chunk of cash and leave."

There was a brief silence while Guilderpost thought that over, and then he said doubtfully, "I suppose we could meet."

"Us and Irwin? And your other partners?"

"Just one other."

"So you're three." Kelp thought about his last meeting with Guilderpost and Irwin. He looked at Tiny, then nodded to himself and said, "I think we're three, too."

"Andy!" came the reproving voice from the phone.

"Well, there's this other fella here, we hang out sometimes. Hold on." To Tiny, he said, "Tiny, you want a piece of this?"

The phone asked, "Tiny?"

Tiny said, "How much?"

"That's a good question. I'll find out." Into the phone, Kelp said, "How much are we talking here, Fitzroy?"

"I'm not going to— What are you—"

"Just ballpark, Fitzroy. I'm not asking for a guarantee. But roughly how much? In total, how many commas?"

Another little pause. A sigh shivered down the phone lines. "Two."

Kelp nodded, and said to Tiny, "Two."

Tiny nodded, and said, "In."

Kelp said to Guilderpost, "Tiny's in, so that's three of us, and if we make this meeting pretty soon, maybe there won't be any more."

"Good."

"So where and when?"

"I'll have to make arrangements," Guilderpost said. "Why don't I phone you tomorrow, say three o'clock? I'll tell you then where we'll meet."

"Gee, I'd rather not do that, Fitzroy," Kelp said, "not after what happened to a friend of mine."

"And what would that be?"

"Well, there was this other fella, and he and my friend had a little misunderstanding, bad blood, threats, that kinda thing, and the other fella called and said why don't we meet someplace neutral and talk it over, and my friend said okay, and the other fella said I'll call you tomorrow at two o'clock and tell you where we'll meet so the next day my friend made sure he was home at two o'clock and the phone didn't ring."

"It didn't?"

"No. The house blew up instead."

"Well, that's terrible," Guilderpost said.

"That's what my friend thought," Kelp said. "Or what he would have thought, you know what I mean. So why don't we just go ahead and meet tomorrow?"

"So soon? I—"

"Won't be able to set anything up. And neither will we. That bridge where we saw each other last?"

"Yes?"

"If you don't go over that little bridge, if you head for Jones Beach, you come to these huge parking lots that fill up in the summer with everybody's cars that are going to the beach."

"Yes, I know them."

"This time of year, there's nobody there," Kelp said. "A fella in a car in the middle of that parking lot, nobody could sneak up on him or stash anything there ahead of time or anything like that. That fella could feel safe."

"You, you mean, Andy," Guilderpost said.

"Well, I meant both of us, Fitzroy," Kelp told him. "How about eleven tomorrow morning in Parking Area Six? Out in the middle of it."

"That's rather early, isn't it?"

"Is it? We could make it earlier. Would ten be better?"

"No, no, I don't want it *earlier.*"

"Let me say this, Fitzroy," Kelp told him. "I'm glad you called when you did, because I was getting tired of the responsibility of Mr. Redcorn. I figured, next week, I was gonna park the van in front of a police station."

"Then I'm glad we chatted this week," Guilderpost said.

"Me, too, Fitzroy. See you eleven tomorrow morning, Parking Area Six." And he hung up and carried the phone back to the bedroom.

When he came out, J.C. pointed a dark red–nailed finger at him and said, "Andy, if you don't tell what that was all about, I'm going to have to throw you out the window."

"No need," Kelp said. "I'll tell you the whole story."

But then Anne Marie appeared in the doorway and said, "Dinner. Andy, help me carry things to the table."

So that was a delay, not Kelp's fault, and now everything had to come out to the other table, next to the dining room table, and Anne Marie had to consult her seating list, and then she had to *change* her seating list, because it was clear that Tiny couldn't sit with somebody else on the side of the table, but had to sit by himself at the end. But then that worked out another way, because when Anne Marie looked at Kelp and said, "So now the question is, who's going to carve?" and Kelp gave her the blankest look anybody's ever seen outside an opium den, Tiny said, "I can be pretty handy with a knife," and there he was, already at the head of the table.

So while Tiny carved and Anne Marie filled the plates that Dortmunder shuttled from the table, Kelp explained to the others the story till now. Then Tiny moved the turkey remnant to the side table and everybody sat down, and J.C. said, "Why did they do it?"

"First," Anne Marie said, "the toast. Andy?"

She'd made him buy a bunch of bottles of red wine with corks in them, so everybody now had a glass of wine in front of their place. Kelp picked up his and said, "Well, Thanksgiving tradition. I think maybe we got us something going here."

"Hear hear," everybody said, and tasted the wine, and agreed it was very good stuff, and picked up their knives and forks, and J.C. said, "All right. So why did they do it?"

"If you mean the switch," Kelp told her, "that's what John and me keep asking them and they keep not wanting to tell us. If you mean anything else, they don't want anybody to know what they're up to, and we figure that's because it's gonna go public and they don't want anybody around that might tip the word on them."

J.C. shook her head. "I've done some cons," she said. "I've done some scams. I tell myself I oughta be able to figure this out."

May said, "Anne Marie, this stuffing is so moist, it's wonderful."

"It's the apples, I think," Anne Marie said.

Dortmunder said to J.C., "I don't think we got enough information yet." To Kelp, he said, "There's another partner, right?"

"That's what he says," Kelp said, and to Anne Marie, he said, "This stuff is really great, hon, we oughta eat like this every night."

"We do, Andy," Anne Marie said.

J.C. said, "So maybe the other partner is what'll tell you."

Dortmunder said to Anne Marie, "Great gravy, really great gravy, goes with the turkey like they were meant for each other." Then he said to J.C., "We'll find out tomorrow morning at eleven o'clock."

"Speaking of which," Tiny said, "that's a very tight schedule, Kelp."

"I didn't want to give them a chance to booby-trap us."

"Tight for *us*."

Dortmunder said, "No, I think Andy's right. We're not trying to blow them up, just talk to them. Doesn't take that much preparation."

"Maybe," Tiny said, and patted Anne Marie, to his right, on the arm—she flinched—and said, "This is a great meal, Anne Marie. Every bit of it. I'm gonna be around for seconds."

"Good," Anne Marie said, smiling at him and favoring her other arm.

Kelp said, "It would be nice if we had a car with a remote control. And a bomb, you know? Send it out there, see what happens. If nothing happens, then we go out there with the other car."

J.C. said, "You're going to have to give me the recipe for these creamed onions, Anne Marie. Isn't she, Tiny?"

"Yes," Tiny said, and turned to Kelp to say, "Hand grenade and duct tape."

Kelp looked at him. "You'd be willing to do that?"

"I done it before," Tiny said. "It always makes people switch over to Plan B, every time."

"Okay, good," Kelp said. "You got the grenade?"

"I know where to get it."

Dortmunder said, "I think I should find us some guns, too."

"Okay," Kelp said. "And in the morning, I'll go steal us a car."

"You know," Anne Marie said, "Thanksgiving dinner conversation in Lancaster, Kansas, wasn't at all like this." And she smiled happily around at her guests.

9

Little Feather knew she had to stay patient with these clowns. They were going to make her very, very rich, so all she had to do was hang in there with them until everything was taken care of, when she wouldn't need them anymore. But right now, they were all indispensable to one another, she and Fitzroy and Irwin, so they had to get along together, so she had to go on being patient, no matter how irritating they might become, Fitzroy with his genius act and Irwin sniffing around her as though she couldn't tell he didn't really want her body, only wanted that money she was going to collect.

Of course, now that Grandpa Elkhorn was installed in that grave out in Queens, she was the most indispensable of the three. Until then, Fitzroy could always have decided to replace her with another Indian maid, even though she was perfect for the job at hand. But now? Now it would take a hell of a lot for them to want to go dig up some third body somewhere.

So, even though they were all still indispensable to one another, now that she had become the most indispensable of them all, she could permit herself to show just the tiniest bit of impatience, peeking around the patience she still maintained. She could permit her voice to rise just the slightest bit when she asked, *"Tell them?"*

"It may be necessary, Little Feather," Fitzroy said apologetically. "We'll have to take that possibility into account."

They were having this discussion shortly after Fitzroy's phone call to the one guy he'd managed to find, and the three of them were now seated around in the rather cramped living room of the quarters Fitzroy had picked up from somewhere to be their base of operations while they were in New York. The quarters were cramped, but they wouldn't be staying in them much longer. Still, it was another reason that Little Feather was finding patience a difficult mode to hold on to. And now this.

"Already I'm having to share with you guys," she pointed out. "And now, how many more are gonna show up?"

"In the first place, Little Feather," Fitzroy said, "you aren't sharing with us, we're all sharing together. Don't forget who conceived of this idea."

"You're the genius, I know that," Little Feather assured him, not for the first time. "I'm not taking anything away from you. But the idea was to deal with these guys the way you dealt with the guys in Nevada, and for a month now, you led me to believe you *did* deal with them, and now all of a sudden they're not only alive but they're gonna be *partners*?"

"Only for a little while," Irwin promised. "Believe me, Little Feather, I don't like those fellows any more than you do. In fact," he said, tenderly touching fingertips to the end of his nose, "I've got more reason than you have not to like them. But Fitzroy's probably right."

"Thank you, Irwin," Fitzroy said, with barely any irony at all.

"They're not as easy to handle as the ones in Nevada," Irwin went on. "So there they are, they're alive, they know about the body switch, and if we keep them out, don't try to work some kind of deal with them, when the story hits the papers and the TV, they could make a lot of trouble for us."

"Out of spite, if nothing else," Fitzroy added.

"Exactly," Irwin said. "But if we bring them in, sooner or later we'll get a shot at them."

"You had your shot at them," Little Feather told him, "the night they did the work."

Fitzroy said, "We underestimated them, Little Feather. I'm afraid I must admit to that. It's my fault, I take full—"

"All right, all right," Little Feather said. "I'm not here to play the blame game. So we're gonna have to see them in the morning. We gonna use this place?"

"I don't see why not," Fitzroy said. "It would be simplest."

"And I could maybe set up a couple booby traps," Irwin said, "so maybe we could get rid of them right away."

Startled, Little Feather said, "What, are you gonna blow it up? I've got all my stuff in here."

"No, no, no," Irwin reassured her, "nothing like that. Just little things. If they work, there might be a little blood in here to clean up afterward, that's all."

"Just so I don't have to move out all my stuff," Little Feather said.

10

In the morning, Dortmunder walked over Nineteenth Street to Third Avenue and waited on the corner there. It was pretty full of pedestrians around that neighborhood, and about three minutes later, down Third Avenue came what appeared to be some sort of sonic wave that moved people to the edges of the sidewalk, opening up a vee behind itself like the wake behind a speedboat. Knowing this was Tiny arriving, Dortmunder turned the other way to look for a nice recent-model car with M.D. license plates.

Andy Kelp always took doctor's cars when he needed to travel, on the theory that doctors, surrounded as they are by the intimations of mortality, are always in favor of treating themselves well while here below, including the cars they choose to drive. "I trust doctors," Kelp often said. "When it comes to cars, that is."

Seeing the approach of no Volvos or Lincolns with M.D. plates, Dortmunder turned back the other way, and yes, here came Tiny. He was dressed for the occasion in a bulky wool olive-drab greatcoat that made him look like an entire platoon going over the top in World War I.

But what were those pink nylon straps curving over each shoulder to retreat into each armpit?

Tiny stopped in front of Dortmunder and nodded his head. "Whadaya say, Dortmunder?"

"I say," Dortmunder told him, "the people we're going to meet don't know my last name."

"Gotcha," Tiny said. "They won't hear it from me."

"Thank you, Tiny. What's with the straps?"

Tiny turned around, and he was wearing a cute pink nylon backpack big enough for two grapefruit but not one pumpkin, the kind of fashion accessory that on most people just looks dorky but which, on that expanse of olive-drab wool, looked like a really bad pimple. Most men wouldn't dare to be seen in such a thing because they'd be afraid people would laugh at them, but, of course, Tiny never had that problem.

Having given Dortmunder a complete eyeful, Tiny turned around again to say, "Somebody left it in the lobby at J.C.'s building about a year ago, and nobody ever claimed it—"

"Well, that makes sense."

"—so after a while, I took it upstairs and threw it in a closet because maybe someday it'd come in handy."

"Tiny? Why today?"

"I didn't want the grenade to stretch my pocket," Tiny said.

"I get it," Dortmunder said, and Tiny looked past him to say, "Here's the doctor now."

When Dortmunder turned, he saw approaching him up Third Avenue one of the larger suburban assault vehicles available, a Grand Cherokee Jeep Laredo, which isn't quite enough name for such an imposing command car.

This one was maraschino cherry red, with huge black waffle-tread tires, and yes, there was the M.D. plate, flanked by a number of bumper stickers recommending we all take great care with the fragile resources of our planet.

"Now that," Tiny rumbled, "is my kinda car."

"Yeah, it is," Dortmunder agreed.

Kelp, at the wheel, was grinning like Christmas morning. He braked to a stop at the curb, and Dortmunder opened the front passenger door while Tiny opened the rear one.

"Watch out for that first step," Kelp advised them.

Tiny unhooked his itty-bitty backpack and tossed it casually onto the backseat, where it bounced once and fell on the floor. Then he lifted his massive self into all of the backseat while Dortmunder climbed up to the seat next to Kelp.

Kelp looked back and down at the pink pack on the floor. "What's with that?"

"The grenade," Dortmunder told him.

Kelp looked at Dortmunder. "Ah," he said, and faced front, and when the doors were closed, he drove them uptown.

Looking around at the plush interior and the dashboard like an electronic major-league scoreboard, Dortmunder said, "Andy, are you sure a doctor owns this? It's more like a drug cartel would own it."

"When I saw it outside New York Hospital," Kelp told him, "I knew I had to steal it. Even if I wasn't going anywhere. Lemme tell you, this is a doctor, he doesn't just want comfort, he doesn't just want convenience, he wants to be immortal."

"I bet he's feeling naked right now," Dortmunder commented.

"Six to one he won't even leave the hospital," Kelp said, and turned toward the Midtown Tunnel.

It was a beautiful clear cold November day, and when they got out to the southern shore of Long Island, with the gray and quicksilver ocean sloping away from them down toward the distant horizon, the sky was a huge empty space, a bright but faded pale blue. There were a few distant cars on Ocean Parkway, but nothing in the day was quite as visible as the red Cherokee zipping along the pale concrete road past the ashy tans of sand and dead beach grass.

The long stretch of Jones Beach was empty, frigid waves lapping ashore, looking for something to take home. From time to time, they passed the entrances to parking areas, mostly blocked by sawhorses, the parking lots themselves screened from the road by hedges and stunted pine trees.

They'd been quiet inside the car for some time, but now Tiny leaned forward and said, "Dortmunder, you can give me a hand."

"Sure, Tiny."

Tiny had opened his pink pack and removed from it a standard U.S. Army hand grenade, known as a pineapple because it looks a little like a pineapple, its cast-iron body serrated to turn the body into many small pieces of shrapnel when the TNT inside goes off. Curved down one side of the grenade was its safety lever, held in place by a safety pin at the top, the pin attached to the pull ring. Pull the pin out by the ring, but keep holding the lever close against the grenade, and everything's fine. Release the lever, and you have ten seconds to remove yourself from the grenade's proximity.

The other item in the pink pack was a small roll of duct tape. Tiny now handed this tape to Dortmunder and said, "Twice around. But under the lever."

"Right, I know."

Tiny held the grenade loosely in his left hand, the lever opposite the side against his palm. Dortmunder wrapped duct tape twice around Tiny's hand and the grenade, leaving the lever free, then said, "Feel okay?"

"Like a rolla nickels," Tiny said. He seemed quite happy this way.

And here was Parking Area 6, as the big Parks Department sign announced, and the sawhorses had already been moved aside. The dashboard clock, when you finally found it among all the tachs and meters, read 10:54, but obviously the others were already here.

"Show time," Tiny said, and they drove through the break in the hedge and out onto the big pale expanse of parking area. And out there in the middle of all that emptiness stood a pastel green and chrome motor home, one of the biggest made, top of the line, a forty-foot Alpine Coach from Western Recreational Vehicles.

"Well, looka that," Kelp said.

"I guess we drive over there," Dortmunder said as the bus door at the right front of the motor home opened and three people stepped out into the pale sunlight.

Tiny leaned forward to peer past Dortmunder's cheek. "That's them, huh?"

Kelp made the introductions: "The fat one in the three-piece suit is Fitzroy Guilderpost and the thin one in the wrinkled suit is Irwin somebody, or maybe somebody Irwin. We don't know the babe."

The babe was tall and very well proportioned, with lustrous black hair in two long braids halfway down her back, almost to her waist. She wore a long white-fringed buckskin jacket and a short white-fringed buckskin skirt and the kind of tall red leather boots that are allegedly meant for walking.

"Too bad I already know Josie," Tiny commented. He was the only one in the world who called J. C. Taylor Josie.

"I don't know," Kelp said. "She looks to me like you could strike matches on her."

And, as their red Jeep rolled closer to the trio at the motor home, it was true. The babe was a babe, all right, but she looked more like an action figure made out of stainless steel than an actual person. She stood with one hand on one hip and one leg cocked, as though ready to show her karate moves at the slightest provocation.

Kelp drove up close and stopped, with his side of the car facing the three people, so that was the side Tiny got out. Dortmunder had to walk around the big red hood of the Jeep, and by then Kelp was already introducing everybody: "Tiny, this is Fitzroy Guilderpost, and that's Irwin, and I don't know the lady."

"I guess you don't," Irwin said.

Guilderpost said, "Forgive me, *this* is Tiny?"

"It's kind of a nickname," Tiny explained.

"I see," Guilderpost said. "Well, may I introduce Little Feather. Little Feather, that says he's Tiny, that's Andy Kelp, also sometimes Andy Kelly, and that's John. John, I'm sorry, I don't know your last name."

"I'm not," Dortmunder said. "Go ahead, Tiny."

"Right."

Tiny stepped forward and showed all assembled the hand grenade taped to his left hand, then closed the hand to keep the lever pressed to the grenade's side as he pulled the pin. Moving closer to Guilderpost, whose eyes had grown considerably wider, he extended the pin, saying, "Hold this for me, will you?"

Guilderpost gaped at the hand grenade. All three of them gaped at the hand grenade. Not taking the pin, Guilderpost said, "What are you *doing*?"

"Well, I'm goin inside there," Tiny said, "look around, see the situation."

"But why— Why *that* thing?"

"Well, if I was to faint or anything in there," Tiny said, "I wouldn't be holding this safety lever anymore, would I?"

Irwin said, "Is that— Is that an actual— Is that *live*?"

"At the moment," Tiny said.

Guilderpost, flabbergasted, said, "But why would you *do* such a thing?"

Dortmunder answered, saying, "Fitzroy, we've got like a few reasons not to trust you a hundred percent. So Tiny sees to it, if something happens to somebody, something happens to everybody."

Tiny turned to the babe. "Little Feather," he said, "*you* hold this pin for me, okay? Don't lose it now."

Little Feather was the first of the three to recover. Grinning at Tiny, she accepted the pin and said, "This is awful sudden. Pinned on the first date."

"That's just how I am," Tiny told her, and said to the rest, "I'll be out in a minute."

Tiny started for the motor home, but Irwin suddenly jumped in front of him, saying, "No, well, wait, why don't you let me go in first? You know, it might be unfamiliar to you and all."

"We'll go in together, then," Tiny said, and turned to Dortmunder to say, "See? Plan B every time."

"I see," Dortmunder said.

Tiny and Irwin went into the motor home and Little Feather gave Guilderpost an angry grin as she said, "Temporary partners. We'll take care of them. Fitzroy, you're *never* going to outsmart these people."

"Little Feather," Guilderpost answered, torn between anger and embarrassment, "we can discuss this privately."

Kelp said, "You know, Little Feather, I think you people need us, wouldn't you say so?"

"You may be right," Little Feather said, and the motor home door opened and Irwin stuck his head out to say, "All clear." Then he hurtled out among them, and it became obvious he'd done that because Tiny had given him a slight shove, and now there was Tiny in the doorway, saying, "They had a couple cute things set up. The electric wire to the toilet, I liked that one."

Kelp shook his head at Guilderpost, saying, "Fitzroy, you disappoint me."

"That was Irwin's idea," Guilderpost told him. "All those booby traps were his idea."

Little Feather said, "And guess who turned out to be the boobies."

"All right, all right," Irwin said. His nose appeared to be out of joint. "He's happy now, so let's go in."

"Nah, let's not," Tiny said. "That's a very small living room you got there."

"Especially for you, I guess," Little Feather said.

"Right." Coming out to join the rest, Tiny said, "So why don't we just stand here in the sunlight and talk this over? But first, Kelp, you and, uh, John, whyn't you put your guns on the ground by your feet?"

"Okay," Dortmunder said, and he and Kelp took out their pistols and put them on the concrete while Tiny said, "And you three, same thing."

Guilderpost said, "Why do you assume we're armed?"

Irwin was already taking two pistols out of his pockets, putting them on the ground as he said, "Oh, come on, Fitzroy, stop playing the fool."

So Guilderpost shrugged and brought out a cannon of his own and grunted as he bent to put it on the ground. "I must say," he commented, "I don't much care for this meeting so far."

"It'll get better," Tiny assured him.

Little Feather's pistol turned out to be a chrome Star .22 in a thigh holster. She looked both fetching and lethal as she drew it, and then she stood holding it, giving Tiny a speculative look.

He raised part of an eyebrow at her. "Yeah?"

"I'm wondering," she said. "If I was to shoot Andy there, would you really blow yourself up?"

"You wouldn't shoot *me*," he pointed out, "so it seems to me all you'd be doing was buy yourself some trouble."

"Very weird," she decided, and did a nice Bunny dip to put the .22 next to her boots.

Kelp said, "Start off anytime, guys."

Guilderpost said, "Shouldn't you, uh, Tiny, shouldn't you put the pin back in now?"

"Nah, I'm fine here," Tiny told him.

Irwin said, "But what if you forget, or stumble, or whatever?"

"Tough on us all, I guess," Tiny said. "Little Feather, you still got the pin?"

She held it up, a round copper-colored ring in the sunlight.

"Good," Tiny said, and turned to Guilderpost to say, "Start here."

"Very well," Guilderpost said. "But I must say I find that hand grenade distracting."

"I'll think about the hand grenade," Tiny promised, "you think about your story."

"Before the story," Little Feather said, "there's one thing we got to get straight."

"Money," Dortmunder said.

"You read my mind," Little Feather told him. Gesturing at Guilderpost and Irwin, she said, "I'm hooked up with these two, and it's a third each, and each of us puts in a third, one way or another. Guilderpost thought it up, Irwin's Mr. Science, and I'm the goods. Now you birds come along, and I can see where maybe you're useful, but I'm not doing any more shares. I'm not into this for a sixth." Nodding at Tiny, she said, "You're gonna have to wear that hand grenade the rest of your life, if you think you're gonna hold me up for a share."

Dortmunder said, "So you have a different idea."

"An offer," Little Feather said. "A cash buyout, once it's over."

Kelp said, "But nothing in front."

Irwin, sounding aggrieved, said, "We're not getting anything in front!"

"Well, that's you," Kelp told him.

Guilderpost explained. "We're operating, I'm sorry to say, with a rather tight budget."

Dortmunder said, "So make your offer."

Tiny said, "But don't make the first offer *too* small, you don't wanna startle me."

Little Feather and Guilderpost and Irwin looked at one another, apparently none of them wanting to say the number they must have earlier agreed on, and then Little Feather shook her head and said, "We've got to offer more."

Guilderpost nodded. "I'm afraid you're right."

"We have to add," Little Feather said, "a zero."

Irwin, still aggrieved, cried, "That much?"

"So you're going," Dortmunder said, "from ten grand to a hundred. Ten grand would have been an insult, I'm glad you didn't say it."

Little Feather said, "But I won't go above a hundred. It isn't a negotiation. We become partners, here today, or we become enemies." Smiling at Tiny, she said, "The old Indian lore I heard says, if there's gonna be an explosion close by, drop to the ground and lie flat, and maybe you'll be okay."

Tiny nodded. "What does the lore say if you're lying *on* it?"

Guilderpost said, "Now, we three have a contract between us—"

"Among," Little Feather said.

"You're kidding," Kelp said to Guilderpost.

Guilderpost seemed a little pompous, a little defensive. "It just seemed a good idea to have our understanding in writing."

Dortmunder said, "It has *never* seemed to me a good idea to put anything in writing."

Guilderpost said, "So you don't feel you need a contract."

"If we ever got a question," Dortmunder assured him, "we'll send Tiny to ask it."

"We know what we're talking about," Kelp said, and offered his cheerful smile to Little Feather. "When you get yours, we each get a hundred K."

"Right," she said.

Kelp turned his smile on Guilderpost. "And now," he said, "the long-awaited story."

Guilderpost nodded. "Yes. Fine. But first, you'll have to bear with a brief history lesson."

"I love school," Kelp said.

"In school," Guilderpost said, "do you remember the French and Indian War?"

"Remind me," Kelp said.

"Essentially," Guilderpost reminded him, "it's how France lost Canada. French and English settlers fought one another from 1754 to 1760. It seemed a very big thing to the people here, but it was actually just a small part of the conflict called the Seven Years War, involving virtually all of the European powers, fought in Europe and America and India. In the American part of the war, both sides made alliances with Indian tribes that did much of the actual fighting. In northern New York State, there were three small tribes that had always been subjugated by the five larger and more powerful tribes of the Iroquois Nation. These three tribes, to free themselves from the Iroquois, made treaties with the English settlers and fought for them, and then renewed the alliance a few years later, fighting for the colonists against the British in the American Revolution. The three tribes were given land in New York State, near the Canadian border, to be their sovereign state forever, but of course the white men reneged on all such treaties, and soon the logging interests moved in, fought the tribes, defeated them, and took over the land."

Irwin said, "There's so much wickedness in this world, you know what I mean?"

"We know," Kelp assured him.

Dortmunder said, "Little Feather's an Indian."

"We're coming to that, John," Guilderpost said. "In the last thirty years or so, the American courts have been redressing many of those wrongs done so long ago. Indians are getting their sacred tribal lands back—"

Dortmunder said, "And putting casinos on them."

Irwin said, "Yeah, sacred tribal lands and casinos just seem to go together naturally, like apple pie and ice cream."

"The tribes have their own sovereignty," Guilderpost said, "their own laws, and casinos are extremely lucrative."

Little Feather laughed, a sound like shaking a bag of walnuts. "This time," she said, "the Indians win."

"The three tribes I've been telling you about," Guilderpost said, "the Pottaknobbees, the Oshkawa and the Kiota, won their cause back in the sixties, and have been operating a thriving casino on their land up by the Canadian border for nearly thirty years now. The tribes had almost died out, but now they're coming back, or at least two of them are. At the time of the settlement, there were only three known full-blooded Pottaknobbees left in the world, and at this point, so far as anyone knows, there are none."

"Wait a minute," Dortmunder said. "I'm getting it."

"Anastasia," Tiny said.

Dortmunder said, "That's it."

Grinning, Kelp pointed at Little Feather. "*You're* the last of the Pottaknobbees."

"You bet," she said.

Tiny said, "But you can't do Anastasia no more. They do DNA now, they can prove you're not it."

Dortmunder said, "No, Tiny, that's what the scheme is, that's the body we dug up." To Guilderpost, he said, "Joseph Redcorn was a Pottaknobbee, right?"

"Definitely," Guilderpost said.

Dortmunder said, "And we took him outta there, and we put in . . ." He pointed at Little Feather.

Who said, "My grampa."

Guilderpost said, "The arrangement is, the tribes share equally in the casino profits, and then the tribal elders distribute the money to their own people. For a long time, there've been only two shares to distribute."

Dortmunder looked at Little Feather with new respect. "A third," he said.

Little Feather smiled, like sunrise. "A third of the casino," she said, "from day one."

11

You hardly know you're leaving the United States. On your way to Dannemora in upstate New York, near the Canadian border, famous as the home of Clinton State Prison, you turn left at the big billboard covered by a not very good painting of a few Indians in a canoe on some body of water, either a river or a lake, surrounded by pine tree–covered mountains. It's either sunrise or sunset, or possibly the mountains are on fire. Printed across this picture, in great thick letters speckled white and tan and black, apparently in an effort to make it seem as though the letters are made of hides of some kind, is the announcement:

WORLD-FAMOUS
SILVER CHASM CASINO
Native American Owned & Operated With Pride
5 Mi.

This billboard is brightly illuminated at night, which makes it seem rather worse than by day. At its top and bottom, arrows have been added, also lit up at night, which point leftward at a well-maintained two-lane concrete road that curves away into the primeval forest.

You are deep in the Adirondacks here, in the state-operated Adirondack Forest Preserve, but once you make that left turn, you have departed the United States of America and entered the Silver Chasm Indian Reservation, home of the Oshkawa and the Kiota, and until recently, also home of the Pottaknobbee. This is a sovereign state, answerable to no one but itself.

As you drive along the neat curving road, at first you see nothing but forest, beautiful, silent, deep, unchanged for a thousand years. Then you round a curve and all at once, in front of you, flanking both sides of the road, are suddenly a pair of competing shopping centers, with big signs promising tax-free cigarettes, beer, whiskey, or whatever you want. Indian blankets made in Taiwan are also available, and illustrated editions of *Hiawatha,* and miniature birch-bark canoes made in a factory outside Chicago and stamped in red "Souvenir of Silver Chasm Indian Reservation." Both shopping centers do very well.

Then there's more forest, as though the shopping centers had only been a horrible mirage, until, around another curve, you come upon a development of small neat tract houses on grids to both sides of the road, surrounded by forest; this is Paradise, home of most of the Kiota. (Most of the Oshkawa live in another part of the forest.)

Beyond Paradise, there's another bit of undisturbed forest and then a vast clearing, which is a parking lot. Signs direct you to enter, to park your car in any available slot, lock it, and wait beside it. Small buses constantly circle the parking area, picking up the new arrivals and driving them the last half mile to the casino itself, a low black-and-silver construction that makes a halfhearted attempt to look like an Art Deco log cabin.

The casino building is enormous, but because it's low, mostly one story high, with some upstairs offices toward the rear, and because it's surrounded by trees and tasteful plantings, it's hard to get a clear idea of just how big it is. But once inside, you begin to realize that the wide, bright, low-ceilinged spaces just go on and on. What seems to be acres of slot machines and poker machines spread off to infinity in one direction, while craps tables and blackjack tables march in long green lines in another. Then there are restaurants, poker rooms, baccarat tables, lounges, bars, and a number of playrooms where the kiddies can be looked after while Mom and Dad are losing the farm.

The casino is not itself a hotel, though there are four motels spaced nearby, and all do well, even in the depths of winter, though they're expected to do better yet once the casino management completes its plan for a motorized subway system to link up parking area, motels, and the main building.

Casino management these days consists of two men. One, Roger Fox, is Oshkawa, while the other, Frank Oglanda, is Kiota. Both are sleek, smooth men in their fifties, their thick black hair slicked back, cigars in their blazer pockets, heavy rings on most of their thick fingers, a smile of contentment almost always visible on both their round faces.

And why not? The casino mints money, they have no government to look over their shoulders, the tribes are happy so long as they all get their "shares" regular as clockwork, and nobody in the world has any reason or desire to examine just how Fox and Oglanda manage casino affairs.

But that happy situation all began to change on Monday, November 27, when a letter arrived from the United States, addressed simply, "Casino Managers, Silver Chasm Casino, Silver Chasm Indian Reservation." Fox was first in the office that afternoon—neither man was ever in the office in the morning—and he read the letter with surprise, unease, and distaste. Twenty minutes later, when Oglanda arrived, Fox carried the letter from his own office to his partner's, and said, "Look at this."

Oglanda took the letter, but kept his eyes on the unwonted frown on Fox's face. "Something wrong?"

"You tell me."

Oglanda removed the letter from its envelope, opened it, and read:

Sirs,

My name is Little Feather Redcorn. I am fifty percent Pottaknobbee, through my mother, Doeface Redcorn, who was born in the village of Chasm in upstate New York, near Dannemora, on September 9, 1942. My mother's mother, Harriet Littlefoot Redcorn, left Chasm in 1945, when word came from the government that her husband, my grandfather, Bearpaw Redcorn, was reported missing in action when his destroyer was sunk in the South Pacific.

My grandmother lived in the West for many years, mainly around Los Angeles, where she worked as a waitress, and raised her daughter, my mother, Doeface Redcorn. I believe Harriet Redcorn died somewhere in California or Oregon around 1960, but I don't know the details.

Doeface had a brief marriage with a full-blooded Choctee in 1970, of which I am the result. They lived together on the reservation for a while, but the marriage was not a good one. My mother soon got a divorce and went back to her maiden name, and she never saw Henry Track-Of-Skunk again.

My mother and I didn't get along well when I was in my teens, I'm sorry to say, and eventually I left her in Pomona and went away to Las Vegas to live on my own. I had some success in show business in Las Vegas, but I had no more contact with my mother. I later heard that she had died, but I don't know the circumstances or where she is buried.

However, I do know that I am Pottaknobbee of the Redcorn clan, through my mother, Doeface, my grandmother Harriet Littlefoot Redcorn, and my great-grandfather Joseph Redcorn.

Recently, I read an article in *Modern Maturity* at my dentist's office about the casino at Silver Chasm and how the Pottaknobbee are part of the owners of the casino, except there aren't any Pottaknobbees anymore. But I am Pottaknobbee. Shouldn't I receive something from the casino?

I have come east to learn more about my situation at Silver Chasm. I am staying now at Whispering Pines Campground outside Plattsburgh, where the phone number is 555-2795. I will phone you Tuesday afternoon, by which time you should have received this letter.

I am very excited at the idea of being united at last with my own people, after having lived my entire life far away.

Sincerely,

Little Feather Redcorn

"It's a phony," Oglanda said when he'd finished reading. Disdainfully, he dropped the letter onto his desk.

"I certainly hope it's a phony," Fox said.

"No, Roger," Oglanda said, "listen to me." Tapping the letter with a hard finger, he said, "This claim is a phony, a definite phony. Do you know why?"

"Why?"

"Because," Oglanda told him, "if this woman is telling the truth, and she's even fifty percent Pottaknobbee, we're going to have to show her the books."

"Oh," Fox said. He picked up the letter, frowned over it. "You're right," he said. "No question. An absolute phony."

12

Dortmunder said, "What's in it for me?"

"Money," Kelp suggested.

"That isn't what I mean," Dortmunder said.

Tiny said, "Money isn't what you mean?"

"That's right," Dortmunder said. "Not this time."

These three were seated in their sitting room as the fire sputtered through green wood in the fireplace and mostly white glistened outside the small windows. They had found this three-bedroom bed-and-breakfast just outside Chazy and had taken the whole thing on a very good weekly rental, because this wasn't yet quite ski season in what, with rare simple truth, the locals called the North Country. Though it seemed to Dortmunder there was enough snow out there on the lawns and streets and car roofs and pine trees for any skier to ski on. But what did he know? His only outside winter sport was slipping on the ice while trying to get to the car. (Extra points if you're carrying groceries. Double points if the groceries include beer bottles.)

Their hosts in the bed-and-breakfast were an elderly male couple who lived at the downstairs back and wore many heavy wool sweaters and scarves; with their wrin-

kled red faces on top, they looked mostly like baked apples on sheep. These were Gregory and Tom, and other
than producing fine stick-to-your-ribs breakfasts of pan-
cakes and fried eggs and French toast and lots of bacon
and orange juice and a huge coffeemaker full of java,
they tended to stay in their own part of the house. They
had a French-Canadian maid, a large young woman
named Odille, who did the laundry and cleaned the rooms
while singing "Frère Jacques" over and over to herself.

Today, Monday, November 27, was their third day
here, and Tom had informed them that winter rates would
kick in two weeks from now, if they were still in residence. They'd promised to take that into account when
considering their future plans.

So far, there hadn't been much to do. They'd driven
north the same day the trio in the motor home had come
up here to turn themselves into a solo in the motor home.
Little Feather was the only one in occupancy over there
in Whispering Pines, while Guilderpost and Irwin had
moved into a motel just south of Plattsburgh, where they
had picture-window views of the wind howling down out
of Canada and across Lake Champlain and into their
rooms.

Although Tea Cosy, which in fact was the name on the
small hanging sign outside the bed-and-breakfast, was
the most comfortable venue among the three available to
the conspirators, with its comfy, warm sitting room,
where even Tiny could feel uncrowded, Dortmunder and
Kelp and Tiny had all agreed they didn't particularly
want Guilderpost and Irwin to know where they were, so
meetings were taking place in Guilderpost's room at the
motel. In the meantime, Dortmunder and Kelp and Tiny

kept body and soul together, and dealt with the modest rent at the Tea Cosy, by committing the occasional minor felony, around and about. Enough to get on with, but not enough to lead local officials to create a task force. It was a living.

But was it an excuse for living? That was the question, and that was why, seated in the sitting room after yet another anchor-sized breakfast, digesting slowly and rather noisily while "Frère Jacques" was sung in counterpoint upstairs, waiting for the moment to go over to the Four Winds motel and read the letter Little Feather had yesterday sent to the casino, Dortmunder had professed his discontent: "What's in it for me?"

"Well, if money isn't what you mean," Kelp said, "then what *do* you mean?"

"I mean," Dortmunder said, "why am I in this place? I'm not a con artist. I'm not a grafter. I'm a thief. There's nothing here to steal. We're just riding Little Feather's coattails—never mind, Tiny, you know what I mean—and we're horning in on somebody else's scam, and if they don't manage to kill us—and you know, Tiny, that's still Plan A they've got over there in their minds, and you can't walk around with a hand grenade strapped on forever, for instance, you're not even wearing it now—what do we get out of it?"

"A hundred K," Kelp said.

"For what? Now, Andy, Tiny, listen to me. I think of myself as a person with a certain dignity and a certain professional ability and a certain standing, but what's happening here is, I'm looking for crumbs from somebody else's table, so why am I here?"

"That's a very good question," Tiny rumbled, and Kelp said, "To be perfectly honest, John—"

"Don't strain yourself."

"No, no, no, in this issue only," Kelp assured him, then said, "The reason you're here, and Tiny's here, and I'm here, is because I screwed up. I misjudged Fitzroy, and essentially you didn't get the gee you were supposed to get to make up for the other gee you didn't get, and—"

"What are these gees?" Tiny demanded. "You two all of a sudden astronauts?"

"Doesn't matter," Dortmunder told him. He did *not* want to get into a description with Tiny of his shopping experience at Speedshop.

"What it is," Kelp said, "one thing leads to another, and that's what happened here, and one thing led to another, and this is the other."

They both looked at him, but Kelp was done. Dortmunder finally said, "That's it? One thing led to another?"

"That's the way it looks from here," Kelp said. "Also, if you remember, we both wanted to know what Fitzroy and them were up to, and see maybe there's a little something in it for us—"

"There's always something in it for me," Tiny grumbled.

"That's right, Tiny, thank you," Kelp said, and to Dortmunder, he said, "Then we got Tiny, and when Tiny's aboard, you know, we always gotta come up with *something*."

"Though sometimes," Tiny said, "the something's been kinda thinner than I'm used to. But I forgive you, Dortmunder. I always forgive you—"

"Thank you, Tiny."

"—because you make me laugh," Tiny said, and laughed, and the Tea Cosy rocked a little. "So here's what it is," he said. "We got these people gonna pull a scam. It looks like it could maybe work, and that's a lotta money. And wherever there's a lotta money, Dortmunder, there's always sooner or later some use for the guy who does the thinking, which is you, and the guy who does the heavy lifting, which is me."

"And don't forget transportation," Kelp pointed out.

"I was gonna mention transportation," Tiny said, "on account it's time to go over to the Four Winds and see how the windbags are coming along."

"Fine," Dortmunder said, rising. "Let's see do we have a use for my talents."

Tiny heaved himself to his feet, and the sofa sighed in gratitude. "And mine," he said.

It hadn't snowed during the night, but the wind had dusted the Jeep with fine cold sparkles of blown snowflake, which was very attractive on its new color. It was now a gleaming black, and sported Massachusetts license plates, with no medical degree but with enough plausibility to survive a trooper's computer check. Now, as they wiped snow off the windows with their gloves, Tiny said, "You know, Dortmunder, time hangs heavy on your hands, why not steal the whole county?"

"And do what with it?"

"Move it farther south," Tiny suggested.

13

Little Feather didn't want to be associated with any of those people, not in anyone else's mind, just in case sometime in the future she might want to be able to deny them, so she'd made Fitzroy sign over the motor home's title to her, making herself more or less legal. She also wouldn't travel from Whispering Pines Campground to the Four Winds motel and back by cab, nor would she permit Irwin and Fitzroy—it was always the two of them, that's how much they trusted each other—to pick her up at the motor home. First, they would agree on a time, and then she would call a cab to take her for the inexpensive run into Plattsburgh, to a big supermarket there, where Irwin and Fitzroy would be waiting for her. They'd meet, discuss, do what they had to do, and then they'd return her to the supermarket, where she'd buy some grapefruit and Swedish flat bread and other necessities, and then call another cab to return her to the campground.

And that's the way it happened today. Cab number one dropped her off at the supermarket. She went in the automatic in door, U-turned, went out the automatic out door, and there were Irwin and Fitzroy in the Voyager, which had never really worked well since the night Irwin had started it without benefit of key. (Which she hadn't learned about, of course, until much later.)

Irwin always drove, Fitzroy beside him, and she traveled in back. Getting aboard, sliding the door shut, she said, "You mailed it?"

As Irwin drove them away across Plattsburgh toward Route 9 southward to the Four Winds, Fitzroy said, "They'll be reading it today."

"And then changing their pants," Irwin commented.

"Good," Little Feather said, meaning the letter having been delivered, not the casino managers changing their pants. But in fact, now that it had begun, she herself was feeling just the least bit nervous.

She wasn't used to anxiety attacks, they didn't suit her lifestyle. Little Feather had made her own way since she was fifteen and still known as Shirley Ann Farraff, when she'd left home and Cher first had become her ideal. She'd been a pony in Vegas shows, she'd gone through dealer's school to become an accredited blackjack dealer, she'd waitressed or worked in department stores when times were bad, and she'd always come out okay. She'd never hooked, she'd never made the mistake of counting on a man instead of herself, and she'd never been proved wrong. When you count on yourself, you know whether or not you're counting on somebody you can trust, and Little Feather was somebody that Little Feather could trust absolutely, so what was there ever to get nervous about?

Well. It wasn't that she was *counting* on Fitzroy and Irwin, but she sure was tied in with them, and she no longer shared their high opinion of themselves, not after this new trio had showed up.

At first, Fitzroy had seemed like the genuine article. He'd met up with her in Reno, where she was dealing at one of the smaller casinos—family trade, crappy tips— and after a few verbal dance steps, during which she hadn't been able to figure out *what* he was up to, he finally introduced her to Irwin, and together they told her the scheme.

Well, who ever knew being an American Indian could be worth that much money? It was almost worth putting up with *Native American* (one of the more redundant of redundancies) from the same clowns who talk about flight attendants and daytime dramas and the height-impaired.

Little Feather had understood from the beginning that although they needed a full-blooded American Indian to work their scheme, one with the right background, they didn't necessarily need *her.* The plains were full of Navajo and Hopi and Apache with dead grandpas. So she'd concentrated her attention on being just the *right* little squaw for their needs, until now, when the game had actually started.

It had started. The letter had gone out, over her signature, giving her whereabouts, telling her story. Would it fly? Or was there something Fitzroy and Irwin had forgotten that would come sneaking up behind her to bite her on the ass?

It was Andy and John and Tiny that had shaken her faith in Fitzroy and Irwin. Until then, she'd thought she was safe in their hands, she'd thought they were brilliant and brutal, and she'd thought nothing could stand in their way. For instance, they'd known the scheme couldn't work if even one extraneous person knew about it, and so they'd made sure the extraneous people along the way, meaning the grave diggers in Nevada, didn't survive their knowledge. Little Feather had never killed anybody, and she hadn't killed those two, or been around when it was happening, but she didn't mind it as a *fact*. A couple of loser winos; they were better off. So long as she didn't have to watch, no big deal.

But now, these new three. They came on kind of goofy, but underneath they were pros in some way Little Feather didn't know about. She'd never quite met their like before, and it seemed to her the most significant thing about them was how they refused to get worried. Well, John, he always looked worried—that was obvious—but worry didn't *interfere* with them, that was the point.

And the picture of Tiny, casually holding the live grenade, was pretty well guaranteed to stick in the memory.

Riding along, thinking it over, watching Lake Champlain's cold, pebbly gray surface off to the left of the road, she said, "Be interesting to know what they think of the letter. Andy and so on."

Irwin kept his concentration on his driving, but Fitzroy half-turned to look back at her. Pretending surprise, he said, "Little Feather? Don't you trust your own judgment?"

"*My* judgment, fine," she told him. "It's your judgment and Irwin's where I'd like a second opinion."

After that, there wasn't much conversation in the car. And then, when they got to the Four Winds, there stood the recently black Jeep, parked in front of Irwin's room, empty. Pulling in beside it, Irwin said, "That is the same Jeep, isn't it?"

"I don't imagine," Fitzroy said, "we're looking at its final color change. But where do you suppose they are?"

They all got out of the Voyager, looking this way and that, and Irwin said, "Suppose they got cold and they're waiting in the office?"

"Wouldn't they see us drive in?"

Little Feather said, "Fitzroy, why don't you look in *your* room?"

They stared at her, then at the closed door of Fitzroy's room. Fitzroy bustled to it, pulling out his key, muttering something about "Can't possibly" or some such, and when he got the door open, there they were, watching a soap, Andy in one of the two chairs, John in the other, Tiny a kind of profane Buddha on the bed, back against the headboard.

"*There* you are," Andy said, cheerful as ever, getting to his feet as John offed the TV with the remote. "Little Feather, here, have my chair."

Fitzroy seemed to have lost some of his self-assurance. "Did you," he asked, "did you ask the maid to let you in?"

"Oh, why bother people when they're working?" Andy said. "Come on, Little Feather, take a load off. We all wanna see this letter of yours."

I'm enjoying these clowns, Little Feather thought as she crossed to say, "Thank you, Andy, you're a gentleman," and take the chair that had lately been his.

Fitzroy, sounding put out, said, "I'm surprised you haven't read the letter already. It's in the drawer over there."

Andy affected hurt surprise. "*We* wouldn't poke around in your personal possessions, Fitzroy. We all respect one another, don't we?"

From the bed, Tiny said, "Yeah, we're all gonna get along now, that's the idea."

John said, "We're all kinda anxious to see this famous letter."

"Show it to them, Fitzroy," Little Feather said. "Let's see how it plays."

Fitzroy could be seen to decide not to make a federal case out of a simple breaking and entering. They'd been invited, and here they were. "Of course," he said, crossing to the room's flimsy little desk. "I'm quite proud of it, in fact," he said, opening the drawer and taking out the copy they'd made at the nearby drugstore. "Only one copy, I'm afraid."

So the way they worked it, Tiny stayed where he was on the double bed, holding the letter, and Andy and John sat to either side of him, scrunched on the edges of the mattress, and all three read it at once. And Irwin took the opportunity to sidle into John's chair.

They finished, and Tiny handed the letter to Andy, who stayed where he was but leaned forward to hand it to Fitzroy, saying, "Has a nice naïve quality to it."

"Thank you," Fitzroy said.

Tiny rumbled, "United at last with my own people."

Irwin grinned. "Heart-tugging, that part."

John said, "How much of it is true?"

"Almost all of it," Fitzroy assured him.

The three stayed where they were. Crowded together on the bed, the wide man in the middle, the other two bracing themselves with feet out to the side, they looked like an altarpiece from some very strange religion, but none of them seemed ready or willing to move.

John said, "All those named in the letter, that family tree?"

Holding the letter, Fitzroy went down the names: "Joseph Redcorn, he's real. You know that, you met him."

Andy said, "You mean, we unburied him."

"Exactly. His daughter-in-law Harriet Littlefoot Redcorn, she's real, or she was. She's dead, but there are records."

John said, "And Doeface?"

"Harriet's daughter," Fitzroy said, nodding. "Completely real. All trace of her is lost."

"And her daughter."

"You mean Little Feather here," Fitzroy said.

"Not yet I don't," John said. "You're telling me what's true in there."

"Very well," Fitzroy said. "Doeface did marry one Henry Track-Of-Skunk, a full-blooded Choctee, and lived with him on the reservation. They did have a daughter in 1970 named Little Feather, and shortly after that the marriage ended."

John said, "Then what?"

Fitzroy shrugged. "They left the reservation, mother and daughter."

"And she took back her maiden name, like it says in the letter?"

"Unlikely," Fitzroy said. "She didn't keep the name Track-Of-Skunk, but I can find no telephone listing for a Doeface Redcorn anywhere in the West throughout the seventies." Turning to Andy, he said, "The Internet is very good on things like that, you know. If there's a list, the Internet will find it, and old phone books are nothing but lists."

John apparently didn't care much about the wonders of the Internet. He said, "So Doeface disappeared, and you don't know what name she used."

"I would guess she married again," Fitzroy said. "And, once they left the reservation, I would imagine the mother changed Little Feather Track-Of-Skunk's name, too. The child would have been less than a year old, and it's unlikely she has any idea she was ever called by that name."

John said, "But you don't know where she is, and you don't know what her name is, but she'll be about the same age as this Little Feather here."

"Yes," Fitzroy said.

"So, when this gets into the news," John said, "and it will, this casino, all this money, inherited all of a sudden by this pretty girl here—"

"Thank you, John."

"Anytime," he said, then said to Fitzroy, "So she's on the news, and the real Little Feather says, 'Hey, that's me.' Then what?"

Irwin said, "Why then, the way to prove out the competing claims is, let's do a DNA test on the only known relative of Little Feather we can find, which is Joseph Redcorn, and guess what?"

Andy said, "What about baby prints?"

Most of the others looked blank, but Irwin said, "You mean footprints of babies taken shortly after birth, for later ID. They didn't do that in a very poor reservation infirmary in 1970."

Tiny said, "What about Skunkface?"

"Track-Of-Skunk," Irwin corrected, and Fitzroy said, "What about him?"

"What if he shows up? And says, 'There's my baby girl.'"

Little Feather knew the answer to that one. "So what?" she asked. "I'm inheriting a third of a casino through my mother, nothing to do with him. Maybe I can get him a job driving the parking lot bus."

Andy said, "What if he says, 'There *isn't* my baby girl'?"

Little Feather said, "Why would he? The last time he saw me, I was ten months old."

Andy said, "Identifying marks? Strawberry birthmarks, stuff like that?"

Fitzroy said, "From what I've learned about Track-Of-Skunk, I doubt his eyes ever focused quite that clearly on his baby daughter. If he's alive, he probably doesn't remember her at all."

John said, "Social Security number."

"Under the name of Shirley Ann Farraff," Little Feather said.

John looked at her. "I have the feeling that's the name you started with."

"Uh-huh."

"So?"

Fitzroy said, "Tell him the story, Little Feather."

"Sure." She gave him her most honest look, which wasn't particularly honest, and said, "My mother, Doeface Redcorn, had me on a reservation somewhere, father unknown, named me Little Feather Redcorn. When I was two, my mother moved in with Frank Farraff. I don't think they ever married, but my mother renamed me

Shirley Ann Farraff, because we weren't living on the reservation. When I was fourteen, Frank tried to rape me, and my mom wouldn't stand up for me, so I left. But by that time, I already had my Social Security card, so I went on being Shirley Ann Farraff."

John said, "How much of that is true?"

"Everything from where my mother moved in with Frank."

"And who was your mother?"

"Doris Elkhorn, full-blooded Choctee."

"So that's what it says on your birth certificate."

Little Feather shook her head. "The only time I ever saw my birth certificate," she said, "my mother had to show it when I started school. I remember it said 'Baby Elkhorn, female, father unknown.' My Little Feather story is, I've never seen a birth certificate, wouldn't know whom to ask. Investigators can look for a birth certificate under Farraff and never find one."

"And under Redcorn and never find one," John pointed out.

Guilderpost said, "John, if people start looking into Little Feather's past, they can't get further back than Shirley Ann Farraff. It's clear she was born under some other name, but no one will ever prove that name wasn't Little Feather Redcorn."

"But," John objected, "she can't prove it *was* Redcorn."

"DNA," said Irwin.

John nodded, absorbing that, then apparently grew tired at last of sitting on half his ass, squeezed in beside Tiny. Standing, shaking himself all over a little like a dog, he said, "Fitzroy, what I want to know is, how come you know all this? How come you can set it up?"

"I've been setting it up," Fitzroy told him, "off and on for six years. I was first putting together some Dutch land grants along the Hudson River, very nice paper, clouding the ownership of any number of valuable properties, and the owners were always relieved, even grateful, at the modest price I would ask to sell them the grants, ending all likelihood of later dispute and making it possible for them to sell their properties if they were ever of a mind to—a very nice enterprise, if I say so myself—when some collateral research led me to the Silver Chasm Casino and the died-off Pottaknobbees. I asked myself, Could one find a Pottaknobbee who could be tweaked into just one more living relative?" He gestured theatrically at Little Feather. "The result, you see before you."

John and Andy and Tiny looked at one another. Tiny shrugged, and the bed groaned, and apparently bounced Andy to his feet, where he turned and said, "Well, Fitzroy, it sounds pretty good."

"Thank you."

John said, "And tomorrow's the day."

"It all depends on Little Feather," Fitzroy said.

"Thanks, I needed that," Little Feather said.

John said to her, "You'll be okay. What time you gonna call them?"

"Two in the afternoon."

"So whatever's gonna happen," John said, "we should all know about it by six, huh?"

Fitzroy said, "We could meet here again tomorrow at six, if that's your suggestion."

"Good," John said.

Fitzroy said, "And, if we're not back yet when you arrive—"

"That's okay," Andy assured him, "we'll just let ourselves in."

"That isn't what I was going to say."

Andy said, "You want us to stand out there in the cold, attracting attention?"

Little Feather said, "No, he doesn't." Rising, she said, "If you three also think we got a shot, that's good. Fitzroy, drive me back now, will you?"

"Of course, my dear."

The two trios parted outside the door, with expressions of warmth and mutual respect, and then Little Feather reversed the process homeward: car to supermarket, shop, cab to Whispering Pines.

Little Feather spent a quiet evening with her exercise tapes and her reading—she particularly liked biographies of famous women, like Messalina and Catherine the Great—and the next afternoon at two, she left the Winnebago to go to the Whispering Pines office to call the casino. She shut the motor home door, turned, and saw two men wearing dark suits under their overcoats walking toward her. One said, "Miss Redcorn?"

Little Feather looked at them. Trouble, she thought. "Yes?"

The man showed a badge. "Police, Miss Redcorn. Would you come with us?"

Bad trouble, she thought. "Why?"

"Well," he said, "you're under arrest."

14

Once again, they got to the Four Winds first. Kelp opened the door to Guilderpost's room and they seated themselves the same as last time, Dortmunder settling himself in to operate the remote, except now what they watched was the local six o'clock news.

Guilderpost and Irwin and Little Feather were really very late, so they still hadn't returned, and Dortmunder and Kelp and Tiny were still watching the local news, at 6:16, when Little Feather walked across the screen, in handcuffs, with hard-eyed guys flanking her, each holding an elbow. Little Feather didn't look at all happy with her situation, and Dortmunder sympathized, a lot.

"Holy shit!" Kelp cried, and Tiny said, "Sharrap."

"Arrested at Whispering Pines Campground on Route Fourteen this afternoon," the voice of the newsperson said, while the perp walk continued, the camera panning to show an official-looking old building, a pile of stone and brick that had probably been moldering there since the twenties, "was a woman claiming to be Little Feather Redcorn, last member of the Pottaknobbee tribe, one of the three tribal owners of Silver Chasm Casino."

Little Feather and her escort, moving amid many

newscasters and newspersons, were engulfed by the pile of stone and brick. The news gatherers remained clustered outside.

"Charged with extortion, the woman, one of whose names is Shirley Ann Farrell, is being held in the Clinton County House of Detention."

Another shot of the pile of stone and brick, apparently taken later in the afternoon, had a newsperson in the foreground, with a microphone, speaking directly to the camera: "News Eight has learned that Ms. Farrell has been a gambler and showgirl in Las Vegas until very recently. Why she is making this claim at this time, police hope to determine."

Now there was a shot of some kind of office, with dark-paneled walls, glass shelves with trophies, head-shot photos of smiling people in frames on the walls, green glass table lamps, and two sleek, smooth guys in their fifties, one seated at an elaborate dark wood desk with a black stone top, the other in a comfortable dark red leather chair just beside him. One of the men was talking, because his lips were moving, but his words couldn't be heard. Off-camera, the newsperson could be heard saying, "Roger Fox and Frank Oglanda, who received the letter of extortion from Ms. Farrell in their position as co-managers of Silver Chasm Casino, and turned it over to the police, say they've never been faced with a matter like this before but are not surprised."

Now the talking man's words became audible: "We've always known it was a possibility that someone would try some fraud like this, and we've guarded against it and we're ready for it, and I want to assure our tribespeople, Mr. Oglanda's Kiota and my own Oshkawa, that their investments in our tribal property are safe from all the flim-flam artists in the world."

The other man, Oglanda, said, "Years ago, both our tribes made an exhaustive search for any surviving Potta-knobbees, and we have the results of that search, every bloodline followed right down to the end, and although it's sad, I'm afraid it's also true, and it must be said, there are no surviving Pottaknobbees. None."

"I feel sorry for this misguided young woman," Fox said, and smiled in an unpleasant way.

Then they were back in the studio with the primary newsperson: "The search for the black box—"

"Off," Tiny said, and Dortmunder offed the set.

In the silence, they looked at one another, until Dort-munder said, "The only question is, do we have time to go back to the Tea Cosy for our stuff, or do we just drive south straight from here?"

Kelp said, "John, don't be such a pessimist."

"Why not?"

Tiny said, "Because Little Feather won't flip."

Kelp said, "If she was going to, the cops would come *here,* not the Tea Cosy. And anyway, Tiny's right. Little Feather's stand-up, we can count on her."

"More than the other two," Tiny said.

"You're probably right," Dortmunder agreed, and sighed, only partially in relief.

Kelp said, "Well, at least now we know why they're so late. How much longer do you suppose they'll hang out at the supermarket and wait for her?"

"Well, however long, we gotta wait for them," Dort-munder said, and the door opened, and in came Guilderpost and Irwin, both looking very worried, Irwin saying, "She didn't show up."

"We know," Dortmunder told him, but before he could add any more, Guilderpost said, "I don't understand it. We all agreed on the time, but we got there and we looked and we waited, and we never saw her."

"We did," Dortmunder told him, and pointed at the television set. "On the six o'clock news."

Guilderpost stared at the blank television set as though expecting to see Little Feather show up on its screen, while Irwin stared more usefully at Dortmunder, saying, "On television? Why?"

"She was arrested," Kelp said.

Tiny said, "Extortion." From him, it sounded like a suggestion.

Dortmunder said, "Not the way we expected to see her on TV."

Guilderpost was having trouble catching up. "But— What went wrong?"

"The casino guys did a preemptive strike," Dortmunder explained. "Turned the letter over to the local cops, let them deal with it. They'll all be buddies here, the casino a big employer, brings in lots of money, it doesn't all stay on the reservation."

"Bum's rush," Tiny commented.

"Oh, I see it," Guilderpost said, calming down. With a sage nod, he said, "In fact, truth to tell, I've seen it in the past. Find a grifter in your territory, pull him in, shake him up a little, convince him to move on elsewhere, to greener pastures."

"The casino guys," Dortmunder said, "don't want to

have to deal with Little Feather, so the local cops lean on her."

"They even gave her the perp walk," Kelp said. "That's how come we got to see her on TV."

"Intimidation," Irwin said.

Guilderpost cocked an eyebrow at his partner. "Intimidate Little Feather?" His smile was almost as unpleasant as the casino guy's. "Anyone who tries to intimidate Little Feather," he said, "is in for an unpleasant surprise."

15

The room was somehow both cluttered and bare. A lot of folding chairs in messy rows on the left faced a raised platform behind a wooden rail on the right, with a long table and more folding chairs on the platform. Straight ahead, opposite the door from the hall, windows showed a nearby stone wall, probably some other official building. The walls of the room were covered with posters to do with fire fighting, drugs, AIDS, the Heimlich maneuver, and the implications of school being open. One man and one woman sat behind the long table, and a few more people were scattered among the scattered folding chairs.

"Sit there," said one of the detectives to Little Feather, pointing at the nearest folding chair, and before she could tell him where *he* could sit, he went off to confer with people at the long table. So she sat.

What Little Feather mostly was was furious. This wasn't the way it was supposed to happen, just hustled off like some penny-ante crook. There was supposed to be a conversation, a dialogue, an unfolding of events. It was as though the world had suddenly jumped to the last chapter.

They'd taken her bag with her ID in it, and now the detectives and the people at the table studied all that for a while, then studied some other papers, and then the detective turned to crook a finger at Little Feather, who mostly by this point wanted to kick him in the shin. But she would contain herself, because sooner or later somebody would have to stop this folderol and pay attention.

Or maybe not. She went over to the long table, and saw on it a three-sided brass plaque in front of the man, reading:

MAGISTRATE
R. G. GOODY IV

R.G. himself didn't much live up to the billing, being a spindly little balding man in a rumpled brown suit and crooked eyeglasses, who had no interest in meeting Little Feather's eye. The woman beside him, schoolmarmish, was a steno or something, with pad and paper at the ready.

"Shirley Ann Farraff," Goody began, and Little Feather nearly corrected him, but why bother? This was clearly a flunky. "You have been charged," Goody went on, and then, not looking up, concentrating on the papers in front of him, he reeled off a list of numbers and sections and subparagraphs, after which he said, "How do you plead?"

"I didn't do anything," Little Feather said.

Goody looked at the steno. "Was that a not guilty plea?"

"Yes, sir," she said.

"So noted." Still not looking directly at Little Feather, he said, "Your Miranda rights were read to you."

"In the car," she agreed. *Mumbled* to her, really.

"Have you an attorney?"

"No. I don't see—"

"Can you afford an attorney?"

"What? No!"

"Would you like the court to appoint an attorney?"

"Well, uh . . ." Not at all what she'd expected. "Maybe I should," she said.

Goody nodded, then beckoned somebody from the spectators, and Little Feather turned to see moving toward her, lugging a big heavy old black battered briefcase, a woman of Little Feather's age, but pretending to be her own grandma, with narrow reading glasses tipped forward on her face, black hair pulled severely back into a bun, and makeup so slight as to be almost not worth the effort. She wore a bulky black sweater, shapeless brown wool slacks, and black hiking shoes, and she gave Little Feather a quick impersonal nod before saying to Goody, "Your Honor, I need time to consult with my client."

"She pleads not guilty," Goody said. "She claims to be indigent. Did you want to seek bail?"

"Your Honor," the woman said, "as I understand it, Miss Farraff has no previous criminal record, and would not be a danger to the community, so her own recognizance would—"

"The defendant," Goody pointed out, "lives in a motor home, which would make the prospect of flight, I should think, very appealing. Five thousand dollars bail."

Five thousand dollars! While Little Feather tried to think where she'd get hold of money like that—Fitzroy? Forget it—more words were handed back and forth by the woman attorney and the magistrate, *remand* and *cal-*

endar and other words not part of her normal vocabulary, and then the woman turned and extended a card to Little Feather, saying, "I'll speak with Judge Higbee."

The card said she actually was an attorney-at-law and her name was Marjorie Dawson. Little Feather said, "Isn't *this* the judge?"

"This is the arraignment," Marjorie Dawson explained. "Judge Higbee will hear the actual trial. I'll report to you after I talk to him."

"But—" Little Feather said, and a hand closed on her elbow and she was taken away from there.

After the arraignment, Little Feather was run through a process that was handled so easily and so calmly that it was clearly routine for these people, and probably routine for most of the arrestees as well, but it wasn't routine for Little Feather, and it shook her confidence. She'd never been arrested, had never had a conversation with a suspicious or hostile cop, had never even had a traffic ticket. Sure, she'd been involved in a number of low-level scams in Nevada, mostly as decoration, but nothing that had ever drawn her to the attention of the law. The world these people lived in inside here contained a lot of assumptions about guilt and innocence, good guys and bad guys, freedom and obedience, that she didn't like at all.

But she had no choice, did she? They just walked her through it, the mug shots and the fingerprinting and the writing down on a long form all the personal effects they were taking away from her. Then a hefty woman deputy sheriff took her in a small bare room for a strip search she didn't care for in the least, after which, her own clothing was taken away, replaced by denim shirt and blue jeans; not the best fit, either one.

"They don't have different ones for women," the deputy said, not quite apologizing, which was about as human as anyone got around here.

And now she was on her way to a cell of her own. They walked down a long corridor, past the cells for male inmates, and Little Feather looked in and saw a concrete-floored communal area with a long wooden table and some folding chairs and a TV set tuned to the Weather Channel. Three losers in denim shirts and blue jeans like hers sprawled around on the chairs, gawking at the set. Down both sides of the communal room were cells with only bars for their inner walls, so you could never be out of sight.

Well, at least, Little Feather thought, they're not putting me in there. And then she thought, what do those clowns care about the weather?

Past the Weather Channel fans at the end of the hall was an iron door. One of the two male deputies escorting her pushed a button beside the door, a nasty electronic buzz sounded, and the door popped open. "You go in there," the deputy said.

She wished she could think of an argument, but at the moment, there didn't seem to be one, so she went in there, and they shut the iron door behind her, and here she was. The women's quarters, looking very much like an afterthought. A fairly large long room had been fitted with vertical bars all around, just inside the real walls and over the large window at the end. When she went over there to look out the window, she could see some old brick walls and, in the distance, a white spire against a gray sky. That was it.

The furniture in the room consisted of two sets of bunk beds on opposite side walls, each with a thin mattress on it, folded in half—you can't fold a thick mattress in half—plus one sheet, one scratchy-looking wool blanket, one pillow, and one pillowcase, all neatly stacked on top of the mattress. There were also a square wooden table and two folding chairs like the men's, but no TV set. For the weather, she'd have to rely on the window.

And also for the time, since they'd taken her watch. So now and then, when the spirit moved her, she could go over to the window to see how much the shadows had lengthened out there, if she wanted to confirm that a whole lot of dead time was passing by.

When the nasty buzzer sounded at the door again, she happened to be over by the window, shoulder leaning on a bar as she looked out at the world, where now the shadows were so very long, they'd definitely combined into nighttime; she'd been in here for hours. At that sound, she moved away toward the center of the room and stood by the table as the door opened and a different deputy stood there, saying, "Visitor."

Visitor? For one fleeting instant, she thought the visitor was Fitzroy, come to say forget it, let's call the whole thing off, let's just go home, we were nuts to think we could try this stunt. But no. A) Fitzroy wouldn't do that. B) Fitzroy wouldn't show his face anywhere near Little Feather. C) They *weren't* nuts to try this stunt, they were going to go ahead with this stunt and it was going to work, and she would have the biggest, whitest, grandest, softest, *cushiest* house on the reservation, and screw everybody.

So she said, "What visitor?"

"Your lawyer, ma'am."

Oh, Marjorie Dawson. About time. Little Feather didn't want to have to spend another *second* in this damn place. "Then let's go," she said, and they went.

Walking past the men's cell compound, she just caught a glimpse of herself, doing the perp walk on TV. God-*damn*! After six o'clock, then—the local news.

Down another corridor, and the deputy opened a door and said, "In here, ma'am."

She stepped inside, and he shut the door behind her, and she looked around. This was a women's cell again, without the bars and the bunk beds, but with the square wooden table and the two wooden chairs, on one of which sat Marjorie Dawson, facing Little Feather but studying papers spread on the table in front of her. Looking over her reading glasses, she said, "Come in, Shirley Ann."

Little Feather stepped forward, rested a hand on the back of the empty chair, and said, "My name is Little Feather."

"Sit down, Shirley Ann," Marjorie Dawson said as though Little Feather hadn't spoken at all.

"My name is Little Feather," Little Feather insisted.

Marjorie Dawson gave her a flat look, as though she were a file put away in the wrong place. "We'll discuss that, if you wish," she said. "In the meantime, please sit down."

Little Feather sat, placed her folded hands on the table

in front of her, and waited. She was not, she sensed, going to warm to Marjorie Dawson.

Looking down at the papers on the table, Dawson said, "You're a very foolish young woman, Shirley Ann, but you're also a very lucky one."

Little Feather waited.

Dawson looked up at her. "Don't you want to know how you're lucky?"

"I already know I'm lucky," Little Feather said. "I want to know how I'm foolish."

Dawson gestured at the top document in the folder, and Little Feather saw it was a copy of her letter. "This isn't even a good attempt at extortion," she said. "If you escape jail time—"

"It isn't an attempt at extortion at all," Little Feather said.

Dawson shook her head and her finger at Little Feather. "I'm afraid you don't realize the seriousness of the situation."

Little Feather frowned at her. "Whose lawyer are you supposed to be?"

"I'm *your* lawyer, as you well know, and I have spoken with Judge Higbee, and— Don't interrupt me!"

Little Feather folded her arms, like Geronimo. "You talk," she said, like Geronimo, "and then I'll talk."

"Very well." Dawson seemed a bit ruffled. She patted her hair, none of which was out of place, and looked down at Little Feather's letter, as though to gain strength from it. "You have attempted here," she said, "to obtain money through false pretenses. Let me finish! I've spoken with Judge Higbee, and I've pled your case, and— *Let* me finish! And I've pointed out to Judge Higbee that you have no prior police record of any kind, that this is your first offense, and that I very strongly suspect others put you up to it. The judge has agreed to let you go with only a warning, *if*."

Again she glowered over her glasses at Little Feather, who this time didn't try to say anything at all, but merely watched, and waited her turn.

"If," Dawson finally went on, "you will sign a statement renouncing the claims in this fraudulent letter, and if you will depart Clinton County at once, never to return, the judge is prepared to release you. I have done the statement," she finished, and then found another document in the folder and pushed it across the table toward Little Feather, who didn't bother to look at it.

Reaching down to her briefcase again, Dawson came up with a fat black pen with a screw top. She unscrewed the top, extended the pen toward Little Feather, and, when Little Feather didn't take it, Dawson at last looked up and met her eye.

Little Feather said, "You done?"

"You really must sign this," Dawson said.

Little Feather said, "You done? You took your turn, and if you're done, it's my turn."

Dawson did an elaborate sigh, put the pen on the table, and leaned back. "I don't know," she said, "what you could possibly have to say."

"And if you don't shut up," Little Feather told her, "you never will."

That did it. Dawson gave her a look of stony disbelief and crossed her own arms like Geronimo.

Little Feather uncrossed her arms and said, "You don't act like you're my lawyer, you act like you're the other guy's lawyer." She pointed to the letter she'd sent. "I *am* Little Feather Redcorn," she said. "My mother was Doeface Redcorn, my grandmother was Harriet Littlefoot Redcorn, my grandfather was Bearpaw Redcorn, who was lost at sea in the United States Navy in World War Two, and they were all Pottaknobbee, and *I'm* Pottaknobbee. I'm Pottaknobbee all the way back to my greatgrandfather Joseph Redcorn, who fell off the Empire State Building."

At that, Dawson blinked and said, "Are you trying to make fun—"

"He was working on it, when they were building it, he was up on top with a bunch of Mohawks. My mama told me the family always believed the Mohawks pushed him, so I believe it, too."

Dawson stared hard at her, thinking. "You *believe* the claims in this letter."

"They aren't claims, they're facts," Little Feather told her. She felt indignant at the way these clowns were treating her, not even giving her a civil conversation, and indignation gave her as much self-assurance as innocence would have done. She said, "I never extorted anybody. I never demanded anything. I just said I want to be back with my own people, and since I don't know any other Pottaknobbees, I wanted to get back with the Kiota and the Oshkawa. And *this* is the way they treat me, their long-lost cousin. Like I was an Iroquois!"

Dawson looked less and less sure of herself. She said, "The tribes are certain there are no more Pottaknobbees."

"The tribes are wrong."

"Well . . ." Dawson was floundering now, looking at her documents for help, finding no help there.

"If you're my lawyer," Little Feather said, "you'll get me out of here."

"Well . . . tomorrow . . ."

"Tomorrow!"

"There's nothing further can be done tonight," Dawson said. "You can't post bail—"

"I thought about that," Little Feather said, "and I can put up property. I can put up my motor home, I've got the title to it. *That's* worth more than five thousand dollars."

"But that would also have to be tomorrow," Dawson said. She looked and sounded worried, as she should. "Shirley Ann, if you—"

Little Feather pointed a very stern finger at her. "My name," she said slowly and distinctly, "is Little Feather, but I think you should call me Ms. Redcorn."

"Whoever you are," Dawson said, trying to rally, "of course if you were willing to sign the statement, you could leave immediately—"

"And forever."

"Well, yes. But, as things stand, and I can see you are adamant about this, I'm afraid there's nothing to be done now until tomorrow."

"And what are you going to do tomorrow?"

"Speak with Judge Higbee, ask the judge to speak with you in chambers, see what's best to be done."

"But I spend tonight in here."

"Well, it's not possible to—"

"Not charged with anything, didn't *do* anything, but I spend the night in here."

"Tomorrow—"

Little Feather rose. She felt very angry, and didn't see any reason to hide it. "I've been in here for hours," she said. "My *real* lawyer would have spent that time getting me out of here and not trying to get me to confess to things I didn't do."

"Tomorrow, we'll—"

"There's still one thing you can do for me tonight," Little Feather told her.

Dawson looked ready, even eager. "Yes? If I can."

"Call the deputy to take me back to my cell," Little Feather said. "I have to make up my *bunk*."

16

Judge T. Wallace Higbee had come to realize that what it was all about was stupidity. All through law school and through his years of private practice, he had believed that the subject was the law itself, but in the last twelve years, since, at the age of fifty-seven, he had been elected to the bench, he had come to realize that all the training and all the experience came down to this: It was his task in this life to acknowledge and then to punish stupidity.

Joe Doakes steals a car, drives it to his girlfriend's house, leaves the engine running while he goes inside to have a loud argument with his girlfriend, causing a neighbor to call the police, who arrive to quiet a domestic dispute but then leave with a car thief, who eventually appears before Judge T. Wallace Higbee, who gives him two to five in Dannemora. For what? Car theft? No; stupidity.

Bobby Doakes, high on various illegal substances, decides he's thirsty and needs a beer, but it's four in the morning and the convenience store is closed, so he breaks in the back door, drinks several beers, falls asleep in the storeroom, is found there in the morning, and Judge Higbee gives him four to eight for stupidity.

Jane Doakes steals a neighbor's checkbook, kites checks at a supermarket and a drugstore, doesn't think about putting the checkbook back until two days later, by which time the neighbor has discovered the theft and reported it and is on watch, and catches Jane in the act. Two to five for stupidity.

Maybe, Judge Higbee told himself from time to time, maybe in big cities like New York and London there are criminal masterminds, geniuses of crime, and judges forced to shake their heads in admiration at the subtlety and brilliance of the felonious behaviors described to them while handing down their sentences. Maybe. But out here in the world, the only true crime, and it just keeps being committed over and over, is stupidity.

Which made the people like Marjorie Dawson so useful. Not the brightest bulb on the legal marquee, she was nevertheless marginally smarter than the clients she accompanied into Judge Higbee's court. She knew the proceedings, she knew the drill, she knew how to move the defendants through the routine without letting them make excess trouble through even greater displays of stupidity, and she did it all without complaint and with the acceptance of the rather miserable stipend offered court-appointed attorneys by the state. She did not make trouble. She did not herself perform overt acts of stupidity.

So why was she in Judge Higbee's chambers this morning, saying this Farraff woman required a hearing? Required? A hearing? Shirley Ann Farraff, an over-the-hill showgirl from Las Vegas, tries an old scam on the proprietors of the Silver Chasm Casino, presenting herself as a nuisance to be bought off, and instead is turned in. It being a first offense, and the proprietors of the casino not wishing to be unduly harsh—nor to receive undue publicity—Judge Higbee acknowledges this particular stupidity with a pass, so long as the defendant agrees to perform all her future acts of stupidity in some other jurisdiction.

So what's the problem? "Tell me, Marjorie," the judge said, lowering his several pounds of white eyebrows in Marjorie's direction, where she sat on the opposite side of the crowded desk, "tell me, what's the problem?"

"She insists," Marjorie said, "that what she said in the letter is true."

"Marjorie, Marjorie," the judge said, "they *all* insist their fantasies are true. After a while, they come to believe they actually *were* afraid they were coming down with appendicitis and needed desperately to get to the hospital, and that's why they were driving at one hundred miles an hour in an uninsured vehicle with an expired driver's license at two in the morning."

Marjorie nodded. "Yes, I remember that one," she said. "But Your Honor, this one's different. I'm afraid she really is."

"Do you believe her story, Marjorie?"

"I don't believe anybody's story, Judge," Marjorie told him, "that's not my job. My job is to get them the best deal I can and make them understand it really is the best deal they can get and make them agree to it."

"And?"

"This one won't agree to it."

"You mean she won't sign the quitclaim," the judge said.

"That's right, Your Honor."

Judge Higbee was a large man, large all over, getting

a little larger every decade. When he frowned, as now, whole great reaches of him bunched and puckered, and his eyes became twin blue sunrises over a mountain range in winter. "I don't like this, Marjorie," he said.

"I knew you wouldn't, Your Honor," she told him.

"Roger Fox and Frank Oglanda have filed a complaint," the judge pointed out, "and they want the problem dealt with. If this damn young woman signs the quitclaim, I can dispose of the matter this morning and have her on the road before lunch, saving the taxpayers close to two dollars. If she refuses to sign, I'll have to hold her over for trial."

"Yes, Your Honor."

"I don't believe Roger and Frank would be happy to have to come to town to testify against this young woman," the judge said, "but I don't see what else could be done, once the complaint has been filed. They're not going to pay her off, you know."

"I don't think she wants to be bought off," Marjorie said. "Not like that at least. She doesn't want to just take some money and disappear. She wants to be *here*."

"Marjorie," the judge told her, "I truly don't want her here."

"I know that, Your Honor. But she won't listen to me. She might listen to you."

"You want me to see her."

"One way or another, Your Honor, you're going to have to see her, either here in your chambers or out there in session. I told her yesterday that I would try to arrange an appointment with you this morning in chambers."

Judge Higbee brooded. In the long march of stupidity that rolled past his eyes day by day, there was rarely anything that required him actually to stop and think, and he didn't like the experience. He found it discomfiting.

Marjorie said, "Your Honor, if we go before Your Honor in court, she'll have to be formally charged, I'll have to apply for a bail hearing, and we'll have to begin a very long process that *does not end.* As you know, Your Honor."

The judge looked at the calendar of the day's events, placed on the desk close to his right hand. "In an hour," he said. "Ten-thirty."

She did not impress. At first glance, anyway, she did not impress, but then she did impress, but not in the right way. She was a very good-looking woman, Judge Higbee supposed, with strong Indian cheekbones and thick black Indian hair, but also with the kind of brassy, aggressive style the judge associated with the phrase "Las Vegas showgirl." There was a hardness about her he found unappealing, not only in the toughness of her look but in the very way she walked, sat, turned her head. The judge judged her to be trouble.

He hadn't spoken when she first walked in, accompanied by Marjorie, because he wanted to observe her before making up his mind. No shrinking violet, that was clear; neither the office nor he himself intimidated her. And her night in detention didn't seem to have had much effect on her.

Marjorie murmured to the young woman, showing her where to sit—in the chair across the desk from the judge. Marjorie herself moved to the second chair, off to the young woman's right.

Judge Higbee let the silence extend a few more seconds. The young woman met his probing eyes without a flinch, gaze for gaze. He suspected she was very angry about something, but holding it in. She did not have the skulking posture that the stupid always present, betraying their guilt while they declare their innocence. She did not blurt into speech, but waited for him.

What, he wondered, without joy, do we have here?

Very well. He began: "Ms. Farraff, Ms. Dawson tells me—"

"My name," she said, quiet but forceful, "is Little Feather Redcorn. That's the name I was born with. Later, when my mama left the reservation and moved in with Frank Farraff, she said I had to have a name like the other people around there or I'd be laughed at, so she changed my name, and that's the name I've lived with ever since. But now I'm going back to my first name."

Quite a statement. She'd probably been rehearsing that for hours, in the detention cell. Well, he had given her time to get it all out, so now was the time to close down this little drama. Almost gently, he said, "And do you have your birth certificate with you, with that name?"

"No, I don't," she said. "I don't have any birth certificate, and I don't know how to get one, because I don't know exactly where I was born."

"There wouldn't be a birth certificate somewhere, would there, that says your father was Frank Farraff?"

"My mama didn't meet Frank Farraff until I was three or four years old," she said, "when we moved off the reservation and into town, because there wasn't any work on the reservation."

With a frosty smile, he said, "There's not much work for a three-year-old anywhere, is there?" Making a joke, because of course he knew she'd meant work for her mother.

But the damn woman said, "There was some. They had me weeding. Sat me down in the rows of beans, told me to pull up those but leave those alone. I remember I was pretty good at it."

Judge Higbee leaned back. That wasn't stupidity, that was truth. How could this young woman possibly be different from the endless army of morons who marched past his uncaring eye? And yet, the three-year-old child set out to weed among the bean plants was a picture he believed.

Very well. She'd mixed some of her true history into this folderol. But the underlying fact remained the same: She was an inept scam artist, to be summarily dealt with and sent on her way. He said, "You have no birth certificate."

"All I know is," she said, "I was born on the reservation."

"And you are certain, are you, we won't be stumbling across a birth certificate in the name of Shirley Ann Farraff?"

"If you find anything like that," she said, completely unfazed, "you can lock me up and throw away the key."

The judge had a copy of the young woman's letter on his desk. Now he scanned it, then said, "You say your mother—Doeface, is that it?"

"That's right, that's my mama, Doeface Redcorn."

"You say," the judge persisted, "that your mother told you your history, that you are of the Pottaknobbee tribe, and these people you name here are your forebears, is that right?"

"Yes, sir," she said, and he noticed the 'sir,' and he knew what it meant. So long as he behaved properly toward her, she would behave properly toward him.

Well, fair enough. He could see now that this actually was a more complicated situation than he was used to. God knows, he didn't want to have to deal with an interesting case, but this just might be one. He said, "Do you have any documentation at all to confirm your story?"

"No, sir."

"Then why should you be believed?"

"Because it's true."

He frowned at the letter some more, then said, "I understand you've been living at Whispering Pines, is that right?"

"Yes, sir, in my motor home."

"And how long have you been there?"

"Four, five days. Five days."

"And how long had you been away?"

She looked blank. "From where?"

"From here."

She smiled, which softened her face, though not enough, and said, "I've never been around here before in my life. My mama left here when she was a little girl, with *her* mama, like it says in my letter. I'm coming home for the first time in my life."

He picked up a pencil to point its eraser at her. "Be very careful, Ms. Farraff."

"Redcorn."

"That has not been established. The only documentation I have on you indicates your name is Farraff. Until you demonstrate to *my* satisfaction that you should be referred to by some other name, I shall continue to call you by the name on your documents, your Social Security card, your driver's license, and so on. Is that clear?"

She shrugged. "Okay," she said. "But once you give up trying to get rid of me, I want to hear you call me Ms. Redcorn a *lot*."

"If and when the time comes," he assured her, "I'll be happy to. Now, where was I?"

Marjorie said, "You asked how long Ms. Farraff had been away from this area." And the faint smirk with which she said it showed that Marjorie, too, had been subjected to the name game and was taking advantage of the judge's victory.

Fine. "Thank you, Marjorie," he said, and returned to Ms. Farraff. "If you have never been in this area before," he said, "and I suppose we can document that by your work history and so on, establishing your whereabouts over the past, say, two years . . ."

"I'll give you my tax returns," she offered.

"That may not be necessary," he told her, nettled, thinking, by God, she's sure of herself. Tapping the letter, he said, "So I must ask you this: Where did you get these names that you claim are the names of Pottaknobbee Native Americans?"

"From my mama," the young woman said. "Only she called them Indians."

"Did she. If there are no Pottaknobbees left in this world, and the evidence seems to indicate there are none," the judge told her, "then there are unlikely to be any methods by which you could prove that any of these people ever existed."

"Well," Ms. Farraff said, "there's my grandfather Bearpaw, who went down with his ship in the U.S. Navy in World War Two. Wouldn't the government have a record of that?"

"Possibly," the judge said. He found that answer had made him grumpy. "But I notice," he went on, tapping the eraser end of the pencil against the letter, "that not one of these people even has a grave that could be looked at, to see what name is on the stone. Your mother and grandmother both disappeared, your grandfather was lost at sea."

"That's what happens," Ms. Farraff said.

Marjorie said, "Your Honor, in fact, in my discussion with Ms. Farraff yesterday, she did mention one more supposed forebear. Your great-grandfather, wasn't it?"

"That's right," she said, with a very cool nod in Marjorie's direction. Don't get along, those two, the judge thought.

"Ms. Farraff tells me," Marjorie said, "that her great-grandfather worked in construction in—"

"Steelworker."

"Yes, thank you, steelworker in New York City, and worked on the Empire State Building, and was killed in a fall there."

"My mama," Ms. Farraff interjected, "said the family always believed the Mohawks pushed him, so I believe it, too."

The judge pulled his pad closer. "Presumably, then," he said, "this particular ancestor is buried where one could take a look at his gravestone, or at least at the record of who is to be found in the grave."

That didn't seem to call for an answer; at least, neither woman answered him. Which gave him time for a further thought. He said, "Do we know this person's name?"

"Joseph Redcorn," Ms. Farraff said, as though she'd been waiting years to say that.

The judge wrote it, and echoed it: "Joseph Redcorn. Very good. Now, it seems to me, someone falling off the Empire State Building, there might be some remembrance of that, record of it among the tribes. Let me just call Frank Oglanda."

They let him call, but when he got through to Frank's secretary, Olga, she said, "I'm sorry, Judge, Frank isn't in yet this morning."

"There's a name I'm trying to track down, Olga," the judge told her. "Someone from seventy years ago or so, who may have been a Pottaknobbee."

"Oh, Judge," she said, "I don't think we have that kind of record here in the casino."

"No, this would be a special case," he told her. "The story is, he was a steelworker in the old days, and was killed while working on the Empire State Building. An event like that, it seemed to—"

"Oh, I know who you mean!" she said.

He blinked. "You do?"

"Yes, I'm trying to remember his name. The plaque is in the other room. I could—"

"Plaque?"

"Well, apparently, at the time, it was a real scandal, and a lot of people around here thought the Mohawks had pushed this man off the girder, and the Mohawks tried to make peace and say they didn't do it and all, and they presented the Three Tribes with a plaque to honor his memory. You know, it was beaten copper, with a representation of the Empire State Building and his name and his dates, and it was dedicated by the Mohawk Nation to his memory. But people still thought the Mohawks pushed him."

"And you have this plaque."

"Yes, sir, Your Honor, it's in the next room. I could go look at it. May I put you on hold?"

"One minute, Olga. You say 'the next room.' Is this a public space?"

"Oh, no, sir, it's the Three Tribes conference room, the public *never* gets in there."

So Ms. Farraff hasn't seen the plaque, he thought, and wondered if she even knew of its existence.

"Your Honor? Shall I go take a look at it? I'll have to put you on hold."

"Yes, fine, Olga, thank you."

While on hold, he listened to Sonny and Cher sing, "The Beat Goes On." He closed his eyes. He knew now that this day was just going to get more complicated and more complicated, and then maybe even *more* complicated.

"Your Honor?"

"Yes, Olga, here I am." Sonny and Cher had gone away.

"I'm in the conference room," the pleasant, efficient voice said in his ear. "Here it is. Yes. 'Joseph Redcorn, July 12, 1907, November 7, 1930. With loving respect to a fallen brave from his comrades, the Mohawk Nation.' Does that help, Judge?"

"Oh, immeasurably," he said. "Thank you, Olga."

He hung up the telephone. He looked at the young woman, and she was smiling, but she was also showing her teeth. "I think, Judge," she said, "it's time for you to start calling me Ms. Redcorn."

17

"The question is," Dortmunder said, "what happens next?"

They were gathered again in Guilderpost's bleak motel room at eleven that morning, this time without Little Feather's sunny presence, and Irwin said, "Next, Little Feather lets them stumble on Joseph Redcorn, they search, there's some sort of tribal history or something—"

"Or something," Tiny said, from his usual perch on the bed.

Irwin gave an impatient shake of the head. "Joseph Redcorn was the only Pottaknobbee who died in a fall off the Empire State Building. They'll have a record."

"Fine," Dortmunder said. "They've got a record. Then what?"

Guilderpost said, "They won't get to the DNA today."

Kelp said, "Isn't that what it's all about?"

Irwin explained: "It has to come from them. It's bad psychology if Little Feather mentions DNA first. So all that'll happen now is, they see it's possible, the family did exist, she says she's part of that family, she can't prove she is, they can't prove she isn't, and sooner or later somebody's going to say—"

"Anastasia," Tiny rumbled.

"Exactly," Irwin said. "But it has to come from them."

Guilderpost said, "And they won't think of it today. They have too much to absorb."

Dortmunder said, "Okay. So what I want to know is, what happens next?"

"They let her go," Guilderpost told him, "she returns to Whispering Pines, and she telephones to us, here."

"Uh-oh," Dortmunder said.

But Guilderpost, with a little superior smirk, waggled a finger at Dortmunder, shook his head, and said, "She says only one word. 'Sorry.' As though it's a wrong number. And hangs up."

Dortmunder nodded. "And makes another call?"

Guilderpost looked surprised. "What?" He and Irwin frowned at each other.

Dortmunder said, "So they know it was code, it was a signal, if they're tapping her phone. And if they want to know, is this woman alone here or is there a gang behind her, they'll tap her phone."

Irwin said, "It's a pay phone, John, at Whispering Pines. There're four of them there in a row."

"All right," Dortmunder said. "So there's a chance. Then what?"

"The usual routine," Guilderpost told him. "And she comes here, to let us know how things went."

"No," Dortmunder said.

Guilderpost didn't believe it. "No?"

"In the first place," Dortmunder told him, "if they let her go, we *know* how things went. In the second place, taxis have trip sheets, what time the pickup, where'd they go, what time the drop-off. It'll take the cops half an hour to see Little Feather spends a hell of a lot of time in that supermarket."

Irwin said, "John, we do have to talk with Little Feather, plan what we do next."

Tiny grunted and pointed at Dortmunder and said, "You listen to Duh—John."

"That's right," Kelp said. "He's the planner, he's the organizer."

Guilderpost looked offended. "I beg your pardon, but this is *my* project. You three have coattailed yourselves to it. *All* right, there's enough for everyone, no need to be greedy or cause trouble, but it's still *my* project."

Dortmunder said, "That's not what they mean. We do different things, Fitzroy, you and me. You figure out someplace where you can make people believe something's true that isn't true. Make them believe you got an old Dutch land grant screws up their title to their property. Make them believe maybe there *is* just one more Pottaknobbee alive in the world. That's not what I do."

"No, of course not," Guilderpost said, and Irwin, sounding slightly snotty, said, "I've been wondering that, John. What *is* it you do?"

"I figure out," Dortmunder told him, "how to go into a place where I'm not supposed to be, and come back out again, without getting caught or having anything stick to me."

"It's like D day," Kelp explained, "only like, you know, smaller."

"We also go for quieter," Dortmunder said.

"So up till now," Kelp said, "you've just been putting the scam together, but now you sprung it, now you got the law and the tribes and everybody taking an interest, now you need John."

"To tell you don't do phone calls in code," Dortmunder said. "And don't just make a meeting without thinking about it, because now you got law sniffing around. All of us in this room, our job now is to not exist."

Irwin said, "You mean leave Little Feather out there completely on her own?"

"No," Dortmunder said. "What we do with Little Feather is, we act like she's the crown jewels of England, and she's for the first time on display in America, in New York, somewhere, at somewhere—"

"Radio City Music Hall," Kelp suggested.

"I don't think so," Dortmunder said. "Maybe the UN. Maybe Carnegie Hall. Somewhere. And there's guards. And now what we gotta do is, we gotta get in there—"

"Metropolitan Museum of Art," Tiny offered.

"Wherever," Dortmunder said. "We gotta get in there, wherever the hell it is, and we gotta get back out again, without those guards even knowing we were there."

"Only in this case," Kelp finished, "without the crown jewels."

"Well, yeah," Dortmunder said. "I'm not suggesting we kidnap Little Feather. What I'm saying is, we got to deal with Little Feather without anybody knowing we're doing it, so let me run this part."

"I am prepared," Guilderpost assured him, "to learn at your feet."

"Good," Dortmunder said. Irony never did make much headway with him.

18

Little Feather got out of the cab, walked into the supermarket through the automatic in door, made a U-turn, aimed for the automatic out door, and Andy came in the automatic in door. He gave her the smallest head shake the world has ever barely seen, though Little Feather saw it loud and clear, he did not look at her, and he moved on into the store.

And so did she. He got a cart, and so did she. He started up and down the aisles, taking his time, adding very few items to his cart but studying many, reading cereal boxes and vitamin supplement labels and safe handling instructions on shrink-wrapped hamburger. Little Feather followed him for a few minutes, until she realized he didn't want her to follow him, and then she went off on her own.

Which was when she realized somebody was following *her*. A chunky little guy of about thirty, very much an Indian from the reservation, dressed in old blue jeans, which had been faded by work and use and not by the designer, and a red plaid shirt of the sort worn by some men upstate and some women in the city, and he was not a very good follower. He kept being in Little Feather's way as she roved about, but he would practically rather fling himself over the high display racks than meet her eye. He also was forgetting to put things in his cart, except that, when she stopped to put something in hers, he'd immediately grab something to his right, at waist level, without looking at it, and dump it in. Did he really need Depends? Poor fellow, and so young, too.

Okay, Little Feather got the picture. The tribes had put somebody on her, to tail her around and see whom she made contact with, and Fitzroy and the others knew about it, or had guessed it would happen, and were warning her not to try to meet the same old way.

Which made her realize, as she wended her slow and thoughtful way through the supermarket, that the cops might be doing exactly the same thing, with a more competent shadow, someone she might not tip to right away, or ever. So what did this mean?

Was she on her own now? Couldn't she meet up with Fitzroy and the others at *all*? That could create a little tension.

Except that Andy was still in the store, wandering around; Little Feather saw him from time to time, down at the end of some aisle. So there was more to come, somehow. But what?

It was fifteen minutes later, when she was in the dairy section once again, this time trying to find the low-fat plain yogurt, as opposed to the no-fat plain yogurt—ya gotta have a *little* fat—when another cart stopped next to hers, and Andy leaned past the end of her cart to reach for a Honey Walnut Lime Rickey Yogurt With No Sodium!, and when he'd moved on away, there was an additional item in her cart. It was a magazine, and it was called *Prevention*.

She didn't read the note tucked inside the magazine until she got back to the Winnebago. It was hand-printed on two small sheets of Four Winds motel stationery, and it said:

> Don't telephone. We think they might be tailing you, to see if you've got what they call "confederates." And they could also be tapping the pay phones there.
>
> At four o'clock, call a cab. There's a big shopping center called SavMall outside of town. Go there, go to the drugstore there, buy something you want, come back.
>
> If you see your tail, mark him, but don't let him know you're onto him.
>
> Everything's fine with us, no problem.

Well, who cares about you people? Little Feather thought. Four o'clock. Another cab ride.

19

Little Feather's a real boon for the taxi industry around here," Kelp said as they watched the cab turn in at Whispering Pines main entrance, over there across the road.

They were all in Guilderpost's Voyager, which was crowded but marginally more roomy than the Jeep, parked on the blacktop beside the kind of liquor store that grows like magic across the road from every campground in the civilized world. Guilderpost was at the wheel, with Dortmunder beside him, now looking past Guilderpost's impressive chin at the taxi turning in at the entrance over there. Tiny took up much of the rest of the vehicle, with Kelp and Irwin tucked in among him.

A minute after the cab drove in, a little chunky guy came trotting out of the entrance, had to stop and bounce on both feet and wait impatiently while two big semis roared by, one north, one south, and then scampered across the road to climb into a small old orange Subaru parked around at the front of the liquor store, facing out. Dortmunder had noticed that vehicle on the way in and had idly wondered if the place was in the process of undergoing a holdup, because why else would you park in front of a liquor store facing out? Well, this was why else.

"The follower," Tiny rumbled.

"From the tribes," Dortmunder agreed as the taxi came out the main entrance and turned right, toward town. The Subaru sputtered and stalled, then bounced out in the taxi's wake.

"Okay, good, let's go," said Irwin, who didn't like sitting under Tiny.

"Wait," Dortmunder said, and across the road a dark gray Chevy they hadn't even noticed, which had been tucked up against the shrubbery that grew along the wooden fence fronting Whispering Pines, suddenly slid forward, like a water moccasin through a shallow stream. "And that's the cop," Dortmunder said.

Tiny laughed (Irwin groaned). "Little Feather's got herself a parade."

"Can we go *now*?" Irwin begged.

"Right," Dortmunder said, and they all climbed out of the Voyager, some more stiffly than others, and walked across the road.

Having been here before, Guilderpost led the way down the curving blacktop road among pine trees and brush and various kinds of motor homes and the occasional actual tent, until they came to the motor home. "She'll have locked it," he said, taking out a key as they approached the vehicle.

"Why?" Kelp asked.

"Habit," Dortmunder suggested.

The motor home's right side, opposite its main door, was tucked up against a few scraggly pines. On the left side, there was a bit of wasteland, and a knee-high yellow rope threaded through metal stakes pounded into the ground to define the area of the campsite, and beyond that four oldsters playing cards at a table they'd set up outside their Space Invaders vehicle. They watched the five men, not suspicious, just watching, the way people watch anything that moves, and Kelp waved to them, calling, "How you doing this afternoon?"

The four cardplayers smiled and nodded and waved, and one of the men said, "Pretty fine."

"Nip in the air," Kelp told them, since Guilderpost was still fumbling with the key.

One of the women said, "The young lady went out."

"To the drugstore," Kelp agreed, and pointed at Guilderpost, who'd finally gotten the door open. "That's her father."

"Oh," they all said, as though they'd just been told an entire story, and they all nodded and waved and smiled at Guilderpost and said, "Afternoon."

Guilderpost managed a smile and a wave of his own, then led the way inside, the others following. "Stepfather, perhaps," he said as he shut the door.

20

"Somebody out there says my father's here," Little Feather said, stepping into the motor home, carrying the plastic shopping bag with the big green cross on it that showed she'd been to the drugstore.

"That was one of Andy's little pleasantries," Guilderpost told her.

Little Feather looked around at them all. The motor home's living room had never seemed so small. "So I guess this is the debriefing," she said. "Wait while I put this stuff away."

She left them and went down the narrow hall to the bathroom, where she unloaded the things she'd bought on her outing, and when she came back to the living room, Irwin had risen and was grinning that fake grin of his in Little Feather's direction—whenever Irwin tried for anything in the smile category, he looked like somebody with heartburn—as he said, "Have my chair, Little Feather."

Andy was already seated on the floor, Tiny on the sofa, Fitzroy on the other chair, and John on the footstool from the kitchen, his knees tucked up under his chin. "Thank you, Irwin," Little Feather said, bounced her own brief false smile off him, and sat down.

Irwin found a place on the floor near Andy, where he, too, could lean his back against the wall, and Fitzroy said, "Well, Little Feather, you've had adventures."

"Tell me about it," she said.

"Well, no," John said. "We're here so you can tell us about it."

"Okay," she said. "They decided to play hardball from the very beginning, arrested me for extortion, put me in a cell. Nobody talked to me till after six at night, then this court-appointed lawyer came in, already cut a deal with the judge, here's a paper to sign, says I'm a lying sack of shit and I'm happy to leave town and never come back."

"This is *your* lawyer," Irwin said.

"That's what it said on the label."

"He's just there to get rid of you," Andy informed her.

"She. Marjorie Dawson."

John said, "What do you think of her?"

"She takes the man's money, she does what the man wants." Little Feather shrugged. "When do I get a real lawyer?"

Fitzroy knew the answer to that. "Not until they talk DNA," he said. "The instant they say anything about DNA, you say, 'Oh, gee, then I better get a lawyer who knows all about that.'"

Little Feather understood the concept, but it was still irritating. "So I'm gonna have to go on dealing with little Marjorie Dawson."

Irwin said, "It won't be long, Little Feather. Once they've given up the idea they can get rid of you just by saying shoo, they'll right away start thinking Tiny's word."

"Anastasia," Tiny rumbled on cue.

"Oh, they've already given up that old idea," Little Feather assured them. "We're past that part."

"How?" Fitzroy demanded, sitting up straighter, but before she could answer, John said, "No, this isn't the way. Little Feather, tell us what happened from the beginning."

So she told them what had happened from the beginning, letting them in on how pissed off she'd been that she had to spend a full night in a cell—"I've never been inside a cell before in my life for even a *minute*"—and then giving them the happy news that great-grandpa Joseph Redcorn was not only remembered out on the reservation but memorialized, in a plaque from the Mohawks, the ones that probably pushed him off the building.

"That's wonderful news!" Irwin told her, as though she didn't know, and Fitzroy said, "In all my researches, I never came across that plaque. God bless the Mohawks."

"Homicidal but thoughtful," Little Feather said.

John said, "What's supposed to happen next?"

"Dawson, the lawyer, is going to talk to the people on the reservation," Little Feather told him, "and then she's supposed to call me tomorrow, and I'll go see her."

Irwin said, "And that's when they'll talk about DNA."

John said, "Okay. And what does Little Feather do then?"

Little Feather had gone over this part a number of times with Fitzroy. She said, "I say, 'Gee, that's a great idea. Now you'll know for sure I'm one of you guys, but I think maybe I oughta have a lawyer who knows this stuff.'"

Andy said, "How do you find this lawyer?"

"Fitzroy's already got him."

"*Will* get him," Fitzroy said, correcting her. "Or her. I don't have the specific lawyer yet. I'll make that call this afternoon."

John looked at him. "There's a part here you didn't set up?"

"Would have been too early before this," Fitzroy explained.

Andy said, "This is some lawyer you already know. Or you don't know."

"I know the firm," Fitzroy said. "Feinberg."

John said, "Fitzroy, fill me in on this."

"There's a New York law firm I use all the time," Fitzroy told him. "It's Feinberg, Kleinberg, Rhineberg, Steinberg, Weinberg & Klatsch, but it's known as Feinberg."

Andy said, "I'd know it as Klatsch."

"Yes, you would," Fitzroy agreed. "But the legal profession lacks your delicate sense of humor."

John said, "Fitzroy, walk me through this Feinberg business. You dealt with these people before?"

"Several times."

"These are bent lawyers, is that it?"

"Not at all." Fitzroy smiled. "Lawyers don't have to be bent, John."

Irwin said, "Their *job* is bent."

"Tell," John said.

Fitzroy said, "All right, John, this is the situation. Feinberg is a large corporate law firm in Manhattan. They have hundreds of lawyers on staff."

"More than just all these bergs."

"The bergs, as you say," Fitzroy explained, "were the original partners, all, I believe, now dead."

"Gone to their reward." Irwin smirked.

"So who do you deal with?"

"That depends."

John kept shaking his head, as though gnats were after him. "Depends on *what*?"

"The job at hand. For instance, with the land grant business, I spoke to the senior man there, who knows me, described enough of what I was doing, and he turned me over to a real estate specialist in the firm. When I was involved with the offshore salvage enterprise, he put me in touch with a specialist there in maritime law. This time, he'll give me their DNA specialist."

"You know," Tiny said, "I think that's the lawyers Josie went to when she set up her country."

Fitzroy looked interested. "You know someone who created a country? For development funds, I should think."

Little Feather would have liked to hear more about that—a person set up a country? what "development funds"?—but Tiny merely said, "Yeah, that's it."

Fitzroy nodded; *he* knew what they were talking about. "Feinberg would be just the firm," he agreed. "They have a number of specialists in international law."

Well, at least John still didn't understand, which made Little Feather feel a little less dumb, because he said, "I don't get it. You mean you tell these lawyers what scam you're working, and—"

"No, no, John, not at all," Fitzroy said, and, to Little Feather, he looked actually shocked at the idea. "We don't want," he said, "our lawyer to think ill of us. I explain what they need to know, but I never, never, never suggest I might intend to do something illegal."

"But they gotta know," John said.

"What they know is up to them," Fitzroy told him. "But what matters is what I *say*."

Still shaking his head, John asked, "But why do they go along with it? You're there with them, and you're talking and talking, and you're not quite saying this is a scam going down, and they *go along* with it? Why?"

"Because that's their job," Fitzroy said. He seemed almost kindly, avuncular, and Little Feather realized that, though both men were lifelong professional criminals, they were of completely different orders, and they would never entirely understand each other. And I am going to need them both, she thought. For a while.

Fitzroy was explaining further: "You see, John, lawyers have much less respect for the law than the rest of us. It's familiarity, you see, doing its little breeding job again. A lawyer isn't there to tell you what the law is, you'll get that from a policeman or a judge. A lawyer is there to tell you what you can do anyway."

Irwin said, "Think of yourself as Dante, and the law as hell."

"Okay," John said.

"Your lawyer is Virgil. He takes you through it, and he gets you out the other side."

John said, "And you're saying he doesn't ask questions."

"John," Fitzroy said, "do you think the lawyers who represent Mafia chieftains ask questions? The lawyers who represent inside traders in the stock market? The lawyers who do personal injury suits, class actions, divorces? Do you really think they ask their clients questions? Why on earth would they want to know those answers?"

Irwin said, "John, I'm not prying, but I would guess you've had a dealing or two with the law yourself, and had a lawyer. Did the lawyer ever ask you if you did it?"

"Well, usually," John said, looking just a bit sheepish, "there wasn't that much doubt. But I see what you mean, I get it. So you've got a history with these bergs. . . ."

"I pay their fees promptly," Fitzroy said, "I bring them interesting legal challenges, and I never embarrass them by suggesting I am anything but a pillar of society."

Andy said, "And what's the pillar's connection with Little Feather? You gonna be the sugar daddy?"

"Not at all." Fitzroy offered Little Feather a bland smile, and she returned it in spades. To the others, Fitzroy said, "Little Feather is a young lady who used to work for an old friend of mine in the hotel business out west. She's alone and defenseless here in the East, but her prospects are excellent once she proves her identity, and I put my reputation on the line to guarantee she *will* prove her identity."

"Your reputation," John said.

Fitzroy preened a little. "We talk that way in lawyers' offices," he said.

Tiny, who'd been turning his head to look from speaker to speaker the whole time, like a man watching a slo-mo volleyball game, said, "So we're all done. Us three can go back to New York."

"No," John said. "This part is done, but we're not done."

Tiny turned his head to look at John. "Why not?"

"Because they hit too hard from the beginning," John said. "The tribes. And they put a tail on Little Feather."

Little Feather said, "They did?"

Tiny turned his head to look at her. "Two tails. The tribes and a cop."

She hadn't known about the cop, and she didn't like it. "Well, well," she said.

John said, "So we'll stay here awhile, and we'll go on being careful. Like, when we're done here, Little Feather—"

"I bet I call another cab."

"You win. You take it into town, catch dinner and a movie, then come back."

She looked around at them all. "And when do we six meet again?"

Fitzroy said, "Well, you should keep us informed of what happens tomorrow."

Little Feather nodded. "So I'm going to the drugstore again."

"You don't have to," John said. "You're going to see this Dawson tomorrow, aren't you?"

"Yeah, but I don't know what time."

"Whatever," John said. "When you come back, you'll have company."

21

Marjorie Dawson didn't understand. She knew the Three Tribes attorney; he was Abner Hicks, with an office in the Laurel Building around the corner on Laurel Avenue, Marjorie herself being in the Frost Building around the corner this way on Frost Avenue. She'd expected she might even run into Abner this morning, on the short walk over to the courthouse to meet with Judge Higbee in chambers.

So why had the judge called this morning, a little before ten, to say the meeting would have to wait until three this afternoon, "because the tribe's attorney has to come up from New York"? Wasn't this a simple, straightforward matter? Either Little Feather Redcorn (had to call her that now) could demonstrate she actually was a Pottaknobbee and would have to be accepted as the third of the Three Tribes or she would fail to prove her case and would be sent packing. So why did the Three Tribes need a lawyer from New York?

After getting that call from the judge—from his secretary, Hilda, actually—Marjorie phoned Whispering Pines and they got Ms. Redcorn to come to the phone so Marjorie could tell her they'd meet in her office in the

Frost Building at 2:30. Then she spent the time until then brooding.

The fact is, she was a little intimidated by the idea of a lawyer coming all the way up from New York, almost four hundred miles, to represent the Three Tribes in this matter. Marjorie, with two partners, Jimmy Hong and Corinne Wadamaker, had a small general practice in the county, mostly house closings and wills and divorces and small disputes, in addition to her work as defense counsel for the court, and she felt comfortable with the lawyers she faced in the normal course of work. They all knew one another, they all knew what the job was, and they never tried to make life difficult for one another. Treat the client decently, of course, but your fellow professionals naturally came first.

Would a lawyer from New York feel that way? Or would that person look down his or her nose at the small-town lawyer and try some tricky New York footwork, just to make Marjorie look bad?

But that was what she simply couldn't understand. What was there to do tricky footwork *about*? It should be a very simple matter, this Little Feather Redcorn business, well within Marjorie's competence, so why were they trying to make her nervous?

The next thought was, why had the Three Tribes reacted with such hostility in the first place? Though the initial letter from Ms. Redcorn could certainly be read as the opening step of an extortion racket, it could equally well be read as a straightforward letter from somebody who believed that what she said was true. Why hadn't the Three Tribes at least talked to the woman first? Why had they immediately turned the letter over to the police so they could scare her off?

They're behaving, Marjorie reluctantly admitted to herself as 2:30 neared, as though they have something to hide. Roger Fox and Frank Oglanda, the casino managers, they were the ones who were handling this affair, not the Tribal Council. The Tribal Council didn't even seem to be involved.

Of course, it was the casino managers to whom Ms. Redcorn had addressed her letter, and the ownership of the casino was the only substantive matter at issue here. Still, it did seem to Marjorie there was some hidden agenda at work in this proceeding, and if that were the case, she knew very well that Marjorie Dawson was not the one to ferret it out.

Cinda, the secretary she shared with Jimmy and Corinna, buzzed her at 2:28 to say, "Ms. Redcorn is here."

"Yes, send her in," Marjorie said, and stood to welcome her unusual and rather alarming client.

Who had dressed more demurely today, Marjorie was happy to note. In jail, Ms. Redcorn had been dressed like the girl singer in an old Western, though somewhat more daringly than a PG rating would have allowed. Of course, when she'd dressed that day, she hadn't yet known she would finish the day in jail.

This morning, though there was still a strong western flavor to Ms. Redcorn's outfit, at least her boots were black, her tan leather skirt knee-length, and her colorful shirt not absolutely formfitting. Her expression, however, was at least as wary as yesterday's, and she entered saying, "I thought we were gonna meet this morning."

"So did I, Ms. Redcorn," Marjorie told her. "Sit down here, please. Let's go over the situation."

Ms. Redcorn remained standing. "Don't we go see the judge?"

"Our appointment is at three. Do sit down."

The two gray-blue vinyl armchairs in front of the desk were comfortable, but not too comfortable. Ms. Redcorn gave them a disapproving look, then sat in the nearest one as Marjorie took her own swivel chair, picked up the pencil she tended to toy with during interviews in this room, and said, "The judge phoned me this morning to say the meeting had to be delayed because the tribes' lawyer had to come up from New York."

This got no reaction except a nod.

Marjorie said, "Let me explain. I *know* the tribes' lawyer. His name is Abner Hicks, and his office is around the corner from here."

"You mean they're bringing in the big guns," Ms. Redcorn said. She didn't seem at all troubled by the idea.

"And I don't know why," Marjorie admitted. "Tell me, Ms. Redcorn, is there anything else about this matter you think I should know?"

Ms. Redcorn cocked her head, like a particularly bright bird. "Like what?"

"Any cloud in your past that might cause us trouble, anything to explain why they've sent to New York for a lawyer to deal with you? In other words, is there more information *I* should have if I'm properly to represent you?"

Ms. Redcorn shrugged. "Nothing I can think of," she said. "My guess is, they just don't want to split the pot."

Then she grinned a little and said, "This New York lawyer scares you, huh?"

"Certainly not," Marjorie said. Ms. Redcorn might be telling the truth about her forebears, and she might be the victim of unfair treatment by the Three Tribes, but she was not at all an easy person to like.

Dropping her pencil to the desk with a little disapproving clatter, Marjorie said, "Well, let's walk over to the courthouse."

The New York lawyer looked like a hawk who hadn't eaten for a week. His beak of a nose seemed to be pointing at prey, his sharp, icy eyes flicked back and forth like an angry cat's tail, and his hands were large and knobby and, when Marjorie shook one of them, cold. His name was Otis Welles and he wore a suit that cost more than Marjorie's car, but somehow, instead of the suit giving some dignity to his bony, gristly body, his body seemed merely to cheapen the suit.

This menacing person was accompanied by Frank Oglanda, the Kiota representative on casino management, whose hands were uncomfortably warm as he murmured over Marjorie with his knowing little smile and impish eyes. Frank had made a pawing pass at her once, a grope really, but it had been done distractedly, as though gallantry required him to at least go through the motions. She'd found the experience distasteful in several ways, and made sure he understood that, and he'd been no more than smirkingly polite with her ever since, in those occasional social or business situations in which their paths crossed.

So that made five of them for the meeting, the two

Native Americans, their two lawyers, and Judge Higbee, who started them off by saying, "Frank, have you looked into Ms. Redcorn's claims any further?"

"As a matter of fact, Your Honor," Frank said, "we have."

"I believe, Your Honor," Otis Welles said, "we should make it clear from the outset that the Three Tribes have found absolutely no proof positive to support the young lady's claims."

Judge Higbee looked at Marjorie, who belatedly realized she shouldn't let that go without comment, so she said, "Nor, I take it, have you found proof positive to void her claim."

"Not yet," Welles said.

"Not ever," Ms. Redcorn said.

Welles looked at the judge as though Ms. Redcorn hadn't spoken. I think he'll regret that later, Marjorie told herself as he said, "Your Honor, the tribes have found records of some of the names mentioned in the young lady's letter." Clearly, he meant to evade the name problem entirely by never calling Ms. Redcorn anything except "the young lady." Of that tactic, Marjorie could only approve and regret it was too late for her to emulate.

Again, it was a look from the judge in her direction that made Marjorie remember she was here to work and not simply to observe. A few seconds late, but at least catching up, she said, "Counsel, were there any names in the letter the tribes did *not* find?"

"Other than the young lady's," Welles told her, "I believe not."

Judge Higbee looked over toward Frank Oglanda, saying, "What have you got, Frank?"

To begin with, Frank had a beautiful briefcase, soft and dark and gleaming, much more desirable and wonderful than the mundane scuffed briefcase Marjorie lugged with her everywhere, and even glossier than the expensive briefcase Welles had carried with him from New York. Dipping into this lovely artifact, Frank came out with several sheets of paper stapled together; copies of documents, it looked like. "Joseph Redcorn," he told them all, "did exist, as I think we already acknowledged."

"The plaque was read to me," the judge told him, deadpan. "Over the phone."

"Yes." Frank looked briefly sour, then recovered. "Very good of the Mohawks," he commented. "I didn't know they were capable of guilt feelings. In any event"—he flipped to the second sheet—"Joseph Redcorn did have a son named Bearpaw, who was reported missing in action in the Pacific Ocean while serving in the U.S. Navy in World War Two." Flip to the next sheet. "There is a record that Bearpaw, in 1940, married one Harriet Littlefoot, also a Pottaknobbee." Flip. "Harriet Littlefoot Redcorn produced a daughter, Doeface, in 1942."

"My mama," Ms. Redcorn said.

Ignoring that, Frank stood and took the sheaf of papers over to the judge's desk, saying, "We have more copies, Your Honor. I brought this one for you."

"I'll need one as well," Marjorie said.

Frank smiled at her. "I have one for you, Marjorie, if you need it. I'll give it to you later."

"Thank you."

Frank sat down again, and Welles said, "The point should be made that these are public records. Anyone can obtain them. The Three Tribes, in fact, have a Web site, including all written histories of the tribes, genealogical details, and other matters."

"I understand that," the judge assured him.

"Thank you, Your Honor. I should also point out that in 1970 and '71, the Three Tribes made every effort to find any Pottaknobbees still alive anywhere in the world. Frank has also brought along examples of the circulars and notices and press releases incident to that search. There was a particular effort to find Harriet Littlefoot Redcorn, who was known to have traveled to the West Coast but who had not been heard of for some years. All efforts failed. Harriet Littlefoot Redcorn and her daughter, Doeface Redcorn, have been presumed dead for many years."

Marjorie said, "Do you have death certificates? Newspaper obituaries?"

"There are no records of any kind," Welles told her.

"Which is why," Frank said, "the Three Tribes are willing to discuss a compromise. It might be that this, er, young woman sincerely believes the history she sent us. We think it's very unlikely she really is a Pottaknobbee, but there's always that one chance in a million, so we're ready to make an offer."

"No," Ms. Redcorn said.

Frank gave her a baffled and exasperated look. "You haven't heard the offer yet," he said.

"I told the judge the last time I was in this room," Ms. Redcorn answered, "this chamber, whatever you call it, I told the judge then I wasn't interested in getting bought off. The Oshkawa and the Kiota are the closest thing to people I've got, and I want to be a part of them and accepted by them."

Frank and Welles looked at each other. Welles said to Marjorie, "Would the young lady be willing to waive her putative interest in the casino in return for acceptance into the Three Tribes?"

Before Marjorie could respond, Ms. Redcorn said, "Why should I?"

"If all she wants," Welles went on, still talking to Marjorie, "is acceptance by her people—"

"I'm Pottaknobbee," Ms. Redcorn announced. "And that means one-third of the casino is mine. Why shouldn't I wanna keep it?"

"Now it's in the open," Welles said to the judge, as though Ms. Redcorn had just made an extremely damaging admission.

"And one thing more," Ms. Redcorn said, her cold, hard face turned toward Welles, regardless of where he was looking.

"Don't, Ms. Redcorn," Marjorie murmured, but this was not a very controllable client, who continued, "I'm no longer young, and I never was a lady. I have a name, and it's Little Feather Redcorn."

Still looking at the judge, Welles said, "I believe that is the matter at dispute."

"I am Little Feather Redcorn," she repeated, and then turned her head to glare at the judge as she added, "and I want justice."

"Everyone does," the judge told her.

"And I think there's more than justice," Frank said, "in the very generous offer we—"

"I don't want to hear it," Ms. Redcorn said.

Frank spread his hands. "Your Honor . . ."

Judge Higbee nodded. "Marjorie," he said, "I think you should advise your client at least to listen to the offer before rejecting it."

"Fine," Ms. Redcorn said, and folded her arms like Geronimo. "Weasel away," she urged Frank.

"Marjorie," Judge Higbee said warningly, and Marjorie said, "Yes, Your Honor, I apologize," and to her fractious client, she murmured, "You shouldn't be disrespectful in judge's chambers."

Ms. Redcorn looked surprised. Apparently, she'd thought she was insulting Frank, not the judge. Unfolding her arms, she looked toward Judge Higbee and said, "I'm sorry, Judge. It won't happen again."

Marjorie saw Judge Higbee come very close to smiling. He quashed it, though, and merely said, "Thank you," before turning back to Frank: "Go ahead."

"Thank you, Your Honor," Frank said, and, as Ms. Redcorn folded her arms like Geronimo again, he brought another multipage document out of his exceptional briefcase. Holding the pages in his lap, not looking at them, he said, "The Three Tribes are prepared to pay, uh, Ms. Redcorn one hundred thousand dollars now, if she relinquishes any claim she might want to make on tribal property, plus ten thousand dollars a year for ten years. We were suggesting in this contract that she might like to live in some other part of the world, but if she would prefer to live on the Chasm Reservation, we can work that out, no problem."

Welles said to the judge, "We will adapt the wording to suit the claimant and her attorney." With a wintry smile, he added, "I'm sure the Three Tribes would be pleased to have living among them such an attractive person, and one so well-off."

"Your Honor," Marjorie said, "it might be a good idea if Ms. Redcorn and I were to have some time alone to—"

"No need," Ms. Redcorn said. "That's about the size of the offer I expected, a little bigger but a little more stretched out. I don't want to sell my birthright for two hundred thousand dollars, or any amount of money. All I want, and I said this before, Judge, is justice."

Welles said, "I'm afraid, Your Honor, we are at an impasse. If Ms. Dawson wishes to institute an action against the Three Tribes on behalf of her client, the matter may be settled in a court of law."

Oh golly, Marjorie thought, knowing full well she wasn't up to the kind of lawsuit Welles was offering, as one might offer a poisoned goblet. But before she could respond, Ms. Redcorn said, "Judge, there's *got* to be some way I can prove who I am. I'll get private detectives, I'll talk to everybody in the tribes, I am *not* gonna give up."

Judge Higbee turned on her an expression that managed to be both caring and stern at once. "Ms. Redcorn," he said, "there is a way to prove or disprove your claim. I've had it in mind for some time. However, it would be expensive."

"I'll be able to afford it, whatever it is," Ms. Redcorn promised.

"If," the judge told her, now more stern than caring, "the evidence turns out to be against you, there would be more than expense involved. There would be criminal penalties as well."

"It won't go against me."

Frank said, "Whatever you're talking about, Judge, I don't know what it is, but if it'll settle this, I'm sure I speak for the Three Tribes when I say, let's do it."

Welles, more cautious, said, "Frank, I believe we'll wait to hear what Judge Higbee has in mind."

"DNA testing," the judge said, and Marjorie was startled to sense an immediate relaxation, a loosening, in her client, who was seated next to her. No one else in the room would be aware of it, but Marjorie was, and she carefully did not look at Ms. Redcorn's profile. She's been waiting for this, Marjorie thought. She didn't want to bring it up herself, but she's been waiting for this.

Wheels within wheels. I'm representing this woman, but I really don't know what's going on.

Frank was saying, "I don't follow that, Judge. DNA testing. Bloodstains?"

"Not at all," the judge told him. "This is the technique whereby it was established that the woman claiming to be Anastasia, the daughter of the last Czar, was, in fact, not related to the Romanovs."

Frank looked at Welles. He seemed a little upset by this turn of events. He's afraid, Marjorie told herself, that Ms. Redcorn really is who she says she is, and he doesn't like it. He doesn't want her in the Three Tribes. Or in the casino.

Frank said to Welles, "How reliable is this stuff?"

"Perfectly reliable," Welles told him, and turned at last to look directly at Ms. Redcorn. "You do understand what the judge is suggesting, do you not?"

"If it's something that can prove I'm a Pottaknobbee," she answered, "I'm all for it."

"Or disprove."

"Not a chance."

Frank said to the judge, "Just explain it to me, Your Honor, okay?"

"We know of one guaranteed Pottaknobbee," the judge told him, "whose grave we can find, and whom Ms. Redcorn claims as a relative. Joseph Redcorn."

"My great-grandpa."

"A sample is taken from Joseph Redcorn, probably hair," the judge went on, "and a sample of hair is taken from Ms. Redcorn. Laboratory analysis of the DNA in the two samples can establish without any question whether or not they're related."

"Well, uh," Frank said. His worry was evident now, and he blinked at his lawyer.

Who said, "In principle, Your Honor, the tribes would have no objection. But this is a new technology, after all, and I believe we should be given the opportunity to consult with scientists, experts in the field."

"Of course."

Frank said, "Wait a minute. You're talking about digging him up."

"Sufficient," Judge Higbee said, "to obtain a hair sample. The coffin would be opened, but probably not even moved."

Frank was determinedly shaking his head. "You can't do that," he said. "The Supreme Court is behind us on this one, the white people can't come in and dig up Indian bodies on our sacred tribal lands. The anthropologists have been trying to pull that, but the courts find for us every time."

Judge Higbee had been trying to stem the flow of Frank's protests, and now, rather loudly, he said, "Frank!"

Frank shut up. "Yes, sir."

"I've looked into the matter," the judge told him, "and Joseph Redcorn is buried in a nondenominational cemetery in the borough of Queens in New York City."

Frank blinked. "He's not here? Why . . . why did they do *that*?"

"Apparently," the judge told him, "the tribes were too cheap to pay to transport the body this far north, and the builder would pay the expenses if the interment were in New York."

"Too poor," Welles said.

The judge nodded. "One way or the other," he said, "the effect is the same."

"Well," Frank said, rallying, "uh, for all I know, uh, that could be sacred tribal land around him just because he's *there*. I'll have to consult with the Tribal Council on this."

"And Mr. Welles," the judge added, "will have to consult with the law."

"I will, Your Honor," Welles agreed.

Ms. Redcorn said, "And *I* gotta have a new lawyer."

They all looked at her with surprise, none more so than Marjorie. Ms. Redcorn gave her a friendly head shake and said, "You do your best, Ms. Dawson, but I need somebody who's a specialist in this DNA business."

Judge Higbee said, "Very sensible, Ms. Redcorn. As a

matter of fact, you know, if we proceed and then the tests go against you, the penalties could be quite severe. No one wants to go to that expense on what could turn out to be a frivolous contention."

"I'm not frivolous, Judge," Ms. Redcorn said. "Trust me."

"Yes, well," he said, "I could, if you like, draw up a list of recommended counsel."

"Thank you, sir, but no," she said. "I've got some friends out west can help me." Then she turned to Welles and said, "Which company you work for?"

"My *firm*," he answered, "is Holliman, Sherman, Beiderman, Tallyman & Funk. You wouldn't be able to use us, of course."

"I know," she told him, "that's why I wanted to ask." Turning back to Judge Higbee, she said, "I'll be all right, Your Honor." Beaming at the judge, she pointed toward Welles and said, "I'm gonna get me one of *them*."

22

Roger Fox had never seen his partner so upset. "Calm down, Frank," he said. "It can't be as bad as all that."

"Well, it can't be worse," Frank told him, "so maybe it *is* as bad as all that. Roger, they've got a way to prove whether or not that damn woman really is Pottaknobbee."

"What, that list of relatives she throws around? All right, they existed, but that doesn't mean they have anything to do with *her.*"

"DNA testing," Frank said. "I want a drink, and so do you."

They were meeting this afternoon in Roger's office, the one that had been shown on TV, and in his office the bar was a mahogany and chrome and mirror construction built into the corner to the right of the desk. (It had been out of sight, to the left of the camera, on television.) Roger had been seated comfortably at his desk when Frank came in from his meeting with Judge Higbee, but now he angled forward, his heavy stuffed swivel chair propelling him to his feet as he said, "DNA? That proves paternity, doesn't it?"

"It can prove it in the other direction, too," Frank said, taking down two of the heavy cut-glass whiskey glasses from the chrome shelf and placing them on the mahogany bar. "*And* prove whether you did the rape," he said, opening the low refrigerator and adding two ice cubes to each glass, "whether you stabbed the person," he said, reaching for the bottle of Wild Turkey on the back bar, "whether you had sex with the boss's wife," he said, pouring a very generous portion into each glass, "whether your goddamn great-grandfather is goddamn Joseph goddamn *Redcorn*!" he yelled, and pushed one glass toward Roger—a little slopped, no matter—then drained his own glass by a third.

When next his glass was away from his face, Roger had crossed the room to the bar and was standing there looking at him, but he hadn't moved a hand toward his own drink. Roger said, "DNA?"

"You said it."

"What does Welles say?"

"One hundred percent reliable."

"No, no, I know that. What does he say about can they do it? Did you mention sacred tribal lands?"

"The son of a bitch is buried in New York City!"

Roger reared back, clasping tighter to the bar with both hands. "What the hell is he doing down there?"

"That's where he fell off the building, the goddamn stumble-footed . . ."

"The rumor was, the Mohawks pushed him."

"The Three Tribes blame the Mohawks for everything, they always have. He was probably drunk," he decided, and drank another third of his Wild Turkey.

Roger said, "But why *there*? The Pottaknobbees, all of us in the Three Tribes, we're buried here on the reservation. Unless somebody moves away, loses touch."

"The builder would pay for the funeral," Frank explained, "only if it was in New York. Nobody up here cared enough, apparently. And Roger, realistically, you know, a lot of the Three Tribes are buried way to hell and gone all over the place."

Roger at last reached for his glass. "So much for sacred tribal lands," he said, and drank, not quite as much nor as rapidly as Frank.

"I tried to suggest," Frank said, "that Redcorn's grave is sacred tribal land just because he's in it, but Welles thinks that won't fly. It could help us stall awhile, but sooner or later a court would order the test to go ahead. And we've gotta be careful not to push that stuff too hard, we don't want to look like we're trying to stiff-arm that woman, whether she's Pottaknobbee or not."

"We are, though."

"Yes, but quietly," Frank said.

Roger considered. "What did *she* think of the idea of DNA testing? She was there, wasn't she, at the meeting? What did *she* think?"

"She loves it," Frank said sourly. " 'That's my great-grandpa,' " he mimicked, and emptied his glass.

Roger followed down that trail, more slowly, and as Frank refilled his own glass, Roger said, "She's pretty damn sure of herself, isn't she?"

"Goddamn it, Roger, *I'm* becoming pretty damn sure of her! I think the goddamn bitch probably *is* the last of the Pottaknobbees, and how we're going to keep her out of these offices, I have no idea."

"If only we were murderers," Roger said, and sipped a little more Wild Turkey. It was very warm going down, very comforting.

Frank shook his head. "Come on, Roger," he said, "you know better than that. I thought of that myself, and of course we could do it. We could find some bum right here on the reservation to do the job for us for five hundred dollars, and guess who the only suspects would be."

"I suppose you're right," Roger said.

"And once we're suspects, Roger," Frank said, "their next question is, what were you boys trying to hide?"

"Oh God," Roger said, and drained his glass. Pushing it toward Frank, he said, "Could we make a deal with her?"

"Never," Frank said, refilling Roger's glass and topping up his own. "She's the coldest, nastiest piece of work *I've* ever seen. Give her an inch and she'll take a foot, and I do mean off your leg."

"Then we have to—" Roger said, and the intercom buzzed, and he turned to give his desk a reproachful look. "And what fresh hell is this?" he asked.

"You might as well answer," Frank said. "I think I'm becoming fatalistic, Roger," he added as Roger crossed to the desk. "Do you suppose the Indians have their own gangs in prison?"

"In the Northeast? I think you'd really get to know what a minority is," Roger told him. "Don't give up yet, Frank."

"Be sure to tell me when to give up," Frank said, and drank some more.

Roger reached over his desk for the phone. "Yes, Audrey."

"Benny's here," came the voice of his secretary.

"Good," Roger said.

Surprised, Audrey said, "Good?"

"Just send him in, Audrey."

Frank, fumbling with the top of the Wild Turkey bottle, said, "Send who in?"

"Benny."

"Oh, him," Frank said, and the door opened, and Benny Whitefish entered.

About thirty, Benny Whitefish was a chunky little guy in faded blue jeans and a red plaid shirt, and his usual expression was hangdog, as though he'd just broken some keepsake of yours and was hoping you wouldn't notice before he left. "Hi, Uncle Roger," he said, because, in fact, he was Roger Fox's nephew, via his otherwise-estimable sister, but there was, in any event, just something essentially nephewish about Benny, as though he would be a nephew at ninety, even with no older relatives to be nephew to. The family gofer, forever.

"Come in, Benny," Roger said, with more warmth than Benny was used to.

Benny came in, shutting the door behind himself, grinning eagerly, and stood hunched in the middle of the room, basking in the rare pleasure of his uncle's approval, while Roger said to Frank, "I was about to say that what we need to do is discredit the woman somehow. Stall as long as we can, while we get something on her."

"Something like what?" Frank asked from out of sight behind the bar, where he was looking for the other bottle of Wild Turkey.

"Something reprehensible. Something that would make people want to shun her even if she *was* Pottaknobbee. Something to make the tribes get together and throw her out, and be damned to DNA."

Frank reappeared, holding the fresh bottle. "I don't know, Roger," he said.

Roger said, "Benny, help your uncle Frank open that bottle."

"Okay!"

Frank readily gave up the job, to lean on the bar instead and say, "What reprehensathing? There are no Commies anymore. Nobody would believe an Indian lesbo. We already know she's got no police record. Thank you, Benny. Pour some in there, and see if your uncle Roger needs any more."

"I do." Benny hurried on his rounds, and Roger said, "If there's nothing else, Frank, how about bad associates?"

Frank peered at him across the room from bar to desk, where Roger stood holding his glass like anyone at a cocktail party, Benny standing beside him, smiling, holding the bottle by the neck, not knowing if he was expected to put it down or keep it at the ready for further pouring, and deciding to hold on to it to be on the safe side. "Bad associates?" Frank demanded. "What bad associates?"

"There've got to be some, Frank," Roger told him. "Where did this Little Feather Redcorn come from? Out of the blue, she's suddenly here with histories and claims. There's *got* to be somebody behind her, some whadayacallit, *puppeteer,* pulling the strings. She can't be doing all this on her own, so the people who put her up to it, why are they hiding? Because they're no good, Frank."

"You lost me somewhere in there," Frank admitted.

Roger offered Benny another encouraging smile. Two, in one day! "That's why," he told Frank, "I've had Benny follow the woman ever since she got out of jail, so he can *tell* us who she associates with. Benny?"

Benny looked alert. "Yes, Uncle Roger?"

"Little Feather Redcorn," Roger said, extremely patient. "Who does she associate with?"

"Nobody," Benny said.

Roger blinked at him. Frank said, "Where's that bottle I just opened?"

"Just a minute, Frank," Roger said. "We have to keep our wits about us now."

Frank looked thoughtful.

Roger said to Benny, "She doesn't talk to *anybody*?"

"Mostly, she stays in that motor home thing, down at Whispering Pines," Benny said. "Sometimes she takes taxis, but only to the supermarket or the drugstore and like that. Last night, she went into Plattsburgh and went to a diner by herself and had dinner and then went to a movie by herself and then took another taxi home again to the motor home. This afternoon, she associated with Judge Higbee and a lawyer woman named Marjorie Dawson and Uncle Frank."

"She didn't *associate* with me," Frank said.

Roger said, "I don't believe it."

Benny looked stricken. "Honest to God, Uncle Roger! I swear I been on her every—"

"No, no, not you, Benny," Roger said. "I'm sure you did the job right."

Benny looked astounded. "You are?"

"Frank," Roger said, "leave that bottle and—"

"I don't *have* the bottle."

"*I* have it, Uncle Frank!"

"Put it *down,* Benny. And Frank, leave your glass then,

and come over to the conversation area, and let's have a conversation, the three of us."

"Me, too?"

"Yes, Benny, come along."

The three went to the burgundy sofas L-ing around the glass and chrome coffee table as Frank said, "What are we going to do?"

"We don't know yet," Roger told him. "That's what the conversation's about. The one thing I know for sure, though, it's got to be something drastic."

23

I don't like this," Dortmunder said.

"What, the pizza?" Kelp asked. "The pizza's fine."

"It's very good pizza," Irwin declared.

"Not the pizza," Dortmunder told them, "the story Little Feather just gave us."

"Well, it's the truth," Little Feather said.

"I know it's the truth," Dortmunder agreed, "that's what I don't like about it."

Since Little Feather hadn't gotten back to the Winnebago until after five, there'd been general agreement that she should order pizza and beer delivered in, even though, as she'd pointed out, that was a hell of an order for a woman living alone. "You'll reheat the leftovers," Kelp had told her.

"I'm ordering *with* pepperoni, *without* pepperoni, with and without extra cheese."

"You're an indecisive person."

So they had the pizza delivered in, and Little Feather reported on her meetings, first with Marjorie Dawson and then with the bunch in judge's chambers, telling part of the story before the pizza arrived and the rest after the pizza left, when Dortmunder announced that he didn't like it.

So now Guilderpost said, "I don't see what the problem is, John. We've reached the first plateau, the DNA."

"From here," Irwin said, "it's plain sailing."

"No," Dortmunder said. "They're fighting it. From the beginning, they're fighting it. They don't want Little Feather in their clubhouse."

"Well, they're going to have to get used to it," Irwin said.

Dortmunder said, "No, listen. You're acting like these people are the same as the people you sold the Dutch land things to, like you come in and scam them and they take it like a sport and that's it. But they aren't like that, not from the get-go."

"I don't believe their attitude matters anymore, John," Guilderpost told him. "At first, it was certainly troubling, particularly for Little Feather—"

"I didn't like the night in jail," Little Feather remarked.

"Of course you didn't, my dear," Guilderpost agreed, and then said to Dortmunder, "But we're past that now. I spoke with my contact at Feinberg today, and he put me in touch with their DNA expert, Max Schreck. Little Feather will phone him in the morning, he'll phone Judge Higbee, and we're well on our way."

"That's right," Irwin said. "From now on, it's simply the lab work, and the judge says, 'Look at that, it's a match. Little Feather is hereby declared a Pottaknobbee. Welcome to the casino.'"

"And you fellows collect a not-inconsiderable recompense," Guilderpost added.

"I don't like it," Dortmunder said.

"You don't like the recompense? We agreed—"

"Not the recompense," Dortmunder said, "the story Little Feather come back with. The meeting she had."

Tiny said, "You listen to Duh—John. He's got a nose for this kind of thing."

"All right, John," Guilderpost said in his most kindly fashion, "tell us what it is you don't like about today's events."

"The whole thing," Dortmunder told him, "starting from yesterday. No, starting from the day before yesterday. Now today the guy from the tribes shows up with a lawyer that isn't even his regular lawyer but is a lawyer from another outfit like your Feinberg outfit from New York, meaning what they declared here is war. And when those guys declare war, I don't think they mean to play fair."

Irwin said, "But, John, what can they do? We've got them cold."

"That's what I'm trying to figure," Dortmunder said. "I'm thinking, if I was them, and I wanted Little Feather out of my hair, and I was beginning to think the DNA thing was gonna go against me, what would I do?"

"Kill me," Little Feather said.

"They thought of it," Dortmunder assured her, "but they know they're too obvious. So they gotta do something else."

Guilderpost said, "I suppose they might try to negotiate with her, buy her off."

"They tried that," Little Feather said.

"If I was them," Dortmunder said, "and I'm in the spot

they're in, what do I do? And I'm beginning to think I know what I do."

Tiny said, "What you did."

Dortmunder nodded. "That's what I'm thinking, Tiny."

Kelp said, "They would, wouldn't they?"

Dortmunder and Kelp and Tiny all nodded, not happy. Guilderpost and Irwin both looked baffled. Guilderpost said, "What do you mean?"

Dortmunder said, "What did we do, to make sure the DNA was gonna be a match?"

"You put grampa in there," Little Feather said.

"So if I'm on the other side," Dortmunder said, "what do I do?"

"No!" Guilderpost cried. "They wouldn't dare!"

"I bet they would," Dortmunder said.

Irwin said, "That isn't fair! We worked hard for this!"

"I told you," Dortmunder said, "these guys don't mean to play fair."

"We'll have to guard the grave," Guilderpost declared, "twenty-four hours a day."

"Yeah, that'll be good," Dortmunder commented, "a bunch of dubious guys hanging around one grave in a cemetery for a week or two, day and night. You don't think anybody's gonna start to wonder something, do you?"

Guilderpost said, "Then what *do* you suggest?"

"I dunno," Dortmunder told him. "That's what I'm trying to think."

Irwin said, "I can't believe anybody would actually do that. Dig the man up and put a different body in there?"

"*We* did it," Guilderpost said, and Irwin frowned deeply.

"I really don't wanna have to dig him up again," Dortmunder said. "Dig him up, put something else in, wait for the tribes to do whatever they do, then dig up the grave *again* and put him back. Once a grave robber could just be circumstances, but three times? By then, it's a career."

"I'm with John," Kelp said.

"Then what can we do?" Guilderpost asked, but nobody answered him.

For a little time, they all just sat there, the six of them, listening to one another digest pizza. Everybody frowned and concentrated. From time to time, one or another sighed.

"Stones," Tiny said.

They all looked at him. Kelp said, "Tiny? That wasn't about the pizza, was it?"

Tiny made a gesture with both hands, like a guy switching the shells over the pea. "Switch the stones," he said.

Dortmunder smiled. A burden lifted from his shoulders. "We could do that," he said. "Thank you, Tiny."

"*I* could do that," Tiny said.

Irwin said, "You mean take the Redcorn headstone, move it to a different grave, replace it with the other headstone."

"Then the tribes come down," Dortmunder said, "they dig up the wrong grave, they do what they do, and then we switch the stones back again."

"A lot better than grave digging," Kelp said.

Irwin said, "And that way, you don't disturb the soil

over the Redcorn grave. It's been six weeks now, the soil won't show any signs of recent digging."

"Particularly," Guilderpost said, "if the tribes dig up the wrong grave."

"Now," Dortmunder said, "I like it."

24

Friday, December 1. The only interesting workweek in Judge T. Wallace Higbee's entire twelve-year career on the bench was at last, thank God, coming to an end.

It had all started on Tuesday, when Frank Oglanda and Roger Fox had filed the charges of fraud and extortion against the young woman who, it seemed, must be known henceforward as Little Feather Redcorn. The case had at first seemed like no more than the normal run of stupidity, this time on the part of someone then named Shirley Ann Farraff, until Marjorie Dawson had come to chambers the next day to say the perp wouldn't play the game.

Then the Mohawks' peacemaking plaque had surfaced to buttress Little Feather Redcorn's story, and at that point, it seemed to the judge, the smart move would have been for Roger and Frank to cut a deal with the young lady. Not try to buy her off and send her on her way, but deal her *in*. That would have been the smart move, and the judge couldn't help but wonder why Frank had decided to be stupid instead.

Damn it, he didn't *want* to think about this stuff. He liked the drowsy progress of his days, the slow shuffle of stupidity that passed his glazed eyes every day like the doomed peasants in a Breughel allegory. So why the hell were Roger and Frank insisting on behaving in mysterious ways, giving poor Judge Higbee's brain tough hardtack to chew on?

It had been so obvious, in chambers yesterday, that Frank Oglanda didn't care if the Redcorn woman were Pottaknobbee or not; he just wanted her *gone*. Which could only mean he and Roger had something to hide, out there on the reservation. Now, what would that be? The casino was a gold mine; wasn't that enough for them? Had they succumbed to the temptation of smuggling, being right there on the Canadian border, or drug dealing, or cooking the books? In other words, had those boys been stupid, even when they didn't have to be? Was Judge Higbee going to have to *think* about them?

Not this week. This week was done. This morning, the judge had rewarded several acts of gross stupidity with room and board at state expense, and he was in the process now of finishing the week's quota of stupidity this afternoon. In between, Hilda, his secretary, had started to tell him about a phone call from some lawyer in New York City who was apparently Ms. Redcorn's replacement for poor hapless Marjorie Dawson, but the judge had had enough for this week, thank you. "Tell me about it on Monday," he'd ordered, not even wanting to listen to the lawyer's name, much less whatever his message might be.

Another smart-ass New York City lawyer; as though the judge didn't have enough trouble. Were they going to start acting like smart-ass New York City lawyers *together* in his court? Were they going to play tricky games, challenge each other's (and the judge's) legal knowledge, come up with obscure precedents, send everybody to the law library, drag it out and drag it out, force poor Judge T. Wallace Higbee to make *decision* after *decision*?

Damn! *Why* didn't Frank and Roger just bite the goddamn bullet, bury the hatchet—well, maybe that wasn't quite the right image, but whatever—get over the shock, fellas, the new girl in town is here to stay. That confidence of hers about the results of DNA testing wasn't feigned, and Frank knew it as well as the judge did.

In the meantime, the soothing sob stories of the severely stupid flowed like a warm bath in the judge's courtroom. Firing a pistol at the dinner table to attract the family's attention; forgetting you'd sold that car to your cousin and just happening to have the other set of keys in your pocket when it was time to drive to Florida for the winter; not knowing the drunk you'd decided to roll outside that bar was an off-duty cop and then complaining bitterly about police brutality for having been shot in the leg while trying to escape. Oh, sing these songs, sing them. Judge T. Wallace Higbee loves you all, see you in three to five.

Midafternoon, the day and the week and the march of these morons nearly done, and a person entered the courtroom to sit in the rear row, near the door. Judge Higbee was immediately aware of him, of course, because from where he sat, he looked directly toward that rear door, but he would have been aware anyway, because who was that person?

Within seconds, everybody else in court also became aware of the stranger, even though their backs were to him and they had to take quick peeks over their shoulders to get a gander at him. He created awareness simply by his existence, because he *was* a stranger, and there were never any strangers in Judge Higbee's court.

This courtroom had been constructed inside this ancient municipal building in the late seventies, and it was still as bright and shiny and impervious as the first day it opened for business. The churchlike pews were a honey-colored wood, and so were the tables for prosecution and defense, and the jury box, and the judge's bench. The floor was pale blue linoleum tile, the walls creamy yellow, the dropped ceiling half white sound deadener and half shiny fluorescents. In this clean, well-lighted, and somehow inhuman space, there were, besides Judge Higbee and the court officers, four categories of persons: perps, lawyers, cops, and witnesses. Very rarely, there were also jurors, but that was an exception, the jury system of American law having long ago been replaced by the more efficient and less chancy plea bargain system.

But, the point was, nobody else ever entered this courtroom, nor ever would. So who the hell was the stranger?

And he was strange indeed. Very tall and very thin, he had a long, pale face that seemed to pucker and shrink behind thick-lensed eyeglasses with heavy black rims. He wore a black suit that looked a little too small for him, a white shirt, a thin black necktie. He sat primly, knees together, pale, bony hands crossed on legs, head straight, face expressionless, black eyes glinting in the fluorescent glare as he watched the activity in the courtroom.

Not much activity left, today. Doing his best to ignore that black-clad figure in the back of the room—he was like a knife slash across a painting—doing his best not to distract himself with questions as to who the fellow might be and what trouble he might portend, Judge Higbee dispensed the rest of the day's justice with dispatch, gaveled the final miscreant on his way to Dannemora, and was about to stand and flee to his chambers, when the stranger rose and moved down the central aisle toward the bench, walking rigidly and holding up one pale finger for attention.

Now what? Judge Higbee wondered, and remained where he was, grasping the gavel as though to ward off attack. As attorneys lugged their briefcases past him on the way out, the spectral man approached the judge and said in a deep but faintly hollow voice, "Good afternoon. I am Max Schreck."

The name meant nothing. Wary, Judge Higbee said, "Good afternoon."

Schreck seemed a bit doubtful. The eyes behind the thick glasses flickered, like a lightbulb thinking of burning out. He said, "My secretary spoke to your secretary this morning."

"Oh my God," the judge said, and the heart within him sank. "You're the new lawyer!"

25

Benny Whitefish could not have been more excited. Intrigue! Danger! Beautiful women! (Well, one beautiful woman anyway.) Responsibility! A really important job at last for Uncle Roger.

"You better not screw up," he told himself, and gazed at his shining eyes in the rearview mirror. "You're gonna be fine," he assured himself, "you're gonna be great."

Of course he was. He'd been doing this shadowing job just perfectly, hadn't he? For three days now, he'd been following the Little Feather Redcorn woman around to see who her accomplices were, following her in and out of supermarkets and drugstores and movie houses, and not once had she even suspected he was there. It must be because I'm an Indian, he told himself; I have a natural genius for tracking.

It was only too bad Little Feather Redcorn didn't *have* any accomplices, because Benny was ready with his disposable camera to take their pictures and deliver the prints straight to Uncle Roger, just to show him how on top of the job Benny really was. But he could console himself anyway with the knowledge that he had a real aptitude for this job. He could just see himself moving swiftly and silently through the mighty forest, and never once stepping on a twig.

But what was even better than discovering he did possess some natural skills and talents after all—the evidence had been pretty much solidly the other way up till now—was the fact that Uncle Roger and his almost-uncle Frank had taken him into their confidence and made him a part of their planning committee. Or should he call that their war party? Whatever; he was in it.

Roger and Frank were conferring with their big-time lawyer today about ways to stall the DNA test as long as possible, while they worked out what steps they would take to eliminate the threat of Little Feather Redcorn for good. (Not eliminate *her,* that would be too dangerous; just the threat of her.) Something drastic, they would have to do—they knew that much—and Benny would be part of it.

He was so excited, he could barely sit still in his little orange Subaru, but he knew he had to be as silent and patient and unmoving as a cat. That was part of the tracking genius. He was working on it.

She was at the drugstore again today. Gee, she did a lot of shopping! Benny supposed women did that, though his mother and his older sisters, the only women he actually knew very well, weren't into shopping much. They were mostly into TV, and snacks.

Anyway, he'd followed her yet again in yet another taxi, and here he was parked in the drugstore's lot, near the entrance, watching the door of the place but mostly watching for the next taxi to arrive. That was the way it always worked; she went into the store, whatever store it was, and then sometime later a taxi would arrive and she'd come out again with her bags of purchases and get into it.

The first few times, he'd followed her into the store to trail around after her, making darn sure she never saw him, but when it became obvious she didn't intend to meet anybody in these stores, he'd decided it would be better to wait outside in the car, so she wouldn't see him too often and maybe start to recognize him and get suspicious. So here he was, not yet really expecting the taxi, because she'd only been in there a few minutes, when out she came, completely unexpected.

Benny stared at her, startled by this change of pattern, and his heart began to pound, his mouth to get dry. What was going on here?

Nothing at first. She had a sort of helpless, lost look to her as she stood in front of the drugstore, gazing around. Benny forgot to look the other way, because he was so flummoxed by her abrupt appearance like that, and then, all of a sudden, she was staring directly at *him.*

Oh no! He quickly looked away, at the sale banners taped to the drugstore windows, but it was too late. Here she came, walking toward him, her brown leather coat open over her red fitted western shirt and short white buckskin skirt and high red boots. She didn't look exactly like a real person at all, but more like one of the pinup posters he had on the walls in his bedroom, the ones that his mother and sisters always ragged him about.

Benny had thought, sometimes, that it might be terrific if someday he could see Little Feather Redcorn in a bikini, his imagination not daring to wish beyond that, but he'd never expected to see her in complete real-life close-up. But that's what was about to happen. She walked directly toward Benny across the asphalt parking lot, and it was hopeless to pretend he didn't see her coming, and didn't see her gesture for him to open his window. There was no way out of it; he rolled the window down.

"Excuse me," she said. She had a surprisingly light and musical voice, and her smile was really very gentle.

Benny blinked at her. Does she suspect? Then why would she smile? He said, "He—hello."

"I feel like such a fool," she confessed. "I came out without my wallet."

Benny nodded spastically. "You did?"

"I got everything I needed, and I was just about to pay for it, and then I realized, No wallet. I can't even take a taxi home."

"Oh," he said. Was she going to ask him for money?

No. She said, "I thought I'd have to walk all the way back to Whispering Pines. Do you know where that is? The campground?"

"Oh, sure," he said. I shouldn't have a long conversation with her, he warned himself, because then she'll be able to recognize me later on.

But now she said, "I wonder. I know it's asking a lot, and you a perfect stranger, but could you possibly drive me there? Or are you waiting for your girlfriend?"

"Oh no," he said, and could feel himself blush. He'd be stammering soon. "I'm not waiting for my girlfriend," he stammered.

"Well, it would only take you ten minutes," she assured him, "and I'd pay you when we got there, just as much as I'd pay the taxi. Could you do that for me?" She made a light little embarrassed laugh, then said, "You see I'm a damsel in distress."

"Uh-huh," he said. "You mean you want me to drive you to the campground?"

"Could you be a dear? Could you be a darling?"

There's no way to say no, he realized. "The car isn't—" he began. "It isn't very clean in here."

"I'm sure it'll be fine," she told him. "And you're a lifesaver. Thank you *so* much."

"Uh-huh," he said, and rolled up his window as she walked around to get into the passenger seat beside him, first tossing the comic books and empty soda cans into the back. "Why, it's nice and cozy in here," she said, and smiled at him again as she slammed her door.

Do it quick and get it over with, he told himself. Ten minutes, and then leave. Don't talk a lot, don't do things to make her remember you.

"My name's Little Feather Redcorn," she said. Her smile beamed into his right cheek like an auger. "What's yours?"

Lie? Tell the truth? Then he realized he had to tell the truth because he couldn't think of any other names, not at this particular moment. "Benny Whitefish," he told her.

She said, "Are you from out on the reservation?"

"Uh-huh."

"I'm going to be living there soon," she said.

Red light. He stopped behind the pickup truck already there and risked a glance in her direction. She just kept looking directly at him with those very bright black eyes, very close to him in this little car. She sat half-turned toward him, her coat open, and her shirt was really very tight. Even without her being in a bikini, he could tell her bosom was exactly like the bosoms on the posters in his bedroom.

Feeling his face flame up, he wrenched his head forward to stare desperately at the rear of that unlovely pickup out there. "You're going to live on the reservation?" he asked when he felt his voice might be reasonably steady.

"Pretty soon," she said. "I'm Pottaknobbee."

"Uh-huh." The pickup moved, so he did, too.

She said, "You know who the Pottaknobbee are, don't you?"

"Oh, sure," he said. "They're the extinct tribe."

She chuckled, a throaty sound, and said, "Do *I* look extinct?"

He didn't dare look at her again, but anyway, he already knew the answer. "No, you don't."

"I think I look pretty alive, don't you?"

"Uh-huh."

"You see, the thing is, Benny—is it all right if I call you Benny?"

"Oh, sure."

"And you can call me Little Feather."

"Okay," he said, doubting he ever would.

"Well, the thing is, Benny," she said, "my grandmama moved out west years and years ago, when my mama was just a little girl, so nobody back here knew I was even born. But now I'm coming home at last. Isn't that nice?"

"Uh-huh," he said, and stopped behind the same pickup at a different traffic light. He hoped he was acting cool and relaxed on the outside, but on the inside, he knew, he was swirling like some huge storm. Hurricane Benny. And the only coherent thought to come out of the eye of that storm was the idea that maybe this accidental meeting could be turned to advantage somehow. Maybe it was a good thing after all that he was in conversation with Little Feather Redcorn, maybe he could just casually chat with her, and cleverly slip some questions in, and find out if maybe she did have some accomplices somewhere, like Uncle Roger and his almost-uncle Frank insisted she must. (And he never stopped to wonder, if she forgot her wallet, how did she pay for the *first* taxi?) So, when this new light turned green and the traffic started forward, Benny said, "You're going to move out to the reservation pretty soon, huh? Do you know when?"

"Well," she said, "the tribes have to be sure I'm really me and not some imposter, so that'll take a few days, and then I'll move out. I think it's very exciting, don't you?"

"Uh-huh," he said.

She said, "Maybe you could show me around, when I move out there. Would you like to do that?"

"Oh, sure," he said. Then he imagined all those creeps from high school who used to put him down all the time, and all those girls from high school who wouldn't go to the movies with him, and he saw himself walking around the reservation, right in front of them all, with Little Feather Redcorn walking right next to him, smiling at him and talking to him. In the summer, maybe she'd wear a bikini.

"You're smiling," she said.

Oops. "Well," he said, noticing that his hands were wet on the steering wheel, "I'm happy for you. Coming home and all."

"Little Feather," she said, her voice low. "You can say it, Benny, come on."

He watched the road, as though it might at any second do something unexpected. He inhaled. "Little Feather," he said.

"Hi, Benny," said that low and honeyed voice.

He took another breath. "Hi, Little Feather," he said.

"Now we're friends," she told him, "and here's Whispering Pines. Just drive in and bear to the right. I'll get money out of my wallet and—"

"You don't have to pay me anything," he said. "Not now that we're friends." He inhaled. "Little Feather," he said.

"Why, thank you, Benny," she said. "Bear to the right here. That's where I live, down there. You see the motor home?"

"Is that yours?" he asked.

"Yes, I drove here in it from Nevada, all by myself," she said. "Park here, right in front of it."

He stopped the Subaru but left the engine running. "That's a long way to drive, all by yourself," he said.

"It got scary sometimes," she admitted, "to be completely on my own like that, but I thought, I'm going home, going to my people, and that made it better."

Gee, Benny thought, if only we could really be friends with Little Feather, if only Uncle Roger and my almost-uncle Frank could talk with her and see how really nice she is. Except, it wasn't really *her* they wanted to keep out, they wanted to keep out anybody who could ask questions about how they were running the casino.

"Isn't it funny," she said, not opening her door, "how we got along right from the beginning? Maybe it's because we're almost from the same tribe, but here I am, and I don't even really know you, and I'm telling you all about myself."

"I like to hear you talk," he said, which he knew was true and thought might be clever.

"I tell you what, Benny," she said, "if you won't take any money because we're friends, at least come in so I can show you where I live. Would you like a cup of coffee?"

"Well, uh . . ." he said, wondering what was best to do, thinking he'd already had more experiences today than he could entirely deal with and it might be best just to go home and lie down for a while.

She rested a hand on his forearm, with a touch like warm electricity. It tingled all the way up to his ear. Smiling at him, leaning closer to him so that a faint but powerful musk crept into his nostrils and his skull and his brain, she said, "Wouldn't you like to come in, Benny?"

He swallowed. He inhaled. He nodded. "Yes," he said. "I would like to come in."

26

"East," Tiny said.

Dortmunder had been half-asleep. Now he turned to look at Tiny, who was spread across the Jeep's backseat, and said, "Tiny? You say something?"

"I said 'East,' " Tiny said.

Dortmunder looked around at the night. It had already been full dark when they'd left the Tea Cosy after dinner for the four-hour drive south, and now it was nearly one in the morning and they'd just crossed the Triborough Bridge onto Grand Central Parkway, bypassing Manhattan, juking over from the Bronx to Queens. Late on a Friday night, but there were still a lot of drivers in passenger cars all around them, most of them likely to be drunk.

"East," Dortmunder commented. "You mean we're driving east," he decided.

"Southeast," Tiny said.

Kelp, at the wheel, had just turned off onto the Brooklyn-Queens Expressway. Dortmunder nodded. "You mean now we're going southeast," he said.

"That's what the car says," Tiny told him.

Dortmunder twisted around again to get a full double-

O of Tiny back there. "Whadaya mean, 'That's what the car says'?"

Tiny pointed to where Dortmunder's halo would be, if he had a halo, and said, "Right there."

So Dortmunder faced front again, put his head way back, and saw, tucked under the Jeep roof, above the windshield, a kind of black box. It had bluish white numbers and letters on the side facing the rear seat, glowing in the dark:

S E 41

As Dortmunder looked, the S E changed to S. He looked out at the road, and it was curving to the right. "So now it's south," he said.

"You got it," Tiny told him. "Comin down, that's what I been doin back here. Watchin the letters. A whole lotta *S*. A little *N* there when Kelp got confused on the Sprain."

"The signage stunk," Kelp said.

Dortmunder looked at Kelp's profile, gleaming like a Halloween mask in the dashboard lights. "Signage," he said. "Is that a word?"

"Not for those pitiful markers they had back there," Kelp said.

Dortmunder decided to go back to conversation number one, and said to Tiny, "And the numbers are the temperature, right? Outside the car."

"You got it again," Tiny told him.

Forgetting about signage, Dortmunder said to Kelp, "Did you know about that?"

"Did I know about what?"

"Southwest," Tiny said.

"The car here," Dortmunder explained to Kelp, "it tells you which way you're going, south, east, whatever, and what the temperature is outside. It's up there."

Kelp looked up there.

"Back on the road!" Dortmunder yelled.

Kelp steered around the truck he'd been going to smash into and said, "That's not bad, is it? The temperature outside, and which way you're going."

"Very useful," Dortmunder suggested.

"A car like this," Kelp said, "you could take this across deserts, jungles, trackless wastes."

"Uh-huh," Dortmunder said. "How many of these things do you suppose have been across deserts and jungles and trackless wastes?"

"Oh, two or three," Kelp said, and took the exit, and Tiny said, "South."

They were coming at the cemeteries from a different highway this time, so they did get a little lost, despite everything the car could do to help. Still, eventually they found Sunnyside Street, and drove slowly down it in the darkness until they reached the broken part of the fence, where Kelp jounced them up over the curb.

Dortmunder found it was a lot easier to move the fence out of the way when Tiny was the other guy doing the lifting. Kelp drove through, they put the fence back to position one, and they walked along behind the Jeep, which from the rear still looked something like a Jeep. "It's just a little ways along here," Dortmunder said, moving his lips.

And there it was. Kelp angled the Jeep off the path, and its lights shone on the gravestone that was now, through no fault of its own, a liar.

Dortmunder said, "What we got to find is another one from that year or close to it."

Peering at Redcorn's dates, Tiny said, "Birth and death both?"

Kelp, joining them from the Jeep, said, "I don't think so. The main thing is, he should be in the box the right length of time."

"Well, let's see how tough this is gonna be," Tiny said. He walked over to Joseph Redcorn's stone and smacked it in the middle of the name with the heel of his hand, and it fell over on its back.

"Well, don't get too mean with it, Tiny," Kelp said. "We don't wanna crack it."

Dortmunder had been looking around the neighborhood, having to squint as he moved farther from the lights of the Jeep, but now he straightened and said, "Here's a good one."

The other two came over to look, and stood solemnly gazing down at the tombstone. It was very like Redcorn's, thin, a foot wide, maybe two feet tall, weather-stained, with rounded upper corners. It said:

BURWICK MOODY
Loving Son and Husband
October 11, 1904–
December 5, 1933

"That's the day Prohibition ended," Dortmunder commented.

Tiny looked at him. "You know stuff like that?"

"I like it when they repeal laws," Dortmunder explained.

Kelp said, "You notice, the wife didn't put up the stone, the mother did."

"The wife was still drunk," Tiny suggested.

Dortmunder said, "Whadaya think, Tiny? Can this go over there?"

Tiny stepped over to Burwick Moody's marker and gently pushed it over onto its back. "Piece of cake," he said. "You guys each take a corner at the bottom there, I'll take the top."

The bottom corner, Dortmunder found, was rough, cold, wet, and nasty. "This job has too many graveyards in it," he muttered, but then he lifted along with the other two.

It was heavy, but not impossible. Tiny walked backward, looking over his shoulder as he detoured them around other tombstones, and Dortmunder and Kelp followed him, hunched side by side over the corners they carried, shoulders touching as they shuffled along, gasping a little, sweat already popping out on their foreheads into the cold night air.

At the former Redcorn place, they put the Moody slab on the ground, picked up the Redcorn slab, and schlepped it the other way. There, while Dortmunder and Kelp held the stone in an upright position, Tiny got to his knees and karate-chopped the loose dirt until it was solidly packed around the base and no longer looked as though anything had been disturbed.

When they'd done the same thing with Moody's monument at Redcorn's previous residence, Tiny stood and whapped the dirt off his hands and the knees of his trousers as he said, "And we get to do this again."

"The night," Dortmunder said, "before they take the

sample. We'll find out when that's gonna be from Little
Feather, and for sure the tribes, if they're gonna pull anything, they'll do it before then."

"Nothing for us to do now," Kelp said, "but leave."

"Well, I'm ready," Dortmunder said.

As they walked along behind the Jeep back toward the
break in the fence, Tiny said, "Be a kick in the head, it
turns out that isn't her grandfather after all."

Dortmunder said, "What? Little Feather? Why not?"

"Well, you never know," Tiny said. "Could be nobody
told her, but she's adopted."

"Thank you, Tiny," Dortmunder said. "I was almost
beginning to relax."

27

The Tribal Council functioned mostly like a zoning board. Back in the good old days, the Tribal Council had waged war against tribal enemies, had overseen the distribution of meat after a hunt, maintained religious orthodoxy (a combination of ancestor and tree worship at that time), punished adultery and theft and treason and other high crimes and misdemeanors, arranged executions, oversaw the torturing of captured enemies, conducted the young men of the tribe through the rites of manhood, and arranged marriages (most of which worked out pretty well). These days, the Tribal Council gave out building permits.

Tommy Dog was chairman of the Tribal Council for this quarter, he being a Kiota and the chairmanship alternating every quarter between the tribes, to be fair to everybody and to distribute the power and the glory equally, and because nobody wanted the damn job.

But it had to be done, so on the first Saturday of every month, in the Tribal Longhouse (aka Town Hall), more or less at 3:00 P.M., the chairman of the Tribal Council would gavel the meeting into session, only hoping there would be a quorum, meaning seven out of the twelve members would be present, and that there would be no new business. There was sometimes a quorum, and there was *always* new business, and today, Saturday, December 2, there were both.

Unfortunately, some of the old business was still around as well, including a festering quarrel between two neighbors over in Paradise concerning the placement of neighbor one's septic vis-à-vis neighbor two's well, and which came first. The neighbors no longer would speak to each other at all, and would speak to other people only at the top of their voices, and neither of them would budge until hell froze over, so it was the usual first-Saturday fun. Everybody sat around on the wooden folding chairs in the knotty pine–paneled meeting room and listened to those two Oshkawa rant and rave about each other. Everybody knew the Oshkawa were overemotional anyway.

In the middle of it all, Tommy noticed a stranger come in and take a wooden chair in the back row. Well, not a stranger exactly—Tommy knew Benny Whitefish, had known Benny Whitefish the little squirt's whole life—but he was a stranger *here,* in that Benny was most unlikely to have any business before the Council, and people who didn't absolutely totally drag-out *have* to be at these meetings for whatever business or permit reasons they might have were never here, the lucky stiffs.

Tommy Dog was sixty-three. Over in the United States, he was an electrician, and a good one, but he didn't work much these days, hadn't worked much for maybe twenty-five years; just enough to keep his union card, really. The casino distributed enough money to everybody on the reservation so nobody had to work if they didn't want to, but Tommy was one of those who'd found life without meaningful activity could be amazingly boring after a while, so he kept on being an electrician from time to time, just to keep his hand in, and otherwise he hung around the reservation and watched the young ones come along. Some of those girls, boy, they could get a man in trouble, he didn't pay attention to himself.

But the point is, Tommy Dog knew Benny Whitefish, knew his entire family, and knew Benny to be a harmless young layabout with no more call to be at a Council meeting than a parakeet. So what was he doing here?

I'm afraid I'm gonna find out, Tommy thought grimly as Benny shyly smiled and waved a greeting at Tommy from his perch at the back of the room.

The septic-vs-well problem was held over to the next meeting, as usual, for the town attorney to consult his law books yet again to see if he could come up with just one more compromise that would be completely unacceptable to both parties. Most of the other old business was also held over, and so was some of the new business, though a couple permits were issued.

Whenever there was a vote, which was about every three minutes, everybody got very solemn as Joan Bakerman, the secretary, read out the motion now to be dealt with, and some member agreed to make the motion, and then another member agreed to second the motion, and then Joan Bakerman polled the present members, calling out each name in turn, and each one responding, "Yeah," or, "Yes," or, "Yep."

Finally, it was done, and they all cleared their throats, scraped their chairs noisily over the floor as they got to their feet, hitched their trousers (men and women both), yawned discreetly, wished one another well, and got the hell out of there. All except for Tommy Dog, who saw Benny rise hesitantly to his feet and knew Benny's moment had come.

Yes. After everybody else left, Benny came down the aisle between the rows of folding chairs and said, "Hi, Mr. Dog."

"Afternoon, Benny," Tommy said. "You wanted to talk to me?"

"Yes, sir, for a minute, if I could, if you got a minute."

"I got a minute," Tommy told him, in a manner that suggested he might not have two minutes. "Sit down here."

They sat in the front row and Benny began grimacing and looking at the floor and twisting the leg of his blue jeans with his fingers and jouncing his foot up and down. Tommy watched this display for a few seconds and then said, "I guess this is where you say you don't know where to start."

"Well, it's Little Feather Redcorn!" Benny blurted out.

Oh boy. What dumb bonehead trouble had Benny wandered into now?

Tommy had not himself seen the Redcorn woman on TV, but a lot of the people he knew had seen her, and everybody agreed this was some tough cookie. A hardened crook and a con-woman criminal. Did she have her hooks in Benny Whitefish?

On the other hand, what would she—or anybody else, really—want her hooks in Benny Whitefish for? Moving toward an answer to that question, Tommy said, "Met up with her, did you?"

"Yes," Benny said, then immediately reddened and jerked upright hard enough to make his chair complain, and cried, "No!" He stared wide-eyed at Tommy, then away, then said, "Uncle Roger told me to watch her."

Tommy hadn't expected this. "Watch her? What do you mean, 'watch her'?"

"To look for her accomplices," Benny said, then leaned toward Tommy, bug-eyed with sincerity, to say, "But she don't *have* any accomplices! Mr. Dog, I think she's telling the truth, you know? I been following her for *days* now, and she don't have any accomplices at all. I think she really is Pottaknobbee."

Tommy said, "Aren't they gonna do something in court?"

"Oh, sure," Benny said, "but Uncle Roger and Uncle Frank, they just don't want her around. Even if it's all true, they don't want her there. They told me so themself."

I thought they were smarter than that, Tommy thought, smarter than to tell Benny Whitefish anything at all. He said, "I suppose they just like things the way they are."

"Boy, they sure do," Benny agreed. Then at last, he got to it: "Mr. Dog," he said, full of earnestness, "could *you* talk to them?"

"What, Roger and Frank?" Tommy recoiled from the idea.

"Sure," Benny said. "Tell them the Tribal Council don't want to throw Little Feather out, not if she's really Pottaknobbee."

Noticing that use of the first name, Tommy said, "I think we all oughta leave that to the courts, don't you, Benny?"

"But— The Tribal Council's the law here, isn't it?"

"Oh, sure," Tommy said. "We got our sovereignty. But I don't see there's anything the Council should do about all this. Let the court decide if she's Pottaknobbee or not."

"Mr. Dog," Benny said, blinking like mad, "would *you* talk to her?"

Tommy couldn't believe it. So that was what the woman had in mind; divide and conquer. "Benny," he said severely, "did *she* tell you to ask me that?"

"Oh *no,* sir!" Benny cried, lying very fervently and very badly. "It's all my own idea, Mr. Dog, honest! I been watching her, and following her, and I just thought, we aren't treating her right, and maybe if the Council—"

"No, Benny," Tommy said. "The Tribal Council is not going to get involved. That isn't our jurisdiction." He could just see himself crossing swords with Roger Fox and Frank Oglanda. They'd run *him* off the reservation. A three-month chairmanship of the Tribal Council had not turned Tommy Dog into a complete idiot. "You go back and tell that Miss Redcorn," he said, "her best hope is the court, and if she wants to talk to Roger and Frank, she should pick up the telephone and make an appointment. And now *I* got an appointment to take Millicent to the mall." Rising, he said, "My advice to you, Benny, is to ask your uncle Roger to put somebody else to following your friend Little Feather around, and *you* keep away from her."

Going out, Tommy paused in the doorway to look back, and Benny was still sitting there, in profile to Tommy, slumped, dejected, head down, gazing hopelessly at the floor. In that position, he looked exactly like that famous statue of the mournful, defeated Indian, except he wasn't on a horse and he wasn't tall and thin. And he didn't hold a lance with its tip down in the dirt. And he didn't have the headdress. But other than that, it was exactly the same: the defeated Indian.

28

By Monday morning, May had decided it was like living with a retiree. John had only been back from the North Country since Friday, but he had never been so *present* before. Everywhere in the apartment she looked, there he was, slumped and leaden, looking surly and bored out of his mind.

She hadn't known it was possible for someone who didn't have a regular job, who'd never had a regular job in his life, to sit around exactly as though he'd just been laid off. But here he was, a sodden lump and no fun at all.

Over breakfast Monday morning, before leaving for her cashier's job at Safeway, May decided to bring it out where they could look at it, discuss the problem, so she said, "John, what's wrong?"

"Nothing," he said. He was slumped over his cereal bowl, looking down into it, at the sugar and the milk and the cornflakes all massing together in there, all in a soggy clump, turning gray somehow. His breakfast had never turned gray before. He held the spoon angled into the gob, as though he might use the stuff to patch a hole somewhere, but not as though he had any intention of eating it.

She said, "John, something's wrong, you're not eating your breakfast."

"Sure I am," he said, but he still didn't lift either his spoon or his eyes. Then he frowned into the bowl more deeply and said, "I just remembered. In the orphanage, you know, the bowls they gave us had cartoon people in the bottom, like Bugs Bunny and Daffy Duck and all, and everybody always ate real fast to see what was in the bottom, even when we had pea soup. I usually got Elmer Fudd."

This was more than John had said in the last three days combined, but he seemed to be talking more to the bowl than to May. Also, he rarely spoke about his upbringing in the orphanage run by the Bleeding Heart Sisters of Eternal Misery, which was fine by her. She said, "John? Would you like some bowls like that?"

"No," he said, and slowly shook his head. Then he let go of the spoon—it didn't drop; it remained angled into the gunk—and at last he looked up at May across the kitchen table and said, "What I want, I think, is, you know what I mean, some purpose in life."

"You don't have a purpose in life?"

"I *usually* got a purpose," he said. "Usually, I kind of know what I'm doing and why I'm doing it, but look at me now."

"I know," she agreed. "I've been looking at you, John. It's this Anastasia thing, isn't it?"

"I mean, what am I *doing* here?" he demanded. Slowly, the spoon eased downward. Silently, it touched the edge of the bowl. "There's nothing for me to do," he complained, "except sit around and wait for other people to scheme things out, and then all of a sudden Little

Feather's supposed to give me a hundred thousand large, and guess how much I believe *that* one."

"You think she'll stiff you?"

"I think she'd stiff her mother, if her mother happened by," John said. "But I also think Tiny doesn't like to be insulted, so I figure we'll get *something* out of it. Sooner or later. But in the meantime, I'm here, and what's going on is going on up in Plattsburgh, where it's cold as *hell*, and there's no point in me going up there, because there's nothing for me to do there any more than there's nothing for me to do here, which is nothing."

"Maybe," May said, "you should look for something else to do, like you normally would. Some armored car or jewelry store or whatever."

"I don't feel like I *can*, May," he said. "I feel like I'm stuck in this thing, and I can't think about anything else, and maybe all of a sudden I *will* be needed after all, and I shouldn't be off doing something else." He shook his head, frowning once more at the bowl. The gray mass in there looked dry now. "I never thought you'd hear me say this, May," he said, "but the problem is, and I know this is it, the problem is, everything's going too easy."

29

Benny Whitefish and his cousin Geerome Sycamore and his other cousin Herbie Antelope loaded the coffin into the rented van and shut the doors. Then Geerome went behind the tombstone and threw up.

Benny was pleased that Geerome had thrown up, because it meant there was at least one person around here who was a bigger goofus than himself, but of course, since Uncle Roger had put him in charge of this mission, he had to say, in a manly kind of fashion, "That's okay, Geerome, it could of happened to anybody. Don't think a thing about it."

"Where's the water?" Geerome asked. He was making the most awful face.

"It's in the van," Herbie said, "but pour it into something else, okay?"

Geerome turned his awful face on Herbie. "Whadaya mean, put it into something else?"

"A cup or something," Herbie said.

Geerome said, "*I* don't have a cup. Benny? You got a cup?"

Herbie said, "Then pour it in the bottle top, drink from that."

"The hell," Geerome said. "You get like a quarter ounce at a time like that. What am I supposed to do all that for?"

Herbie made his own awful face and said, "I don't want your mouth on that bottle, all right? Not if the rest of us are gonna drink from it."

"Well, tough noogies on you," Geerome told him, and stomped off to the front of the van.

Benny said, "Come on, Herbie, don't worry about it. We'll buy another bottle at the Trading Post," which was the name of the shopping mall he preferred.

"*You'll* buy," Herbie said.

Benny sighed; the lonely responsibility of command. "All right, all right," he said. "So let's get going."

The fact is, this was a pretty awful task they had in front of them, and that's why it was making them all kind of nervous and testy. Geerome's mouth wasn't any worse than it usually was, but their nerves were kind of off.

Here they were, in the old Three Tribes cemetery, way toward the back, late on Monday afternoon, almost dark, the shadows of the tombstones reaching out black and spooky, like ghostly fingers, and Benny and his crew had just finished digging up a grave. The person they'd dug down to and now transferred to the van was named Ichabod Derek, and he was one of the few people in the Three Tribes cemetery who wasn't from one of the three tribes, he having been a Lakota from out west who had married a Kiota woman and moved east to her reservation with her so she could support him. He'd died a long long time ago, around 1940 or something, but the main point about him was, there wasn't one chance in a million that he had any Pottaknobbee blood in him. Or DNA.

This was the drastic measure the uncles had come up with, and that Benny was charged to act upon. Dig up Ichabod Derek, transport him (inside his coffin, thank goodness, at least they didn't have to open any coffins on this expedition) to New York City, and find the graveyard where Joseph Redcorn was buried. Then dig up Redcorn—this would be *way* after dark, and in New York City, which was full of who knew what kind of menaces and terrors—and plant Derek where Redcorn had been, then drive Redcorn all the way back up to Silver Chasm and put him in Derek's grave, where nobody would ever find him. And then probably have nightmares for weeks.

There was one thing Uncle Roger had insisted Benny do that he just wasn't going to do, because neither Geerome nor Herbie was going to do it, and he couldn't do it alone, and that was fill in the grave after taking Derek out, which would mean having to dig it all up and fill it all in again twice, and the heck with it. Uncle Roger was afraid somebody might stumble across—or into, more likely—the grave if they left it open, but who would be coming out here to the oldest part of the cemetery, even in the daytime? Nobody at night, certainly. So let the damn grave yawn; they'd fill it in when they got back.

The drive to New York City was very long and boring, but at least it was all on good roads. They took the Northway for the first 150 miles, as far as Albany, where they stopped for a lot of hamburgers and french fries and beer, which made them fill the interior of the van with less than sweet airs during the second stage of the trip, the 150 miles down the thruway to New York City. Despite the cold, they spent a lot of that travel segment with the van windows open.

Benny did most of the driving, because he meant to make Geerome and Herbie do most of the driving back north, when Benny would want to sleep. If he could get to sleep. Since he'd met Little Feather, he wasn't having much success with sleep. Nor with Little Feather. Nor with his own tumbled emotions.

The whole trip down, while Geerome and Herbie squabbled and sniped beside him, blaming each other for the aromas in the van, Benny thought about Little Feather. And what he thought was that he didn't know what to think.

He knew he liked to be in her presence. He liked to sit in the living room of the motor home and watch her walk or sit, watch her smile, listen to her voice, smell the wonderful musks that flowed out from her; a zillion times better than these little polecats beside him.

Would she one day let him kiss her? She seemed so open and inviting, and yet there was something about her that told him not to rush things, not to take chances, not to spoil what he already had. So maybe someday she would let him know he could come closer, but until then, he'd just sit there and watch her and listen to her and smell her and think how much better she was in every way than those posters on his walls.

Or maybe someday she'd find out what he was doing tonight, and how he was responsible for her losing her only chance to prove she was really Pottaknobbee, and then she'd never speak to him again, or let him see her or come anywhere near her. But what could he do? What else could he do?

He couldn't refuse Uncle Roger. And he couldn't just pretend to switch these coffins, even if he could get Geerome and Herbie to go along with the idea, because then the DNA would prove Little Feather was Potta-knobbee and Uncle Roger would know that Benny hadn't done the job.

At the same time, he couldn't warn Little Feather what he was doing, because she'd naturally try to find some way to stop it, maybe even tell that judge she'd been describing to Benny, how nice he was, and how fair, and how secure she felt in his hands, so that Benny was beginning to gnash his teeth with jealousy over some *judge,* who was anyway a hundred years old and he wasn't around Little Feather in that kind of way at all.

He was sorry her idea of asking the Tribal Council for help hadn't worked out. He'd never thought much about the Tribal Council before, just knew it was there and people sometimes went to it to ask questions and get permits and things, but he'd always assumed it was something important, like the United States government or something. But when he saw Mr. Dog there, in the Town Hall, and saw what the meeting was like, he knew even before he talked to Mr. Dog that there wasn't much chance Little Feather would find any help there. So that was another avenue closed.

Driving south, his fantasy was that, when this was all over, Uncle Roger would really give Benny that very good high-paying job at the casino he'd been hinting about, and Benny would go to Little Feather and tell her how bad he felt about her not getting to be Pottaknobbee on the reservation, and he would offer to build her a house on the reservation that would be all hers—he wouldn't even live there—and she could ask him to visit sometimes or not; it would be strictly up to her.

And after all, she was a licensed blackjack dealer in Nevada; she could surely get a job at Silver Chasm casino, and Benny happened to know those dealers made very good money. So in his fantasy, Little Feather was robbed of her birthright without knowing it or knowing who'd done it to her, and Benny would make it up to her with a house on the reservation and a job at the casino and the presence of his company whenever she wanted it.

Phew. No wonder he couldn't sleep.

Uncle Frank Oglanda had flown in a chartered plane from Plattsburgh yesterday to La Guardia Airport in New York City, and had taken a taxi to the graveyard where Joseph Redcorn was buried, where he had found the grave and marked it on a little map he made. He had also learned that the graveyard was locked at night, but he'd wandered around and come across a broken part of the fence where people could get through, and he'd marked that on his map as well. Then he'd taxied back to La Guardia and flown back to Plattsburgh and BMW'd back to Silver Chasm, and this morning he'd described it all to Benny, saying, "You'll have to carry the coffin in through the break in the fence, sort of carry it sideways to get it through there, but it isn't far from there to the grave. It'll be easy, strong young fellas like you."

It wasn't easy. They found the right graveyard, no trouble, and down a long, dark, deserted, silent street surrounded by cemeteries, they found the small opening in the fence and parked the yellow van right next to it. When they got out of the van, there was a cold, nasty little wind that nipped at them and picked at them like ghosts, ice-cold invisible spirits coming at them out of the graveyard. Even though, naturally, they didn't believe in all that stuff.

Now they had to wrestle this big heavy box out of the van and across the grass and through the narrow opening. The box was kind of slimy and dirty and kept wanting to slip out of everybody's hands and crash onto the ground, which would be very bad if it happened. Also, it was hard for more than two people to carry the box, even when they weren't trying to ootch it sideways through the opening in the fence, but the box was certainly too heavy to be carried by any fewer than three people, so the whole trip was difficult and exhausting and more than a little scary.

Also, though all three had brought along flashlights, it proved to be impossible to hold a flashlight and carry a coffin at the same time, so they did most of the carrying in the dark. Above them stretched a partly cloudy winter sky, with a very high half-moon sometimes laying its platinum wash over everything and sometimes hiding behind a cloud as though a light had been switched off. That was when the icy fingers of the wind plucked at them the worst.

When they finally reached the Redcorn grave and could put the coffin down, they were all completely worn-out, and the real work hadn't even started yet. Panting, gasping, plodding through the last of the fallen leaves, shining their flashlights around at last, they trudged back to the van and got the shovels and the plastic tarp they would use to pile the dirt on, and brought it all to the grave. And then, with a communal sigh, they got to it.

The way it worked, two of them dug while the third kept a flashlight on them. Benny was in charge, saying when it was time for the flashlight guy to switch to a shovel, and he didn't even cheat, but ran it as fair as he knew how, because he knew Geerome and Herbie were watching him and would put up a terrible bitch if they thought he was trying to pull a fast one.

The work was hard but mindless. They dug and dug and dug, and then at last Geerome's shovel hit something that went *thunk* and he said, "Here it is."

"Finally," Herbie said.

Yes, finally. It was almost eleven at night by now, and they still had a lot to do. Benny was the one with the flashlight at this point, and he leaned down closer to shine its beam on Geerome's shovel. There was wood down there all right, dark brown and solid under the crumbly lighter brown of the soil. "Okay, great," he said. "I think we just clear one end, and then maybe we can pry it up."

"Wait a minute, Benny," Geerome said. "It's my turn with the flashlight. Come on down here."

The other two were now waist-deep in the hole. Benny said, "I'm not sure I can jump down there. What if I busted the wood or something?"

"We'll help you," Geerome said, and leaned his shovel against the side of the hole to show he was serious. Then he and Herbie held their hands up, and Benny leaned forward even more, and half-jumped, half-fell into the grave, all three of them tottering a bit. They might have fallen over if it weren't for the sides of the hole pressing in on them.

"Give me the flashlight," Geerome said, and a *huge* white light suddenly glared all over them. Benny, wide-eyed, astounded, terrified, could still make out every crumb of dirt on the cheeks of Geerome and Herbie, the light was that bright, that intense.

And so was the voice. It came from a bullhorn, and it sounded like the voice of God, and it said, *"Freeze. Stop right where you are."*

They froze; well, they were already frozen. The three Indian lads standing in a row in the grave squinted into the glare, and out of it, like a scene in a science-fiction movie, came a lot of people in dark blue uniforms. Policemen. New York City policemen.

And with them came a capering old man in a thread-bare cardigan and a rumpled hat, who cackled, actually cackled, as he cried, "Gotcha *this* time! You think you can just traipse around in here with all your flashlights and I'm not gonna know about it? You come back once too often, you did! I *gotcha!*"

30

When things got slow, Kelp liked to go to the safes. They were in the closet in the other room, which was all he could think to call a room with a bed in it that you didn't sleep in. Anne Marie called it the guest room, but Kelp had never happened across any guests anytime he'd ever gone in there, if you didn't count the occasional cockroach, which can happen in even the best-cared-for apartment in New York. So it was the other room. And in its closet were the safes; four of them at the moment, in a row on the floor.

This is a kind of safe that isn't much made anymore, but your better-quality house or apartment wall is very likely to contain one. They are round and black and made of thick iron, and are a little smaller than a bowling ball. They have a round steel door on the front with a dial in it, and they have little iron ears, pierced, that angle out for mounting the safe on the studs inside the wall.

They are very hard to get into. Being round, they are almost impervious to explosives, and being thick black iron, they are impossible to crack or break with any known tool. The round door is also thick, and inset in such a way as to make it inaccessible to any lever or pry bar. The combination dial is cunning and clever and cannot be conquered in a matter of minutes. Most slickers coming across one of these safes just pass it by and settle for the television set.

Not Kelp. His practice, if he had a vehicle handy when he discovered one of these coconuts, was to gouge it out of the wall, toss it into the vehicle, take it home, and fiddle with it from time to time when nothing much was happening. It was kind of a hobby, and also a way to keep his talents honed. Sooner or later, he managed to open every one of those doors, by which time, what he found inside was almost beside the point. And what he found inside ranged from a very nice line in jewelry all the way down through stocks of defunct corporations to absolute nothing. Still, it was the journey that mattered, not the destination.

This morning, around ten, with Anne Marie off to the New School at her course on the history of constitutional law in the Balkans, Kelp was seated lotus-style, more or less, on the floor in the other room, in front of the open closet, one of the safes having been drawn out and tilted back, so that it now looked up at him with its one skeptical eye, when the phone rang. Deep in communion with this dial before him, he almost didn't answer, but he could never resist a ringing phone—except in a doctor's car, when he knew it would only be the doctor, wanting his car back—so he finally sighed, shifted so he could reach into his pants pocket, brought out the little cordless, and said dubiously, "Hello?"

He'd been right to be dubious; it was Fitzroy Guilderpost. And he was excited, agitated, upset, blowing bubbles in the middles of his words: "Andy, we're coming down! We've got to meet, we'll meet at your place, call John and Tiny, we're leaving now, we'll be there no later than three, Irwin's ready, we must fly, see you then!"

"Fitzroy," Kelp said, "what are you talking about?"

There was a startled silence down the phone line, with bubbles, and then Fitzroy said, "You don't *know*?"

"If you'll think back, Fitzroy," Kelp said, "you'll realize you haven't told me yet. And if you don't tell me, Fitzroy, I can pretty well guarantee I won't be here at three o'clock."

"It was on the news!" Fitzroy jabbered. "Surely, if it was on the news up here, it was on the news down there!"

"It may be on the news," Kelp pointed out, "but I don't have the news on. So why don't you just tell me?"

"The Indians were caught!"

This sounded like something from the world of sports, but Kelp knew that couldn't be right. He said, "More, Fitzroy. Open it a little wider."

"The Indians," Fitzroy said, damping himself down, obviously as though he thought he were talking to a nincompoop, "took a coffin to the cemetery in Queens last night to switch bodies, just the way John said they would."

Then Kelp saw it. "Oh, oh," he said. "And they got caught?"

"Right in the middle of it, the hole dug, the three of them in the grave, standing on the box."

"This is bad news, Fitzroy," Kelp said.

"Yes! It is! I know it!"

"We better talk this over," Kelp decided.

"Irwin and I are on our way, that's what I've been trying to *tell* you!"

"And Little Feather?"

"She has to stay here, be in court, there's a *great* coruscation over this."

Kelp assumed that word was a legal term of some sort, and let it go. He said, "Okay, we'll see you and Irwin then."

"Because, Andy," Fitzroy said, "because of what those idiots did, there is now a *guard* on that grave."

"Oh boy."

"The tribes have been trying to stall the DNA test," Fitzroy said, "but this will certainly accelerate the process."

"Uh-huh."

"When they take that DNA sample out of that casket," Fitzroy complained, "it will not be Little Feather's grandfather in there."

"It will be Burwick Moody."

"I think I hate Burwick Moody," Fitzroy said.

"Aw, naw, Fitzroy," Kelp said, "he's as much an innocent victim in this as we are."

"I did not get involved in this operation," Fitzroy told him, "to be an innocent victim."

"Yeah, it does feel a little odd," Kelp agreed. "Okay, Fitzroy, we'll see you this afternoon. I'll call John now, though I don't think he's gonna thank me for it."

31

Judge T. Wallace Higbee felt a lot better this morning. Last week, it had looked as though he would be sucked relentlessly into the vortex of the kind of case that law schools later use in moot court, but by now, Tuesday morning, he could see it was going to be all right. It was just the usual stupidity after all.

They were all in court this morning, at three minutes past eleven, when Judge Higbee took his seat on the raised platform to gaze fondly down upon his people. The high-powered New York lawyers, Max Schreck of Feinberg, Kleinberg, Rhineberg, Steinberg, Weinberg & Klatsch, for the Redcorn woman, and Otis Welles of Holliman, Sherman, Beiderman, Tallyman & Funk, for the casino, were in position at their flanking tables, both this morning with assistants up from New York, and masses of briefcases, and flaming red neckties, obviously ready—nay, eager—to do intricate and arcane legal battle on Judge Higbee's turf, but as far as he was concerned, they had become toothless tigers.

Little Feather Redcorn was also here, looking more and more like an unvarnished seeker of justice, hard though that might be to believe. Roger Fox and Frank

Oglanda, whose stupidity had rolled the clouds away from over Judge Higbee's head, were here, trying not to look sheepish, which made for a change; usually, they tried not to look lupine. Even little Marjorie Dawson, Ms. Redcorn's first and extremely local lawyer, was here, blinking in the glare of all this high-wattage legal talent, and serving by her presence, her dimness, her simplicity, to reassure Judge Higbee that it is still the meek who will inherit the earth. After everybody else dies, of course.

In the expectant silence, after he settled himself at the bench, everybody looked at Judge Higbee, and Judge Higbee contentedly gazed back upon them all. Then he lifted a hand, palm upward, and crooked a finger. "Counselors," he said.

Schreck and Welles immediately got to their feet to stride shoulder-to-shoulder toward the bench. Schreck as tall and skinny as a crane, or some darker bird of ill omen, Welles as bony and angular as an Exercycle in pinstripes, they were physically unalike but, nevertheless, obviously twins in their souls. Neither would ever give an inch, and neither would ever become emotionally involved in the work at hand.

Judge Higbee crooked his finger again, so the two lawyers would lean closer and their conversation could be private. Then he said, "We have a changed situation this morning, gentlemen."

Welles said, "I hope to speak to that, Your Honor. The depth of feeling in the Indian community is now manifest. We—"

The judge held up a hand. "Save the speech, Mr. Welles," he advised. "You'll want it on the record."

"Thank you, Your Honor," Welles said, without apparent irony.

Schreck said, "I would also like to address the changed circumstances, Your Honor, by requesting summary judgment in Little Feather Redcorn's favor. By their actions, the casino owners have—"

"Not *their* action," Welles interrupted. "Those young lads—"

"Stop," the judge suggested, and they stopped. He looked from one to the other, and then he said, "The reason I called you to this preliminary off-the-record discussion is because I'm afraid emotions may run high today, and I would prefer that nothing disturb the tranquillity of my court. Mr. Welles, just now you interrupted Mr. Schreck. You will not do that again. Nor will Mr. Schreck interrupt you. When I want one of you to speak, I will tell you so. Is that clear?"

Before Welles could speak, Schreck said, "Your Honor, there are those occasions when one's honorable opponent makes a misstatement that requires a timely response."

"If either of you interrupts the other, ever," the judge told him, "I will declare an immediate thirty-minute recess. And what will happen to your timely response then? I suggest you take notes as we go along."

"Thank you, Your Honor," Schreck said, without apparent irony.

"We'll begin," the judge said, and made a little shooing gesture that sent the lawyers back to their respective tables. Once they'd gotten there and seated themselves, Judge Higbee said, "Mr. Welles, I believe you would like to make a statement to the Court concerning some recent events."

Welles popped to his feet. "I do, Your Honor, thank you. As you know, we have an action in the appeals court in Albany at this moment, on your ruling that the Redcorn grave in Queens cannot be considered sacred tribal burial grounds. It has been our contention, not to resubmit the entire case in this venue, Your Honor, that the protections afforded Native American burial sites in previous court decisions are not limited to current tribal lands. As a part of our argument, we have made reference to the strong tribal and religious feelings among the Kiota and Oshkawa concerning the resting places of their ancestors. And now, bearing out that contention, three young lads from the Silver Chasm reservation have actually gone to the Redcorn grave in Queens to rescue their forebear from what they consider violated land. This entirely voluntary act, done without consultation with any of the tribal elders, simply—"

Max Schreck lunged upward with opening mouth. Judge Higbee raised his gavel. Max Schreck saw that movement, clasped his left hand over his open mouth, lunged back down, and began to write slashingly on a long yellow legal pad.

Meantime, Welles had continued to speak: "—serves to reinforce the contentions we have already made to the appeals court, and cocounsel down in Albany will be addressing that court today, to add this bit of evidence to our argument. Thank you, Your Honor."

Schreck took his hand from his mouth and his pen from his pad and waggled his eyebrows at Judge Higbee, who ignored him and said instead, to Welles, "You see this grave robbing as a further argument in your appeal?"

"We do, Your Honor," Welles said.

"The three young men involved are all nephews of Roger Fox."

"And Mr. Fox," Welles said, while Roger Fox tried to look stoic, "has confessed to me that although the part of him that is a mature adult of course deplores the young lads' actions, the part of him that is always Oshkawa cannot help but be proud of their actions, however rash."

Roger Fox tried to look proud.

Judge Higbee said, "Mr. Welles, I have the police report from New York City here in front of me. The van that was used was rented by Mr. Fox."

"The lads asked him to rent it for them," Welles replied. "They told him they intended to go fishing."

"In a van with a sixteen-foot-long storage area?" the judge asked. "How many fish did they expect to catch?"

"I believe they also intended to help a friend move some furniture."

"It will be interesting to watch you produce that friend, Mr. Welles," the judge told him, "and his furniture. There is also the question of the second coffin, apparently removed from a grave on the reservation. I have a report that an open grave was found in the older cemetery on the reservation."

"It is my understanding," Welles said, "that the person in question was not a member of the Three Tribes, and the lads felt the protection afforded by sacred tribal lands was of little or no moment to him. As they needed a grave in the proper area for the late Mr. Redcorn, they merely intended to reverse the positions of the two decedents."

"Thereby," Judge Higbee pointed out, "invalidating any DNA test that might be done."

Shaking his head, Welles said, "Your Honor, I doubt those lads have ever even thought about DNA."

"Their uncle thinks about DNA," the judge said. "However, this is a police matter in New York City, and not to be adjudicated by this court. I was interested to hear what your explanation of those events might be, Mr. Welles. Thank you. And now, Mr. Schreck, I believe you have a premature application you wish to make."

Clearly, Max Schreck had sniffed the prevailing breeze this morning and understood that the court this week, though it had the same personnel in the same physical location, was not the same as the court last week. It was a more dangerous court this week. Therefore, Schreck did not pop to his feet, but rose cautiously, even rustily, to say, "Your Honor, obviously we don't believe our motion is premature, but I'm happy to hear you at least acknowledge its potential, and I hope my learned cocounsel will be able to convince you that its time is not later, but now."

Learned cocounsel? Some other specialist up from New York, full of obscure citations? Judge Higbee prepared himself for boredom. But then, Schreck turned to bow to Marjorie Dawson, who flickered a nervous smile and rose as Schreck sat down.

Oh, I see, the judge thought. He's throwing her out of the sled. So I'm the wolf, am I? Smiling as though Marjorie were Little Red Riding Hood, he said, "Good morning, Marjorie."

"Good morning, Your Honor." That smile flickered again, and she glanced down at her note-riddled yellow pad. "Judge—Your Honor. In attempting to remove the body of Joseph Redcorn from its legitimate—and presumably final—resting place, the casino managers have—"

"Your Honor, I pro—" called Welles.

"Thirty-minute recess," Judge Higbee declared. *Thock* went the gavel, and off went the judge, to watch thirty minutes of soap opera in chambers.

"Proceed, Marjorie."

"Thank you, Your Honor. In attempting to remove the body of Joseph Redcorn from its legitimate—and presum—" She coughed, having remembered she'd already made that feeble joke "—legitimate resting place, the casino managers have made it clear that they believe Little Feather Redcorn *is* Pottaknobbee, and their actions since she first arrived in this area to press her claim have not been based on their belief in her fraudulence, but in their belief in her *veracity.* They want to keep her from her proper share in the casino *even though* they know full well she is Pottaknobbee. By their actions, they demonstrate that their presence in this court is a sham, meant to gain time while they protect themselves by more devious measures. Since they have demonstrated their belief that Little Feather Redcorn is what she claims to be, and since there is no one else who disputes her claim, we see no reason for this action to go forward before the Court, and we therefore request dismissal of all charges against Little Feather Redcorn."

"Very nice, Marjorie," the judge said.

Now her smile was real, and surprised. The judge could see that Schreck was surprised, too, having expected him to give the proposer of dismissal of all charges a rough time indeed, which is exactly what he would have given Schreck himself: a brusque dismissal. But what Schreck didn't yet understand was that not only are all politics local but so is all law. When this farrago was finished, Schreck and Welles and all their cocounsels and their briefcases and their red neckties would go hallooing back to New York City, but Judge T. Wallace Higbee and counselor Marjorie Dawson would be dealing with each other in this courtroom for years to come.

"Thank you, Your Honor," Marjorie said. "I hope this means you will give our motion strong consideration."

"Henry David Thoreau," he told her, and everybody else in court, "said, 'Some circumstantial evidence is very strong, as when you find a trout in the milk.' There is definitely a trout in the milk this morning—you're right to that extent—but so far, we do not have anything like proof positive that Roger Fox and Frank Oglanda are the ones who watered the milk. Marjorie, if *you* interrupt me, we'll recess until after lunch. Good. It is up to the officials in New York City to decide who is responsible for the trout in this morning's milk, Marjorie, and if they decide Fox and Oglanda are the diluters, I will be happy to entertain your motion at that time."

"Thank you, Your Honor," Marjorie said, and sat.

Welles stood. "Your Honor, may I speak?"

"Of course, Mr. Welles."

"Since Your Honor himself has pointed out," Welles began, "that the matter of the prank by the three lads is in another venue, and since the process of our appeal is in yet a different venue, it might be best to hold these proceedings in abeyance until decisions are made, in one venue or another."

"Oh, I don't think we need wait, Mr. Welles," the judge told him. "In fact, my main purpose in calling this session today is to order the DNA test to proceed at once, without delay."

Welles looked astonished. "But Your Honor! That's the very issue before the appeals court!"

"No, I don't believe it is," the judge corrected him. "You are not disputing DNA tests in your appeal. You are disputing the right of the Court to order the exhumation of the body of Joseph Redcorn. But that is now moot, Mr. Welles. Mr. Fox's nephews, all full-blooded members of the Three Tribes, have already done the exhumation, presumably within the strictures of their native religion. The grave is open, Mr. Welles. The cat is out of the bag."

Judge Higbee smiled at the silent turmoil in front of him. Life among the stupid could be so sweet sometimes. "Marjorie," he said, "arrange with your client for the taking of a sample for the test."

"Yes, Your Honor."

Thock went the gavel.

32

Everybody rose, including Marjorie. Everybody, including Marjorie, watched Judge Higbee stride from the room, smiling like a cat full of cream. But what Marjorie was thinking was, what's wrong here?

This was the second time she'd picked up a secret reaction from Little Feather Redcorn, and once again it had to do with DNA. When the prospect of a DNA test was first raised, in chambers, Marjorie had been the only one close enough to Little Feather to realize the idea wasn't new to her. She'd been waiting for it, and she was relieved and pleased when it finally arose, but she didn't want to admit it. Marjorie hadn't been able to figure that out, and now, just as strongly, when Judge Higbee made that startling announcement that the DNA test could proceed right away, Little Feather's reaction, no matter how much she tried to hide it, had been dismay.

Was Marjorie imagining all this? How could Little Feather have been expectant and eager and already aware of DNA tests last Thursday, and then dismayed at the prospect today? I have to find out about this, she told herself.

Across the aisle, Otis Welles and his associates packed

their briefcases, Welles now like a broken Exercycle in a suit, Roger Fox and Frank Oglanda yattering away at the lawyers with demands, questions, outrage. On this side of the aisle, Max Schreck smiled like a coyote as he packed his briefcase and whispered an encouraging word to Little Feather, as though this morning's outcome were his own work, cleverly and agilely accomplished.

Marjorie stood silent beside Little Feather until Schreck turned away, and then she said, "Well, Little Feather, this is wonderful news, isn't it?"

"It sure is," Little Feather agreed, but Marjorie could see the panic deep in Little Feather's eyes and knew the woman could hardly wait to get alone somewhere by herself, so she could scream and stamp her feet and tear her hair.

No, not yet. "Little Feather," Marjorie said, "let me take you to lunch."

"Oh, that's nice of you, Ms. Dawson," Little Feather said, smiling to beat the band, "but I think I ought to just—"

"*I* think," Marjorie told her, "you should accept my invitation to lunch. I'm speaking as your attorney, Little Feather."

Little Feather frowned at her. Marjorie could see the calculations going by behind those shrewd eyes, and then, all at once, Little Feather switched on the sunny smile once more and said, "I think that would be really nice. Just us girls."

Traditionally, the lawyers had lunch at Chez Laurentian, half a block from the courthouse, so Marjorie took Little Feather the other way, a block and a half to the County

Seat Diner, where the bailiffs and clerks and police ate. Over at Chez Laurentian, the smoking section was two tables at the back, by the kitchen, while here in the County Seat Diner, the nonsmoking section was two booths down at the left end, with windows on one side and the rest rooms on the other.

Having their choice of booths, Marjorie and Little Feather took the one marginally farther from the rest rooms, and while they waited for the waitress to bring their menus, Little Feather said, "That Judge Higbee is quite a card."

"He doesn't usually get to show what he can do," Marjorie said. "I think he's probably having fun."

Then the menus came, and they didn't go on with their conversation until after they'd given in their orders. Then Marjorie said, "Little Feather, you know I'm your lawyer."

"One of my lawyers," Little Feather said.

"Your first lawyer."

"Court-appointed lawyer."

"Little Feather," Marjorie said, beginning to be exasperated, "I'm your lawyer, all right? Will you at least accept that?"

Little Feather shrugged. "Sure."

"And as your lawyer," Marjorie went on, "I am required to keep in confidence anything you tell me. The lawyer-client privilege, have you heard of that?"

Another shrug. "Sure."

"Unless you tell me you're going to commit a crime," Marjorie explained, "which I don't expect you to do—"

A crooked grin from Little Feather. "You can pretty well count on it."

"Well, barring that," Marjorie said, "which, as your attorney, I wouldn't, in fact, be bound by law to report, but, barring that, everything you say to me is strictly private between us and will go no further."

A nod. "Good."

"So tell me what the problem is," Marjorie said.

Little Feather cocked her head, like a bird deciding if that thing in front of her is a twig or a worm. She said, "What problem? Everything's great."

"I've been watching you," Marjorie told her. "I know you don't think much of me—"

"Hey!" Little Feather cried, showing surprise and anger. "What gives you *that* idea?"

"Don't worry about it," Marjorie said, "nobody thinks much of me. But I can *see,* and last Thursday, when Judge Higbee first mentioned DNA, you already knew all about it."

"I thought it was terrific," Little Feather said. "I was happy."

"You were relieved," Marjorie told her. "You'd been thinking about DNA, and waiting for somebody to mention it, but you didn't want to be the one who brought it up yourself. I suppose that's because you don't want people to think you planned this all out beforehand."

Little Feather shrugged. "You got that wrong," she said, "but I guess it doesn't matter."

"Well, my question is," Marjorie said, "why did it upset you today, when Judge Higbee said the test could go ahead?"

Little Feather's frown got deeper and deeper. "Upset me? I thought it was great, we're finally gonna get moving on this."

"I could tell, Little Feather," Marjorie said. "Something happened between last Thursday and today. Then you thought a DNA test would solve all your problems. Today, the DNA test *is* the problem."

"You couldn't be more wrong, lady," Little Feather said.

The food came then, and they both waited. When the waitress left, Marjorie leaned over her BLT and said, "Little Feather, you're in some kind of trouble. You can lie to me if you want, and you can go back to Whispering Pines and cry your heart out all by yourself if you want to, but I'm telling you I'm on your side."

"Court-appointed."

"To be *your* representative." Marjorie shook her head. "Little Feather, I know we got off to a bad start last week, but you *know* I've been on your side ever since, really on your side. And it would be against the *law* if I told anybody anything you confided in me. You're in some kind of trouble. Can I help? How do I know, if you won't tell me what the trouble is?"

Little Feather chomped into her cheeseburger as though she intended never to speak again, but there was a vertical worry line on her brow, and her eyes were thoughtful, so Marjorie said nothing more, just went to work on her BLT.

Little Feather drank some of her diet Coke. "Nobody can help me," she said.

Marjorie put down the BLT, sipped some seltzer, and said, "Try me."

Little Feather seemed to be figuring out how to organize her story. At last, she shrugged and said, "You know how I got my lawyer. My other lawyer."

"Somebody you know out west recommended him," Marjorie said. "That's what you said, anyway."

"Yeah, well, that's it, only a little more complicated. The guy's one of the owners at a place in Vegas where I was a dealer. We never had anything like *that,* you know, between us, you know what I mean—"

"I know what you mean," Marjorie agreed.

"He's just a nice guy," Little Feather said, "so when I needed help, I called him, and he told me to see this other guy who's in the East, named Fitzroy Guilderpost, so I called him, and he's the one put me together with Mr. Schreck."

"Fitzroy Guilderpost."

"That's it. There's something funny about him, Ms. Dawson. I'm not sure, but maybe he's some kind of crook. I'd like to keep away from him, and the people he's with, but I don't know, then I'm gonna be alone again. And now we've got this mess."

"What mess?"

"Well, it wasn't Fitzroy thought of this," Little Feather said. "He's got these friends of his he hangs out with, and they all knew what was happening up here with me, and one of the others, he *said* the tribes were gonna do what they did, switch bodies so the DNA won't match."

Marjorie, surprised, said, "This person guessed that? In advance?"

"I think that's the way they think themselves," Little Feather said, and shrugged, then added, "Anyway, they thought they'd help me out."

"Oh dear," Marjorie said. "They did something."

"They switched tombstones," Little Feather said.

Which was about the last thing Marjorie had expected. She said, "*What* did they do?"

"They went out there to the cemetery," Little Feather explained, "and they switched the tombstones over two graves, and they figured to go back out the night before the DNA test and switch them back. They didn't figure on the tribes getting caught."

Marjorie said, "So, as of right now, Joseph Redcorn's headstone is on some other grave."

"And it's got a guard on it," Little Feather said.

Marjorie sat there, BLT forgotten. Little Feather grinned crookedly at her and said, "That's the way I've been feeling, Ms. Dawson, exactly like you look. And we figured, we figured the tribes were gonna go on stalling, so we had time to work this out, and maybe somebody could come up with a solution before the test, but now the test is gonna be immediately."

"Oh my God," Marjorie said.

Little Feather nodded. "So that's it, Ms. Dawson," she said. "You got any good advice for me?"

33

No more Tea Cosy. Gregory was very sorry, but the skiers had arrived, so the Tea Cosy was full. No more comfortable living room, no more huge breakfasts put out by the cheery Gregory and Tom, no more Odille singing "Frère Jacques" while she changed the beds.

Dortmunder hadn't realized he'd miss the Tea Cosy, hadn't realized he'd miss anything in the North Country, but there you are. Stay at the Four Winds motel in December, on the icy shores of Lake Champlain, and you, too, will miss the Tea Cosy.

The Four Winds was also full of skiers, or at least people dressed for the part. Every time Dortmunder opened his motel room door, somebody was going by through the snowy wind with skis on their shoulder and great clomping boots on their feet and huge goggles on their faces and thick wool caps on their heads. Their bodies were dressed mostly in what looked like shiny vinyl duffel bags. Probably some of them were men and some were women, but from anything Dortmunder could tell they might all have been kodiak bears.

Since either someone had stolen the Grand Cherokee Jeep Laredo or some police person had spotted its potential for a good career mark, Kelp had found them instead a Subaru Outback, which, in addition to the standard M.D. plates, also had four-wheel drive, a good thing in the frozen wastes north of New York City. Kelp was happy with it, but apparently the official owner of this vehicle was a woman doctor, with children; Tiny kept complaining that the backseat was sticky.

The only thing about the Subaru that bothered Dortmunder was the fact that it was the only vehicle within a hundred miles without a ski rack on the roof, which made it very recognizable. "We oughta steal a ski rack from one of these people," he suggested. "Blend in, like."

Kelp said, "Nah, we won't be here that long. Besides, next you'll want skis."

"No, I won't," Dortmunder said.

They'd driven up here this morning, the day after Fitzroy's call about the Indians getting caught in the cemetery, to see what they could do, even though everybody knew they couldn't do anything. The wrong body was being guarded, and the wrong body would be tested against Little Feather, who had about one chance in a billion to turn out to be related to Burwick Moody, so that was that, right?

Except apparently not. After his first call to Kelp, Guilderpost had decided he and Irwin would not go down to New York. Since then, he and Kelp had been E-mailing back and forth enough to get carpal tunnel syndrome, and what they'd finally decided on was a meet, a get-together, all six of them, back up in the North Country.

"Why can't those three come down here?" Dortmunder had complained, and Kelp had said, "Because Little Feather can't leave until the game is over."

"The game *is* over," Dortmunder had announced, but here they were anyway.

The Four Winds motel was also full. Guilderpost had made their reservations and managed to find all three of them rooms, but they weren't together. They didn't feel they should hold conversations on motel room phones, which went through the motel office, so every time one of them thought of something to say to another one, he had to get completely dressed for the wintry outdoors and tramp over through the wind and the snow to the other one's room, and then tramp back again. Dortmunder *really* missed the living room at the Tea Cosy.

What they were waiting for was Guilderpost and Irwin, who were supposedly off finding some safe, quiet, unnoticeable location for them all to meet, and a way to get in touch with Little Feather that wouldn't queer the deal even further than it already was, which wasn't possible, but they would try anyway. In the meantime, Dortmunder and Kelp and Tiny had settled more or less into their rooms, and visited one another anytime they had something to say, and otherwise watched the ski-toters plod around in the snowy wind. And what Dortmunder missed even more than the Tea Cosy was *home*.

A little before three, his phone rang in his room, where he was alone at the moment, looking out the window at the ski-haulers. He crossed to the phone and demanded, "Hello."

It was Guilderpost, who said, "Hello, John. Does your room face the front of the motel?"

Dortmunder frowned at the window. "I got wind with snow in it, and cars with ski racks, and a road, and way over there is a frozen lake. Everything is gray."

"That's the front," Guilderpost said. "If you don't mind, I'll have Andy come wait with you in your room, because his is at the back."

"Wait for what?"

"Little Feather. She's coming over, in the motor home."

"That sounds real secure," Dortmunder said.

"Apparently," Guilderpost said, "the situation has changed. We can all come out of hiding now."

"Because it's all over," Dortmunder said.

"I don't think that's why," Guilderpost said. "She should be here in fifteen minutes or so."

She was. The motor home made a big sweep around the parking lot, so everybody in the group would get a chance to see it, and then it parked way over in the far corner of the lot, away from the other vehicles and as close as possible to the frozen lake.

Dortmunder and Kelp put on a lot of outdoor clothes and headed out over the parking lot, the wind with the snow in it rushing at them from across the lake, trying to push them back into the room, and Dortmunder was almost ready to go along with that idea. But from the right, here came Guilderpost and Irwin, and from the left, here came Tiny, so Dortmunder, too, kept slogging forward.

The motor home was rocking slightly in the wind. It didn't like being out here in all this weather any more than Dortmunder did. As they all arrived, Little Feather opened the door and stood hugging her arms, saying, "Come on in. Come in, come in, it's *freezing* out there."

"You're right," Dortmunder said.

As they all climbed into the motor home, Little

Feather said, low voiced, to each of them, "We got a guest. Follow my lead."

A guest? They trooped into the living room, peeling off their coats, dropping them on the floor, and a woman stood there, tension in her face as though she'd agreed to sit in a poker game with a bunch of people she'd just met and only now remembered she didn't know how to play poker. She stared at each of them in turn but didn't say anything, nor did any of them. Dortmunder didn't know about the others, but the reason he kept quiet was, he figured that if anybody said anything to this woman right now, she was likely to explode all over the room, like Tiny's hand grenade.

Little Feather followed them into the living room, which was more crowded than ever, and with a bright smile she said, "This is Marjorie Dawson. My lawyer. My *first* lawyer."

Her lawyer? Dortmunder tried very hard not to stare at Little Feather, but what was going on here? She was showing her coconspirators, every last one of them, to a local *lawyer*?

This lawyer looked to be in her thirties, but just as Little Feather embraced a kind of flashy beauty, this woman obviously recoiled from any concept of beauty at all. Her black hair was pulled back into a tight bun, her face was pale and plain, and her clothing was all bulky and shapeless, sort of the indoor version of what the ski-carriers wore outside.

"Everybody sit," Little Feather said, "and I'll tell you what happened."

The way to make it possible for everybody to sit, this time around, was that the two women got the sofa, while

Tiny perched like a performing elephant on the chair Little Feather had used last time. Once they were all uncomfortable, Little Feather dealt out a round of her bright, perky, untrustworthy smile, and said, "When Judge Higbee said yesterday we should go right ahead with the DNA test, no more delays, I just didn't know what to do, so finally I told Marjorie the whole story."

Quickly, before anybody could say anything (like the wrong thing, for instance), she added, "I told her how I called my old friend Jack Hall in Nevada, and how he sent me to Mr. Guilderpost in New York, and he's the one who found me the DNA specialist lawyer. And I told her how you all are friends of Mr. Guilderpost, and how you took an interest in my case, and how you, John, just somehow *knew* that the tribes would try to cheat and switch bodies, so you all, just to help me out, switched the tombstones, never thinking for a second that those young Indians would get caught."

Well, that was a nice-enough story, as far as it went. It got Marjorie Dawson aboard, and explained the presence of this mob here, sort of, and Little Feather had tap-danced it all out from a standing start. Not bad.

The Dawson woman, now that nobody had killed her, had gotten her lawyer's confidence back, and she said, "I have to admit that your thinking was very imaginative, very good, uh . . . John, was it?"

"Yeah, John," Dortmunder admitted. "Thanks."

Little Feather said, "Oh, let me introduce everybody. That's Mr. Fitzroy Guilderpost, and that's Irwin Gabel, and that's Andy Kelly, and that's Tiny Bulcher, and that's John. John, I'm sorry, but I don't know your last name."

He hadn't expected that, suddenly out of left field and

all. "Diddums," he said, which was what he said every time he was abruptly asked his name. Somehow, that was the only name he could ever think of.

Marjorie Dawson frowned. "Diddums?"

"It's Welsh," he explained.

"Oh," she said. "Well, Mr. Diddums—"

"John."

"Very well. John. It was clever of you to guess what the tribes might do, but very dangerous to go into that cemetery and start moving gravestones around."

"It didn't work out too good," Dortmunder admitted.

Dawson said, "Can any of you think of any way to reverse the procedure, to make it possible for Little Feather to be tested against her actual ancestor?"

Dortmunder said, "When? The DNA thing's supposed to happen right now, isn't it?"

Beaming, Little Feather said, "I was so lucky I talked to Marjorie! She's on my side, John, she really is, and she did something right away to help."

Guilderpost, who'd been looking flabbergasted since they'd come in here, said, "Help? How can she possibly help?"

"By buying you some time," Dawson said.

Guilderpost said, "But, Ms. Dawson, *you* can't request a delay, that puts suspicion squarely where we don't want it. We have to *pretend* we want that test at once."

"I realize that," Dawson told him, acting like someone who didn't need advice from amateurs. "Here's what happened," she explained. "Mr. Welles, the tribes' main counsel, immediately appealed Judge Higbee's ruling in the state appeals court in Albany. It's a ridiculous argument, based on the idea that the grave robbers acted without the consent of the Tribal Council, it won't hold up for a second."

Kelp said, "Then what good does it do us?"

"As Little Feather's primary counsel," Dawson explained, "I received the notice of appeal in my office here in Plattsburgh. Mr. Schreck, though, would be the one to appear before the court in Albany. However, very stupidly, through an oversight, I neglected to pass the notice on to Mr. Schreck's office in New York, so when Mr. Welles makes his argument to the appeals court, there will be no one there to make the counterargument."

Tiny did his rumbling chuckle and said, "Nice, lady. Nice."

Guilderpost said, "When is this appeal to take place?"

"Right now," Dawson told him. "Mr. Schreck, of course, will find out about it tomorrow, and he'll insist on another hearing, but that's another delay. Today is Wednesday. I don't see how it can all be sorted out this week. I believe you now have at least until Monday to solve the problem in the cemetery."

Kelp said, "Aren't you gonna get in trouble for this?"

"Oh no," she said. "Everybody thinks I'm a dimwit anyway, I'll just be flustered and embarrassed, and apologize to everybody, and they'll all shrug their shoulders and get on with it."

Little Feather said, "So now we have five days to think of a solution. Surely *one* of you people can have an idea by then."

Irwin said, "What if we use a knockout gas and spray the guards, and we wear gas masks? Then we go in before they wake up and switch the stones back, and nobody knows the difference."

Kelp said, "One, they'll know they've been asleep."

Dortmunder said, "Two, the grave is open."

Guilderpost said, "Three, we don't have any knockout gas, and, Irwin, *you* don't know where to get any."

"It was just an idea," Irwin said.

Dortmunder said, "No, it wasn't. But we just might find one, somewhere, now that we got all this extra time. Thank you, Miss Dawson."

She blushed with pleasure. "Call me Marjorie," she said. "And I want you all to come over to my house for take-out pizza."

34

Benny Whitefish had never been so scared in his life. *Two* nights in the New York City jail at Rikers Island, a terrible place, where even the name sounds like some obscure punishment: The rikers are there, and if you aren't careful, you'll get riked.

Benny and Herbie and Geerome, the three little Indian boys, cowered together in the middle of a great horde of mean, tough men, hoping only not to attract attention to themselves. They couldn't sleep at night; they had to keep staring and gulping and feeling their hearts beat up in their throats while they listened to all the *whuffle*s and *snrr*s and *phoot*s of the great resting rabble all around them. And they could only catnap by day, when the herd shuffled and grunted and just kept *moving around*. Meals were impossible, though they did manage to drink coffee, which forced them into the lavatory a lot, all together. None of them wanted to go in there by himself.

A very junior partner of Otis Welles, the tribes' high-powered, high-priced New York lawyer, came to see them Tuesday afternoon, following their first night of terror, to assure them they would be spending Tuesday night at Rikers Island as well. His name was O. Osgood Osborne, and he could not have been more indifferent. He didn't see three terrorized country boys from the reservation in front of him, *way* out of their depth in the big city; all he saw was a case. You handle the case this way, and it comes out that way, and you charge for your time, which includes travel time. That was how he saw it, and he made no attempt to hide the fact.

Anyway, when Benny, through chattering teeth, begged this ally to explain at least what was going *on,* what was going to *happen,* he did oblige. They had committed, it seemed, several misdemeanors, plus a few class C felonies—which was the first Benny knew that felonies come in classes, like air travel—and they would eventually have to plea-bargain to community service or suspended sentence or possibly a brief incarceration (the three moaned in unison, which O.O.O. didn't notice, or anyway didn't react to), but for the moment, the first issue was to get on a judicial docket to get before a judge to have bail set. Once bail was set, Uncle Roger would pay it—the thought of Uncle Roger doubled Benny's terror—and they would be free to depart from Rikers Island and return to the reservation. That would be leaving the United States, of course, which was technically a violation of bail terms, but they wouldn't be leaving New York State, so that made it all right.

The other thing O.O.O. wanted to tell them, straight from Uncle Roger, was that this episode had been all their own idea; they'd done it because they were very religious and wanted to rescue Joseph Redcorn from nonsacred ground, and that's why they chose someone not from the Three Tribes to take Redcorn's place. DNA had had noth-

ing to do with it, and, in fact, they'd never even thought
about DNA and didn't know what it was.

Furthermore, *no one* had put them up to it, nor had
anyone discussed the idea with them, nor had they discussed it with anybody else. Was that clear? The three little Indians nodded their heads convulsively, and then
they were taken away from O.O.O., back to Satan's
Brigade, and another night of trembling wakefulness.

The next and last time they saw O.O.O. was Wednesday afternoon at two, in a courtroom in Queens in a building that had been put up by the federal government
during the McKinley administration, which was a long
time ago. Additions and alterations had been performed
on the building over the years, all as cheaply as possible,
to save the taxpayers money and leave a little something
for the contractor's uncle, the alderman. Electric wires
and steam-heat pipes snaked and sliced this way and that,
a sprinkler system spiderwebbed overhead, and air-
conditioning ducts had recently been jammed in somewhere. The result was that the courtroom looked like a
basement, although it was on the third floor.

In this courtroom, Benny and Herbie and Geerome
stood penitently beside O.O.O. and before a fat, mum-
bling black female judge who never looked up from the
writing she was doing on several documents. Benny
never did understand what she was saying or what was
happening, partly because of the judge and the place itself, but mostly because Uncle Roger was behind them,
seated on a spectator's bench amid a number of hook-
ers, pimps, grandparents, people with bandages on their
heads, and cops. Uncle Roger didn't look happy.

The ritual in front of the judge took five minutes, and

then more ritual in front of a cashier's cage took twenty
minutes more. The three little Indians signed their names
to things without knowing or caring what the things
might say, while O.O.O. told them with bored indiffer-
ence what to do but not why. Then he shook their hands,
startling them all, but that, too, was apparently part of the
ritual, because he did it without exactly making eye contact with anybody, and then he left, and in his place stood
Uncle Roger.

"Nice work," he said.

In the car, on the long drive north, Uncle Roger had more
to say. Benny got the brunt of it, because Uncle Roger
had made him sit in front, while Herbie and Geerome
perched like choirboys on the backseat. "A simple matter," Uncle Roger kept saying. "It's a simple matter. You
go down there and dig a hole and fill it in again. You
don't attract attention to yourself!"

"I'm sorry, Uncle Roger."

"Why the *hell* did you do it at ten o'clock, when
there's still *people* around? *Any* idiot knows you go there
at two, three in the morning."

Benny didn't feel he could answer that with the truth,
which was that he and Herbie and Geerome had agreed it
would be too frightening to go to a cemetery that late at
night, so he said, "That's just when we got there, I guess.
We just didn't think, I guess, Uncle Roger."

"Didn't think! *I'll* say you didn't think! Flashing a lot
of lights around, I suppose. Were you playing the goddamn *radio*?"

"*No,* sir!"

It went on like that, Uncle Roger mostly chewing them

out for being such meatheads, but occasionally wondering out loud what the hell they were going to do *now* about the Little Feather problem, with a *guard* on the *grave* and an *order* from the *judge* that their *stupidity* had made *possible*.

After a while, during a pause in the tirade, Benny found himself thinking about his own relationship with Little Feather, which he supposed was pretty much on the rocks now. He wondered briefly if somehow that relationship, the fact that he'd gotten to know Little Feather and she'd gotten to like him and trust him, if that could be used to help Uncle Roger with this problem, but then he decided the smart move was not to mention his relationship with Little Feather at all. It would be better, most likely, if Uncle Roger never knew about that.

Don't volunteer, Benny told himself, inching toward wisdom. Keep your mouth shut, he told himself, and except for the occasional "Yes, sir," "No, sir," "I'm sorry, Uncle Roger," that's what he did.

The one thing he knew for sure was, he never wanted to get riked again.

35

At the Four Winds motel, you didn't get a nice full stick-to-your-ribs breakfast from the cheerful likes of Gregory and Tom. At the Four Winds motel, you put on a lot of coats and boots and hats and gloves and went *outdoors* and down along the parking lot to the office, at the center of the place, and then indoors again and past the check-in counter to the café, a bland, pale place lit by fluorescents all day long.

Dortmunder found Kelp and Tiny there at 8:30 Thursday morning, seated at a booth for six, with cups of coffee in front of them. He'd had a wakeful night, trying to think, trying to figure out *what* to do about that mix-up at the cemetery, and had just started to get some decent shut-eye half an hour ago, when Guilderpost rang him up to say everybody was gathering in the café in thirty minutes, for breakfast before heading south. A shower had helped a little, particularly because the water temperature kept changing all the time, encouraging alertness, so now here he was.

"(grunt)," he said, as he slid in next to Kelp and across from Tiny.

"You look like shit, Dortmunder," Tiny said.

"Diddums," Dortmunder corrected. "It's Welsh. I've been trying to think of what we could do. You know, we got these five days, so why don't we do something?"

"Four days," Tiny said.

"How time flies," Kelp said. He, too, looked like shit, but Dortmunder noticed nobody was commenting on *that*. He grinned at Dortmunder and said, "Say, gang, we got four days, let's put on a show!"

Dortmunder didn't like to start the day with humor. He liked to start the day with silence, particularly when he hadn't had that much sleep the night before. So, avoiding Kelp's bright-eyed look, he gazed down at the paper place mat that doubled in here for a menu, and a hand put a cup of coffee on top of it. "Okay," he told the coffee. "What else do I want?"

"That's up to you, hon," said a whiskey voice just at ten o'clock, above his left ear.

He looked up, and she was what you'd expect from a waitress who calls strangers "hon" at 8:30 in the morning. "Cornflakes," he said. "O—"

Pointing her pencil, eraser end first for politeness, she said, "Little boxes on the serving table over there."

"Oh. Okay. Orange juice then."

Another eraser point: "Big jugs on the serving table over there."

"Oh. Okay," Dortmunder said, and frowned at her. In the nonpencil hand, she held her little order pad. He said, "The coffee's it? Then your part's done?"

"You want hash browns and eggs over, hon," she said, "I bring 'em to you."

"I don't want hash browns and eggs over."

"Waffles, side of sausage, I go get 'em."

"Don't want those, either."

Eraser point: "Serving table over there," she said, and turned away as Guilderpost and Irwin arrived.

Most of the group said good morning, and the waitress said, "More customers. I'll just get your coffee, fellas," she added, which was apparently the plural of *hon,* but before she could leave, Irwin said, "I know what I want. Waffles, side of sausage."

Guilderpost said, "And I would like hash browns and eggs over, please."

The point end of the pencil now hovered over the pad. "Over how, hon?"

"Easy."

The pencil flew over the pad. The waitress seemed pleased to have some actual customers, rather than a virtual customer like Dortmunder. "I'll just get your coffee, fellas," she promised again, and off she went.

Guilderpost slid in beside Tiny. Irwin would have taken the spot next to Dortmunder, putting Dortmunder in the middle, but Dortmunder said, "Hold on, let me up. I gotta go to the serving table."

The serving table, he could see, when he got there, was for wimps. Orange juice was about the most manly thing on display there, among the bowls of kiwi fruit and containers of yogurt and tiny packages of sugar substitute. He found his cornflakes in little weeny boxes and took two. He found little weeny glasses for his orange juice and filled two. He found a small pitcher of milk and took it along. Back at the table, he found Irwin in his former seat, drinking coffee, so he sat at the end and started opening boxes and drinking out of glasses.

The others were talking about the problem in vague

terms. Dortmunder was *thinking* about the problem while clawing his way into the cornflakes boxes, but the others were all talking about it.

"The problem with twenty-four-hour guards," Irwin said, "is that there's never any time when they're not there."

"I believe that's the point," Guilderpost told him.

"But," Kelp said, "there's nothing else we can do except get in there. We got to get in there, sometime between now and Monday, and get that tombstone back over Little Feather's grandpa, where it belongs."

Tiny said, "You got more than that, you know. You got your hole."

"That's right," Irwin said. "The wrong grave is open. Somehow, we'd also have to get in there and fill up the wrong grave and make it look right, and then dig up the right grave, and *then* switch the tombstones."

"Take an hour," Tiny decided. "All of us together. Maybe a little more."

"One hour out of twenty-four," Kelp said, "and every one of those twenty-four hours guarded."

Dortmunder sighed. Although this yakking all around him was something of a distraction, it was also helpful, because it was defining what the job was *not*. The job was not sneaking in past guards in order to neaten up. It was too late to neaten up. So, if that wasn't the job, what *was* the job?

Irwin said, "Who are these guards, anyway? Are they rent-a-cops?"

"New York City police," Tiny told him. "Two of them, in their blue suits, in a prowl car, parked next to the grave. I went and looked."

Kelp said, "So did I. I didn't know you went there, Tiny."

"Neither did they," Tiny said.

To Irwin, Kelp said, "I can tell you also, they got a generator and a floodlight, for after dark. You could play night baseball at that grave."

Irwin said, "Could we create a distraction? Some other crime happening, someplace nearby. If they're police, don't they have to respond?"

"They call it in," Kelp told him. "A hundred thousand *other* cops come, and roll your distraction up into a ball, and take it off to a cell."

"This is a serious situation," Guilderpost said. "If the comment weren't beneath me, I would say it was a grave situation."

"Oh, go ahead and say it, Fitzroy," Kelp advised him. "Let yourself go."

What if the job was from the other end? Was that possible? They were still talking, but Dortmunder wasn't listening, and so he didn't know or care who he interrupted when he said, "Fitzroy, this Internet thing of yours."

Everybody stopped yakking to look at Dortmunder, not knowing what he was on about. Guilderpost said, "Yes, John?"

"You told me once," Dortmunder reminded him, "you checked the Redcorn family out west with old phone books, you could do that on the Internet."

"Lists, John," Guilderpost told him. "If a topic is compiled, you can find it on the Internet."

"Can you find out," Dortmunder asked him, "if Burwick Moody had any descendants?"

The waitress brought waffles, sausage, hash browns,

and eggs over easy while the looks of awe and either understanding or confusion slowly spread across the faces at the table. She distributed the food, along with one or two *hons,* a couple *fellas,* and departed.

Dortmunder said to Guilderpost, "Well? Can you do it?"

Guilderpost said, "If Moody left issue, I don't see why I can't trace it."

Irwin, one of those whose expression had showed and still showed confusion, said, "John? What are you thinking here? Burwick Moody's descendants demand something? Stay away from our ancestor's grave?"

"Hair," Dortmunder said. This was suddenly absolutely clear in his mind. "We find a descendant with black hair, we figure out a way to get a little buncha that hair, we give it to Little Feather, and when they come to take hair for the test, she gives them Moody hair."

Kelp said, "John, I knew you'd do it. The Moody hair matches the Moody body, and Little Feather's in."

"If we can find an heir," Dortmunder said.

Irwin laughed. "This is wonderful," he said. "The absolute accuracy of DNA testing! First, we put in a wrong body to match our wrong heiress, then we get a *wrong* wrong body, and now we're gonna get the wrong wrong hair. One switched sample is gonna get compared with another switched sample. Absolutely *nothing* in the test is kosher."

Kelp said, "Irwin, that's the kind of test we like."

Guilderpost said, "*If* there's Moody issue."

"That's up to you to find out," Dortmunder told him.

"I know it is, I know it is," Guilderpost agreed. Looking at the food on his plate, brow furrowed, he said, "I can't eat. I have to know. I have to go to my room and start the search." Looking at Dortmunder, he said, "That was brilliant, John. Here, *you* have my breakfast, I can't wait. Good-bye." And he was up and out of there.

Dortmunder had by now drunk his coffee and both his orange juices and finished one little box of cornflakes. Tiny pushed Guilderpost's plate toward him and said, "You don't eat enough, Dibble."

"John," Dortmunder said. He looked at Guilderpost's hash browns and eggs over easy, untouched. "What the hell," he said, and dug in.

The waitress came by a minute later to give them all more coffee, whether they liked it or not, and she paused to frown at the plate in front of Dortmunder. "I could of brought you that, hon, if you'd asked me," she said.

Dortmunder pointed the business end of his fork at where Guilderpost had lately sat. "He got a sudden attack a the runs."

"Oh, that can be tough, hon," the waitress said. "Believe me, I know. You won't be seeing *him* for a while."

An hour and five minutes, actually, before Guilderpost returned. He seemed to be smiling and frowning at the same time, as though he wasn't sure what he thought about what he'd learned.

At this point, their breakfasts had all been cleared away, and the four had only coffee cups in front of them, from which they didn't dare take even one sip, or the waitress would come back and fill the cup again. So everybody looked up from all that cooling coffee to try to read Guilderpost's face, and Irwin said, "Well, Fitzroy? Did you find it?"

"It isn't," Guilderpost answered, "that I have good news and bad news. It's that my good news *is* my bad news. Yes, I found her. No, you'll never get close to her *or* her hair."

Dortmunder, brow furrowing, said, "Why not?"

"Because she's the Thurbush heiress," Guilderpost told him. "She lives at Thurstead."

Dortmunder and Kelp looked at each other. Kelp said, "I think Fitzroy thinks he just said something."

Guilderpost said, "You never—" and the waitress appeared beside him, solicitous, to say, "You feeling any better, hon?"

"In a way," he said, not understanding the question.

She said, "Would you like a glass of milk, hon?"

"As a matter of fact," he told her, "I would like another order of hash browns and eggs over easy. I find I'm famished."

She looked dazed. "Hash browns? And eggs over easy?"

"And coffee. Thank you, dear."

She nodded, forgot to call him hon, and left.

Guilderpost started his sentence again: "You never heard of Russell Thurbush."

"Never," Dortmunder agreed.

"Well, it happens I learned quite a bit about Russell Thurbush some years ago," Guilderpost told them, "when it was happily my opportunity to sell several paintings at gratifyingly high prices that might very well have *been* Thurbushes, for all anybody knew."

Dortmunder said, "He's a painter."

"*Was* a painter," Guilderpost corrected. "His dates are 1901 to 1972, and he was one of the principal figures of the Delaware River School, portrait and landscape painters who flourished between the world wars. He became very famous and very rich, traveled throughout Europe doing portraits of royalty, made a *lot* of money, invested wisely during the Depression, and by the time World War Two came along and the Delaware River School was looked on as old hat, he was rich enough to retire to Thurstead, the mansion he designed himself and built in the mountains of northern New Jersey, overlooking the Delaware River."

Dortmunder said, "And the Moody family has something to do with this guy."

"Russell Thurbush married Burwick Moody's only sister, Ellen," Guilderpost told him, and took a sheet of motel stationery out of his pocket. A hasty family tree was scribbled on it. "Burwick himself died without issue," he went on, "so the descendants have to be through Ellen, his sister."

Dortmunder said, "But she did have descendants."

"Oh, yes." Guilderpost studied his notes. "The family just keeps daughtering out," he said. "Ellen and Russell Thurbush had three daughters. Eileen became a nun. Reading between the lines, Eleanor was a lesbian. That leaves Emily Thurbush, who married Allistair Valentine in 1946, at the age of eighteen. She had two daughters. The older, Eloise, died at sixteen in an automobile accident. The younger, Elizabeth Valentine, married Walter Deigh in 1968 and produced one daughter, Viveca, in 1970. Elizabeth died in 1997, at the age of fifty, leaving Viveca the sole bearer of the Moody DNA. Viveca is also the sole inheritor of Thurstead, where she lives with her husband, Frank Quinlan, and their three daughters, Vanessa, Virginia, and Victoria."

Dortmunder said, "In New Jersey."

"That's right," Guilderpost said. "Overlooking the Delaware River, in a rustic, forested mountain area with majestic views Thurbush frequently memorialized in his paintings, or so it says on the Thurstead Web page."

Dortmunder said, "So what we do, we go to this place—"

"Thurstead," Irwin interpolated.

"Fitzroy knows the place I mean," Dortmunder said. Back to Guilderpost, he said, "We go to this place, like Irwin says, and we sneak in and grab this Virginia, Viveca, whichever one it is, grab her hairbrush, and gedadda there."

Guilderpost had been shaking his head through almost this entire sentence, which Dortmunder had been doing his best to ignore, but now Guilderpost added to the video with audio: "No."

"Why not?"

"Thurstead is on the National Register of Historic Places," Guilderpost told him. "It is operated by a nonprofit trust. The house and grounds are open to the public at certain prescribed hours. In addition to hundreds of thousands of dollars' worth of paintings, by Thurbush and others, the house also contains the jewels, the silver goblets, the rare golden stilettos, and all the other treasures Thurbush brought back with him from his travels around the world. The place is very tightly guarded, with a private security force and alarm system. The Quinlans live in a portion of the house, the rest devoted to the museum, the entire place under extremely tight protection. You'll never get *at* that hairbrush, John. I'm sorry."

"That's awful," Irwin said. "That's a goddamn shame. We were so close."

"Your idea was brilliant, John," Guilderpost said, "but it just won't work out."

Irwin said, "John? Why are you smiling?"

"At last," Dortmunder said. "A job for *me*."

36

There's no point driving the getaway car if nobody's going to get away. Stan Murch, a stocky, open-faced guy with carroty hair, had been sitting in the black Honda Accord, engine idling, just up the block from the bank, for maybe five minutes after his passengers had gone in there, when the three cop cars arrived. No sirens; they just arrived, two angling into the No Parking area in front of the bank, the third angling curbward just past the Accord's front bumper.

At the first flash of arriving white, Stan had switched off the engine, and as the men in blue piled out of their cars, putting on their hats and pulling out their gats, Stan pocketed his big ball of car keys and slowly eased out to the street. Not a good idea to make rapid movements around excited people with guns in their hands.

One cop from the nearest car gave Stan a quick suspicious glare over his shoulder, but Stan rested a forearm on the Honda's roof and looked very interested in what all the cops were doing, so he gave up that suspicion and trotted on with his pals. They all went on into the bank, and Stan walked around the corner.

He hadn't known any of those guys well, and he

doubted he'd be getting to know them any better, not for several years, anyway. But none of them would expect their chauffeur still to be there, outside the bank, amid the cop cars, when they were led out. All the surprises would be over by then.

This bank and this town were way the hell and gone out on Long Island, so those had been Suffolk County cops who would be taking a belated look at the recently stolen Accord, in which Stan had worn nice leather driving gloves, only partly because it was December. If the one cop who'd glared at him tried to reconstruct the suspect from memory later, all he'd come up with would be a bland and unremarkable pale face under a black knit cap; not even the red hair had been visible.

On the other hand, this was no longer a neighborhood and a town—and a county—in which Stan wanted to linger, so once he was out of sight of the bank, he walked briskly, looking for wheels.

A supermarket. In front of it and to one side of it, a blacktop parking lot. A bunch of cars clustered in the general area of the entrance, and another smaller clump of cars were gathered in the far corner around the side. Those would belong to the employees, ordered to leave the better parking spaces for the customers. None of them would pop out the supermarket door, arms full of grocery sacks, while Stan was choosing his next transportation, so that's where he went, deciding on the manager's car, a blue Chrysler Cirrus—much nicer and more expensive than the resold clunkers all around it—which his third key opened like a flip-top box.

If he had noticed when he switched on the engine that the damn car was almost out of gas, he'd have left it where it sat and taken one of the cashiers' cars instead. But he was busy looking for other things, like Suffolk County cops or the supermarket manager, so he was all the way to the on-ramp for the Long Island Expressway before the lit *Fuel* warning attracted his attention.

Well, hell. It was miles from here to Maximilian's Used Cars, where Stan had decided he would deliver the Cirrus, so that the day wouldn't be a total loss. But first he would have to put in a couple bucks' gas.

The next exit, three miles west of where he'd gotten on the LIE, had two huge gas stations handy on the service road, both with convenience stores and car washes attached, plus gigantic signs stuck high enough up in the air to interfere with planes landing at La Guardia. Both were doing very good business.

Stan pulled in behind a late-model black Mercedes-Benz, whose driver, a big bulky bald man in a creamy tan camel's hair coat, was just finishing at the pump. As Stan got out of the Cirrus behind the Mercedes, he could hear that guy juking those last few drops into the tank: *gluk-gluk-gluk.*

Stan stood at his pump and read all the options, the different grades of gasoline and the different payment methods, cash or credit, as the bald guy put his nozzle away and screwed on his tank cap. Stan chose cash, and so did the bald guy, who was walking over to the convenience store. Stan put the nozzle in the gas tank filler neck of the Cirrus, then walked over to the Mercedes, got behind the wheel, and drove off.

The Mercedes was a much better car. Also, the gas tank was full.

*   *   *

Maximilian's Used Cars existed in a kind of neverland that was not quite Brooklyn, not quite Queens, and certainly not Nassau County. A small pink stucco structure blushed at the rear of the lot, behind a display of clapped-out gas guzzlers horrible enough to make any self-respecting building blush. Triangular plastic pennants in gaudy colors strung around the perimeter of the lot did their best to distract attention from the heaps on offer, as did the sentiments scrawled on many of the windshields with whitewash: !!ultraspecial!! !!better than new!! !!a gift!!

Stan Murch drove past this automotive fool's paradise, turned at the side street just beyond it, and turned again into an anonymous weedy driveway. He pulled to a stop in a scraggly area of beaten ground flanked by the white clapboard walls of garages. Leaving the Benz, he stepped through an unlocked gate in a chain-link fence, followed a path through winter's dead leaves and weeds, and entered the pink building through its rear door.

He was now in a simple gray-paneled office, where Max himself stood like a snarling beast over the seated figure of his secretary, Harriet, a skinny, severe, hatchet-faced woman who typed away like a robot while Max barked words into her ear: "And I don't wanna hear from you birds again. Screw you, Maximilian Charfont."

Stan said, "Charfont?"

"Hi, Stan," Harriet said.

"Hi, Harriet."

"What's it to you?" Max wanted to know. "Read that back to me, Harriet."

Leaving the paper in the typewriter, Harriet read while Max, a bulky older man with heavy jowls and thin white hair, his white shirt under the black vest smudged from leaning against used cars, listened and paced. He no longer smoked his old cigars, but ethereal cigar smoke wafted behind him anyway as he paced.

Harriet read: " 'Better Business Bureau of Greater New York. Gentlemen: When you first made contact with me, I assumed it was your purpose to bring me better business. Now I see your hope is to drive me out of business entirely, by aligning yourselves with these malcontents and mouth-breathers who apparently can neither see the particular automobile they are in the process of purchasing nor read the standard contract relating to that purchase. The Royally Mounted A-One Collection Agency knows these people better than you do, and I suggest you check with them before leaving any of them alone in your office. As for me, the laws of the State of New York are good enough for me, and your Boy Scout pledges are not needed, thank you very much. I would prefer that our correspondence end at this point. Sincerely, Maximilian Charfont.' "

Max stopped his pacing. He said, "Didn't I have some swear words in there?"

"Yes, you did."

"Well, what happened to them?"

"This is a very old typewriter," Harriet pointed out. "From the Victorian era. It won't type dirty words. If you got me a nice new computer, I could type *Portnoy's Complaint* in here."

"You don't want a computer," Max informed her, "and I don't want no complaint." Rounding on Stan, he said, "And wadda *you* want?"

"Well, I'd like to call my Mom, if it's okay."

Max lowered an eyebrow. "Local call?"

"Sure, a local call," Stan said. "You expect my Mom to leave the five boroughs?"

"I don't expect anything," Max said. "That's it, you drop by, use the phone? You wanna flush the toilet, too, drop a few notes to absent loved ones?"

"No, just the phone call," Stan said. "And out back, there's a Mercedes you might like."

"Ah-huh," Max said.

"Gas tank's full," Stan told his departing back.

Harriet had replaced Max's letter with some Motor Vehicle form and was typing again, full tilt. She said, "Use the phone over there, okay?"

Meaning the room's second desk. "Sure," Stan said, and sat at desk number two and dialed his Mom's cell phone, which she now kept in her cab, while she was working, so they could keep in constant touch.

"Hello!"

"Don't shout, Mom."

"I gotta shout, I'm next to a cement mixer!"

"You want me to call you back?"

"What?"

"You want me to call you back?"

"No, that's okay," Mom said, at a much more reasonable volume. "He turned off. How you doing out on Long Island?"

"Well, that's what I'm—"

"Hold on, I got a fare, a fare!"

"Okay."

Mom must have put the phone on the front seat next to her, amid the newspapers and take-out crap that always accumulated in there. He could hear a male voice, but not what it said, and then he heard his Mom's distant voice say, "You got it," and a few seconds later, she was back, very pleased. "JFK," she said.

"Oh, yeah? Listen, that's good, because things worked out different."

"Long Island, you mean?"

"Well, it didn't happen," Stan said. "The rest of them all went off to discuss things with the officials, you know?"

"Uh-oh."

"So it turns out," Stan said, "I'll be home for dinner after all."

"No, you won't," Mom said.

"Why not?"

"John called, he's got something. He wants a meet at the O.J., six o'clock."

"Okay, then," Stan said as Max came back in, trailing the memory of cigar smoke. "Where I am instead, I'm at Maximilian's. When you're done at Kennedy, come over here, pick me up, and we'll go up to the O.J. together."

"Don't let that Maximilian cheat you, Stan."

"What an idea," Stan said, and hung up, and said, "Well, Max? Is that attractive?"

"But what does it attract?" Max wanted to know. "Truthfully, Stanley, how hot is that vehicle?"

"Well," Stan said, "if it happened you wanted to fry an egg . . ."

"That's what I thought. So that means," Max explained, "a lotta work in the shop, changing parts, changing numbers on things, getting paperwork that doesn't turn into dust in your hand. This is all expensive, Stanley, it's time-consuming, the boys in the shop, it's gonna take a lot of time away from their regular work, I'm not sure it's even worth my while to get into it. But I know you, I like you, and I know you're anxious to get movin outta here—"

"As a matter of fact, no," Stan told him. "My Mom's got a fare to Kennedy, and then she's coming here to pick me up. So we got all the time in the world to discuss this. Isn't that nice?"

"My lucky day," Max said.

The phone rang, and Harriet answered: "Maximilian's Used Cars, Miss Caroline speaking. Oh, I'm sorry, no, Mr. Maximilian is no longer with us, he retired to Minsk. Yes, I'll pass that along. You, too." Hanging up, she returned to her machine-gun typing. "The one with the machete," she said.

37

When Dortmunder walked into the O.J. Bar & Grill on Amsterdam Avenue at four minutes before six that evening, Rollo, the bulky, balding bartender, was painting MERY XM on the extremely dusty mirror over the back bar, using some kind of white foam from a spray can, possibly shaving cream, while the regulars, clustered at one end of the bar, were discussing the names of Santa's reindeer. "I know it starts," the first regular said, " 'Now, Flasher, now, Lancer, now—' "

"Now, now, wait a second," the second regular said. "One of those is wrong."

Dortmunder walked over to stand at the bar, somewhat to the right of the regulars and directly behind Rollo, whose tongue was stuck slightly out of the left corner of his mouth as, with deep concentration, he painted downward a left-trending diagonal next to *M*.

"Oh yeah?" said the first regular. "Which one?"

"I think Flasher," said the second regular.

A third regular joined in at that point, saying, "Naw, Lancer."

Rollo started the second leg of the next letter.

"So what are you telling me?" demanded the first regular. "They're *both* wrong?"

A fourth regular, who had been communing with the spheres of the universe, or maybe with the bottles on the back bar, inhaled, apparently for the first time in several days, and said, "Rupert."

All the regulars looked at him. Rollo started the horizontal.

"Rupert *what*?" demanded the second regular.

"Rupert Reindeer," the fourth regular told him.

The third regular, in total disdain, said, "*Wait* a minute. You mean the one with the red nose?"

"Yeah!"

"*That's* not a reindeer!" the third regular informed him.

"Oh yeah?" Transition complete, the fourth regular was at this point fully in the here and now. "Then why do they call him Rupert Reindeer?"

"He's not one of *these* reindeer," the first regular explained.

"He's not even Rupert," the third regular said. "He's Rodney. Rodney, the red-nosed—"

"They won't let him play," the second regular said, "unless it's foggy."

"And *you*," the third regular said, pointing a definitive finger at the fourth regular, "are foggy."

"Hey!" the fourth regular said. "How'm I supposed to take that?"

Rollo added an extremely accomplished apostrophe just to the right of XMA, then paused to contemplate that next bare space.

"Any way you want," the third regular said.

The fourth regular frowned, thinking that over.

Rollo shook his head, then turned slightly to glance toward Dortmunder. "How you doin," he said.

"Fine," Dortmunder assured him.

Rollo shook the spray can in the direction of the space next to XMA'. "It's all curves from now on," he said.

"You did good with the *R,*" Dortmunder told him.

Rollo was cheered by that. "You think so? It's in the wrist, I believe."

"You're probably right," Dortmunder said.

"I think one of them is Dopey," the second regular said.

"Yeah," the third regular said, "and I know which one, too."

The first regular said, "I *think* the next two are Masher and Nixon."

"*Nix*on!" snorted the third regular. "He wasn't even alive yet."

"Well, it's Masher and somebody."

"Donner," said the second regular. "I know Donner goes in there somewhere."

"No, no, no," said the first regular. "Donner's that place where they ate the people."

Everybody was interested in that. "Who ate the people?" asked the fourth regular, who had decided not to make a federal case out of being called foggy, or whatever it was.

"Some other people," the first regular explained. "They got stuck in the snow, on a bus."

"Now wait a minute," the third regular said. "It wasn't a bus. I know what you're talkin about, it was a long time ago, it was one of those wagons, Saratoga wagons."

"It wasn't Saratoga," the second regular said. "Maybe you mean station wagon."

As Rollo started the slow circuitous path of the final letter on the mirror, the first regular said, "*Station* wagon! If it's too long ago for a bus, whada they doin in a station wagon?"

"I dunno, Mac," the second regular said, "it's your story."

Rollo finished a somewhat recognizable *S,* and the first regular called over, "Hey, Rollo, you got that misspelled there!"

Rollo looked at the regular, then at his handiwork. MERY XMA'S. He didn't seem particularly worried. "Oh yeah?" he said.

"You gotta spell merry," the first regular told him, "with an *a.*"

The third regular said, "What are you, nuts? When you spell it with an *a,* that's what you call it when you get married."

"Only if that's her name," the fourth regular said, and received massive frowns of bewilderment in response.

Rollo at last put down the spray can and faced Dortmunder. "It's the thought that counts," he said.

"You're right about that."

"You'll be wanting the back room."

"Sure. We're gonna be the other bourbon, the vodka and red wine, the beer and salt, and the beer and salt's Mom. I think she's a beer, too."

"She is," Rollo agreed. A professional to his fingertips, he identified his customers exclusively by their choice of beverage. "I'll give you the other bourbon's glass," he said, "and send everybody back when they get here. You're the first."

"I'm kind of the host," Dortmunder said.

As Rollo went off to get glasses and ice and a bottle of Amsterdam Liquor Store Bourbon—Our Own Brand, as it said on the label, the regulars spent some time trying to decide if it was Mary that was a grand old name or Ulysses S. Grant that was a grand old name. Ulysses S. Grant certainly *sounded* grander. Probably older, too.

Rollo brought over a round enameled metal Rheingold Beer tray containing two plain water glasses, a shallow ironstone bowl with ice cubes in it, and the alleged bourbon, which, beyond the brave statement of its label, was a muddy brown liquid that looked as if it might have been scooped from a river somewhere in Azerbaijan. "See me on the way out," he advised.

"Sure," Dortmunder said. "Merry exmas," he added, and carried the tray past the regulars, most of whom were pretty sure at this point that Nerdy was *not* one of the original Seven Dwarfs. Dortmunder went on down beyond the end of the bar and down the hall past doors decorated with black metal dog silhouettes labeled POINTERS and SETTERS and past the phone booth, where a new string now dangled from the quarter slot, and on through the green door at the very back, into a small square room with a concrete floor. All the walls were completely covered from floor to ceiling by beer and liquor cases, leaving a minimal space in the middle for a battered old round table with a stained felt top that had once been pool-table green but now looked as though some Amsterdam Liquor Store bourbon had been poured all over it a long time ago and let dry. This table was surrounded by half a dozen armless wooden chairs.

This room had been dark when Dortmunder opened the door, but when he hit the switch beside the door, it all sprang to life, illuminated by one bare bulb under a round tin reflector hanging low over the table on a long black wire. Dortmunder walked all around the table to sit in the chair that faced the door; the first arrival always did that. Setting the tray on the table, near his right hand, he shrugged out of his coat and let it drape behind him on the chair. Then he put two ice cubes into one of the glasses, poured muddy liquid on top, took a sip, and leaned back to gaze around the room in contentment. Small, cramped, windowless; what a nice place to be.

Tiny Bulcher appeared in the doorway. Barely visible in his left fist was a tall glass containing what looked like, but was not, cherry soda. He paused to cock his head and say, "Dortmunder. What's that on your face?"

With his free hand, Dortmunder brushed at his face. "What, I got a smutch?"

"No," Tiny said, coming in, moving around the table to put his glass at the place to Dortmunder's left, "it almost looked like a smile." He was wearing his World War I infantry coat again, which he dropped on the floor behind him, then sat down. "So what's," he said, picking up his glass, "with the giggling all at once? It ain't like you."

"Well, it coulda been I was thinking," Dortmunder said, "that at last I know what I'm doing. Or maybe it's just I'm somewhere at last that at least I *should* know what I'm doing because at least it's the right place. Or maybe it's just that Fitzroy and Irwin aren't gonna be here."

"So who is," Tiny asked, "besides us?"

"Kelp, and Stan Murch, and I think Murch's Mom."

Tiny looked around at the table and the chairs. "You're early," he said, "which is right, and I'm on time."

"So am I," Kelp said, coming in, waving a thick manila envelope. "I brought the stuff," he said. "Copies for all of us." He took the chair to Dortmunder's right, putting the envelope down there, shucking his coat, seating himself, reaching for the other glass on the tray.

"Which makes Murch late," Tiny said. Tiny was known to disapprove of people who weren't punctual.

"I *wouldn't* be," said a voice in the hall, approaching, "if we'd come the way *I* wanted to come." Stan Murch appeared, walking briskly. "But no," he said. "Whada they say? A boy should listen to his mother? Wrong again!"

"I couldn't know there was gonna be an *accident* up ahead of us," Murch's Mom said, coming in behind her son. Both carried glasses of beer, and Murch also carried a salt shaker. Being a driver, he limited his alcohol intake to the point where his beer tended to go flat before he was finished with it, so from time to time he'd shake a little salt into it to bring the head right back up again.

"The accident wasn't the point," Murch said as he put his glass and shaker down beside Kelp. "Atlantic Avenue is the point," he said.

"Hello, all," Murch's Mom said, electing to come over and sit beside Tiny instead of next to her son.

"Hello," all said.

"Every known religion," Murch went on, shucking out of his coat, "has some big-deal event or celebration or thing in December, and every known ethnic, too, and for every known religion and every known ethnic, there's three other blocks of stores on Atlantic Avenue in Brooklyn that has everything especially for them, and in December on Atlantic Avenue in Brooklyn, every known religion and every known ethnic is *shopping,* and not one in a million of those people, that came here from thousands of places that you don't even *know* about, ever learned how to drive."

Tiny said gently to Murch's Mom, "Would you wanna close the door there, okay?"

"Sure," Murch's Mom said. "It was the accident," she confided, and went over to shut the door.

Taking his seat, Murch said, "To drive on Atlantic Avenue in Brooklyn in December is to make a serious statement that you don't really wanna *go* anywhere."

Tiny patted the air in Murch's direction with one big palm. "Okay, Stan, thank you," he said. "You weren't that late."

"Fine," Murch said. "I was an obedient son, that's what you get."

They were all seated now as though the door were the television set they were going to watch. The chairs facing away from the door got very little use, all in all.

Dortmunder said, "Okay, what we got *here,* we got an ongoing situation that Murch and Murch's Mom should be brought up-to-date on, so what it comes down to, for the benefit of the recent arrivals, we got a place to go into that's loaded with stuff, out in the boonies, and while we're there, we gotta get some hair from a hairbrush. Or a comb."

Murch and his Mom continued to look at Dortmunder, who considered himself finished. Murch said, "That's it? We're up-to-date now?"

"I don't feel," Murch's Mom said, "like I'm fully aboard here, somehow. How about you, Stanley?"

Murch, who'd forgotten about the horrors of Atlantic Avenue, shook his head and said, "No, Mom, I gotta admit. Aboard? No."

Dortmunder sighed. "We gotta go through all this DNA and the Indians and all this?"

"I think so," Murch's Mom said.

"I'm feeling kind of at a loss without it," Murch said.

Kelp said, "John, let me take a whack at it."

"It's all yours," Dortmunder said.

Kelp said, "John and Tiny and me got involved with some people doing an Anastasia, and we need a right DNA sample, and it's gonna be on a comb in a place with hundreds of thousands of dollars of valuable stuff, so while we're there, anyway, why don't we take it all."

"Sounds good," Murch said.

"I'm glad you called," his Mom said.

Dortmunder said, "That's it? Now you're satisfied?"

"Well, when it's explained," Murch's Mom said.

Kelp said, "Okay, what I got here is the stuff from the Thurstead Web site." Pulling a stack of papers from his envelope, he said, "All in color, and it's free. What we got here is a whole brand-new way to case a joint." Dealing out stapled-together pages, he said, "We can all take a look at this place."

The top page was a very nice color photograph of an imposing and vaguely Oriental building, made of stone blocks, different sizes and different colors, so that one wall was a kind of rusty rosy red, while the other wall you could see in this picture was more of a faded pea-soup green. The photo had been taken in the summer, and muted purple-and-gold awnings angled out over all the windows. The windows themselves were different sizes and shapes, and some of them had panes of colored glass. The roof was molasses-colored shingles, and the three onion domes were different shades of dark blue. It all came together, somehow, probably because all the colors were muted and calm.

"Some snazzy place," Murch's Mom decided.

Murch said, "I don't remember ever driving past this place. Where is it?"

"Jersey," Kelp told him. "Way out by the Delaware Water Gap. In fact, if you look at what it says under the picture, it's inside the national park there, the Delaware Water Gap National Recreation Area."

Murch said, "So what've you got there, park rangers?"

"No," Kelp said, "they were there before the park went in, so they're like grandfathered. Read about it. On page two is very nice."

They all read about it, how Russell Thurbush, the famous painter, had designed and built the house high on a hilltop overlooking the Delaware River, how he'd filled it with valuable art and stuff he brought back from his worldwide travels, how it was on the National Register of Historic Places and was maintained by a nonprofit private foundation run by Thurbush's great-granddaughter and her husband, Viveca and Frank Quinlan, who live on the property. Most of the downstairs was open to the public, with guided tours, from April until November.

"So it's shut now," Murch's Mom said.

"Another reason we case it on the Web," Kelp pointed out.

Page two, as Kelp had promised, was very nice. Among the paragraphs about the art and the history and

the architectural innovations and all the rest of it was a
paragraph concerning security:

> The Thurstead Foundation maintains its own pri-
> vate security arrangements, with support available
> from the New Jersey State Police. Motion-activated
> floodlights encircle the house. In addition, security
> cameras are mounted in trees about the property,
> monitored at all times in the security office in the
> barn, just behind the visitor center.

"How do you like that?" Kelp said. "They tell us their
security."

Tiny said, "They don't say what's inside the house."

"That's on page three."

Page two had been almost completely print, with only
one small photo of a hookah at center left, part of Russell
Thurbush's worldwide swag, but page three was half-
devoted to a photo of a room so crammed with *art,* paintings in big frames all over the walls, fur rugs all over the
floors, whatnots and knickknacks all over every flat surface, ornate furniture and lamps like hussars, that it was a
true relief for the eye to move on down to the words, in
which the key sentences were: "Although the private
quarters have been modernized, the areas open to the public have been left exactly as Russell Thurbush knew them.
Modern heat is delivered through the original grates, and
even electricity has not been added to these spaces."

Dortmunder said, "All their security is outside."

"But it's pretty good," Murch said. "Floodlights with
motion sensors, observation cameras in the trees. Maybe

we oughta do this thing in April, when they're open, when we can go look it over."

"Well, that's the problem," Dortmunder said. "Normally, that's the way I'd like to do it, visit once or twice, maybe take some of our own pictures, see what's what on the scene. The only reason I'm going along with Andy here on this World Wide Web thing is, we got kind of a deadline."

Murch's Mom said, "Before April, I bet."

"Well, yeah," Dortmunder agreed. "Today is Friday, and we gotta get that hair sample back upstate by Monday."

Murch said, "Whoops. You wanna plan it, and organize it, and do it, all this *weekend*?"

"No, I don't want to do that," Dortmunder said, "but that's what we got."

"Then," Murch said, "I don't know we got much."

"Well, it could be that luck is with us," Dortmunder told him. Then he stopped and looked around at everybody and said, "I can't believe what I just heard me say."

Kelp said, "I'm a little taken aback myself, John."

"And yet, and yet," Dortmunder said, "it might even be the truth. See, the thing is, I looked at the weather report, the old-fashioned way, on the television, and comin outta Pennsylvania on Sunday is supposed to be our first winter storm of the season. A nice big one."

Murch said, "This is the luck? We've also got a storm?"

"That's right," Dortmunder told him. "You know what happens when a big snowstorm goes through? In a rural part of the world? The electricity goes out. And nobody thinks a thing about it."

38

Everything that happens with weather in the greater New York City area has already happened in Cleveland two days before, so on Saturday morning, when Kelp and Murch flew from La Guardia Airport in New York to Hopkins Airport in Cleveland, they sailed over the storm, which was then ruffling feathers in Pittsburgh, and landed in an exhausted city that no longer had any present use for the vehicle they intended to borrow.

In fact, the municipal parking lot where they went looking for what they needed was deserted. City workers had just finished a twenty-seven-hour war against the snowstorm, and they were now all home in bed, with their beepers on the bedside table. The locks on the gate in the chain-link fence that surrounded the parking lot did not hold Kelp's and Murch's attention for long, and then off they went, down the rows of garbage trucks, snow-plows, morgue vans, and cherry pickers, till they found just the vehicle they'd had in mind.

It was big, with big tires. It was red and had many sparkly yellow and white and red lights mounted all over it. It had begun life as an ordinary dump truck, but it had been fitted to a specific use: sand spreader. On the front of it was a big yellow V-shaped snowplow blade, and inside the open bed was a slanting metal floor with runnels that led back to the spigots where salt or sand would be ejected onto the roadway behind the truck, with controls operated by the driver. The rear wall of the truck body was mostly a pair of metal doors that would swing open outward from the center to give maintenance access to the spigots and other equipment inside.

The spreader's most recent operator had been too tired to top up the gas tank when he'd brought the machine back from its municipal duty, so that was another lock they had to go through, on the gas pump, before the computer inside it would give them any fuel. Then they took time out for a quick lunch, and were on the road by one.

It's just about four hundred miles from Cleveland to Port Jervis, New York, where New York and New Jersey and Pennsylvania meet, just a little north of the Delaware Water Gap. On an ordinary day, in an ordinary car, traveling Interstate 80, they'd have made it in under six hours, but this was not an ordinary car, and straight ahead of them was something that would keep this from being at all an ordinary day. The storm they'd flown over, they would now drive through, which would slow them down a bit. On the other hand, you couldn't ask for better wheels than this, if what you planned to do was drive through a snowstorm.

They caught up with it in western Pennsylvania, just as they were crossing the Allegheny River. The sky in Ohio, after the storm, had been pale, almost ivory, with a small cold-looking sun far, far away, its weak beams glaring white from all this fresh snow round and about, but once past Youngstown and into Pennsylvania, the sun faded to nothing, the sky was slate, and the fresh snow in the mountains was deeper, duller-looking, as though it hadn't settled yet from its recent journey. And then, just east of the Allegheny, the sky turned darker; they could see wind whipping tree branches, and snow began to swirl in the air in front of them.

Half an hour later, they were in the storm, and Murch had turned on every running light the truck possessed. All about them, cars were sliding, trucks were stopped beside the highway, visibility was not much farther than the end of your nose, snow was everywhere, on the ground, in the air, in the sky above, and they were creeping along at thirty, tops. "I think," Murch said, "it's time to figure out how to lower this plow."

39

The girls, of course, thought it was an absolute waste to have a big winter storm on the weekend, when school was closed anyway. "Don't be silly," Viveca told them. "You'll have a great time out on the slope tomorrow, you know you will."

"We could have just as fine a time on a Tuesday," Victoria replied.

There was never any point arguing with the girls. "I'm busy," Viveca told them, which was perfectly true. "Go on down to the barn, the three of you, and get out all of our winter things. The toboggan, both sleds, the snowshoes. Put them all in the visitor center. Who's on duty down there today?"

"Matt," Vanessa said, and all three girls giggled. They all had a crush on Matt, whom they considered the only member of the security staff who could be thought of as a serious hunk.

"Well, ask Matt to help," Viveca said. "And don't tease him."

They all giggled again, then raced out of the kitchen, and Viveca turned back to her list. Here it was midafternoon on a Saturday, a storm was coming, they were actually quite isolated here on this mountain, and, as usual, Viveca had waited till the last minute to see which provisions might be running low. Frank always used to take care of details like that, damn him.

Viveca and Mrs. Bunnion, the housekeeper, sat across from each other at the kitchen table. Mrs. Bunnion would drive down to Port Jervis to do the shopping, but she quite sensibly wanted it done and over with before dark, and also before the onset of the storm, so there was a certain amount of hurry in this list compiling. "Milk," Viveca said.

"That we have," Mrs. Bunnion answered. "You don't want too much of the perishables, in case the electric goes out."

"The refrigerator's on the backup generator," Viveca pointed out, "but I suppose you're right, that we shouldn't bring in too much. Cereal, though, I know we'll need more of that. And buy some nice soup for lunch tomorrow."

"Yes'm."

They were comfortable together, employer and employee, though not quite as comfortable as they'd been before Frank left. Viveca knew Mrs. Bunnion considered her a bit scatterbrained, which was of more moment now that there wasn't a man around to hold the reins, and she supposed Mrs. Bunnion was right, but there really was an awful lot to do here, even in winter, when the house was closed to the public. And particularly with a storm coming.

Thurstead was the only home Viveca had ever known, born here as Viveca Deigh, daughter of Walter and Elizabeth Deigh, granddaughter of Emily and Allistair Valentine, and great-granddaughter of Russell Thurbush, who had built this magnificent pile and then left his descendants the endless task of caring for it.

In a way, it was an easy life. The nonprofit corporation maintained the place and provided the family with an income, in addition to the roof over their heads. In season, volunteers worked as cashiers and docents, so the family never actually had to look at any of the thousands of visitors who trooped through the downstairs every year. Also, Russell Thurbush's reputation meant the family was automatically welcomed at the uppermost social levels in both Philadelphia and New York; Viveca could attend a museum opening a week, if she cared to.

But in another way, as Frank had increasingly felt, Thurstead was a kind of soft prison, an indentured servitude. Frank had his M.B.A., but there was little enough business to conduct, and that was all done by the Thurstead Foundation. The family could never go very far from the house for very long, but, on the other hand, they weren't free to alter it or add to it or do any of the things normal families did with normal houses. No wonder Frank wanted his own place, in New York City, and his own job, with Standard Chemicals, and his own life, which Viveca believed he was sharing at the moment with a woman named Rachel.

This so-called trial separation was well into its second year now, with many visits all year long from Frank and summertime excursions for the girls to Frank's apartment in New York, all the new little systems and rituals in place. Viveca knew that Frank was right when he said he'd left Thurstead more than he'd left her, but, damn it, it sure *felt* as though he'd left her.

"There," she said, pushing the list across the table to Mrs. Bunnion. "I can't think of anything else, can you?"

"No, we'll be fine," Mrs. Bunnion said, then rose and carried the list with her out of the room.

We'll be fine. Viveca got up from the table, feeling vague and a little uncertain, probably because of the coming storm. She wandered through their rooms to the parlor, with its large windows overlooking the view that had attracted Russell Thurbush in the first place. The four hundred acres owned by the Thurstead Foundation covered this entire eastern slope of the mountain, plus land around to the south. From here, the view was southeastward over a roughly tumbling downslope falling away to the deep gorge of the river, and then the rocky face of Pennsylvania on the other side.

Mrs. Bunnion's red Ford Explorer appeared and disappeared, heading down the twisty road to the highway far below.

One of the windows in this room consisted of a large pane of pale yellow glass; through it, even a day like today was sunny. Gazing through that window, the red of the Explorer brighter, the black of the trees darker, Viveca sighed. We'll be all right. We'll be all right because nothing ever happens. And which of her daughters, she wondered, would wind up sentenced to this soft life?

She felt like a princess in a fairy tale, locked in a tower, which for a semi-single mother of three was a little late in the day. She'd already been rescued by her prince, who was now in New York City with a woman named Rachel.

Above Pennsylvania, far away, she could see the storm clouds coming.

40

The storm reached Port Jervis at eight, but Kelp and Murch did not. Dortmunder and Tiny and Murch's Mom had taken rooms at a motel south of town, which, the clerk had assured them, would be full of skiers once this weekend's storm passed through. "We'll be outta here by then," Dortmunder said.

They'd eaten an early dinner in a nearby diner, partly to be ready when Kelp and Murch arrived, but mostly because Murch's Mom "got peckish" if she didn't have an early dinner, and nobody wanted Murch's Mom peckish. Then, a little before eight, just ahead of the storm, they all gathered in Dortmunder's room, which he had paid for with a credit card named Livingston Van Peek, and waited for the other two and the truck to arrive.

And waited. The motel had cable, so at least they didn't have to watch network television, but, on the other hand, there wasn't very much out there on the airwaves that this particular trio could all agree on. So they sat around and watched things none of them particularly cared about, and from time to time whoever hated the current program the worst would get up and go over to look out the window and say, "Sure is snowing," or "Still snowing," or "Looka that snow."

There was no deadline problem here; it was merely that the wait was boring. Just so Kelp and Murch showed up before dawn, at least an hour before dawn, the plan could still work the same as ever.

They were definitely going to cut Thurstead's electricity and phone. They had no doubt a place like that would have a backup generator, but backup generators can't carry the entire normal load of even an ordinary house, so what would they use their limited supply of electricity for? The refrigerator, the water pump in the well, the furnace igniter, a few lights. The exterior motion sensors in the trees might or might not be included, probably not, but even if they were, it didn't matter. The plan included the idea that they'd be eyeballed from the house. But the electricity and phone being off would mean that the security office would certainly be shut down, and all the people present at Thurstead would be compressed into a smaller than usual space. That was all Dortmunder and the others needed, or at least that was the idea.

At eleven, they gave up on the wonders of worldwide broadcasting to watch the local news instead, which was all about the storm that continued to rage outside. There were dramatic pictures of trees lying on automobiles, intrepid reporters standing in wind-whipped snow to report to *you*, snowplows chugging along, ambulances with many flashing red lights, and some cheerful clown with a ski report.

Eleven-forty-two, according to the clock screwed to the table beside the bed, when the phone rang. Dortmunder answered, and Kelp's voice said, "I gotta admit, it was kind of fun."

"Slowed you down a little."

"You should see the other guys."

"You all set now?"

"Sure. When you go out, go way down to the end, away from the office here. I'll head back down there now."

"Right."

The idea was, Kelp and Murch couldn't exactly check in at this motel because they didn't have a vehicle they could mention on the register card, and if they didn't have a vehicle, how did they get here? So Kelp had merely walked into the lobby to use the house phone, and now they'd all meet outside. And later, when they were done, Kelp would illegally share Dortmunder's room and Murch would illegally share Tiny's room.

Kelp said, "Bring along the WD-40, we got a squeaky door in the back."

"Right."

"And don't forget the tin snips."

For cutting the electric and phone wires, of course. Dortmunder said, "Don't need them."

"But we gotta cut off the, *you* know."

"It was on the news half an hour ago," Dortmunder told him. "That part of the country down there, they're already out, electric and phone both. The storm did the job for us."

41

The holiday special the girls wanted to watch on television this evening, *The New Adventures of the Virgin Mary and the Seven Dwarfs at the North Pole*, started at eight, but had barely gotten the dwarfs out of F.A.O. Schwarz inside a shiny new Beetle—bright red—when the power went. "Oh hell," Viveca said. Now the girls would have to be entertained.

Around them in the fresh darkness, the house purred almost as much as normal, because the backup generator automatically kicked in when the power went out, but the television set was not part of that grid, which had been installed years ago, at a time when the house was not full of young children. Today, the decision might have been different; too bad.

Matt, the hunk from security, had gone home at six, so it was Hughie, a gruff, stout, older man, a former New York City policeman who preferred to keep himself to himself, who came from the now-dark barn, grumpily following his flashlight beam. "Phone's out, too," he announced when he came tromping up the stairs.

Viveca had already lit the Coleman lantern and was carrying it by its looped handle as she stood at the top of the stairs, watching Hughie come up. At this point, there was no other light in the house, though they did have candles and flashlights, as needed. "I'm sure they'll plow us out in the morning," she said as he came in and took off his pea jacket to hang it on one of the wooden pegs on the kitchen wall near the door. "Do you know Uno?"

He gave her an exasperated look; but then, all of Hughie's looks were exasperated. He said, "Do I know I know?"

"It's a game," Viveca told him. "It's a lot of fun, really."

"We play it whenever the electricity goes out," Virginia explained. "It keeps us entertained."

"You don't have to play if you don't want to," Viveca threatened.

Hughie looked alert, waiting to be given the same option, but not a chance. The more the merrier with Uno, and Hughie was the closest thing they had at this point to a man around the house, so this was not a time when he could be permitted to keep himself to himself. This was a time for Hughie to play Uno.

They all trooped into the living room, Viveca leading the way with the Coleman lantern, Virginia and Vanessa and Victoria following, Hughie grumpily bringing up the rear, and while Viveca hung the lantern from the hook at the bottom of the chandelier that they always used in these circumstances, the girls took the whatnots off the side table and brought it out to center it under the light. Hughie, catching on, helped bring over the chairs, while Viveca got the Uno deck from the drawer in the end table beside the sofa. Then they all sat down, explained the rules of the game to Hughie three times, and began.

The first hour, the game was, in fact, a lot of fun for all concerned. Hughie showed an unexpected competitive streak, and his grumpiness turned out to be a kind of bearish good nature. Not for the first time, Viveca was actually getting to know a member of the security staff while playing Uno during a blackout.

The second hour dragged a little, though nobody would yet admit it. Outside the large windows, the storm whipped around in darkness, lashing the mountainside. It was pitch-black out there, so nothing could be seen, but the storm could be heard as the wind swooped past the house and occasionally sleet rattled against the windows. Inside, they were warm and dry. When one of them had to go to the bathroom, they had water. To occupy themselves, they had Uno. And later on, for Hughie, there would be the guest room.

The third hour, the girls began to yawn, and Hughie had started to show a certain absence of mind that might suggest he'd now plumbed the depths of the complexities of Uno and was ready to go on to some other challenge, but nobody wanted to go to bed, and there was nothing else to do, really, but sit in a circle under this one light. If they were going to sit here anyway, they might as well play Uno.

At midnight, Viveca said, "That's it, now. Time to go to bed."

"Just one more round," Vanessa said, as one of them always did.

"Hughie will be the last dealer," Virginia announced.

"*That's* good," Victoria said.

Once again, they'd outnumbered her. "Just the one round," Viveca said, as though it were her idea.

"Good," Hughie said.

They were midway through that last round when Victoria exclaimed, "*Look* at all those lights!"

Everyone turned toward the windows, and now all at once there was something to see out there. It was some kind of vehicle, absolutely festooned with bright lights in red and white and yellow, and it was climbing slowly but inexorably up the mountain, toward the house.

"*How* can it do that?" Viveca wondered. "Nobody could drive up that road tonight."

"It's a snowplow," Hughie informed them, from his years of experience as a New York City policeman. Rising from the table with a certain evident pleasure to have done with Uno even before his final deal, he went over to one of the windows—not the yellow-paned one—and said, "It's a snowplow coming up to the house."

"But they don't do that," Viveca said, standing and walking over to also stare out the window at the approaching lights. "That looks like some kind of big highway department thing. Jerry from the gas station plows us out, tomorrow, when the storm's over."

"Well, here he is," Hughie said. "I better go see what it's all about."

"We'll all go," Vanessa said, dropping her cards on the table and getting to her feet.

"Definitely not," Viveca told her. "You girls are not going out into that storm."

"Oh, Mom, yes," Virginia said.

"We're just going outside the *door*," Victoria said.

"Absolutely not," Viveca said.

42

I'd like a cab like this," Murch's Mom said.

"Be tough for the customers to get in," Murch suggested.

"I wasn't thinking about the customers," Murch's Mom said.

The two of them were warm and cosy in the cab of Cleveland's top sand spreader, plowing the twisty, steep road up to Thurstead. Dortmunder and Kelp and Tiny were undergoing who knows what agonies behind them in the open bed of the truck, but that was them, and anyway, they'd be making a bunch of money out of this trip.

The snow was heavy and wet, which, from their point of view, was good. The sand spreader didn't care how heavy anything was, but a lot of ice on this steep road might have given it pause.

There was nothing out there so far on this mountain but the snow-piled road, the snow-laden wind, and the snow-burdened trees all around them; beyond the multi-colored lights of the truck, there was only darkness. But then, far upslope, Murch's Mom saw a faint glow, like a dim light left on in an empty attic, seen up the long and creaky stairs. "I guess that's it," she said.

Her son was concentrating on the road; mostly on finding it, under all this snow. "You guess what's what?" he asked, turning the big wheel this way, then turning it that way, goosing the gas, easing up, goosing the gas.

"There's a light up there," Murch's Mom said. "What you call your ghostly little light."

"Good," Murch said. "I'm glad they got a light, because that's what we're gonna say we saw."

The trio in the back of the sand spreader couldn't see anything at all, and they weren't even trying. They'd all huddled as close as possible to the cab of the truck, to be in its lee, where the wind was maybe one mile an hour less vicious and the snowflakes maybe seven per minute less frequent. They'd brought hotel blankets to wrap precious items in, but they had started by wrapping themselves inside the blankets, so that they now looked like snow-covered bags of laundry that the driver from the cleaners had forgotten. Every time the truck jolted, which it did all the time, it made them bump into one another and the metal cab wall behind them.

"Dortmunder," Tiny growled through his blanket, "when this is all over, we're gonna have a little discussion about this plan of yours."

Fortunately, given the wind and all, Dortmunder didn't hear that.

"The light's moving," said Murch, who had also spotted it by now.

"That *is* spooky," his Mom said.

They could almost make out the house now, as they neared it, though mostly they were remembering what they'd seen on the Thurstead Web page. Up there on the second floor of the house, that one spot of light had started to move, shifting past windows, some of which had panes of glass of all different colors, as though the light were semaphoring to some ship long since lost at sea. During a storm like this.

"They saw us is what it is," Murch said. "They're coming down."

"Good."

Their study of the Thurstead Web page had showed them that a door at the right side of the building, toward the rear, led to a kind of foyer and then the stairs going up to the family's living quarters. Farther forward in that wall was an entrance to the lower floor; not the main entrance, but a secondary one, to the old original kitchen. Now Murch drove and plowed and steered his way up to the house and along the right side, losing sight of that illumination up above, and stopped with the cab near the family's entrance and the rear of the vehicle near that other entrance.

No sooner had Murch shifted the big floor-mounted gear lever into Park than the family's door over there opened, and out came a guy in a big dark wool hat and a bulky dark pea jacket, pointing a flashlight ahead of himself in the general direction of the truck. Somebody behind him, still in the house, had a lantern of some kind, in which the guy could be more or less seen, and to Murch, he looked like a cop. Ex-cop. Retired cop.

His Mom said, "They got a cop."

"I see that," Murch said. "Well, here goes nothing," he said, and opened his door.

*   *   *

Dortmunder and Kelp and Tiny came out from inside their blankets, slowly, cautiously, something like butterflies emerging from their cocoons, but not a lot like that. They shook themselves, and kept the blankets around their shoulders, and duck-walked back to the rear of the truck, where the hinges on the doors had been recently drenched in the lubricant called WD-40.

Dortmunder cautiously opened the left-hand door, which would open away from the house and would not be seen by anybody standing over by the family entrance. Stiff, aching all over, he let himself down onto the black-top, which was already covered with snow, even though Murch had just this minute plowed it. Then he waited to hear conversation.

Murch climbed down out of the cab and waved at the ex-cop. "Harya," he yelled.

"Come on in here," the ex-cop yelled back, more order than invitation, and led Murch through the doorway into the warm foyer, where the other people stood. As he crossed the threshold, Murch took a quick look to his left, where he saw the dark figure of Dortmunder hobble stiffly, like Frankenstein's monster, toward that other door, whose lock he would now pick.

There was a mother in the foyer, carrying a Coleman lantern, and there were three girl children. There was supposed to be a father, too, which couldn't possibly be the ex-cop, who was obviously the guy from the security company. Maybe the father was stuck in town or something. "Evening," Murch said to everybody.

The mother looked bewildered, maybe even anxious.

She said, "I don't understand. You highway people never plow this road."

"And I go along with us," Murch assured her. "But I got this lady in the truck," he explained, "and I saw your light."

The truck cab's windows were opaque at the moment, but everybody stared in that direction anyway as the ex-cop said, "You got a lady in the cab?"

"Her car went off the road," Murch explained, "and I come across her, and she's gonna die in there, you know? So I took her along, but I still got another hour out here before my shift is over, and that truck is no place for this lady. I wondered, you know, you look like you got things okay here, could I leave her with you for an hour?"

The ex-cop said, "You want to leave her with us?"

"Yeah, just for an hour, then I'll come back up and get her and drive her to Port Jervis. But I can't do that now, I got my route I gotta do. And everything else is dark, it's cold, there's nothing around here but you people."

The mother said, "Of *course* she can stay here. That was wonderful of you, to rescue her."

"Well, she wasn't gonna make it," Murch said. "Wait, I'll get her."

Dortmunder and Kelp and Tiny made their way through the downstairs to the living room, where windows showed them the many lights of the sand spreader. Here they sat down in nice antique chairs and caught their breath a little. There was nothing to do now until the sand spreader went away.

The downstairs heat was on, but not very high, since nobody lived down here. The family kept the temperature in this part of the house at fifty, warm enough so the pipes wouldn't burst. Normally, Dortmunder and Kelp and Tiny might have found that a little chilly. After their ride up the mountain in the back of the open truck, this dark living room was toasty. Toasty.

"I really wanna thank you," Murch's Mom told the people who gathered her into the house, all clustered together at the foot of these stairs. "And I really wanna thank you, too, young man," she told her son, who was standing at the closed door, his hand on the knob.

"All in a day's work, ma'am," Murch assured her. "Well, I gotta get back on the job." He waved to everybody and went out to drive the truck back down the mountain, park it just off the road down there, and nap for an hour. Then the alarm on his wristwatch would wake him, for the return trip.

Dortmunder awoke, to see the lights of the sand spreader recede down the mountain. He nodded at it, closed his eyes, then jolted upright. Asleep!

Man, that had been close. He'd no sooner sat down here on this comfortable chair in this comfortable living room in the dark than he'd fallen asleep. What if he'd slept the whole time until Murch came back, and even went on sleeping then? Huh? What if *that* had happened?

Well, Kelp or Tiny would have woken him. Everything would have been okay.

Tiny snored. It was a low sound, but powerful, a sound you might hear from deep inside the cave where the virgins are sacrificed.

The truck was gone now and the room was very dark.

Dortmunder stood and peered around at his companions, as best he could in all this darkness, and they were *both* asleep, Kelp just a little more quietly.

Dortmunder went to Kelp first, shook his shoulder, and whispered, "Andy! Wake up!"

"Oh, sure," Kelp said.

Tiny snored.

"No," Dortmunder said, "I mean really awake."

"You got it," Kelp said.

"I mean awake with your eyes open and maybe even standing up," Dortmunder said.

Tiny snored.

"Absolutely," Kelp said.

So Dortmunder gave up and went to Tiny and said, "Tiny, we gotta wake up now and steal a lot of stuff."

Tiny opened his eyes. He looked around and said, "It's nighttime."

"In Thurstead," Dortmunder reminded him. "We're here to burgle the place."

"Or rob," Tiny suggested, and heaved himself to his feet. "When is it, do you happen to know, Dortmunder? When is it you burgle, and when is it you rob?"

"When I get the chance," Dortmunder said.

Tiny looked around. "I can't see in here," he complained. "Hold on."

A second later, light appeared. They had all brought flashlights along, which they'd adapted for the night's work by covering most of the lens with black electric tape, so that only a narrow band of light could emerge. Tiny had switched his on, and now he waved it around at all the treasures in the room. He said, "Where's Kelp?"

"Right there, asleep," Dortmunder said.

Tiny tapped Kelp on the side of the head. "Up," he said.

Kelp got up.

"I love Uno," Murch's Mom said. She'd told these people her name was Margaret Crabtree, so the mother, Viveca, called her Margaret, and the three children, very polite and well brought up, called her Mrs. Crabtree. Hughie, the ex-cop, hadn't figured out yet what to call her.

"Margaret," Viveca said, "it's so late for the girls."

"But it's a special night, isn't it?" Murch's Mom said. "With the storm and everything." She wanted everybody talking and involved in one place together, not off alone and silent in their individual rooms, listening to unusual noises from downstairs.

"Oh, Mom, please," or variations on "Oh, Mom, please," said the three girls, and Viveca said, "Well, just for a little while."

"Yeah," Hughie the ex-cop said. "Just for a little while."

Everywhere you go these days, if there's a group that's sponsoring where it is you are, the group gives you a tote bag. The tote bag has something written on it that is supposed to make you remember the group and the occasion every time later on that you use the tote bag, but when will you ever use all those tote bags? The only real use for your fourteenth tote bag is to hold the other thirteen tote bags, which is what most people do and why most people say they don't have enough closet space. However, if you happen to be a burglar by profession—or maybe a robber—tote bags are very handy.

The public rooms of Thurstead were full of many valuable items, both large and small, but, given the circumstances, the three robbers now shining their muted flashlight beams this way and that way in those rooms were interested only in items that were both valuable *and* small; thus the two tote bags that each of them carried.

The paintings on the walls in here might be worth two or three fortunes in money, but they would never survive a trip down the mountain through this storm in the back of an open truck, so unfortunately they had to be left where they were. But gold would survive, in a tote bag. Jewels would survive, jade would survive, marble would survive, scrimshaw would survive.

Tiny's left-hand tote bag said *National Scrabble Championship 1994* and his right-hand tote bag said, many, many times all over it, *Holland America Line*. Kelp, somehow a more literary type, carried in his left hand a tote bag that said *LARC—Library Association of Rockland County* and in his right hand one bearing a stylized giant *W* and the name *Warner Books*. And Dortmunder's two tote bags read *Temporis Vitae Libri* and *Saratoga*.

They didn't rush to fill these bags. They had an hour, and each of them wanted to be carrying only really very valuable items when the job was done. They used their experience from previous dealings with resalable merchandise, they occasionally consulted together over an item such as a dagger with a ruby-encrusted hilt, and slowly they made their way through the treasures of Thurstead, leaving many of them, but not all, behind.

Murch's Mom said, "Could I, uh, could I be excused?"

"Of course," Viveca said.

Rising, Murch's Mom said quietly to Viveca, "Where's the, uh, you know, facilities?"

"Oh, use my bathroom," Viveca told her. "It's just to the left, and then the first door on the right, and through the bedroom."

"Here, take my flashlight," Hughie said.

"Thanks," Murch's Mom said, and went away, followed directions, and in the bedroom went straight to the hairbrush on the vanity table. From her pocket, she removed a small Ziploc bag, and into it went all the stray hair from the brush. Then back into the pocket went the Ziploc bag and, after a quick visit to the bathroom, back to the Uno game went Murch's Mom.

The tote bags were full, and lined up in a row near the door. They had time to kill, so they wandered the rooms some more, this time acting like regular visitors, eyeballing the paintings, the furniture, the fur throws. "We oughta come back here sometime," Tiny said, "with a semi."

"I think the family would notice," Dortmunder said.

"Helicopter," Kelp suggested. "Stan knows how to fly a helicopter, remember?"

Dortmunder said, "I think the family would notice a helicopter even more than a semi."

"You can fit more in a semi," Tiny said.

Kelp said, "We pretend we're a movie company, shooting on location. Use one of the big trucks they use. Borrow Little Feather's motor home to be the star's dressing room, steal a camera and some lights somewhere."

Dortmunder said, "And do what?"

"I dunno," Kelp said. "You're the planner. I'm just giving you the big picture."

"Thank you," Dortmunder said.

"You girls are yawning," Vickie said. In fact, so was Hughie, but Viveca didn't think it would be right to mention that.

"Oh, Mom, please."

"Well, now, young ladies," Margaret Crabtree said, "you look to me as though you could sleep. It's quarter to one, isn't it?"

"It is," Hughie said, and *hugely* yawned.

"There you go," Margaret said, "*I* bet you'll all be asleep the minute your head hits the pillow."

"I won't take that bet," Hughie said. "Miz Crabtree, Miz Quinlan, I think I gotta say good night."

"Don't let me keep you all up," Margaret said. "I'll wait here for that nice young man to come back, and I'll turn that lantern off when I go."

Viveca, who didn't feel at all like sleeping, said, "Oh, no, I'll stay up with you. We can chat. Hughie, you know where the guest room is."

"Rrrr," Hughie said, which would have been *yes* if he hadn't been yawning.

The girls, too, were actually very sleepy, and did only a little more pro forma pleading before finally marching off, Hughie among them, to bed. Viveca left the Coleman lamp hanging where it was, but she and Margaret went over to sit in comfortable chairs where they could see the snowplow when it came back up the mountain.

"Quite an adventure for you," Viveca said once they were settled.

"More than I had in mind," Margaret said. "I hope your husband isn't stuck out someplace in all this."

To her astonishment and embarrassment, Viveca abruptly began to cry. "He isn't here," she said, and turned her face away, wishing she had a tissue, hoping Margaret wouldn't notice these te̲a̲ ̲ ̲n the dim light.

But she did. Soundi̲n̲ ̲ ̲very concerned, she said, "Viveca? What is it? He isn't hurt or anything, is he? In the hospital?"

"We're . . ." Viveca swallowed, wiped her eyes with her fingers, and said, "We're separated."

"He left you?"

"It's a separation," Viveca said.

"Then *he* separated," Margaret insisted. "How come he left you?"

"Well, the truth is," Viveca said, "Frank left this house more than he left me."

"I don't get it," Margaret admitted.

Viveca had kept all this bottled up for so long, it was a relief to suddenly be able to unburden herself, to a stranger, someone she didn't really know and would never see again, who would be leaving here forever any minute in a snowplow. "My great-grandfather built this house," she explained. "He was a famous painter, and the house is a national monument, open to the public from April to November, just the downstairs, and the family lives here and takes care of everything."

"Why you?" Margaret asked. "Why not somebody else in the family?"

"I'm an only child."

Margaret nodded. "And your husband decided he doesn't like the house."

"He grew to hate it," Viveca said. "It was boring and confining and he felt he was wasting his life here, and I had to agree with him."

"So he waltzes off and leaves you and the kids. *That's* nice."

"Oh, no, it's not like that," Viveca said. "He sees the children all the time, they spend weekends at his apartment in the city."

"New *York* City?"

"Yes."

"He's got a big place there, big enough for the kids?"

"Yes."

Margaret shook her head. "So whadaya doing here?"

"Well," Viveca said, "the family's always lived here, ever since my great-grandfather built the place."

"Yeah? What happens if you leave?"

"Leave? Oh, I couldn't possibly leave."

Margaret nodded. "Why not?" she said.

"Well . . . I was brought up to live here."

"So, if you leave, does the house fall down?"

"No, there's a nonprofit corporation that takes care of everything."

Margaret said, "So you're just like, here's the famous painter's family on display. Do you have to wear like Colonial costumes?"

"He wasn't from *that* long ago," Viveca said.

"Okay, flapper skirts," Margaret suggested. "Is that what you wear?"

"No, we don't wear costumes or do things like that. We don't even *see* the visitors, they're just downstairs and we're up— Oh, did you hear that?"

Margaret looked very open-eyed and blank. "Hear? Hear what?"

"There was a rustling sound downstairs," Viveca said.

"Didn't hear it," Margaret said.

Viveca leaned close and dropped her voice. "It's mice," she confided.

Margaret looked interested. "Oh yeah?"

"In the winter," Viveca said, "there's just no way to keep them out, since there's nobody ever down there."

"Huh," Margaret said. "Tell me about this husband of yours."

"Frank."

"Be as frank as you want," Margaret said, but then she shook her head and patted the air and said, "No, just a joke, I get it, the name is Frank. And Frank said he was leaving the house, not you."

"Yes. And I know it's true."

"You want him back, you feel like shit, you—whoops, sorry, you feel really terrible all the time, and you can't control your daughters because you don't feel good enough about yourself, and you don't know what's gonna happen next. Have I got the story here?"

"Yes," Viveca said. She felt humble in the presence of this wise older woman.

"Okay," the wise older woman said, "I tell you what you do. Tomorrow, when you get your phone back, you call this Frank. You tell him, 'Honey, rent a truck and come get us, all of us, we're blowin this mausoleum.'"

"Oh dear," Viveca said. "I don't know, Margaret."

"What you tell him is," Margaret insisted, "this separation is over. Come on, Frank, rent a truck or hire a lawyer, because we're either gettin together or we're gettin a divorce. And if it's a divorce—"

"Neither of us wants a divorce," Viveca said. "I'm sure of that."

"Great," Margaret said. "But if he wants one anyway—He isn't alone there in that apartment in New York, is he?"

"No," Viveca whispered.

"Men," Margaret concluded. "So if it *is* a divorce—This guy's pretty well-off, am I right?"

"Yes," Viveca whispered. "He's an executive with a chemical company."

"So if it *is* divorce," Margaret told her, "you rent the truck yourself and move the hell outta here. Take the girls and go where you want and meet a guy and never even tell him about this place."

Viveca laughed, surprising herself as thoroughly as when she'd cried before. "I shouldn't have told Frank about it, that's for sure," she said.

Looking out the window, Margaret said, "Here comes my ride."

Yes, here came all those lights, back up the mountain. Both women rose, and Viveca said, "Thank you, Margaret."

"Anytime," Margaret said. "Remember, soon as you get your phone back, call Frank."

"I will." Viveca smiled. "And I'll tell him I was a fool to let a house get between us."

"Well, don't give him *all* the marbles," Margaret said. "Negotiate a little. Come on, I gotta go."

Viveca carried the Coleman lamp, and they made their way through the house to the kitchen. "I can find my way down the stairs," Margaret said.

"Margaret," Viveca said, "I can't tell you how grateful I am."

"Nah," Margaret said, "it was just me and my big mouth."

"God bless it," Viveca said, and kissed the wise older woman on the cheek.

"Oh, come on," Margaret said, and turned hurriedly to the door.

Viveca said, "I'll never forget what you did here tonight, Margaret."

Margaret gave her an odd look. "Good," she said.

Murch saw the downstairs door just beginning to open as he drove past it to stop at the family's entrance to Thurstead. He climbed down out of the cab, and off to his left he saw three huddled figures swathed in motel blankets and toting tote bags hotfoot it across the snow to the rear of the truck.

The family door opened before Murch got to it, and his Mom stepped out, waving to her son, then turning back to shout up the stairs, "You be sure to make that phone call!"

The only interior light source had stayed upstairs, and now it swayed like the signalman's lantern in movies about nineteenth-century train rides. Murch's Mom waved up the stairs, then came out and slammed the door, and hurried around to her side of the cab.

They both climbed up and in, away from the storm, slamming their doors. Murch said, "What was that all about?"

"Just a conversation we were having."

"Oh."

They waited about another ten seconds, and then a

quick *rat-tat-tat* sounded on the metal wall behind their seats. Then Murch put the monster in gear and drove it around in a great circle to head down the mountain once more.

"Well," Murch's Mom said, "I think maybe I did some good in there tonight."

"I think we all did," Murch said.

"That, too," his Mom said.

Two days later, Viveca and Mrs. Bunnion and Vanessa and Virginia and Victoria all piled into Mrs. Bunnion's red Ford Explorer and drove to New York City, where every trace of Rachel had been expunged from Frank's apartment. The following month, January, the Thurstead Foundation hired a couple—Hughie, the ex-cop, in fact, and his wife, Helen—to live in the upstairs rooms and take care of the place. In April, when the downstairs was opened to the public, some of the docents, the nice lady volunteers who would lead the tours through Russell Thurbush's mansion, noticed some items missing, but no one commented. Some of the docents assumed that Viveca had taken a few small pieces with her, and why not, while others assumed the Thurstead Foundation was merely quietly selling off a few less important knickknacks to help with expenses, and why not. No one ever noticed the burglary—or robbery.

At last, the perfect crime.

43

Little Feather didn't know *what* to do. Here it was Monday morning, almost noon, and everything was going according to plan, and yet nothing was going according to plan.

The part that was Marjorie Dawson's plan had ticked along like a charm. Her lapse in failing to send the announcement of appeal on to Max Schreck's office in New York had created exactly the delay it was supposed to create, stalling the DNA test over the weekend, so that Fitzroy or John or *somebody* could come up with the solution to the open Burwick Moody grave. But that left the part of the plan that included the solution to the open grave, and so far Little Feather didn't see any solution forthcoming.

It was true that John, when he and the others had left here last Thursday, had seemed almost cheerful, and certainly self-confident, saying this, at last, was a job for *him*, exactly the way Clark Kent says, "This is a job for Superman." And it was also true that Andy had E-mailed Fitzroy on Friday evening that everything would soon be okay, and had E-mailed Fitzroy again yesterday that somebody would be coming up from the city today, but since then, Fitzroy hadn't been able to reach Andy or anybody else—it was never possible to reach John—so what did this mean? *Was* somebody coming up from the city today? Who? And what difference would it make?

Little Feather and Marjorie and Fitzroy and Irwin were all gathered in the motor home this morning, hunched over Marjorie's cell phone like a group of early settlers over a campfire. Max Schreck, still miffed over Marjorie's "error," had phoned from Albany at twenty minutes past ten to say the Three Tribes' appeal had been denied, so the DNA test could go forward forthwith, and an investigator from the local DA's office would be coming to the motor home between twelve and one today to collect the hair sample. And here it was 11:30, and now what?

Little Feather asked Marjorie the question direct: "Now what?"

"We can only hope," Marjorie answered, "that someone, John or Andy or whoever, actually does come up here this morning, and that he or they actually do have some solution to offer to our problem."

Irwin said, "What if Little Feather were kidnapped?"

They all looked at him. Sounding wary, Marjorie said, "I don't follow, Irwin." Ever since their shared pizza the other night, they were all on a first-name basis.

"Well," Irwin said, "here you've got this heiress, gonna be worth millions any minute now, so maybe somebody came in here last night and kidnapped her and left a ransom note—we can use those magazines there, cut out words for the ransom note—and now she's disappeared and it's not *our* fault, but we just can't do the DNA."

"One," Marjorie said, "we'd have to call the police, and once they discovered the fraud, which they would, we'd *all* go to jail."

"Two," Little Feather said, "where am I gonna hide around this neck of the woods that they wouldn't find me in twenty minutes?"

"Three," Fitzroy said, "to whom is this ransom note directed?"

"Well," Irwin said, "the tribes."

They all hoorawed at that. "The tribes!" Fitzroy exclaimed. "Irwin, that's 'The Ransom Of Red Chief'! The tribes would pay the kidnappers to *keep* Little Feather!"

"Well," Irwin said, "it was just an idea."

"No, it wasn't, Irwin," Marjorie told him, but in a kindly way.

"So what I'd still like to know is," Little Feather said, "what am I gonna do when the DA's person gets here? Maybe I should just run away right now."

"Oh no, Little Feather," Marjorie said, "don't do that."

"Never give up, Little Feather," Fitzroy said.

Little Feather said, "Why not? I can't give any investigator my own hair, cause Judge Higbee will put me in jail if the DNA doesn't match. So what do I—"

A knock at the door.

They all leaped like startled fawns, except Fitzroy, who leaped like a startled yak.

"Oh no!" cried Little Feather. "He's early!"

"Maybe," Marjorie said, "it's Andy, or someone like that."

"We shouldn't," Fitzroy said, "be in this room, if indeed the investigator is who that is."

"We'll be in the bedroom, Little Feather," Irwin said, as they all faded from view.

"And I'll be in the bathroom," Little Feather muttered, "as soon as I can."

The knock at the door was repeated.

"All right, all right," Little Feather complained.

What was she going to do? *What* was she going to do? Trying to think of a way out, fretting, frightened, furious with herself for getting into this mess in the first place, she went over to open the bus-type door and look out at a guy she'd never seen before in her life. A blunt-featured, stocky-bodied guy with carroty hair and a calmly indifferent manner that suggested he was nothing to do with her at all, but had knocked on the wrong motor home.

"Who," she said, "are you?"

"You're Little Feather, right?" this fellow said. "I'm Stan. Andy sent me."

"Andy! Come in, come in."

Stan came in, and Little Feather shut the door behind him as she called to the others, "It's okay! He's one of us!"

The other three came out to look curiously at Stan. Fitzroy said, "One of us? Which one?"

"Stan," Stan said. "They asked me to come up because I'm the best driver, I'll make the best time. I would of come yesterday except for the snow, and I didn't have the plow anymore."

Marjorie said, "Do you have a message for us?"

"Naw," Stan said. "I got this." And from his carcoat he pulled a Ziploc bag, which he extended toward Little Feather.

Who looked at it with some revulsion. Inside the bag were some strands of black hair. Unwilling to touch it, she said, "What's that?"

"Your DNA," Stan told her.

"Did that—did it come from a grave?"

Stan looked both astonished and disgusted. "A grave? No, whadawe wanna do with a grave? This come from a lady in New Jersey. Well, from her hairbrush."

Fitzroy, sounding awed, said, "You got into Thurstead?"

"Sure," Stan said. "Why not?"

"But—" Fitzroy was having a lot of trouble here. "It's so well guarded. There are many valuable works of art at Thurstead."

"There sure are," Stan said. "We made out like bandits. Well, I guess we are bandits, so that's how we made out."

Little Feather had unzipped the bag and taken out most of the hair. It was a little finer than hers, but black, and mostly straight like hers. She sorted it into a kind of swatch while the others continued to talk.

Irwin said, "Do you mean you robbed the place? Thurstead?"

"Well, we were there," Stan said.

"I'm not hearing this," Marjorie stated.

Fitzroy said, "But what if the police catch you? Isn't it possible they'll, they'll find *us*?"

"I don't think they're looking," Stan told him. "Nothing in the paper yet. There was that big snowstorm over the weekend, you know, maybe they won't even know it happened until weeks from now."

"Oh-*kay,*" Little Feather said.

They all looked at her, and she held up the swatch of hair, which she'd arranged between her thumb and first finger so that it looked as though she'd just cut it off her own head herself just this minute. "*Now* it's gonna be okay," she said.

Fitzroy said, "Little Feather? Are you sure you can make the investigator believe that's your hair?"

"Watch me," Little Feather advised. "You don't get a blackjack dealer's license in Nevada without knowing how to use your hands." She had gone in an instant from confusion and fear directly to absolute self-assurance. "Bring on that investigator," she said.

"And if I can just make a quick pit stop," Stan said, "I'm outta here."

Marjorie said, "You're going to drive all the way back? Today?"

"You bet," Stan told her. "My pals down there are waiting for me. We're gonna sell some property we just come into, and we all want to be there to cut up the jackpot. So, could I?"

"Oh, the bathroom," Little Feather said. "Sure. It's right down the hall there."

"Thanks."

Stan went down the hall, Marjorie moved into a corner to use her cell phone, to find out exactly when the investigator would arrive, and Fitzroy said, "Irwin. We're off."

"Right," Irwin said.

As they shrugged into their coats, Little Feather said, "Where you two going?"

"We shall follow," Fitzroy told her, "our new friend Stan. I believe he shall lead us to our former partners."

"Former," Little Feather said.

Irwin said, "And I believe we'll find them counting a jackpot. See you, Little Feather."

44

He isn't in that much of a hurry," Irwin commented. He was behind the wheel of the Voyager, Fitzroy beside him, the courier Stan in a recent red Lexus some distance ahead, southbound on the Northway.

"Then neither are we," Fitzroy told him, smiling like a man who's had an advance look at the test answers. Which, in a way, is exactly what he was.

Everything was about to come out right after all, and at long last. His simple but profitable scheme to produce the missing Pottaknobbee heiress had almost derailed several times, had been forced to undergo all the complications produced by Andy Kelp and Tiny Bulcher and John Whatever his name was—and their timely assistance once or twice as well, it had to be admitted—but through it all, the original concept had remained intact. The hair in Little Feather's hand would prove her ancestry and open the casino coffers to her and to her partners. Oh, happy day.

Of course, Fitzroy had no doubt a little intimidation would be required to keep Little Feather from *forgetting* she had partners, but Fitzroy also knew that he and Irwin were up to whatever persuasive methods were called for.

And the bozos—Irwin's word, which Fitzroy was happy to borrow, now that they were in endgame—were about to be dealt with for good and all.

In addition to the usual sidearms that he and Irwin packed on their persons, they now had a pair of Glock machine pistols under the Voyager's front seats, and Fitzroy firmly expected to use them before this day was done.

And with a profit attached as well. Not only would they rid themselves of all these unwelcome associates but those associates, according to Stan, had just performed a very profitable robbery. That profit would do just as nicely in Fitzroy's pocket.

The only remaining problem that he foresaw was Irwin himself, and those blasted tapes of his. While the tapes existed, perforce Irwin must also continue to exist. Well, once the bozos were dealt with, and once Little Feather was installed as the new full partner in the casino, Fitzroy would be able to turn his attention to the problem of Irwin. He had no doubt it was a problem that would eventually be solved.

In the meantime, on this cold and sunny day, Monday, the eleventh of December, while Little Feather was palming off another person's hair on an unsuspecting investigator, Fitzroy and Irwin drove south, following that red Lexus, staying well back, observing that Stan was in no rush to be once again among his fellow thieves, but was taking his time, staying with the general flow of traffic, barely above the speed limit.

Nearly two hours after they'd started, they came to Albany, then made the transition from the Northway to the

Thruway, and shortly afterward, the Lexus began to signal for a right. "It's a rest area," Irwin said.

"Good," Fitzroy commented. "I've been feeling for some time I could use a rest area."

"We need gas, too," Irwin told him. "I'll take care of that while you're in the gents."

"If I can find a bottle of soda or a sweet roll," Fitzroy offered, "without our friend Stan piping me, I shall do so."

"Just don't still be gone when he comes back," Irwin said. "I'm following him if you're here or not."

"Oh, I'll be back in plenty of time," Fitzroy assured him as they followed the Lexus into the rest area and to the passenger car parking lot next to the fast-food restaurant.

Irwin dawdled while they watched Stan on his car phone in there, absorbed in what he was doing, paying no attention to the world around him. "Reporting in," Irwin commented.

"Establishing a rendezvous," Fitzroy concluded.

Finally, Stan, too, concluded his phone call, and emerged from the Lexus, to lock it and head for the restaurant.

"Good," Fitzroy said, "he's decided to have lunch."

"You can get me a sweet roll *and* a bottle of soda," Irwin said.

"I shall."

Irwin stopped in front of the restaurant entrance long enough for Fitzroy to climb down from the Voyager, then headed on for the gas pumps while Fitzroy went into the building and followed the sign to the men's room, which was full of skier daddies and their tiny sons. Moving through all these elbow-height people, Fitzroy entered a stall and spent some time in there, listening to the families bond outside; it sounded like an aviary.

At last, ready to leave, he took down his coat, heavy with weaponry, from the hook on the back of the door, shrugged into it, opened the door, and Tiny Bulcher stepped in, pushing Fitzroy backward so that he sat abruptly on the toilet, while the big man came on in, squeezing into the space, pushing the door closed behind him.

There really wasn't room for both of them in here. Fitzroy was about to say so, perhaps with some vehemence, when Tiny reached out, delicately, with thumb and first finger of his right hand, like someone choosing just the one perfect grape from a bowl of grapes, and grasped hold of Fitzroy's Adam's apple. Fitzroy froze, eyes and mouth wide open, and Tiny leaned down to speak to him very quietly, but with impact: "John is a humanitarian," he explained. "He says I should let you stay alive unless you irritate me. It's more complicated that way, but I'm willing to go along with it, not have this major mess on the floor in here with all these kiddies about, if we can do it that way. You gonna irritate me?"

Fitzroy didn't trust himself to speak. Also, his throat was in extreme pain. Instead, understanding now why Stan had taken his time on the drive south and to whom he had been communicating on his car phone, Fitzroy spastically shook his head. No, he would certainly not irritate Tiny.

"Good." Tiny released the Adam's apple, which went on hurting anyway. He leaned his back against the door and said, "I'll take the coat. Might as well leave the guns in it."

Not questioning, Fitzroy removed his bulky coat and extended it toward Tiny, who said, "Just drop it on the floor."

"It'll get dirty."

"There are worse problems," Tiny said.

So Fitzroy dropped his coat on the floor, and Tiny kicked it backward through the space under the door, where hands at once grabbed and removed it.

And Tiny said, "Now the sweater."

"It's terribly cold out there, Tiny," Fitzroy reminded him.

For answer, Tiny extended that thumb and first finger again, but this time he didn't reach for the Adam's apple. This time, he shot a marble from Fitzroy's forehead.

Fitzroy's head rang like a temple gong. He took off the sweater and reached it toward Tiny, who pointed at the floor. So he dropped it on the floor, and Tiny kicked it back out of sight and said, "The shirt."

"Tiny, what are you—"

The thumb and forefinger showed themselves. Fitzroy went to work on the shirt buttons.

Watching him, Tiny said, "What I really liked, Fitzroy, was those Glock machine pistols under the front seat. Don't stop unbuttoning, Fitzroy."

Unbuttoning, Fitzroy said, "You saw those? We had no intention to use them, of course."

"I know," Tiny said.

Feeling sudden urgency, Fitzroy said, "Tiny, where's Irwin?"

"At the moment," Tiny told him, "he's wrapped in

about a mile of duct tape and resting comfortably in a great big tractor-trailer full of raincoats."

"Raincoats?"

"On their way to Oregon," Tiny explained, "nonstop. Get there in maybe five days."

As the shirt went under the door, Fitzroy said, "Tiny, I need Irwin."

"I don't," Tiny said. "Shoes."

"Shoes?"

"Shoes."

Fitzroy considered resistance, then unlaced his shoes. His problems were more severe than shoes. He said, "Tiny, Irwin has concealed some audiotapes that could be very incriminating for me."

"Kick the shoes under the door."

Fitzroy kicked the shoes under the door. "If Irwin isn't around to take care of those tapes," he said, "they'll be turned over to the police."

"Socks."

"Tiny, don't you understand? If Irwin—"

Tiny showed the thumb and forefinger again. He said, "Sounds like you're gonna be in some trouble. Good thing you're taking a trip."

"I'm taking a trip?"

"Socks, Fitzroy."

So off came the socks, and away under the door, and Tiny said, "T-shirt."

Fitzroy said, "Tiny, how far are you going with this? You don't mean to leave me here, do you? Naked?"

"Oh, naw, Fitzroy," Tiny assured him, "we ain't mean guys, not like some. There you go, kick that T-shirt. And now let's do the pants and the shorts all at once. You got the rhythm here, Fitzroy, don't falter now."

"I could shout," Fitzroy said.

Tiny looked interested. "You think you could? With all these little chirping kiddies out here? And for what fraction of a second, do you figure, Fitzroy? And then what happens next?"

Fitzroy, embarrassed and humiliated beyond belief, trying to assure himself that someday he'd get even for this but having great difficulty fleshing out that fantasy, finished stripping himself, saw the last of his garments kicked under the door and out of sight, and sat, miserable, cold and naked, on the toilet for a few seconds, until something else slid in under the door from outside. A garment of some kind, a deep, rich red.

"There you go," Tiny said, looking down at this new apparel with approval. "Try that on, there, Fitzroy."

Fitzroy stooped, grunting, to pick up the garment, which turned out to be a jumpsuit, cotton, many times laundered. On the back, in big white block letters on the deep red material, was printed C H C I. "What are the—What are these letters?"

"Central Hudson Correctional Institution. It's your medium-tough kind of place. They're bad guys, but they pull their punches. Like me with you, right now. Put it on, Fitzroy."

They're going to put me in this prison, Fitzroy thought in panic and despair. How are they going to do such a thing? Slipping on the legs of the jumpsuit, he said, "Are you going to put me there?"

"What?" Tiny chuckled, a sound from the bass drum section of the orchestra. "Naw, we don't want you *found,*

Fitzroy, we want you *lost*. And I guess you do, too. Okay, get up, boy, sleeves in, zip it up, that's good, turn around, hands behind you, Fitzroy."

Fitzroy felt the cool, rigid metal as the cuffs went on his wrists.

"Now," Tiny said, "let's do the perp walk."

"Tiny," Fitzroy said, "this is no way to treat a person who has never been anything—"

His head rang like a temple gong. He blinked and shut up, and Tiny reached past him to open the stall door.

They were all out there, in a cluster, facing the other way, Andy and John and Stan, obscuring the action at this one stall here for all the daddies and kiddies in the room. Tiny nudged Fitzroy in the back, and the five of them marched across the gents and out to the restaurant and out to the parking lot. Fascinated and horrified eyes followed them every step of the way.

It was so obvious what this was. Here was a criminal, a convict, probably been off to New York City or somewhere to testify in some gruesome, horrible crime, being taken back to prison, surrounded by four plainclothes deputies because he's such a dangerous felon, and to whom, at this point, should Fitzroy call for help? That sneaking, despicable, rotten turncoat of an Irwin was on his way to Oregon in a truckload of raincoats. These tourists all around him weren't likely to want to abet the escape of a desperate and dangerous criminal. Oh, *damn*.

They were walking him toward the separate truck parking area, so apparently he, too, was to take a voyage. They had left the family groups now, the observant eyes. The big trucks were parked in long, crowded rows, with very short sight lines, and nobody around anyway. They were leaving the world of witnesses. The ground was cold under Fitzroy's bare feet; his future was all at once too horrible to contemplate, but all he could think now was, where are they sending me?

Andy walked to his right, John to his left, Tiny and Stan behind him. Fitzroy said, "Andy, is there any chance at all I could appeal to your better nature?"

"Every chance, Fitzroy," Andy told him. "You already did. That's why me and John told Tiny not to unplug you unless he had to. And I'm really glad he didn't have to, you know what I mean?"

Fitzroy sighed. This was the *good* news. What might have happened otherwise was the bad news. He said, "Where am I going, Andy?"

"You're gonna like it," Andy told him. "See that big rig up there, the shiny silver one?"

"Yes."

"Got a crew of two, got a bunk up in the cab, drive twenty-four hours a day. Back is loaded up with cardboard cartons, big soft cardboard cartons because they're all full of Nerf balls. You're gonna go in luxury, Fitzroy, on a cushion of Nerf balls."

"Go where, Andy?"

"Nerf balls," Andy repeated. "Where else? San Francisco. You'll be there in no time, Fitzroy."

45

What I especially don't like about Arnie Albright," Dortmunder said, "is everything."

"He must have *some* qualities," Stan said.

"No, I don't think so," Dortmunder answered. "I think Arnie Albright is the one guy around and about with absolutely zero qualities. I think Arnie Albright is composed one hundred percent of deficits."

They were having this conversation on the West Side Highway, having driven south in a two-car caravan after completing Fitzroy and Irwin's travel arrangements. Stan and Dortmunder were in the Lexus, Kelp and Tiny behind them in some doctor's dark green Bentley, and they were on their way to West Eighty-ninth Street, where a fence lived named Arnie Albright, who was the only fence Dortmunder knew who was neither in jail nor actually a cop running an undercover sting operation.

(The thing to do with those sting operations is know when to stop being a customer. The money's always very good, and you know the cops aren't going to rip you off. Also, they keep the neighborhood safe. So long as you aren't present on roundup day, where's the downside?)

The unfortunate part about selling stolen goods to

Arnie Albright was, you had to be in his presence to do
so. "I don't see," Dortmunder groused, "why Andy can't
go up and talk to him, *he* knows Arnie as well as I do."

"Andy says," Stan told him, "he barely knows Arnie at
all, and only through you."

"Everybody claims to barely know Arnie at all," Dortmunder said, but he knew there was no way out of this.
An Arnie Albright encounter was coming his way, like it
or not; like one of those movies where the Earth is going
along, minding its own business, and an asteroid crashes
into it.

Both cars left the highway at Ninety-sixth Street, went
past the argument in front of the parking building on the
north side of the street just past the underpass that has
been going on for three generations now, went east over
to Broadway, then south to Eighty-ninth Street.

When they made the turn, they saw that the van was
still where they'd left it. It was a blue Econoline van with
white waves painted on its sides, plus the information:

ERSTWHILE FISH EMPORIUM
Estab. since 1947
J. Erstwhile, Founder

This van possessed commercial license plates, which
meant it wouldn't be towed away, which everything else
is, sooner or later. It was not a found object, like the
Lexus or the Bentley, but had been borrowed from a
friend of Kelp's, one Jerry Erstwhile, ne'er-do-well
grandson of the original Jake. Since it was now full of
everything the group had liberated from Thurstead, and
since they hadn't known exactly how long they'd have to

leave it unattended at the curb, they'd wanted to be sure they had a vehicle that would not draw attention from anybody for any reason whatsoever, and so far, it had apparently worked.

As they drove past the fish van, Stan said, "I'm done with this car, unless you want it for something."

"Not me," Dortmunder said.

"No prints around?"

"Not me," Dortmunder said, showing his gloves.

"Fine, then," Stan said, and parked next to a fire hydrant, since there were, as usual, no legal places to park within several miles of this location.

Apparently, Kelp had had enough of the Bentley as well, because he took the next hydrant along, and the four gathered on the sidewalk, where Kelp said, "John, we'll just loiter and make ourselves nondescript and unremarkable while you go have a word with Arnie."

Dortmunder had too much dignity to try to get out of it with everybody watching, so he said, "I'll be back," much as General MacArthur once did, and marched down the block past Erstwhile to Arnie's place, an apartment over a tanning salon that used to be a video shop and before that a bookstore.

As he walked, Dortmunder remembered various moments with Arnie Albright over the years, like the time Arnie had said, "It's my personality. Don't tell me different, Dortmunder, I happen to know. I rub people the wrong way. Don't argue with me." Or when he'd explained, "I know what a scumbag I am. People in this town, they call a restaurant, before they make the reservation, they say, 'Is Arnie Albright gonna be there?'"

And the weird thing, as Dortmunder well knew, was

that Arnie considered Dortmunder himself the closest thing he had to a friend. As he'd once said, "At least you lie to me. Most people, I'm so detestable, they can't *wait* to tell me what a turd I am." Which was probably true.

All Dortmunder hoped was that Arnie was healthy at the moment. Arnie got little diseases from time to time, each one more disgusting than the last. Recently, when Dortmunder had been forced by circumstance to have business dealings with Arnie, the fence had just broken out in something so horrible (salsa oozing from every pore on his body) that, he'd explained, "My doctor says, 'Would you mind staying in the waiting room and just shout to me your symptoms?'" May Arnie today, Dortmunder prayed, to Whoever might be Listening, at least be healthy.

Dortmunder entered the tiny vestibule of Arnie's building, rang the button, and waited for Arnie's snarl of greeting over the intercom. Instead of which, without a word being said, the buzzer sounded, unlocking the door.

Dortmunder simultaneously pushed on the door and recoiled. No challenge? No "Who the hell goes there?"

Cops. Had to be. Like most fences, Arnie was occasionally visited by marauding bands of cops, who have a proprietary view of fencing, not liking civilians to horn in on their sting operations. So was this the middle of a cop visit? And had the cops said, "Just let them in, Arnie, let's see who's coming to visit"? Was this, in short, a trap?

"Hal-*loo*-ooo."

That was somebody calling down the stairs. Could that possibly have been Arnie? Curious despite himself, Dortmunder pushed the door farther open and looked up the staircase, and there at the top, *smiling*, stood Arnie Albright himself, a grizzled, gnarly guy with a tree-root nose.

Dortmunder, not trusting the evidence of his senses, said, "Arnie?"

"Why, it's John Dortmunder!" Arnie cried with evident delight. "Come on up, John Dortmunder, it's been too long since I seen you!"

Dortmunder stepped all the way into the hall, letting the door snick shut behind himself. He peered hard, but there didn't seem to be anybody behind Arnie holding a gun to his head. He said, "Arnie? Is that you?"

"The *new* me, John Dortmunder!" Arnie announced, and waved a beckoning arm. "Comon up, I'll tell you all about it."

"Well," Dortmunder said, "we got some stuff in a van out here."

"In a minute, in a minute, I'll get my coat. But come up first, let's visit."

Visit? With Arnie Albright? Wondering if he had somehow fallen into a parallel universe, Dortmunder went on up the stairs, the smiling Arnie receding before him like a friendly vampire. "Come in, come in for a minute, John Dortmunder," this new Arnie said, backing into his apartment. "You wanna cuppa tea?"

"Well, Arnie," Dortmunder said, following him across the threshold, "I got these guys downstairs, you know, by the van, they just wanna show you this stuff we got."

"Oh, sure," Arnie said, "we don't wanna keep nobody waiting. Hold on, I'll just get my coat."

Arnie's apartment, small underfurnished rooms with big dirty windows showing no views, was decorated mostly with his calendar collection, walls festooned in

Januarys from all over the twentieth century, under pictures of girls in short skirts in high winds, kittens in wicker baskets with balls of yarn, paddle-wheel steamers, and much, much more. *Much* more.

While Arnie went on into his bedroom to get his coat, Dortmunder waited in the living room among the Januarys, and some Mays and Novembers, too (incompletes), and called after him, "Arnie? How come you're the *new* you?"

Arnie came back, shrugging into a drab and raggedy black coat you wouldn't let a barn cat sleep on, and said, "You remember, last time you was here, I'd come down with something."

Salsa. "You were ill," Dortmunder understated.

"I looked like a torture victim," Arnie said, more accurately. "Finally, my doctor wouldn't see me no more, wouldn't even *hear* me no more, he said I was the reason the Board of Health shut down his waiting room, so he passed me on to this like referral doctor, you know, the doctor all the other doctors refer you to whenever they're away."

"Which is whenever," Dortmunder said.

"You got it. Well, this guy, this referral doctor, turns out, he's okay, he's like making a comeback from parole, and after he cured me of the ooze thing he said, 'Lemme give you a second opinion, you're also obnoxious,' and I said, 'I know it, doctor, you don't have to tell *me,* I'm so hard to be around I sometimes shave with my back to the mirror,' and he said take these pills, so I'm taking them."

Dortmunder said, "Pills. You mean like Prozac?"

"This stuff is to Prozac," Arnie said, "like sour mash is to sassafras. How in hell it's legal I will never know, and if *this* is legal how in hell anything else is *il*legal I'll also never know."

"But it did the job, huh?" Dortmunder said. "You aren't obnoxious anymore."

"Oh, no, John Dortmunder, not like that," Arnie said. "I'm as obnoxious as I ever was, believe me, when the shock wears off, you'll begin to notice for yourself, but I'm not *angry* about it anymore. I have come to accept my inner scumbag. It makes all the difference."

"Well, that's great, Arnie," Dortmunder said, though not as enthusiastically as he'd hoped. Apparently, he was going to lie to the new Arnie as much as he used to lie to the old one.

Arnie once again showed Dortmunder his new smile. His teeth were not of the best. "So, John Dortmunder," he said, "you're doin so good these days, you're bringin me the stuff in vanloads, is that it?"

"Pretty much," Dortmunder agreed. "We got a variety of stuff down here."

"Do I want my loupe?"

"Maybe so."

"And my Polaroid camera?"

"Could be."

"And my gold-weighing scale?"

"I'm beginning to wonder," Dortmunder said, "if maybe we should just drive the van up the stairs and into the apartment."

"Nah, never mind, John Dortmunder. We'll go down and see what you got."

So they went down to see what they got, and what they got was three guys loitering very obviously around the

Erstwhile van. Fortunately, no law-enforcement elements had yet noticed them, so it was okay.

"Well, hey, Andy Kelp," Arnie said, coming down the stoop with his very best new smile, "John Dortmunder didn't say we was *all* gonna be old friends around here."

Kelp blinked, looked glazed, and said, "Arnie?"

"But we're *not* all old friends," Arnie corrected himself, looking at the other two. "John Dortmunder, introduce me to your pals."

"This is Arnie," Dortmunder said, "and that's Stan and that's Tiny."

"And how do you do? I won't offer to shake hands," Arnie said, to general relief, "because I know some people got feelings about germs, in fact, I got feelings about germs myself, for very good reasons, which we needn't go into," he said, to general relief, "except believe me, I know, my experiences have not all been sunny ones, and I take it this is the van here."

Dortmunder recovered first. "Yeah, this is it, Andy's got the key to the rear door."

"Oh, yeah," Kelp said, "I do, don't I?" Reaching in his pocket, he waggled eyebrows at Dortmunder behind Arnie's back: What's with Arnie? Dortmunder rolled his eyes and shook his head: Don't ask.

Kelp unlocked the rear doors of the van and opened the left one, to shield the loot from pedestrians. Arnie leaned forward to peer in, then paused and sniffed and said, "Scrod. Wait a minute, halibut. Wait a minute, perch."

Dortmunder said, "Arnie, we aren't selling you fish."

Arnie nodded over his shoulder at Dortmunder. "Oh, I know," he said. "I'm just trying out my new nose. The pills have this side effect, they improve my sense of smell, which, given me, you know, is a mixed blessing. Hold on, lemme see what we got here."

"Sure," Dortmunder said.

Arnie climbed into the van and started whistling. Unless it was Schoenberg, it was off-key.

"A little of your friend here," Tiny said, "goes a long way."

Stan said, "I'm ready for him to go a long way. I'll help him pick out the route."

"This is the improved version," Dortmunder assured them.

"Actually, John," Kelp said, "he *is* better than he was. Different anyway."

"He's being treated by a doctor," Dortmunder explained.

Tiny said, "Yeah? No doctor ever stood *me* a round."

"Everybody knows my feelings about doctors," Kelp said, and Arnie backed out of the van, still whistling. Then he stopped whistling, nodded at everybody, and said, "What you got there is your basic mixed bag in there."

Tiny said, "It all come from one place."

"Maybe," Arnie acknowledged, "but before that, it all come from all over the place."

Dortmunder explained, "The guy was a collector."

"You said it," Arnie agreed. "Okay, some of this I can move to antiques guys upstate, some has to go out of the country and come back in to be museum-worthy, and some we'll have to melt down for whatever. In any event, it should be nice. Worth the detour."

"How much?" Dortmunder asked.

"Eventually, it could be nice," Arnie told him. "You know me, John Dortmunder, I give top dollar. Even now when people can maybe stand to be around me, at least for a little while, even now, when maybe I wouldn't have to give top dollar no more, even now, the habit is so strong, and my new pleasantness is so intense, even now I give top dollar."

"Okay," Dortmunder said.

"But not today," Arnie said. "And by the way, I got no use for the van."

"Not the van," Kelp said. "I gotta return the van."

Arnie nodded. "I take it, Andy Kelp," he said, "you are the driver of the van."

"Sure," Kelp said.

"I'm gonna give you an address in Queens," Arnie told him, "a bathroom fixtures wholesaler, you're gonna go there and ask for Maureen, who I'm gonna call, and she'll have a box there for you to unload everything in, and from time to time, as we lower this inventory here, you'll get a little something."

Stan said, "What about today?"

"Today," Arnie said, "I can give you four G, on account."

Tiny said, "On accounta what?"

"On accounta that's how much cash I got upstairs," Arnie explained. "So come along, Andy Kelp, come upstairs, I'll give you that address and the cash and I'll show you some new incompletes, they'll knock your eyes out. I got one from a hospital, you won't believe it, the picture's their ER's new waiting room."

"Uh," Kelp said.

Dortmunder beamed. "Yeah, Andy Kelp," he said, "go on up with the new Arnie, we'll wait here."

"Or," Arnie said, "you could all come up for herbal tea."

"No, that's okay," Stan said, "we gotta keep an eye on the van."

"That's right," Arnie agreed. "So long, then. Come along, Andy Kelp."

Kelp, with one last mutinous look over his shoulder, followed Arnie into the building.

Tiny said, "This is really a changed individual?"

"I'm not sure," Dortmunder admitted. "You know, there's like a jacket, and you can get the jacket in blue or you can get the jacket in green? I think this is Arnie green, but somehow it's still Arnie."

"It is true," Tiny said, "the downside of this profession is, some a the people you gotta associate with."

Kelp hurtled out of the building. "I told him I had an appointment with my accountant," he explained. "Gather close, I've got this cash here."

Stan said, "Is it okay to touch?"

"Yeah, it was in a plastic bag when he gave it to me," Kelp said, and pulled a plastic bag out from under his windbreaker. "Just lemme . . ."

For the next minute or two, while New Yorkers all around them passed on by, minding their own business, Kelp pulled bills out of the plastic bag and distributed them. "There we are," he said at the end, "a grand apiece."

Dortmunder had already pocketed his. "So," he said, "I finally get my thousand dollars. May *is* gonna be pleased."

46

By Wednesday, Little Feather couldn't stand it anymore. The last thing that had happened was Monday, when Fitzroy and Irwin went off to dissolve the partnership with the other three, after which the DA's investigator, a very pleasant woman with unfortunate hips, had come for the hair sample, which Little Feather had palmed and presented with the aplomb of Blackstone the magician himself, while Marjorie Dawson had stood there pop-eyed, ashen with fear. Then the investigator went away, bearing the ringer hair sample in another plastic bag, tagged and dated and even more official than a notification from Publishers Clearing House, and after that, nothing.

Well, it would be at least a week before the lab would produce the DNA results, so there was nothing to do on that side except wait. But what about Fitzroy and Irwin? Not a word. Tuesday and today, both, Little Feather had left messages for Fitzroy at the Four Winds motel, but no response. What was going on? What was happening? By Wednesday, Little Feather couldn't stand it anymore.

When Fitzroy and Irwin had left Monday morning, planning to follow Stan the courier back to wherever the other three were holed up, Little Feather had felt a bit of a pang, knowing what was on the schedule next and having grown—not fond—*used to,* maybe—used to Tiny and Andy and John. She also, she thought, had a higher regard for that trio's capabilities than Fitzroy and Irwin did, so she didn't consider it a shoo-in at all that Fitzroy and Irwin would come out on top in whatever events would next take place. But *something* had to have happened.

So what happened? Who was still standing? Why didn't anybody get in touch with Little Feather and bring her up to speed on this thing?

Another frustration was not having a car. She was not only tired of taxis; she couldn't afford many more of them. She was going to be very rich any minute now, but at the moment, she was running low on the ready. And the motor home wasn't exactly transportation; it wasn't *that* mobile a home. Once you brought it somewhere and attached all the hookups, you didn't then take the motor home out two or three times a day for a spin around town.

Which meant Little Feather was mostly stuck in this strange dwelling, all alone, with no idea what was going to happen next, or when, or if she was in the gravy or in the soup, or what in *hell* was going on. By Wednesday, she couldn't stand it anymore.

Which was too bad, because nothing else happened until Thursday.

Two-something in the afternoon, it was, when the knock sounded at the motor home door. Little Feather was reduced by then to watching daytime talk shows, hating herself for it, remembering with new nostalgia the good old days in Nevada, dealing blackjack in cheap joints,

fending off cheap drunks, driving around in her own little blue Neon; sold, when she'd moved east.

The estranged couple on this particular program had
not quite come to blows yet when the knock sounded at
the door, and Little Feather, with some embarrassment,
realized she wanted to stay seated here in front of the television set; she wanted to see what would happen next in
those people's lives, rather than respond to something
happening in her own. "I gotta get out of this," she muttered to herself, offed the set with an angry gesture, and
hurried over to open the door.

Andy. And with him a woman, late thirties, attractive
without fussing over it, bundled up in a fox fur coat, grinning uncertainly as though afraid Little Feather might belong to PETA. "Hello," Little Feather said, thinking, if
Andy's up, Fitzroy and Irwin are down.

"What say, Little Feather," Andy greeted her. "I'd like
you to meet Anne Marie Carpinaw."

"Hi," Anne Marie Carpinaw said. "I've heard a lot
about you."

"I haven't heard a thing about you," Little Feather
said, thinking, this is why I never picked up any vibes
from Andy. "Come in," she invited, "and tell me all about
yourself."

"Thanks, we will."

They came in and went through the process of uncoat-
ing and accepting an offer of coffee and generally settling
in, so it was a good five minutes before they sat together
in the living room and Little Feather said, "Okay, Andy,
what's happening?"

"Beats me," Andy said. "I come north to find out
what's doing with the DNA. In fact, we called Gregory

and Tom, you know, over at the Tea Cosy, and turned out they had a cancellation, some guy already broke his leg at some other fun spot, so Anne Marie and me, we thought we'd take a few days in the North Country, kick back."

"But don't ski," Little Feather suggested.

"I skied in my teens," Anne Marie told her, "and my thighs began to turn into rock-hard hams, so I decided my real sport was après-ski, and I was right."

Little Feather nodded. "I'm pretty good at après-ski myself," she said. "And with Andy talking DNA in front of you, I take it that means you're in the loop on this thing."

"Well, sure," Andy said. "Pillow talk, you know."

Anne Marie said, "Pillow talk. I don't know why they call it pillow talk. When we're talking, there's no pillow around, and when there's a pillow around, we aren't talking."

"It's a whadayacallit," Andy explained.

Little Feather said, "What I really want to know is, how are things with Fitzroy and Irwin?"

"Well, they had to leave," Andy told her.

Little Feather had suspected that. "Permanently?"

"Oh, yeah, they won't—" Then Andy shook his head, and said, "Not like *that*. You know, there's permanent and there's permanent."

"Yes."

"Well," Andy said, "they are permanently retired from this particular little operation here, because they've got a lot of stuff to take care of out west all of a sudden, so that's where they went."

"They're out west," Little Feather echoed.

"On their way," Andy said. "So how you doing here?"

"I've got cabin fever," Little Feather said, "and I'm going nuts, and nothing is happening, and it won't be until next week sometime that the DNA comes back, and I'm stuck here. I've been leaving messages over at the Four Winds, because I didn't know what was going on, and I hope you don't think I was in on anything with those guys."

"Little Feather," Andy said, "we all understand that you were a helpless pawn in the hands of those guys, and we know you're gonna be glad about the new situation."

"Helpless pawn" hadn't exactly been the self-image Little Feather had been hoping to project, but what the hell; leave it alone. She said, "Thank you, Andy, I'm already glad."

Andy said, "We thought we'd find a nice restaurant tonight, one of those on the slopes, where you can sit there and dine at your leisure and watch the skiers fall down the mountain. You wanna come along?"

"I'd love to," Little Feather said.

"Great." Getting to his feet, Andy said, "We'll pick you up at seven."

"I'm looking forward to it."

At the door, Anne Marie smiled at Little Feather and said, "I just know we're going to be chums."

Meaning, Little Feather knew, don't you dare look cross-eyed at my man. "Chums it is," she reassured Anne Marie.

47

Ah, but what of Fitzroy Guilderpost and Irwin Gabel? Well, in the first place, by the time they arrived in San Francisco and Portland, respectively, they were both extremely hungry. And messy as well, unfortunately. Both had tried to attract attention by shouting a lot every time their transportation had paused on the journeys across the continent, but raincoats and Nerf balls had muffled their cries, so it wasn't until their respective semis were unloaded that they were discovered and, er, rescued.

In Fitzroy's case, rescue initially took the form of arrest, since he gave every indication of being an escaped convict. Fearing the effects of Irwin's tapes, damn his sniveling eyes, Fitzroy had been reluctant to divulge his true identity, but when the officials of Central Hudson Correctional Institution in Swell Haven, New York, faxed a response to the police of San Francisco that they were missing none of their inmates at the moment, Fitzroy had no choice but to submit to fingerprinting and to reveal his true identity to all questioners.

Whereupon it turned out the tapes had *not* surfaced, but a few California state warrants did surface, referring to scams and other outrages he'd performed in the

Golden State some years ago (which had caused him to relocate eastward in the first place), warrants that had not at all stale-dated. Bail was not granted, conviction was slow but certain, and off Fitzroy went to a small but sometimes sunny room to write his memoirs.

As for Irwin, he had not, in fact, given those tapes for safekeeping to a trusted friend, for the simple reason that Irwin had no trusted friends. In his original concept, he would have hidden the tapes until it was time to threaten Fitzroy with them. Once Fitzroy had become aware prematurely of the tapes' existence, that fact had seemed sufficient to Irwin to assure his own future in the partnership. Now, the partnership was finished, and so very nearly was Irwin. Fitzroy and the tapes had forever lost their urgency in his mind.

Having been plucked from the raincoats, hosed down, and temporarily hospitalized, Irwin at last got to tell the story he'd concocted during all those idle hours in Missouri and Nebraska and so on, that he had been kidnapped from a Greyhound bus at that rest area on the New York State Thruway by the friends of a jealous husband. No, he didn't want to press charges, nor even mention the husband's name, to spare the lady embarrassment. All he wanted was to eat a lot, and then be released from the hospital.

When all of that had transpired, Irwin arranged to have his luggage and other scant possessions forwarded from the residential hotel in which he'd been living in New York to the residential hotel into which he'd moved in Portland, having absolutely no desire to confront Tiny and Andy and John ever again; who knew what they'd think up to do next?

Instead, using dubious but passable credentials from his recently arrived luggage, he got himself a job as a chemistry teacher in a suburban high school, and if he hadn't subsequently been discovered in the backseat of that car in the school parking lot with that fifteen-year-old girl student, he would no doubt be there still.

48

Judge T. Wallace Higbee would have described himself, if asked, as guardedly optimistic. It seemed to him that at long last this excessively interesting Pottaknobbee case was nearing its conclusion. The DNA results had been in his chambers when he'd arrived this Monday morning, the eighteenth of December, just a week after the samples had been collected from the quick and the dead, and Judge Higbee had immediately alerted all the principals in the case to be in his courtroom at 3:30 that afternoon, which was the earliest he could be certain to have finished with the mounds of stupidity that would have piled up over the weekend.

And now, here was the time and here were the people. At the table on the left sat the Three Tribes, in the persons of Roger Fox and Frank Oglanda and Otis Welles, this morning armed with only one assistant. Roger and Frank looked very worried indeed, and Welles looked like a lawyer. In the first spectator row behind them sat four actual members of the Three Tribes, of whom Judge Higbee recognized only Tommy Dog, not because Dog had ever called upon the judge to certify his stupidity but because Dog was an electrician, when he could bother to work, and a good one, who'd done some of the rewiring when the judge had installed the indoor swimming pool.

Come to think of it— He made a note: *Swim more.* Everyone in the courtroom attentively watched him make the note.

At the other table, to the right, sat Little Feather Redcorn, looking as prim as such a person could, and exceedingly sure of herself. With her were Marjorie Dawson, as tense as though it were her own DNA at issue here, and Max Schreck, as pleased behind his great black-frame eyeglasses as though he'd just finished dining on a corpse. They had their own rooting section in the row behind them, a motley crew the judge had never seen before, consisting of a fairly ordinary-looking couple, some sort of man monster in a black suit that made him look like an entire funeral party, and a shabbily dressed, slump-shouldered fellow with the kind of hangdog look with which Judge Higbee was very familiar. He knew immediately that *that* fellow had never before in his life been inside a courtroom when he wasn't the defendant.

Well, well, he thought. Now that it's all over, Miss Redcorn's shadow cabinet puts in its appearance. Disappointing; he'd hoped for once in his life to meet a mastermind.

Well, time to get on with it. "I have asked you to come here," he said, not entirely accurately, "to inform you that the test results are in, and that there is no longer any question but that Miss Little Feather Redcorn is a descendant of Joseph Redcorn, a full-blooded Pottaknobbee, and is therefore a member of the Pottaknobbee tribe herself."

Miss Redcorn beamed, having had no doubt. Marjorie

Dawson nearly fainted, having had every doubt. Max Schreck looked hungry.

Across the aisle, "Consternation" was the only possible title for the tableau being presented, at least by Roger and Frank. Welles, getting to his feet, said, "Your Honor, naturally we will request a second series of tests to be done at a laboratory of our own selection."

"And naturally," the judge told him, "I will turn down that request." Hefting the sheaf of papers that consisted of the test report, he said, "This is not a private lab, Mr. Welles, this is a federal facility, and I have no intention of questioning their report."

"Your Honor," Welles said, "federal facilities have in certain cases in the past—"

"They have not," the judge told him. "There have been accusations, there have been no cases. If you wish to appeal my decision, by all means do so, but it will not impede the *effect* of my decision. Miss Redcorn."

She snapped to seated attention, but couldn't help the grin. "*Yes,* Your Honor."

"Have you an accountant, Miss Redcorn?"

Schreck stood to answer: "We will have accountants here, Your Honor, by tomorrow."

"By one P.M. tomorrow?"

"Certainly, Your Honor."

"Mr. Welles, at one P.M. tomorrow, your clients will be prepared to show every courtesy and the casino's books to Miss Redcorn and her accountants."

"Your Honor, the casino is on sovereign land of the Three—"

"Mr. Welles, if your clients attempt to delay this process one second past one P.M. tomorrow, I shall jail them, in the United States, for contempt of court. Miss Redcorn, a Pottaknobbee, a member of the Three Tribes, has come to this court for redress, and the court has accepted jurisdiction."

Tommy Dog popped to his feet behind Welles, exhibiting both stage fright and determination. "Your Honor?"

Now what? Judge Higbee lowered several great white eyebrows in Tommy Dog's direction. No more complications, damn it. "Yes, Mr. Dog?"

"Your Honor," Tommy Dog said, "I'm head of the Tribal Council this quarter, and I just want to say the tribes are perfectly happy to accept that test result you got there, and we accept Miss Redcorn, and we're happy to know there's still a Pottaknobbee around, and every one of us is gonna welcome her."

I can think of two who won't, the judge thought, looking at the horrified faces of Roger and Frank. "Thank you, Mr. Dog," he said. "I'm encouraged by your statement." He looked down at his pad and saw the note: *Swim more.* Exactly. "Court adjourned," he said, and went home and swam.

49

So where was Roger? Frank had no idea, that's where Roger was. No idea. And the hell with him.

Just when you need, Frank thought, and stooped for another bottle of Wild Turkey, and lost the thought. But found the bottle. Straightening with it, slowly, not wanting to get dizzy again, he placed the bottle carefully on the mahogany bar, then concentrated himself to the task of opening the damn thing.

He was here in Roger's office, later than two in the morning of a sleepless night after that damn session in court, here in Roger's office instead of over there in his own office, for three reasons. First, he wanted to talk with Roger, who somehow wasn't here. Where was he?

Anyway, the second reason was, this was the office with the bar with the bottles of Wild Turkey on the shelf underneath. And the third reason was, this was where they kept the books.

Books as in books, the old-fashioned way. The casino had started without computers, just before computers had become ubiquitous, and because of the way Roger and Frank operated their business, it had always seemed to them a good idea to let computer ubiquity end at the reservation border. Computers lose half what you tell them anyway, except that, when the feds show up, everything is still in there all along, particularly the stuff you *tried* to erase. What with one thing and another, stick with books.

All the books. All three sets of books.

They had to have three sets of books because they had different needs at different times. They had to have an accurate set of books because they themselves at least had to know what the package was they were skimming from, and they had to know enough about the operation to be able to run it efficiently. But *those* books couldn't be shown to anybody else, because *those* books were streaked with the hands of Roger and Frank, reaching in and taking out.

While it was true that the casino was free of federal taxes, it was also true that there were certain taxing and regulatory agencies who did keep track of things here, sales of alcohol and tobacco, gambling income, things like that. These official snoops were mostly from New York State, but also from Ottawa, since the reservation spread over into Canada. For those outfits, there was the second set of books, in which income and outgo were more or less similar to events in the real world, but the skimming hands of Roger and Frank were replaced by other, perhaps plausible expenses.

And then there was the Three Tribes. From time to time, Roger and Frank had to present an accounting of their stewardship to the tribes—it was never a big deal, just pro forma, nobody wanting to rock a very successful boat—and for that purpose, neither the first *nor* the second set of books would do, because both showed far too high a cash flow, and it wouldn't take the tribes long to realize they were getting just about 50 percent of the money that was actually due them. So for the tribes, and only for the tribes, there were the books, variant number three.

So there they were, the three sets of books. The straight books, the cooked books, and the fried-to-a-crisp books. And they were all kept in Roger's office, because that's where the safe was.

And where the hell *was* Roger anyway? It seemed to Frank there was only one thing they could do now, but before he got started on it, he wanted to run the idea past Roger, bounce the notion off old Roger, run it around the block with Roger. So where was Roger? Where was old Roger anyway?

Not at home, or at least he hadn't been home two hours ago, when Frank had last phoned there and had last spoken to Roger's increasingly irritated wife, Anne, who had said, "Frank, stop calling here. He isn't here, I don't know *where* the hell he is, and when he does come home, I intend to take a baseball bat to him. Tell him that when you see him."

"Oh, okay," he'd said, so he knew he shouldn't phone Roger at home anymore. But where *was* he?

Here. In came Roger all at once, moving fast, still in his topcoat. "Roger!" Frank cried.

Roger gave him a sour look. "Frank," he said, "this is no time to drink."

Frank stared at him in astonishment. "Roger? If *this* isn't a time to drink, when the hell *is* a time to drink?"

"When we're safe," Roger said.

"Safe? How can we be safe? Don't you remember,

Roger? That damn woman is coming here *tomorrow* to look at the *books*!"

"Today," Roger said, looking at his watch.

"Today," Frank agreed. *"There!"* he cried, having finally gotten the damn bottle open. "Roger, have a drink."

"No," Roger said.

Frank paused before refilling his glass. "Roger," he said, "they want to look at the books. They're *going* to look at the books. Do you know what that means?"

"I know precisely what it means," Roger said.

"That judge—"

"The judge doesn't worry me," Roger said. "None of that legal shit worries me. Frank, what we have to worry about is the tribes."

"Oh, I know that, Roger."

"Once the tribes find out what we've done," Roger said, "they'll kill us. They'll flat out kill us."

"That's a very strong possibility," Frank agreed, filling his glass. "Very strong possibility."

"I have just fini—" Roger started.

But Frank wasn't done. "What we have to do, Roger," he said, "and I've just been waiting to discuss it with you, but what we have to do is burn those books. All of them, all three sets. Just burn them all."

"No," Roger said.

"We have to, Roger. We can't let anybody see those books."

"And what are you going to say?" Roger demanded. "You were careless with cigarettes?"

"We'll say," Frank told him, "they disappeared, we have no idea where they are, and everybody can search all they want."

"You'll never get away with it," Roger told him. "The only possible thing for us to do, Frank, is flee."

Frank gaped. "Flee? Whadaya mean, *leave*?"

"That's what flee means, yes."

"But Roger," Frank said. He knew that Roger and Anne had been on the outs for some time, that Roger wouldn't at all mind flight if flight from Anne were included in the package, but that wasn't Frank's situation at all. His marriage was a good one, with good kids, and nothing he wanted to leave. "No, Roger," he said. "This is where I live, I *live* here."

"And you'll die here," Roger told him, "probably hanging from a lamppost. Frank, don't you realize what two or three thousand angry Kiota and Oshkawa could *do*?"

"With some hotheads," Frank agreed, nodding. Then he drank some Wild Turkey.

"I have just finished," Roger said, getting back to the sentence that had been interrupted, "cleaning out every account we control, transferring *all* those funds. I am about to leave this reservation forever, out the back way, into Canada, and be on a plane out of Canada in the morning. Frank, we've been partners for a long time. I'm telling you, this is the thing to do. Put that damn glass down and come with me. We'll be rich, we'll be happy, we'll be on an island somewhere."

Frank felt very sad. "Roger," he said, "I don't want to leave Silver Chasm. This is my *home,* Roger."

"Last chance, Frank," Roger said.

Frank shook his head. "I can't do it, Roger. That's why I gotta burn the books."

"Well, good luck to you," Roger said, and came over to stick out his hand. "We had a good long run, Frank."

"Yes, we did," Frank said.

Solemnly, they shook hands. Then Roger pointed at the glass, as Frank picked it up again, and said, "I wouldn't drink any more, Frank, if I were you."

"Oh, Roger," Frank said. "If you were me, you'd drink a *lot* more." And he proceeded to.

When he next lowered the glass, he was alone in the office. Roger had gone.

Could he get away with it? What other choice did he have? Roger had always been the sophisticated one, taking the long vacations, learning French. Frank had just liked the soft life at home. Was it somehow possible to keep that soft life, even after this disaster?

We should have had her killed, he thought, and took our chances.

He was suddenly feeling nostalgic for himself, as though he, too, had gone, like Roger, and now he was missing himself. Putting down his glass, he left Roger's office to take a slow amble around the casino. He liked to do that almost every day, just walk around his domain, watch the gamblers slide their money into his pockets.

That's what he did now, as though for the last time, though he certainly hoped it was *not* for the last time. This late on a Monday night in winter, there was very sparse action, but that was okay, there was always some. One blackjack table open, one craps table, no roulette. Three or four players among the platoons of slot machines. Restaurants closed, coffee shop open but empty. Frank considered having a cup of coffee, then decided against it. Time to get to work.

Back in Roger's office, he dragged into the middle of the room the big mahogany coffee table with the large round hammered copper disk in the center of it. Then he went to the safe behind Roger's desk, knelt before it to open it, and pulled out all the books, all those heavy ledgers—black for the true ones, red for the officials, green for the tribes—all those pages full of tiny inaccurate writing.

They wouldn't burn in clumps. They were in loose-leaf binders, and he had to open the binders and take out pages and feed them to the fire he'd started in the copper disk in the coffee table. He pulled up a chair, set the bottle and glass on the floor beside him, fed pages to the fire, fed more pages to the cheery little blaze in the middle of the coffee table, and when he woke up the office was on fire.

This is where Frank made his Mistake. He'd made a number of mistakes before this, but this one was the Mistake. He opened the office door.

What Frank did here, he completely forgot to consider the fact, which normally he well knew, that, like most casinos in America, between midnight and eight in the morning, the air pumped into the windowless gambling areas is sweetened with just a little extra oxygen, just enough to make the players feel awake, happy, positive, uninterested in quitting, unneedful of sleep. Just a little extra oxygen.

Frank opened the office door, thinking to run to Security to come put out the fire, and the fire behind him *lunged* at that oxygen. All at once, he was running in the middle of the blaze, his clothes were catching fire, his hair was catching fire, and out in front of him the few employees and customers still around were fleeing for their lives.

Everybody ran, the customers and employees from the fire, Frank with the fire, and when he got outdoors, he flung himself into the nearest snowbank and rolled there for quite a while. And when next he sat up, the casino was gone.

50

Dortmunder walked west across Tenth Street, hands in his pockets, head down as he watched his shoes scuffle along. A cold, nasty wind was in his face, having come all the way across the continent just to get up his nose before heading on eastward toward Long Island and the ocean and all of Europe, full of people to annoy. At the moment, the wind was Dortmunder's problem; perhaps the least of them.

Sunday, December 31, 4:00 P.M. A pretty miserable year was finally slinking off, and Dortmunder was out in this nasty wind to help send it on its way. He was headed now toward the intersection of West Tenth Street and West Fourth Street in Greenwich Village, the only place in the world likely to *have* an intersection of West Tenth Street and West Fourth Street, for what should be the final meet on the casino problem; perhaps the worst of them.

And there was the intersection up ahead, with the familiar motor home parked at the far corner on the right, facing away from him. And seated on the curb, back to Dortmunder, hunched over, scrunched in between the motor home's rear wheel and the corner streetlight post, wasn't that Kelp? Yes, it was.

It was Kelp who had called him to this meet. It seemed that he and Little Feather had been in unsatisfactory communication the last few days and it was time to find out what was what.

The only thing Dortmunder had known in the last two weeks was that the casino had burned to the ground. It was all over the TV news, even the national TV news, because these days, nothing happens anywhere without at least three video cameras coincidentally right there on the scene, ready to roll. At Silver Chasm Casino, both tourists *and* casino employees had been on tap with their cams.

Mixed in with the wobbly shots of crashing walls and gouting fireballs had been nonamateur footage of a very dumbfounded Little Feather, who, because she was the last of the Pottaknobbees and also extremely photogenic, pretty much took over the story once the ashes had cooled. By the fourth day, though, she, too, was gone from public view, and since then, Dortmunder hadn't known nothing from nothing.

Until yesterday, when Kelp had called to tell him the story since then. After a week of silence from the North Country, Little Feather had started making collect phone calls to Kelp, he being the only coconspirator she could find. These phone calls were more irritating than informative, however, not only because Kelp had to pay for them but also because she was making them on the reservation, from the home of somebody apparently named Dog, who had taken her in now that her money had run out and she was a certified Pottaknobbee. In that house, she had to be careful what she said on the phone, which meant she couldn't say much of anything on the phone, which made Kelp quickly begin to wish she'd quit calling all the time. As he'd explained to Dortmunder, he'd finally made an oblique reference to the problem: "If you don't have anything to say, why do you keep saying it?"

"Well, I'm stuck here, Andy," she'd explained. "I got no money, and no place to go. If the casino was up, I could get a job dealing, but if the casino was up, I wouldn't *need* a job dealing." But then she'd lowered her voice and said, "I think I may be getting a check at Christmas. Like a present from the tribes, now that I'm one of them. I hope it's enough so I can put some gas in my apartment, so I can drive down and meet with you guys and we discuss the situation."

So here it was, New Year's Eve, yesterday being the earliest she could get away from all her new relatives, and Kelp had arranged the meet here and was just straightening up out of the confined space between motor home and lamppost as Dortmunder arrived. "That's got it," he said. His hands and left cheek were very dirty.

"That's got what?" Dortmunder asked. "Your face is dirty."

"I'll wash it inside," Kelp said, and gestured at the space where he'd been hunkered. "I tapped into the power cable inside the pole, so we can have light and heat in there without the engine on all the time. Too bad they don't have a waste pipe in there. Come on in. I want to hear Little Feather's story."

"So do I," Dortmunder agreed.

"I mean, I want to hear it without paying for it collect," Kelp said, and knocked on the door.

The Little Feather who opened the door was just sub-
tly different; still looking mostly like an action toy in a
western setting, but now after a tough day in the sandbox.
"You might as well come in," she said.

"Happy New Year," Dortmunder said glumly.

"You think so, huh? Come in, it's cold out there. Andy,
thanks for the electricity."

"De nada," he said. He followed Dortmunder in, shut
the door behind himself, and somebody knocked on it.

"The big city," Little Feather commented. "Always
something happening."

"That'll be Tiny," Kelp said as he went away to wash
his face.

Little Feather opened the door, and it was. "Happy
New Year's," Tiny snarled, climbing in.

"Another one," Little Feather said. "I hope you didn't
bring your grenade this time."

"I can go back for it, you want."

"That's okay," she said as Kelp returned, fresh-faced
as a schoolboy. "I got beer, if you want."

They did, and then sat, Tiny on the sofa, Kelp and Little Feather on the chairs, and Dortmunder on his footstool
from the kitchen. Kelp said, "Now that we're face-to-
face, Little Feather, what's going on up north?"

"Snow," she said.

"Thank you," Kelp said.

"But not much else," she went on. "The casino's a
dead loss, burnt flat. Roger Fox is gone, and so's all the
casino's money."

Dortmunder said, "The cash on hand, you mean."

"Everything," Little Feather said. "That last day, Fox
was a busy man. Every bank account and IRA and money

market account and anything else he could get his hands on, set-aside money for withholding taxes, everything, cleaned out. So the casino's broke *and* it owes a bundle. They traced all the money to the Turks and Caicos islands, but by then, he'd moved it again. So it's gone, and so is Fox, and nobody will *ever* find him."

Dortmunder said, "And the other one's in jail, I guess."

Little Feather offered a sour grin. "Frank Oglanda begged to go to jail," she said. "The tribes were gonna string him up, they had to call in the feds, Huey him out of there."

Tiny said, "Too bad the tribes don't have ground-to-air."

"They wished they did," Little Feather said. "Everybody's plotting and planning up there right now, they say the trial can't be secret, when it starts, wherever it is, they're gonna rush the courthouse. Which they even might, but I don't think so, because they're not gonna have the time for it."

Dortmunder said, "Why not?"

"Well, now we get to the real problem," Little Feather said. "Not only is the casino gone, turns out, Fox and Oglanda, they were so greedy, they didn't even insure the place to its full value, so it's going to take a while to get it up and going again. The people all have to get jobs, which is probably a good thing, if you ask me."

"A while to get the casino up and going again," Kelp echoed. "How long is a while?"

"Right now, they figure eight years."

There was general consternation at that. Dortmunder said, "How come?"

"Casinos cost a lot to build," Little Feather pointed out. "There's no money in the tribe, no insurance, and Fox and Oglanda paid off as little of the debt from the first construction as they could, so the tribes can't get any more from those banks. Everybody's tithing, but that's gonna take a while."

"Borrow from somebody else," Kelp suggested.

"Well, the problem with that," Little Feather told him, "anybody that wants to invest in a casino, they gotta be investigated by the government, make sure they're not mobbed up. Only, most people that want to invest in casinos *are* mobbed up, so it takes a while to prove you're not."

Dortmunder said, "How long?"

Kelp said, "She's gonna say eight years."

"If everything goes smoothly," Little Feather said.

"Everything goes smoothly," Dortmunder repeated in a quiet and contemplative way, as though wondering what those pretty-sounding words meant.

Tiny said to Little Feather, "So what it comes down to is, we don't get no money because you didn't get no money, and you aren't gonna get no money because there isn't any casino."

Kelp said, "It sounds pretty final when you put it that way."

Tiny, looking like Grendel between meals, said, "How'd I wind up here anyway?"

"Fitzroy," Little Feather promptly answered. "Fitzroy and Irwin got us into this."

Kelp said, "Well, don't leave out Oglanda and Fox."

"Maybe *I'll* rush the courthouse, too," Tiny decided.

"Well," Dortmunder said, "I'm gonna forget the whole

thing, if I possibly can. Tomorrow, we start a whole new
year, and it's gonna be a better year, I just believe it is,
and I'm gonna start it by going over to Jersey and pick up
some cameras I left there."

"I know you meant to ask me to come along," Kelp
told him, "and just forgot, but in fact, I'm gonna be busy.
When I leave here, I gotta go over to St. Vincent's hospital."

They looked at him. Little Feather said, "Why, you
sick?" as though she was about to go for the Lysol.

"No, I need a car," Kelp said. "Anne Marie wants us
to drive to Kansas, start tomorrow, there's some people
there she wants to show me to."

Tiny grumbled and moved his shoulders around. "It's
New Year's Eve," he said. "I'm goin down to Brooklyn,
find a good bar, start a fight."

Dortmunder said, "How about you, Little Feather?
You heading back north?"

"In a few days," she said. "We're gonna stick around
the city awhile, take in some shows."

Kelp said, "We?"

"Well, if the business part of the meeting is over," she
said, "I'll bring him out." Turning, she called over her
shoulder, "Benny!"

Benny Whitefish appeared in the doorway, in the suit
and tie he'd worn to court, but the face above the raiment
was very different. His smile was both awed and grateful,
like a lottery winner who hadn't known he was playing
the lottery. "Hi," he said, and gave a little wave.

Dortmunder and Kelp and Tiny had nothing to say.
Little Feather gave them her own unreadable smile and
said, "Benny's my protector now, aren't you, Benny?"

"Uh-huh," he said, and gulped, his Adam's apple bouncing like a golf ball.

"That's nice," Dortmunder managed to say.

"I been needing a protector," Little Feather said. "Benny, bring out the pretzels, let's make it a party."

Benny trotted off on his errand.

More
Donald E. Westlake!

Please turn this page
for a
bonus excerpt
from

*PUT A LID
ON IT*

available
wherever books are sold.

THE ELEVENTH DAY MEEHAN WAS IN THE MCC, THE barbers came around to 9 South; two barbers, a white one for the white inmates, a black one for the rest. Each dragged a chair behind himself, with a guard following, and they set up in opposite triangles of the communal room, which was shaped like a six-pointed star, the cells outside that, in two facing lines in sword hilts sunk into five of the star's crotches: the exit to the concrete room where the elevators came was at the sixth.

So that was another difference from state or county jugs; no separate room for the barbers to ply their trade. After eleven days, Meehan was thinking he might write a monograph on the subject, was already writing it in his head. Never put anything on paper in stir: that was one of the ten thousand rules.

Of course, the primary difference between the Manhattan Correctional Center, which was where bail-less federal prisoners in the borough of Manhattan, city and state of

New York, waited before and during their trials, was the attitude of the guards. The guards thought the prisoners were animals, of course, as usual, and treated them as such. But in this place the guards thought they themselves were not animals; that was the difference.

You get into a state pen, any state pen in the country—well, any state Meehan had been a guest in, and he felt he could extrapolate—and there was a real sense of everybody being stinking fetid swine shoveled into this shithole together, inmates and staff alike. There was something, Meehan realized, now that he was missing it, strangely comforting about that, about guards who, with every breath they took, with every ooze from their pores, said, "You're a piece of shit and so am I, so you got no reason to expect anything but the worst from me if you irritate my ass." These guards here, in the MCC, they buttoned all their shirt buttons. What were they, fucking Mormons?

Meehan had never been held on a federal charge before, and he didn't like it. He didn't like how inhuman the feds were, how unemotional, how you could never get around the Book to the man. Never get around the Book. They were like a place where the speed limit's 55, and they enforce 55. Everybody *knows* you enforce 70.

Shit. From now on, Meehan promised himself, no more federal crimes.

And this one was a wuss, this one was so lame. Him and three guys, whose names he would no longer remember, had a little hijack thing, off a truckstop, Interstate 84, upstate fifty miles north of the city, there was *no way* to know that truck held registered mail. Not a post office truck, a private carrier, no special notices on it at all. The truck Meehan and his former allies wanted, from the same carrier, was full of computer shit from Mexico. Meehan wasn't looking forward to making that plea to some jury.

But in the meantime, for who knows how long, here he was in the MCC, downtown Manhattan, convenient to the federal courts, thinking about his monograph on the differences between federal and non-federal pounds.

There were a number of ragheads on 9 South, Meehan presumed either terrorists with bombs or assholes who strangled their sisters for fucking around, and they all lined up to get their hair cut by the white barber. Johnson, a white inmate who'd been friendly and palsy with Meehan since he got here and who Meehan took it for granted was a plant, came over to help him watch the barbering, the two of them seated at one of the plastic tables in the middle of the communal room. "Every time," Johnson said, "those guys are first in line, get their hairs cut, never does any good."

Meehan, polite, said, "Oh?"

"Their hair grows too fast," Johnson told him. "It's something about the sand or something, where there's no water, you look at these guys, haircut haircut, end of the day they're back the way they were, they still look like a Chia toy."

"Chia toys take water," Meehan said.

"And sparrows take shit," Johnson said.

What was that supposed to mean? Meehan watched the piles of curly black oily hair mount up around the raghead in the chair, like they were gonna finish with a Joan of Arc here, and it occurred to him to wonder, as it had never occurred to him to wonder in a state pen, how come barbers were such a total criminal class. Everywhere you went, the barbers were inmates who happened on the outside to be barbers, so this was how they made bad money and good time on the inside, but the question was, how come so many barbers were felons? And what kind of *federal* crime can a barber pull? Maybe what happened, every jail around, whenever a barber was gonna finish his time, the word went out to the police forces of the world, keep your eyes on the barbers, we need one May 15. Could be.

A guard came into the block. His tan uniform was so neat, he looked like he thought he was in the Pentagon. Maybe he really was in the Pentagon; who knew?

The guard came over to Meehan: "Lawyer visit."

That was a bit of a surprise. There wasn't much Meehan and his lawyer had to say to one another. But any distraction was welcome; rising, Meehan said, "I'm with you."

Johnson, friendly and genial, said, "Expecting good news?"

"Maybe I'm being adopted," Meehan said.

Turned out, he was.